St. Elmo's Fire

Oliver Theakston

MMXXII

For Grandad.

A Note On Names

Many in the English-speaking world will know Fernão de Magalhães (pronounced *Fer-now de Mag-a-laysh*) by his Anglicised name, Ferdinand Magellan.

Our names ought to be our most treasured possession. As foreign speakers, we should do our best to learn and pronounce them properly, to let the music of their native tongues ring through them.

In that spirit, the Magellan of this book is called by his Portuguese name.

Part I

Chapter 1

The labourers sweat and swear as they wrestle medical supplies from the packed port of Los Cristianos onto the main deck of the Trinidad. Juan de Morales watches them work from the dock, his brow knotted with anxiety. The men are reckless, impatient to get the job done quickly and return to hiding in the shade of the taverns lining the port. They are likely to damage something in their haste.

De Morales sighs, turns away from the careless labourers and looks east across the low hills of Tenerife, barely discernible beyond the midday haze. Three hundred leagues away lies his native Sevilla, from where the armada sailed two weeks ago. He looks back, but he feels no longing for its choked streets, swarming markets and memories. A life long settled in the dust of the past.

On his way to the armada that waited on the Guadalquivir, de Morales had passed through Sevilla. For the first time in six years, he had walked familiar streets filled with bittersweet memories. He had even stopped at the road in San Vicente that led to his town house, empty since his wife's passing. But he could not bring himself to enter that tomb. He had not the courage to face whatever ghosts waited for him there. The phantom life his wife now lives, her spectral, pregnant belly swelling into the space before her where a child should have played, could continue undisturbed.

But now, de Morales turns his back on Sevilla. Rather than face the past, he looks out to the sea, to the west, to the future.

When a call was put out from the Casa de Contratación for doctors to join a mysterious venture led by a Portuguese exile, de Morales eagerly volunteered. For thirty years he had served Castile, first as a surgeon in Ferdinand's armies and then as a physician to Juana la Loca. To be rid of the rivalry, bickering and scrutiny of court was too good an opportunity to turn down.

Around him, the port is fraught with anticipation and the five ships of the Armada de Molucca, smeared with black pitch, dot the azure harbour. They stand motionless in the dazzling ocean, weighed down with food, wine, water and men, awaiting their absent Capitán General.

The other captains are all already here. The smallest ship of the armada, the Santiago, rests beside the Trinidad. Its captain, Juan Rodríguez Serrano, speaks to a man in the open air on the main deck. Next in line is the colossal San Antonio, a massive ship that dwarfs the rest of the armada, its vast sails stowed against lofty masts. Cartagena, the San Antonio's captain, is hiding from the midday heat of the sun in his cabin along with Gaspar de Quesada. His ship, the Concepción, is smaller with a patched-up hull showing its age. Finally, is the Victoria, captained by Luis de Mendoza, standing at the farthest pier of the harbour.

As he lists their names in his mind, de Morales tries to imagine some aspect of the captain's personalities that accompany them. For some, he need not imagine. Cartagena is already constantly questioning the Capitán General, despite the fact their Portuguese leader has yet to arrive. Quesada and Mendoza are quieter, aloof and distant, but never check their companion's words. They are a close triumvirate, always passing between one another's ships and exchanging knowing glances across the harbour. It is only the final captain who has kept to himself. Since his arrival, Serrano has yet to even leave the Santiago. Perhaps that is what the other captains ought to be doing. Perhaps they ought to be seeing to their own ships rather than scheming together in one another's cabins.

Despite the hushed conversations and conspiratorial visits of the past few days, de Morales has tried not to catastrophise the situation. He is a man who, against his better judgement, tries to see the good in his fellow man. After all, he has seen every other part of them strewn across the battlefields of Tripoli, Ravenna, La Motta and Navarra or hanging from the gibbets of San Jorge. In amongst all that gore, all that blood, bone and gristle, why should there not also be goodness?

But for all de Morales' shaky optimism and speculation, these captains are a mystery. As much a mystery as what life at sea has in store for him. The extent of his experience on the ocean amounts to the short crossings between Italy and North Africa he took to tend the wounded on the battlefields there nine years ago.

Then there is that final mystery: their leader. The captain of the Trinidad and the Capitán General of the Armada: Fernão de Magalhães. A man absent but present in the minds of every other captain, cabin boy and sailor in the fleet. A man who has masterminded this entire endeavour. A man who claims to know the location of a fabled strait through the New World to the distant riches of the Spice Islands. Sail west to go east. On the face of it, the idea seems absurd. If the rumours that have filtered back to Castile are to be believed, the New World is vast. A virgin land, guarded by savage natives, malicious jungles and sea monsters. And Magalhães plans to pass right through it and out the other side? The Capitán General must have maps and charts no others have seen.

The men have finished moving the crates now and, to escape the midday heat, de Morales takes shelter in his cabin. Though the ship is anchored and tied up at the port, he feels unsteady on his feet as he climbs the gangplank onto the main deck of the Trinidad. He is acutely aware that below him is a few feet of oak and then the abyss awaits. He cannot swim. After all, if he should fall into the depths, what use is swimming? He would only prolong his death at the hands of a lungful of water or the jaws of a monstrous sea creature.

To take his mind off the ocean, de Morales instead focuses on the ship that is to be his home for the voyage. It is a squat thing of the usual design of Spanish naos, with its prow and stern raised out of the ocean as if it is reluctant to get wet. High above, the masts stand imperious and naked with their sails furled. He turns to aftcastle, with its three low, narrow doors opening into separate cabins. On the left is Magalhães' cabin, as yet empty but for the Capitán General's belongings and items of furniture. In the centre is a cabin serving as a dining room and meeting place for Magalhães and the Trinidad's senior officers. Finally, on the right, is de Morales' cabin.

He is to share his cabin with another man he is yet to meet. An Italian and the fleet's chronicler, he has been told, by the name of Antonio Pigafetta. Their cabin is small and made smaller now by the crates and sacks of medicines and other provisions provided by the Casa de Contratación. The labourers have left them dumped in a messy pile in the centre of the room. Still resting on his bed, where he left it that morning, is de Morales' case of surgical tools. Pliers, scissors, scalpels, knives of every size and shape, saws, hammers, a pelican for the removal of rotten teeth, a mortar and pestle, a set of brass scales. All the instruments to cut and mend human flesh and, thereby, save lives. He takes good care of the tools of his trade, keeping them clean and impeccably sharp. He will need them and, when he does, he wants them to be in perfect order.

He passes the rest of the afternoon taking stock of the medicines. Their value is immense, and everything must be in order before the armada leaves. In the stuffy cabin it is hot work but suited to his methodical nature and keeps his mind from wandering into the past.

There are boxes of unguents, nostrums and dried bunches of garlic, wormwood, cropleek and hollowleek. Others contain skullcap and aqua vitae to dull pain during operations as well as mandrake, gall of boar and hemlock. Smaller crates, packed with sawdust, contain a dozen of tiny ampoules of mercury and opium, strictly reserved for the captains' use should they need surgery. Then there are distillations of fennel and chicory as well as dried bunches of rosemary, thyme and sage to clear miasmas. Two large sacks of clean

5

linen cut into strips of various sizes to dress wounds and soak up blood, bile and phlegm. There is honey to treat septic wounds, incense to clean bad airs and chamomile to aid in sleep. Most important, and most precious, is a quart barrel of vinegar to treat that scourge of the Spanish empire at sea: scurvy.

It is all here, thankfully. De Morales did not relish the idea of chasing up lost orders in the few hours left before the armada leaves. Next, he turns his attention to tidying the mess of boxes, crates and sacks, piling them neatly against the far wall of the cabin beside a short stool and table. As he organises the medicines, he keeps half an eye on the open door for the coming of his cabin-mate.

The afternoon slides by in that languid way time passes during spells of hot weather. The calls and shouts from the dock dwindle as the workers, street sellers, merchants and prostitutes hide indoors, taking siestas or fanning themselves in whatever shade they can find. De Morales continues to organise, enjoying the quiet that descends over the Trinidad. Beads of sweat fall from his forehead and, despite the open door of the cabin, the room is soon filled with oppressive heat.

He hears footsteps outside and turns to find a short man standing in the doorway. 'It is hot,' the man says in accented Spanish, blowing air from his inflated cheeks. He drops the case he is carrying in the doorway and steps inside. 'Antonio Pigafetta,' he says. He pulls a silken handkerchief from somewhere inside the green brocade doublet he is wearing and wipes the sheen of sweat from his brow.

De Morales, standing now, removes his hat and bows to

Pigafetta. His eyes rove across the Italian's face, taking in the features quickly. The cropped hair, the neat beard, high brows and dark, almost sullen eyes. 'You are the fleet's chronicler.' he says.

With more than a hint of impatience, Pigafetta offers the slightest of bows in reply. He lifts his case and crosses the room in short, quick steps. 'And what an honour it is,' he says, the loose fabric of his Venetian breeches billowing with his movements, 'to play a part, however small, in such an incredible adventure.' The chronicler sits quickly on the stool, opens his case and pulls a quill, ink and parchment from it. 'You are the physician, correct?' He asks, without looking up.

De Morales nods, for the time being bemused by this strange, rodent-like man before him. 'Juan de Morales,' he says, finding his tongue.

'Physician,' Pigafetta says, scribbling on the parchment.

De Morales, still standing, watches Pigafetta scratching away, expecting him to ask more questions. When it becomes apparent that none will come, he turns back to his organising. The two men work in awkward silence as the shimmering sun is chased into the ocean by the dusk, de Morales organising and Pigafetta writing. Night comes, but the heat remains. Torches are lit, their dancing flames glowing into the darkness, and Los Cristianos awakens from its siesta. The port heaves with men, women, children, animals and slaves. All of them drawn out into the night air. Bartering, begging, drinking and laughing the night away.

When Fernão de Magalhães joins the armada late the following afternoon, he does so without fanfare or ceremony. De Morales hears the Capitán General enter the dining cabin beside his own, a train of companions following on his heels. Furniture grunts and growls as it is dragged across the floor next door and thuds into the thin dividing wall. Though he cannot understand the Portuguese they are speaking, de Morales can hear the muffled voice of the armada's leader and his companions. They sound agitated. One voice, Magalhães' he supposes, is more persistent than the others, the frantic words flowing into one another with barely an interruption.

Soon after sunset yesterday, Pigafetta left the cabin and did not return. Now, de Morales hears the chronicler's muffled voice through the wall. Like the rest of the señores with nothing yet to do aboard the ships, Pigafetta probably slept at an inn in Los Cristianos. De Morales could have joined them, but he preferred the quiet of the flagship. But now everyone is aboard the ship, that quiet has been replaced by cacophonic chaos. The deck of the Trinidad echoes with thuds as men walk this way and that. The heat has yet to let up and the boatswains and masters call to lethargic sailors high up in the rigging, barking orders and threats as the fleet makes its final preparations to depart.

A whistle sounds, piercing through the tumult, and the crew of the Trinidad are called to the main deck. De Morales leaves his cabin. Evening is coming, but the heat of day lingers despite the lengthening shadows and is made worse by the mass of bodies crammed shoulder to shoulder. Sailors come and go, sliding between their comrades while calling and jostling one another. Just visible above the heads of the crew, the ensign of the Capitán General quivers from the flagship's bowsprit, the deep burgundy cross on its white background contorted in the confusion of its folds.

De Morales is pushed aside by a sailor and almost walks into a stocky, rough-looking man standing beside him. He is about to ask the man to step aside when a señor he recognises as the Trinidad's supernumerary, Barbosa, appears beside him. 'Capitán General,' Barbosa says, gesturing toward de Morales, 'this is the physician sent by the Casa de Contratación.'

So, this is Fernão de Magalhães. The Capitán General nods indifferently to de Morales, not noticing or ignoring the hand the physician has extended to him. Magalhães is short and heavily built with a long but well-kept beard covering his throat. His eyes are deeply set, his brow furrowed, his mouth downcast at the corners. His clothing is the familiar baggy shirt and zaragüelles trousers cut off at the knee. On his head, Magalhães wears a wide, deep blue cap with a flattened top. All in all, the Capitán General makes for a shabby sight, far from the lordly image de Morales had conjured up of him. Behind the Capitán General stands a dark-skinned man with a mop of loosely curled black hair. Magalhães' slave, no doubt. The slave is dressed as a Spaniard, in a loose linen shirt and wide breeches. He may stand out on the deck of the Trinidad, but in Sevilla, his like are not an uncommon sight.

'You are fully stocked from the Casa?' Magalhães asks. His voice is low and his eyes search de Morales' face.

'I believe I am fully prepared, come what may,' de Morales says.

The Capitán General nods. 'Good,' is all he says before he turns away. Barbosa begins shoving sailors aside, calling for them to make way as Magalhães follows. The Capitán General has a severe limp and he drags his right leg behind him as he heads towards the forecastle of the Trinidad.

Pedro Sánchez de la Reina, a bishop, and Pedro Valderrama, the fleet's chaplain, stand on the forecastle of the Trinidad. Magalhães joins them, shaking their hands and offering the barest of smiles. Despite being the younger of the two clergymen, Valderrama leads the crew in a prayer for good fortune and the safe return of the fleet. The Trinidad quietens, its crew shuffling into position, their heads bowed.

As the men pray, de Morales takes in the ships of the Armada de Molucca, gathered around the Trinidad, cornering the flagship. The main decks of the Victoria, the Concepción, the San Antonio and the Santiago are thick with the two hundred and forty-two strong crew, craning their necks to see their Capitán General for the first time. Their hulls glisten with inky black pitch juxtaposing with the clean cream of their pristine canvas sails, tightly furled on towering masts. Above them, gulls circle overhead, snapping and screaming at one another in the air.

His eye is drawn to the captain of the Victoria. Mendoza stands stern and austere, a severe look on his aristocratic face. De Morales notices a handsome man beside the captain with black hair and a sharp, spade-shaped beard of perhaps forty years of age. In his arms, the man cradles a white cat. The cat stretches its neck, lifting its head towards the man's fingers as he scratches its brow and ears. The domestic image strikes de Morales as strange in such a foreign setting.

Valderrama is finished and Pigafetta strides towards the Capitán General who, de Morales notices, greets the chronicler with a warm smile. The Italian joins the assembly of family and friends surrounding Magalhães on the forecastle. They joke in Portuguese, shoving each other and laughing, excited for their adventure to begin.

But Magalhães' smile has faded now. He becomes stern and serious amid the joviality of his comrades. He looks south, out to the sea or, possibly, at his armada. From the deck of the massive San Antonio, Cartagena leers back at the Capitán General. His cruel face twisted with a venomous sneer.

The Armada de Molucca finally leaves Los Cristianos as evening falls and it does so to the triumphant boom of cannon fire. The guns wheeze acrid smoke, turning the air to sulphur and hiding the port from view. The live pigs, to be butchered in the coming days, scream and squeal from the holds of the San Antonio at the thunderous salvo. The sails are loosed and catch the wind in their greedy jaws, billowing triumphantly.

Even with their anchors raised, the massive ships packed with men, food, weapons, animals, ballast, wine and water sink low into the ocean. The very fact they are afloat seems astonishing to de Morales, let alone that they can be moved by nothing more than the wind. But move they do and they steadily pick up speed. Slowly, the armada leaves the smoke and tumult of the port behind as it advances from Tenerife, plunging into the endless ocean ahead.

There is no turning back now. De Morales watches Tenerife, the last outpost of Spain and a past he has finally escaped, dwindle into the horizon.

He breathes a sigh of relief.

Chapter 2

September 1519

Sails on the horizon. White sails, bearing the flag of Portugal.

As they passed by, the armada gave the Cape Verde Islands a wide berth but, it seems, they were spotted nonetheless. The Portuguese surely patrol these waters ceaselessly, alert and intent on finding the Armada de Molucca and bringing its renegade Capitán General back to Lisboa in chains.

The caravels are already better designed than the armada's Spanish naos and are certainly faster, not least because they are not weighed down by so many provisions. Whether deliberately so or because of local currents, however, they remain at a distance; their amorphous shapes rippling in the heat coming from the ocean. Nevertheless. they send a shiver of foreboding through de Morales whenever he sees them. Is he imagining it, or are they closing the distance?

The well-charted coasts of western Africa give the Capitán General the confidence to order the fleet to continue sailing through the night. That, he says, ought to put distance between themselves and their pursuers.

Despite the ominous sails on the horizon, the crew quickly settle into life at sea and the deck of the Trinidad is alive with their comings and goings. The boards squeak and groan under their stamping feet and the fresh rigging, still stiff from the factories of Sevilla, creaks as the sails are dropped and raised in response to changes in the wind. Sailors climb the shrouds acrobatically like the Barbary Macaques of Gibraltar, while below the boatswains bark their orders. De Morales keeps his door open to the new sights, sounds and smells of life at sea, carried in by the breeze.

The next day the Capitán General orders his captains to attend a meeting with him in the Trinidad's dining cabin. They are ferried, one by one, in skiffs from their ships. De Morales can hear the conversation taking place next door as Magalhães orders the captains to each hang a signal light from the stern of their ships. The light will allow him to keep track of the locations of the ships of his armada after nightfall. The order does not seem to go down well and is met with loud objections. The captains argue over one another and so their words are incomprehensible, but the tone is clear enough. Incredulity that their allegiance is being questioned gives way to anger when their protestations are ignored.

Eventually, the voices settle, the captains concede defeat, the meeting ends and Serrano, Mendoza, Quesada and Cartagena file out onto the main deck of the Trinidad. As they pass by de Morales' open door, heading towards their waiting skiffs, he hears Cartagena quietly grumble to a silent Quesada.

When dusk falls that evening, one by one the other ships of the armada slow their speed, falling back beside the flagship to allow their captains to hail Magalhães. 'God keep you, Capitán General and master, and good company,' they call, before signal lights swinging from the stern of their ships are lit.

Their greetings are echoic but their tone belies their true thoughts. Serrano is earnest in his salutation and the first to appear. Mendoza is impatient. Quesada is bored and aloof. And then there is Cartagena, hardly bothering to hide his antipathy. Slowly, as the days pass by, Mendoza, Quesada and Cartagena become slothful in their timekeeping and lazy in their delivery, as if the whole spectacle is tiresome to them.

The days lumber by, each one like the last. De Morales lies in his bed, sleep evading him as he imagines caravels closing in from all sides. Pigafetta is scribbling away in the corner on the small writing desk, their gloomy cabin lit by a single candle burning beside the chronicler. The sea has grown more restless and the ship keels and undulates.

Something about the movements in the darkness brings on a roiling sickness. It begins in de Morales' head, his eyes rolling in their sockets, searching for an unmoving anchor in the darkness. A cold sweat smears across his forehead and soaks his shirt. His stomach twists itself into a knot, then lurches with the ship and he feels his throat stretch open. He launches up from the bed, reaches for the bedpan on the floor and vomits copiously into it.

Pigafetta cries out, throws his quill down and quickly stands from his stool. 'What ails you, doctor?' He demands. De Morales retches again and the chronicler staggers away from him, pressing himself against the far wall of their cabin, between the foot of his bed and his writing desk.

De Morales wipes his mouth and examines the yellow bile within the bedpan, sloshing and rolling with the ship's movement. There is no sign of blood nor black bile and so there should be no sickness to worry about. With the excess of yellow bile and phlegm gone, the sickness, he hopes, will pass soon enough.

It is nothing,' he says breathlessly and spits into the bedpan. 'Seasickness.'

'If I come down with something I shall blame you,' Pigafetta says coldly. He shakily returns to his writing, holding his hand over his mouth and nose.

De Morales rises slowly from his bed. He reaches out a shaking hand, leans against the wall for support and takes a sip of water. Then he walks out onto the main deck, leaving the door to the cabin open as he leaves, allowing the breeze to dispel the bad airs.

The night air outside is cool on his damp skin and he inhales deeply through his nose. Estêvão Gomes stands at the whipstaff. With a hand lazily draped over the handle, the ship's pilot guides the Trinidad. Ahead, the signal lights of the Concepción, the Victoria, the San Antonio and the Santiago bob and rock in the darkness. De Morales can just make out the shapes of the armada against the night sky. Dark silhouettes on a darker background.

He crosses to the gunwale and empties the chamber pot overboard. He is careful not to look at the sea slapping and splashing against the hull of the ship, fearing it will bring on another bout of sickness.

He turns to find Gomes looking at him from across the deck through the darkness. 'Seasickness, señor doctor?'

'Yes.' De Morales is surprised to find a note of shame in his voice.

'Drink wine and wormwood,' Gomes says. He winks, 'an old sailor's trick.'

'Thank you, I shall try that.' To make conversation, though he knows he will not understand the answer, de Morales asks how things go.

'Well enough,' Gomes answers. 'We are sailing further south than most ships heading to New Spain. I think the Capitán General means to confuse the caravels pursuing us.'

De Morales avoids the temptation to lean over the gunwale and search in the darkness behind them for the ships, knowing to do so will reveal the ocean to him and bring on more sickness. But he knows they are there. 'How did they know we had left?' He asks.

Gomes scoffs. 'The whole of Europe knows what we are about. The King likes to boast of Spanish achievements, despite the fact he is Flemish. Anyway, you can be certain Portugal has its spies in Tenerife. It makes sense, does it not, that Manuel would want to stop an expedition led by his former subject. Especially given their parting was not exactly friendly.'

'How so?' De Morales clears his throat of bile and leans against the wall of the aftcastle, crossing his arms to stop their shaking. This conversation is welcome to him, if only to take his mind off his rolling stomach.

'Some years ago, Magalhães went to Manuel requesting repayments of debts he said he incurred while fighting in some war or other for the Portuguese crown. But we all know what kings are like. Manuel refused to pay and Magalhães launched into an irate tirade against his king.' Gomes smiles wryly and nods at de Morales' shocked face. 'He was lucky to keep his head. This all happened long before Magalhães befriended Ruy Faleiro and learned of the strait.'

'Ruy Faleiro?'

'You know nothing, do you, señor doctor?'

'I know only what I was told,' he says, feeling self-conscious.

'Ruy Faleiro was a Portuguese cartographer, of sorts. A man of no skill, no worth and no standing. Somehow, he came across the exact location of a strait long rumoured to exist through the New World. Magalhães befriended him and together they approached Manuel with a plan to find this strait. Manuel, perhaps understandably, already disliked Magalhães after his previous visit and refused. Spurned by his king, Magalhães scarpered from Lisboa and approached Castile with the same plan. And, well, here we are.'

'But if Ruy Faleiro knows the location of the strait, why is he not among us now?'

'That,' Gomes says slowly, 'is the question.' He lowers his voice, casts a conspiratorial eye across the empty main deck of the Trinidad and leans closer to de Morales. 'Some say he went mad, others that he is dead. Either way, the discoverer of the strait is not here. And now Manuel's caravels pursue us.'

'Then we are in danger?'

'There is always danger,' Gomes says, standing upright once more, 'as long as one is at sea.'

'But where did you learn of all this?' De Morales asks. Gomes is full of information and more forthcoming with it than anyone involved in the armada has yet been.

Gomes shrugs and flashes that wry smile once again. 'You would be surprised what you can overhear if you sit near the captains' table in the taverns.'

The captains. Surely he means Mendoza, Quesada and Cartagena. From the moment he saw them, de Morales had a bad sense about the Spanish captains. But surely even they could not fabricate such an intricate story. Even if they have inflated it, in every tall tale there is always a kernel of truth. Ruy Faleiro is the missing piece of the puzzle that explains Magalhães' knowledge of a strait. But could he truly have murdered his friend?

De Morales feels another wave of sickness wash over him as the ship lurches. His eyes roll and he staggers sideways.

'You look very unwell, señor doctor.' Gomes' tone is blunt, but his eyes give away his concern.

De Morales breathes through his nose and swallows fresh bile. He bids Gomes goodnight, wishing him well for the night's sailing ahead and slides through the open door to his cabin.

The cramped room is darkened now and Pigafetta, facing the wall, is seemingly asleep. Closing the door behind him, de Morales stumbles back into his bed, hoping beyond hope the seasickness will not return and wondering at the rumours Gomes spoke of.

The next morning, he is called to the Concepción. A sailor was found crying into his hands with deep scratches on his forearms, face and thighs, whimpering of blood and wine. Bustamante, the fleet's barber surgeon posted on board the Concepción, is already here. He stands, with an indifferent look on his face over a pathetic figure, curled up in the cramped hold between two crates of hardtack.

For a moment, de Morales is a youth again standing in the Hospital Cristiano Nuestra Señora. His father is before him, chained to the wall, head shaved, sobbing and filthy. Beside de Morales is his brother, who would inherit what little wealth their father had and to whom de Morales would soon have to beg for the money to study medicine at the Universidad de Salamanca. He looks at the man who created him, who raised him, the man who beat and rebuked him and marvels at what he has become. A bull of a man, worthy now of little more than pity. So many nights of de Morales' youth were spent staring into the darkness, turning over carefully crafted fantasies of violent revenge and finally facing up to the one man he has ever truly hated. Over the long years of adolescence that followed, those fantasies of rage and violence had distilled into little more than a desire for acknowledgement. Now they are reduced further still to nothing. It was just like his father, to deny him even that.

He sighs back into the present, to the cramped hold of the lurching Concepción and the weeping sailor before him. 'Did you treat him?' He asks Bustamante.

'This cannot be treated.' Barbers are all alike: stuck in the past. For them, what cannot be treated immediately cannot be treated at all.

'I will be the judge of that,' de Morales says. 'He can be trepanned if it is necessary. Though that may have to wait until we are on land. Do you know his name?'

'The crew call him Juan la Loca,' Bustamante says sardonically. 'For the queen,' he adds.

All his life, it seems, de Morales has been surrounded by the mad. For most, like his father, madness is but the final stage in a lifetime of living with the pox. But Juana la Loca was different. Mad from birth, had she been anything but a queen, she would have been left outside a nunnery or else swung into a wall by her legs.

He kneels, reaches out a hand, touches the sailor's shoulder. 'What is your name?'

The sailor continues whimpering into his hands, ignoring de Morales' touch. 'He will not answer,' Bustamante says. 'He is beyond help.'

Rolling his eyes, de Morales moves closer to the sailor. 'You must let me help you,' he says.

The sailor lashes out with a clawed hand and gnashing teeth and de Morales jumps backwards. Before he can react, the sailor is on his feet, darting for the ladder. He follows the sailor, as quickly as he can, up onto the main deck while Bustamante lags behind.

De Morales bursts into dazzling sunlight bouncing off bright sails, and whirls around, searching. 'Where did he go?' He asks desperately.

Sailors point to the aftcastle and he bounds up to it only to find Quesada already there. The captain's back is to him, his balding head is bowed as he is looking down at the sea behind the Concepción. De Morales hurriedly moves beside the captain. He sees the body in the water, already sinking below the surface.

'You must save him,' de Morales says.

'He wants to die,' Quesada says still staring into the ocean, the brown smudge of the sailor slowly disappearing into the darkness. 'Let him go.'

'You cannot let a man die.'

Quesada turns his grey eyes on de Morales. 'Madness is bad luck at sea,' he says, apparently unbothered by de Morales' lack of respect. 'If I pulled him in, the crew would only cast him back again.' He nods towards the body in the water. 'See how he does not fight? He knows what must be done.'

The mad sailor is lost now. The Trinidad surges past the foam swelling across the ocean's surface, the only memorial to where he drowned.

Dinner and the Capitán General's comrades line the table. He sees familiar faces from Tenerife. Magalhães at the head of the table. His slave, Enrique, surreptitiously leaning against the wall behind his master, resting his back. At the right hand of the Capitán General sits Valderrama, ascetic and serious, his bland face set in the pious self-righteousness of the clergy. At Magalhães' left is Pigafetta with Barbosa next in line. Across from him is Cristóvão Rebêlo, the illegitimate son of Magalhães, perhaps bored or perhaps drunk, it is difficult to tell. Sitting beside him is Álvaro Mesquita, the Capitán General's cousin. The ship's master-at-arms, Gonzalo Gómez de Espinosa, sits on a chest in the corner of the room, chewing on bread and massaging his shoulder.

'Stop making a show of it,' Barbosa says with mock exasperation. 'No one asked you to dance around the forecastle with your sword all day.' The diners laugh. Espinosa, de Morales notices, does not.

The master-at-arms rises from the chest, his face serious. 'I was training a few of the sailors,' he says. 'You will thank me, Duarte, when they save your life.' Like de Morales, Espinosa is not a seasoned sailor. The master-at-arms, instead, is a former warrior and the only trained soldier onboard the armada.

Espinosa crosses the room and grunts into the empty

chair beside Pigafetta. De Morales does the same, seating himself beside Barbosa, at the end of the table.

Always de Morales tries to appear late to these things, even when there is no excuse. He would rather be late. He would rather enter into a room where the stage is already set, the players already in place. Those who approach him are those who feel he is worthy of approaching. It saves time. And disappointment.

'How do you settle into life at sea?' Barbosa asks him.

'Well enough, thank you,' de Morales replies, aware of the seven pairs of scrutinising eyes settling on him.

'He vomited like a dog last night,' Pigafetta bawls.

The joke is brutish and uncalled for and the laughter that follows is cruel. The stage is set then. De Morales reddens and involuntarily shrinks into himself.

'Be kind, Antonio,' Barbosa says. 'Should you fall ill, you will be under de Morales' scalpel, remember.'

''Tis but a jest,' Pigafetta says, waving a hand dismissively.

'Did he spatter your scribbling?' Espinosa asks. 'God forbid.'

'Thankfully he did not,' Pigafetta answers. He becomes serious. 'I would be loath to lose my records. They must be kept safe,' He turns to Magalhães, 'for posterity.' The Capitán General remains silent at the head of the table. Behind his beard, his face is unreadable but his dark eyes roam the table.

'We have all suffered at some point,' Rebêlo says. 'Anyone who claims to have never had seasickness is a liar for my money.'

'I had a rough night myself,' Valderrama says. 'Though praise be I believe I am through the worst of it.'

'It is how it always goes,' Barbosa says casually, as a man who has travelled extensively at sea only can. 'One feels awful at first and it will come and go over the coming week or so. But eventually, your stomach will settle and life at sea will be second nature.'

The cook, Cristobal Rodriguez, enters the room, a cabin boy on his heels. A pig on the San Antonio must have been slaughtered for the pewter tray he carries is piled with steaming pork, glistening and succulent. Cloves, sizzling in the fat, breathe their warm, woody scent into the air.

De Morales' stomach heaves at the sight of the food and the pungent scent of the spices. As prayers are said by Valderrama, the scent of the cloves settles itself into de Morales' mind, heightening his awareness of what the armada hopes to achieve.

The others eye the food greedily, waiting for the Capitán General to take the first serving. Before he eats, Magalhães leans back in his chair. Enrique moves from the shadows of the cabin, leans over his master and lifts a scrap of pork from the tray. He places it on his tongue, chews slowly and swallows. The other diners, focusing on the food, the wine or themselves, ignore Enrique. Can the Capitán General truly be this paranoid? True enough in Castile, it is common for slaves to taste the food of their masters for poisons, but surely it is not necessary here? On a ship, utterly separated from anyone who might wish Magalhães harm.

De Morales studies the Capitán General's blank expression, searching for any clue to the rumours Gomes spoke of last night. Could this man truly have murdered Faleiro? He turns and notices Pigafetta's cold eyes watching him from across the table.

The other men are talking now and, feeling he must take part, de Morales asks, 'how did you injure your leg, Capitán General?'

Rebêlo answers, 'my father was injured on the battlefields of Azamor fighting for Manuel.' A wave of irritation crosses Magalhães' face. Could it be this is the same war Gomes spoke of last night, the war that caused the rift between Magalhães and his king?

The Capitán General exhales heavily. 'It did not heal properly,' he says quickly. 'The surgeons did what they could. But I have lived with it for many years. It is what it is.'

'God's will be done,' Valderrama says quietly.

'Hear hear,' Pigafetta says, raising his goblet. 'It led you here, after all, Capitán General. Injury and mishap can lead to good things.'

'Tell that to the men left on the battlefield,' Espinosa says.

'It is all God's will,' Valderrama says seriously. 'Whether we understand it or not, His will be done.' The priest crosses himself slowly, deliberately. Magalhães follows suit. 'Pain is the inheritance of sin,' Valderrama says.

'Pain should be soothed, as much as possible,' Espinosa says. 'Why else would we bother with medicine at all. Would you prefer we leave men to suffer in agony, believing their pain will purify them before death?'

'If it is necessary,' Valderrama says.

Espinosa shakes his head in disbelief. 'With all due respect, Father, you know nothing of pain.'

'I have given succour to countless men in their final agony,' Valderrama says.

'I am sure you have, but yours is a spiritual relief administered at a deathbed. I am talking of physical pain, of the pain found upon a battlefield.' Espinosa turns to de Morales. 'Señor doctor, surely you can see what I mean.'

De Morales pulls his eyes from the glistening pork before him, looking so much like the smear of humanity strewn across the battlefields as he pieced screaming men back together. 'The medical world is divided,' he says slowly. 'Some universities teach to alleviate pain. Others are more traditional and tell us illness is sin and pain is part of the cleansing process. The Protomedicato are happy to let both sides exist.'

'And you, de Morales?' Valderrama asks. 'What were you taught?'

The diner's eyes turn on de Morales once more, scrutinising this newcomer in their midst, anticipating what he will say. He must be careful. One wrong word and any one of them could report him to the Inquisition when the Armada returns. 'I was taught that physical pain should be soothed and softened as much as possible,' he says, choosing his words carefully. 'I leave the state of the soul to holy men such as yourself, Father, but the body is of flesh and it is my duty to care for it.'

Espinosa shrugs. Valderrama nods. De Morales breathes a silent sigh of relief. He has navigated those treacherous waters well.

The conversation turns to mundane anecdotes of the past, littered with childish jokes and boisterous laughter from Pigafetta and Rebêlo. De Morales stays on the periphery, eating little and speaking of harmless matters with Barbosa until the meal is finished and he excuses himself.

The diners stay in the cabin long into the night. Next door, de Morales tosses and turns, listening to the muffled conversations echoing through the dividing wall, pierced every so often by cackling laughter. His mind returns time and again to the image of the mad sailor sinking below the waves in the wake of the Concepción.

He imagines the ocean pressing in, blotting out all light and sound from the world. He cannot imagine a lonelier death.

Chapter 3

October 1519

The armada is spread across the sea, limp sails bathed in the orange glow of evening, the heat from the desert of western Africa slides into the Great Ocean. The sea and the air are still, as they have been now for thirteen days.

The crew have grown lethargic with inactivity. There are things to be done, as there always are aboard a ship, but knowing one is going nowhere while one does them is depressing to the mind and soul for those who signed up to an expedition in search of adventure, fortune and spices. One can look at the same landscape for only so long before one becomes as languid as the surrounding ocean.

The Portuguese caravels have disappeared, melting into

the haze of the horizon. But the crew of the armada is on edge nonetheless. They are in Portuguese waters and have been since they left Tenerife over a fortnight ago. The only saving grace is that any Portuguese ships nearby will have hit the same doldrums. If the Capitán General had only sailed west, like most expeditions to the New World, they would be well rid of them by now and far away from the becalmed weather. But he continued south for countless leagues, following the western coast of Africa almost to the equator.

The Capitán General will tell no one of what his exact plans are and his tendency toward secrecy is exasperating the Spanish captains of the other ships. The whole situation came to a head four days ago during a meeting Magalhães had ordered the other captains to attend. The meeting took place in the Trinidad's dining cabin on a stifling evening of still, sticky air. Though he was not party to it, de Morales, taking the air on the deck, had heard Cartagena's shrill voice as the captain of the San Antonio furiously slammed his fist onto a table. *Traitor.* He had screamed. What followed de Morales cannot say. The voices quickly returned to their muffled conversation and the sailors around him, at least pretending to have heard nothing, continued with their work.

The problem appears to have been resolved but, de Morales suspects, not for long.

There is an insubordinate air about Cartagena. In the weeks since the armada left Tenerife, his sulky salutations to the Capitán General each evening have become scornful and his bad mood has turned to open dissent. How much longer before the dissent matures further still, into something more direct? De Morales gets the sense that this motionlessness cannot end soon enough for the Capitán General. As long the fleet remains immobile, it will be easy for Cartagena to stir up

28

trouble amongst the bored men.

The terse company de Morales and Pigafetta kept has also soured, cooling into little more than words spoken in passing. Since the doldrums hit, de Morales has seen little of Pigafetta. The Italian has spent his days with Magalhães, staying with the Capitán General long into the night. For whatever reason, the chronicler seems to dislike de Morales' company. It is as if he feels sharing a cabin with a mere physician is beneath him. Whereas he used to greet the chronicler on his return, de Morales now ignores Pigafetta when he stumbles into the cabin, instead choosing to feign sleep or preoccupation. There is only so much cold indifference a man can take before he, too, becomes apathetic.

As yet, there has been little call for de Morales to use his trade. Mesquita has complained of a sore tooth, for which he prescribed a compress soaked in a mixture of wine, vinegar and seawater. There have been other small injuries and mishaps – burns, sprains and cuts – but nothing mortal nor, even, severe. To pass the days of inaction, de Morales and Barbosa have taken to conversing in the evenings. Tonight, they are sitting in de Morales' cabin, fanning themselves with sheets of Pigafetta's parchment. The chronicler is elsewhere, most likely ingratiating himself to Magalhães in his cabin.

'In Sanlúcar de Barrameda, I ordered servings of quince for each captain and señor in the armada,' Barbosa says, passing de Morales a small clay jar. The surgeon pulls the cork stopper. The lancinating scent of oranges fills the cabin, transporting him to Sevilla and the Patio de los Naranjos. He sees the vivid green of the trees in the midday sun, smells their citrus tang in the air and remembers the fluttering white of a dress, the flash of a smile, the feel of his wife's hair falling across his face.

He closes the jar carefully, putting away the memories. 'You are most kind,' he says heavily. 'I am truly thankful.'

'Think nothing of it,' Barbosa's reply is jovial. 'I ask only that you call me Duarte, you need not be so formal. With me, at least.'

Judging the time to be right, de Morales risks asking Barbosa a question that has been on his mind since he first met Magalhães in Los Cristianos. 'I sense the Capitán General does not trust me,' he says, choosing his words carefully. 'Have I done something to arouse his suspicions?'

'What brought you to the Casa de Contratación?'

Sensing it best to answer Barbosa's seemingly evasive question, de Morales says, 'I served as a physician to Juana of Castile for six years.' He pauses, remembering the court with its labyrinthine corridors, politics and scheming, the sense he always had of the oppressive weight of hundreds of years of history and ghosts pushing down around him. 'I could live with life in Castile no longer. I saw the request for physicians from the Casa de Contratación. In truth, I believe I was the only trained surgeon to apply, for I was granted the role in a letter before I had even arrived in Sevilla for an interview with their physicians. But what does this have to do with the Capitán General's suspicions?'

'You had no previous dealings with the Casa?' Barbosa asks.

'No,' de Morales says simply. 'How could I? Why would I?'

'Good.' Barbosa thinks for some time before continuing. 'You are trustworthy,' he says, 'and so I will tell you this, but you must keep it to yourself. The last thing this armada needs is more gossip.'

'On my honour.'

Barbosa sighs deeply. 'Fernão is an excellent leader, but I am sure you have wondered at a Portuguese Capitán General of a Spanish armada?'

De Morales knows he must be careful not to reveal all Gomes told him of Magalhães' past a fortnight ago. 'In truth, I have not,' he says. 'Was not Cristoforo Genoan? Vespucci a Florentine? I have been in the service of the Spanish royalty for much of my life, not always happily. But even I would concede that what sets the Spanish court apart from all others is that a man is judged by his merits, not the land of his birth.'

'I am sure that is true in respect of the court of Castile,' Barbosa says, 'but the Casa de Contratación is a whole other beast. Its head, Juan Rodríguez Fonseca, is a conniving and jealous man. When I introduced you to Magalhães, I mentioned the Casa and that was enough to raise his suspicions. I ought not have said that and I apologise for it.'

Well, that answers half of de Morales' question but not the whole. 'But why is the Capitán General so suspicious of those sent by the Casa de Contratación?'

'None of the other captains of the armada were chosen by Magalhães,' Barbosa says. 'When Fonseca saw the Capitán General's list of proposed captains, he threw the parchment upon which they were written to the floor and launched into a tirade, accusing Magalhães of nepotism. Fernao's list was made up almost entirely of Portuguese relatives or Spanish in-laws. My own father was to be captain of the San Antonio.'

'Forgive me,' de Morales says, 'but surely, he knew that was unwise?'

'I would call it ill-advised rather than unwise,' Barbosa shrugs. 'But remember, the Portuguese are far more experienced than us Spanish in exploring the New World; and as for my father, he has travelled the Indies perhaps more than any man living. Anyway, Serrano, Mendoza, Quesada and Cartagena were appointed by Fonseca, countermanding the authority the king had granted Magalhães to select his own captains and crew. But Cartagena's appointment, especially, is nothing more than the nepotism Fonseca accused the Capitán General of.'

'Why is that?'

'Because Cartagena is the bastard child of Fonseca,' Barbosa says. 'He has no experience at sea to qualify him as captain of a ship, let alone the largest ship in the armada. We believe he has been put in place by his father with the sole intention of subverting the Magalhães' authority.'

'Well, that would explain a lot,' de Morales says. 'Judging by the events of the meeting the other day, Cartagena is more than fulfilling his charge.'

'Exactly. We are not a month into our journey and already Cartagena is showing his true purpose here. Be mindful, de Morales,' Barbosa says seriously. 'There is much conspiracy amongst this armada and you would do well to stay vigilant of it.'

With that Barbosa rises to leave. He stops at the threshold, turns back to de Morales. 'Enjoy the quince, señor doctor,' he says. 'Ration it well, it may have to last some time.' He smiles brightly and stoops out of the doorway, leaving de Morales alone in the cabin.

The surgeon thinks back to the harbour in Los Cristianos. The screaming gulls, the booming cannons and Cartagena in the midst, staring venomously at Magalhães from the deck of the San Antonio. Fonseca's bastard. Magalhães' past. The Spanish captains. The picture is becoming clearer.

Three days pass and still, the wind does not come.

The night is quiet and a heavy mist has melted from the coast of Africa into the ocean, dampening all sound. The signal lights from the other four ships send their dull, weak glow into the night, bruises of yellow light breaking the blackness.

De Morales has taken up the habit of walking lengths of the Trinidad in the quieter, cooler night; if only to clear his head and break the monotony of his days and the silence of his cabin. Until illness and malady strike the armada, there is little for him to do. He makes his way along the port side of the Trinidad, Africa on his right and the vast emptiness of the Great Ocean on his left.

In the corner of the main deck, hidden in the shadows cast by the eaves of the forecastle, three sailors quietly throw dice while others watch. Their stifled jeers and hoots break the silence of the night. Gambling is strictly forbidden and, were they caught, a whipping would be the least of their punishments. De Morales looks at them, imagines from where they came and who they left behind.

He reaches the aftcastle, turns and immediately notices the lights of the San Antonio disappear. His eye is drawn to the black shape of the Concepción as its lights are also dimmed. Between the Trinidad and the coast, the Victoria stands black and imposing, its signal light still wavering in the heavy fog.

Cartagena first, then Quesada. The signs seem evident. It is mutiny, then.

He is about to call out for Barbosa. But then the signal light of the San Antonio shimmers back to its dull glow. Seconds pass and the same happens to the Concepción's light.

This cannot be a mutiny. But it could, possibly, be

something much worse. Something is passing between the ships. De Morales' mind jumps to the Portuguese caravels. If they have been discovered then the expedition is doomed before it ever really began.

But it cannot be. Whatever this black shape that cuts through the water is, it is doing so noiselessly. Not the slightest splash or ripple can be heard. But even if the ship's crew were working in complete silence, how can this vessel be moving in a wind that does not exist?

A sea monster, then? One of the leviathans that come upon ships and rip them apart. De Morales imagines furious jaws below the ocean's surface and sees them crushing the hull of the Trinidad, men and provisions spilling out into the sea. His throat dries out and his skin prickles at the thought.

Forty feet above, a blue light plumes through the mist. It pulsates and flickers, sending a shiver down de Morales' spine. From its bleak glow, he can make out a bent and splintered mainmast, rising out of the mist, shockingly naked without its sail. Other masts appear from the gloom: the bowsprit, lateen and the mizzen, all crooked, their torn sails limp and bathed in the dismal glow. Despite the heated air spilling from the coast, he feels cold to his bones, as if all warmth and hope are being stolen from him by that cold and empty blue light.

De Morales tries to cry out, but his voice is stolen from him. With great effort, he pulls his gaze from the light and looks around him. The sailors gambling on the main deck don't seem to have noticed this lurid, broken ship that is drawing itself past the flagship, sliding slow and fateful through the unmoving water.

The vessel drifts closer, its prow is beside him now. If he were to reach out his hand, he could almost touch its slimy, battered hull. But horror has stricken him immobile. The ship bears a name that makes his blood run cold. Though the paint is cracked and the hull chipped, worn and matted in weeds, lichen and algae the name is perfectly legible to him.

The Victoria.

Before his mind can catch up to what his eyes are seeing, the smell hits him. A foetid blend of rotting wood, mildew and human filth. But cutting through all that putrid stink is a smell that hits him like an Inquisitor's lash. Spices. The ship is giving off the warm, beguiling scent of cloves and, following fast on its heels, is the sick, earthly scent of cinnamon.

De Morales looks along the waterlogged hull of the spectral Victoria, taking in its derelict beakhead and empty gun ports. His eye is drawn to the main deck where figures stagger and stumble. Their clothes are tattered. Their faces are gaunt, lips swollen and cracked. Their glazed eyes are sunken in dark sockets surrounded by crusted sea salt and seem to see nothing before them. The apparitions listlessly wander the deck like the dead of Hades, indifferent to the world around them.

He looks past the phantom ship at the Victoria behind its ghastly twin. Its pristine sails and perfect masts, rising straight and true, glow in the light of braziers and torches. How can the ship be in two places at once? It is only then, as his eye wanders down the phantom Victoria's hull to the waterline, that he sees this ship is leaving no wake. The ocean is completely undisturbed by its passage.

Almost of their own accord, his eyes return to where he expects to find the deck, but the ship has moved on on its slow, unceasing journey. It passes into the darkness, leaving only the memory of its bloated, waterlogged hull, emaciated crew and hopeless blue light to haunt his thoughts.

A sleepless night follows. De Morales tosses and turns but every time he closes his eyes, he sees those pallid faces staring back at him and the bloated bulk of the ghastly Victoria, stinking to high heaven of cloves and water rot. All of it draped in the ethereal, blue light.

At some point, he hears Pigafetta enter the cabin, the door squeaks on its hinge, spilling the dull glow of candlelight into the room. The chronicler's footsteps thud against the wooden boards before he spills into his creaking bed.

He could tell Pigafetta what he saw. He feels himself already sinking into the relief of sharing his vision. But he thinks better of it. The chronicler has shown nothing but contempt for de Morales thus far. Surely Pigafetta would use anything de Morales told him now as a way to be rid of him. After all, who would want to sleep in the same cabin as a madman? The realisation hits him: he cannot speak to anyone of what he saw. He fears inciting a wave of superstition and terror amongst the crew, not to mention how they would treat him. De Morales has seen first-hand how the mad are treated on land and Quesada could not have been clearer in explaining how they are dealt with at sea. He swallows hard as he thinks back to the body of the mad sailor, sinking below the waves behind the Concepción.

He rolls over, faces the wall and stares into the darkness.

He gives up on the farce of sleep and rises just after dawn breaks. Leaving the cabin, he makes his way onto the main deck, blood pumping in his ears at his wild imaginings of seeing that awful ship again. But the air outside is warm and pleasant and the mist has gone. It is only the four, real, ships that surround the Trinidad on the ocean. A light breeze brushes his face.

Magalhães is already standing on the main deck, looking out from the starboard side of the Trinidad at the Great Ocean stretching out endless and empty. The night watchmen, nearing the end of their shifts, watch him pass by from under their caps with tired eyes and hunched backs.

The deck creaks under his feet, catching the Capitán General by surprise, awakening him from some dark thought. Magalhães turns quickly, sees him and seems to relax. 'It is a sorry thing,' he says, turning back to the ocean, 'to see sedition rise against you. Pray you may never face it.'

De Morales can tell, from the wanness of his skin and the darkness of his eyes, that the Capitán General has also had a sleepless night. What apparitions did you see? He wonders. 'I think, señor Capitán General, I need not worry about that happening,' he says.

Beneath his beard, Magalhães' face twists into a joyless smile. For a moment, de Morales thinks he will tell the Capitán General of his vision. But he quickly decides against it. Magalhães is under much strain already and who can say how he would react?

'I know Duarte spoke with you,' Magalhães says quietly. 'He feels you can be trusted.' De Morales remains silent, knowing the Capitán General has more to say. After some thought, Magalhães continues, 'I wonder if you could assist me with something?' He turns his stern eyes on de Morales, searching his face.

'Of course. Anything.'

'The armada is rife with insubordination. My father-in-law warned me of it in a letter I received from him in Los

Cristianos. He told me of rumours of mutiny. Those rumours and my suspicions have been confirmed over these past days. Fonseca has poisoned this expedition against me.' There is no self-pity, no bitterness in Magalhães' voice. He has resigned himself to the facts that lie before him. For his part, de Morales is as unsurprised by the revelation of mutiny as Magalhães appears to be.

'As you come and go between the ships, going about your work, you may hear fragments of evil intent,' Magalhães continues. 'Do not put yourself in any danger, but anything you do hear you must report to Barbosa or myself. I am sure, every chance they get, the Spanish captains will speak ill of me. I have no interest in slander. But be vigilant of talk of mutiny.'

'Thus far I have had little reason to pass between the ships,' de Morales says.

'I am sure bad luck will befall our armada at some point,' Magalhães says. 'When it does, all I ask is that you keep your eyes and ears open.'

The Capitán General looks out once again at the rippling waters of the Great Ocean. From the bowsprit, his ensign flickers restlessly. The wind has risen even as they have spoken.

A cry comes from the forecastle. 'To the sails. Raise anchor.' Behind them, the hatch bursts open and seamen spill onto the main deck, jostling and shoving past one another.

Magalhães turns to leave, stops, turns back and looks de Morales in the eye. 'I fear I was mistaken in keeping so many of my allies aboard the Trinidad,' he says mournfully. Then he is gone, lost among his crew.

Chapter 4

November 1519

The warm breeze pushes at the sails, steadily building to a gust, then a gale and, finally, a squall. As the wind rises, Magalhães gives the order for the fleet to turn west, towards the New World.

The tempest they plunge into is terrifying in its violence. Wanting to make up for so much time lost off the coast of Africa, Magalhães orders the fleet to continue under full sail despite the high winds. The masts bend and creak as the sails balloon, dragging the Armada de Molucca onwards. De Morales has never known such a fierce windstorm. The only small blessing is that the seasickness now seems to have passed.

In the midst of the storm, men begin to lose their minds. Rumours find their way to the Trinidad of a sailor from one of the other ships, some say it was the Concepción, others the

San Antonio, who simply jumped over the gunwale into the churning waters below.

It is a cruel irony that not two weeks ago every man prayed for salvation from the doldrums and now, for ten days, they have been at the mercy of this heartless ocean. Buffeted and battered by the cruel and relentless winds. Their only salvation is that they are being sent in the correct direction.

Only the most necessary crew venture out onto the deck. For de Morales a cramped, squalid life is all he knows. But the unfortunate sailors on duty have it far worse. They are soaked and chilled to the bone in seconds not by rain but by seawater whipped into the air by the gale.

Even Pigafetta stays in the cramped cabin with de Morales. The two sit and work in silence. Pigafetta, tightly gripping the corner of the small desk as the ship lurches and pitches on the waves while he scribbles away. De Morales, checking unguents, preparing herbs, cleaning tools, doing anything to keep his mind busy.

Though it is difficult to tell the difference between day and night in the heavy gloom of the now permanent low hanging clouds, evening is doubtless coming. Tired of the silence between them, de Morales says, more to the walls than to Pigafetta, 'I find myself thinking of those who came before us to these very waters. Those who disappeared in them.'

Pigafetta puts down his quill and turns on his stool to face the physician. The Trinidad drops suddenly, falling into the trough of a wave. 'What are you saying?'

'Just that this storm puts me in mind of the lives these waters have claimed. The Vivaldi brothers died, what, two hundred and fifty years ago? And there was Van Olman in the 1480's. How many other names have been lost in the folding waves of this Great Ocean?'

Pigafetta watches de Morales in silence, his face cast half in shadow by the guttering flame of the lone candle on the desk. The Trinidad groans as the ocean pitches and rolls beneath it. Another wave slaps the hull of the ship. An inky smear of dark water spills over the sill and into the cabin. De Morales lifts his feet as the puddle grows. He looks into the shallow pool, imagines the depths from whence it came surging outside.

'What an absurd thing,' he says slowly, hypnotised by the broadening pool, 'to cast men into such a vast, unfathomably violent ocean with nothing between them and a watery grave than not two inches of slowly rotting oak and a thin coating of pitch.'

'Shut up,' Pigafetta says. His bluntness snaps de Morales from his dark thoughts. He blinks and looks up at Pigafetta. Now standing, the chronicler's knuckles are white and harsh as he grips the table tighter still. Pigafetta lurches as the Trinidad climbs a wave and corrects his balance as it slaps back down into the trench behind it. 'You are a pessimistic brute,' he says finally. 'I do not want to hear your morbid musings, nor do I want to hear you challenge the Capitán General. Magalhães will have you whipped when he hears of this.'

'For what?' De Morales demands.

'You are undermining his authority,' Pigafetta fires back. Another wave comes and the prow of the Trinidad rises as it climbs to its crest. Pigafetta takes a faltering step towards de Morales, letting go of the table. At the same moment, the Trinidad surges down, crashing into the trough of the wave. Pigafetta is launched forwards. He raises his hands just in time to protect his face before he smashes into the cabin

41

door. The latch snaps and the door bursts open.

'Antonio,' de Morales cries. The howling wind invades the cabin, whipping parchment and herbs into the air. He stands, desperately trying to find his feet as the Trinidad tosses on the waves. Around him, the cabin is in chaos. He grasps the door frame tightly as a torrent of water surges across the main deck of the ship, soaking the prostrate form of Pigafetta lying in the doorway.

A faceless sailor, wrapped in a cloak and cap, turns towards the chasmic opening of the cabin. He shouts something, his words lost in the storm, then waves his arms. But de Morales is not looking at the sailor. He is looking past him. Into the gloom and the violent storm of the rolling waves thrashing and boiling, dwarfing the armada. Dotted across their vast peaks are the four flickering signal torches of the San Antonio, the Santiago, the Concepción and the Victoria.

The Victoria. That ominous shape that still recalls in his mind the horror of the vision on the stagnant African coast, the ship cuts boldly through the ocean leading the advance. From the topmost spear of its mainmast a light, white at first but deepening to a Cerulean blue, stutters and pulsates toward the heavens. Others have noticed it now and, despite the tumult around them, every man stops where he is. They stare in fascination at the otherworldly image before them.

Pigafetta struggles onto his knees, bleeding hands clasped in front of him as if in prayer. 'St. Elmo's Fire,' he shouts into the wind and rain. 'The blessed saint of Formia is with us.' He crosses himself quickly, sending splashes of blood into the wind. 'We will not lose friends. Take heart. God is with us.'

Others on deck follow Pigafetta's lead and cross themselves or fall to their knees, hands folded above their heads, their prayers stolen from their lips by the wind. Surrounded by the vast and terrible storm, they find comfort in a light sent from heaven, a light that will guide them to safety in the arms of the patron saint of sailors.

But de Morales feels no comfort. Standing behind Pigafetta in the doorway of the cabin, his clothes already soaked through, the wind lashing at his face, he stares wide-eyed at the Victoria. He sees the eerie blue light towering from the mainmast of the ship and his heart pounds in his chest. The colour drains from his face as before him the Victoria becomes that ghost ship he saw off the coast of Africa. The supernatural light pulses and brings flashes to his mind of the starved crew stumbling about the deck. He is filled with a profound terror of that light and the cursed ship from which it comes.

There is no hope here, in this massive, indifferent ocean. God cannot find them and Saint Elmo is not guiding them. That light is the light of hell, drawing the armada towards a fate de Morales saw off the coast of Africa.

The windstorm passed several days ago and the sea now undulates with silken waves. Though the ferocity has gone, the strength of the wind remains and the sails billow and snap, pulling the armada onwards.

De Morales has passed between several ships since the storm passed. While the crews have set to repair the damage to the ships, the physician has set to repair the broken bodies. While he does so, at the back of his mind, is the instruction Magalhães gave him: *Keep your eyes and ears open. Report anything you hear to myself or Barbosa.*

Today a skiff arrives from the Santiago with news that a cabin boy has been vomiting since the first day of the storms. At this stage in the journey, it is unlikely to be seasickness. Even the most inexperienced among the crew, of which de Morales was certainly one, have long ago become used to the constant pitching of the ships.

He makes his way to the smallest ship of the fleet in a skiff, bouncing and slapping off the ocean. The sailor at the oars powerfully rows against the wind and waves. When he climbs over the taffrail, de Morales comes face to face, for the first time, with the Santiago's captain, Juan Serrano.

Their first meeting is short and formal. Serrano is a quietly spoken man with a long and grave face. His hair and beard are cropped short and he wears a pair of wide beige slopes and a blue leather jerkin over a woollen doublet undulating in the wind. The short introduction he receives from the captain of the Santiago teaches de Morales nothing more than he already knew: Serrano is a solitary, serious man and is here to do his job and nothing more.

The ailing cabin boy's excess of yellow bile is easily cured. De Morales tells him to fast until the ailment clears and gives him peppermint leaves to chew.

Others are worse affected.

Also aboard the Santiago, he sets the bone of a seaman whose arm was broken when he slipped and fell onto the main deck. The sailor feels no pain, which is fortunate because de Morales must be sparing with his medicines. He has so little and the strongest remedies he has are reserved for the captains and señores.

The next day, de Morales is called to the San Antonio to view the corpse of a sailor who was stabbed at some point during the storm. It is the first time he has been to

Cartagena's ship and, as his skiff approaches it, he is weighed down by the expectancy of what he will find onboard.

But his imaginings of a wild ship, teeming with unruly pirates are unfounded. The ship instead is well-managed and the crew are worked hard and kept in line. Cartagena is nowhere to be seen. The captain must be hiding from the wind, comfortable and warm in his cabin.

He is led into the orlop hold of the massive San Antonio, where rats scurry and the darkness is filled with the creak of the rudder. His presence is unnecessary, for the sailor has been dead now for some days.

Already decaying, the body lies where it was found, slumped against the wall in a dark corner of the hold. The rats have gotten to the cadaver and have already gorged on the softest parts of the body. The face is a glistening mess and, eyeless, the corpse stares into the darkness.

De Morales pulls apart the sailor's shirt, crusted with dried blood. The rats have found their way there too and have chewed their way deep into the abdomen. But even with that mutilation, de Morales can easily make out the single, deep stab wound in the side of the sailor's belly. His was a slow and painful death. He hopes the man was long dead before the rats began their feast.

The body is hauled onto the deck and cast into the sea, accompanied by a few disinterested words from de la Reina. His duty done, the bishop shuffles across the main deck into the captain's cabin. Still there is no sign of Cartagena.

After what de Morales assumes to be a half-hearted investigation, Cartagena eventually reports to the Capitán General that evening that he has found no evidence of foul play. The sailor, he says, died by his own hand. Magalhães, apparently satisfied, dismisses Cartagena. The whole meeting

45

is brusque, formal and filled with tension.

Nobody bothers to ask de Morales his opinion. Though if they had, he would point out that there are far easier ways to commit suicide than to stab oneself in the gut and wait to bleed to death in agony.

What's more, where was the weapon?

'Have you learnt anything at all?' Barbosa asks later that evening in de Morales' cabin. They are alone. Since their argument during the storm, Pigafetta has yet to return to the cabin. Once he composed himself, the Italian went into the dining cabin of the flagship where, de Morales assumes, he has taken up residence. The better to be closer to the Capitán General.

'No,' de Morales replies. 'I have heard nothing of mutiny nor any hint of conspiracy.'

After his conversation with Magalhães off the African coast, Barbosa had come to him warning him that de Morales might be asked to convey letters between the conspirators as he passed between their ships. But they are far too devious for such overt tactics and he tells him so now. 'Whatever plans they have, it seems, I have no part in them.'

Barbosa looks concerned by his report, not knowing whether to take the news as a good sign or ill.

'I do wonder,' de Morales continues, 'that perhaps the conspirators suspect me as being Magalhães' spy. After all, I am posted aboard the flagship' He leaves the sentence unfinished.

'Well,' Barbosa says, 'whether they suspect you or not makes little difference. They cannot act either way and they will not, knowing how valuable you are to the armada.

Continue to keep your ears and eyes open. They could let slip some remark or you may overhear something.'

It was worth a try. In truth, de Morales does not believe the captains suspect him as being the Capitán General's man. But he would like to be done with this unwanted charge that has weighed on his mind. Espionage ill suits him.

'I did have my suspicions about the death of the sailor on the San Antonio,' he says.

'Hmm?'

'He was stabbed in the belly. His death was probably slow and certainly agonising. Cartagena told the Capitán General it was suicide, but I disagree.'

'How so?'

'If you were to take your life, would you not do so in the quickest way possible? The least painful?' He shakes his head, seeing again the mess of the sailor's corpse. 'I suspect foul play.'

'Then why call you in the first place? Why not throw the body overboard and be done with it? No one would have known. Anyway,' Barbosa says, 'we cannot act against Cartagena for the sake of a single dead sailor. It must be conspiracy or nothing. But there is doubtless an evil air in this armada. We must remain vigilant. To disregard or underestimate the situation would spell our doom.'

We. Our.

That evening de Morales sits alone in his cabin considering how events have conspired against him. He left Castile to be done with intrigue and suspicion and now, a thousand leagues from Spain, he finds himself wrapped up in plotting and scheming once more. He would prefer to be in league with neither side.

He imagines what life aboard Serrano's ship might have

been like. The Santiago seems to exist in an entirely separate world from the rest of the armada. Serrano's focus is entirely on the task at hand, as it should be. The magnitude of what the armada has set out to do, the vast distances involved and the lives of so many men at stake demand their task be taken seriously. All other distractions should be pushed from the captains' minds. After all, are they not the leaders? The men upon whose shoulders rest the fates of two hundred and thirty-nine souls.

He curses Quesada and Mendoza. But he especially curses Cartagena. For the root of the insubordinate mood that seems to have taken hold of the fleet is certainly wrapped tightly around Fonseca's vicious little bastard.

The following morning, he is called to the Victoria. The ship has an outbreak of the flux. As his skiff approaches the towering bulk of the ship, de Morales looks up. He imagines an eerie blue light, flickering amid the lines of rigging and folded sails.

But there is no ruined woodwork, no staggering men and no St. Elmo's Fire. Just a ship, slightly the worse of wear after the storms, but far from the apparition he knows it is destined to become.

He climbs the Jacob's ladder and immediately recognises the sailor who meets him on the main deck. 'You had a white cat at Los Cristianos, did you not?' De Morales asks him.

The man laughs. 'Yes,' he says, still smiling. 'Her name is Amaya. She is beautiful is she not? Though she is a fierce hunter,' he adds with mock seriousness.

'Very wise,' de Morales says. 'It is a wonder no one else thinks to bring a cat aboard.'

'It is an old Basque method for dealing with vermin,' the sailor says. 'Amaya will keep the rats and mice in check. I am Juan Sebastian Elcano,' he says, bowing and extending a hand. 'I am the Victoria's pilot.'

De Morales returns the bow. He cannot help but be surprised at Elcano's effortless warmth. Besides Barbosa, this is the first friendly face he seems to have found in the armada. He asks Elcano about the illness sweeping through the Victoria.

'As yet only the common seamen suffer with it. Thus far none have died but those who are ill are in great discomfort. Captain Mendoza and the other senior staff are unaffected.'

'Have all the crew eaten of the same food?' De Morales asks.

'Of course,' Elcano says, leaning over a brazier burning beneath the mainmast. He struggles to light a candle, the jealous wind snatching at the flame.

While he waits, de Morales takes in the Victoria. It seems only the fittest men are on deck and their numbers are greatly reduced. He quickly learnt there ought to be at least twenty-five men working a shift at a time on a ship of this size but, currently, only eighteen or so meander about. Even those on the deck and working have a pallid look about them. As if they have only just recovered from the illness or fear catching it themselves.

Finally, the candle is lit. 'If you will follow me, señor doctor,' Elcano says, shielding the flame from the wind.

De Morales takes a gauze of scented herbs from his pocket and passes another to Elcano who accepts it gratefully, then follows the Basque master below into the crew's quarters. The stench that meets him in the murky air is obscene. A sickening medley of sweat, bile and faeces. Vomit sloshes in buckets hidden away in the corners of the foetid hold. He holds the gauze tightly to his nose.

'These men need to be in the open air on the main deck,' de Morales says. 'Those who are well enough must thoroughly clean the boards and walls of this hold. Diluted vinegar should do the job. One part vinegar to five parts seawater. Do not allow the healthy into this place until it has been thoroughly cleaned and aired of the miasma. The bad airs must be removed.'

'Where are we to put the sick?' asks Elcano.

'You must find space above decks. Section off an area of the deck. The aftcastle, perhaps. If the sick remain down here, the miasma will begin claiming lives in no time.'

'Mendoza will not like it,' Elcano says. 'The aftcastle should strictly be for the officers.'

'Needs must. But worry not, Elcano,' de Morales says, noticing the look of concern on the Basque's face, 'this flux will not affect the healthy as long as the sick are kept outside in the fresh air. Where do you store your food? Would you take me there?'

Elcano steps with care around the stricken men. The pilot leads de Morales to the rear of the Victoria's hold and the trapdoor on the floor. He kneels, pulls a ring of keys from his belt. 'Strange,' Elcano says. 'This door should be kept locked.'

He pulls the handle and the trapdoor opens, turning noiselessly on well-oiled hinges, then gently rests it against a beam rising through the floor. De Morales, meanwhile, opens his case. He takes a twisted bunch of rosemary and lavender from it and hangs it from a beam in the ceiling of the hold. That ought to be enough to clear some of the bad airs of the improvised sickbay until it can be cleaned more thoroughly.

They descend into another, much darker space below.

Elcano takes a small unlit candle from a sconce on the wall and lights it from the one he carries with him. He passes the candle to de Morales and they begin to make their way to the prow of the ship.

Fresh water and fortified wine splash behind them in great barrels. So too do the bilges, with their faint smell of urine. Elcano's cat, Amaya, lounges lazily on a crate, taking no notice of them as they pass by.

'I let her down here every so often,' Elcano says quietly. 'It gives her reprieve from the noise of the upper decks and she catches a few rats.'

Elcano holds up a hand and de Morales stops behind him. The surgeon heard it too. A faint, rasping groan. Surely there cannot be a dying man down here too, like the one that was found in the hold of the San Antonio yesterday.

Elcano cautiously continues forward, the groans continuing into a rhythmic chorus. De Morales listens intently, confusion wrinkling his brow. He follows Elcano, treading carefully. Could he be mistaken, or was that second voice?

As the weak light from the dim candles gradually breaks the darkness before them, a figure is revealed. It is hunched over, strangely large and misshapen. A pig, maybe? Forgotten during the slaughter of the cattle after they first left Los Cristianos. But surely a pig could not go unnoticed for six weeks and anyway, there were no live animals aboard the Victoria.

Both de Morales and Elcano are drawn forwards in anxious silence. As they approach the unnatural mass of movement the light spreads further still. De Morales sees two figures and...

'Christ above.' The blasphemy leaves his lips before de

51

Morales can think to stop it. Elcano quickly crosses himself but stands rooted to the spot, silenced by what is before them.

Lighted by the dim candle are two figures, one much larger than the other. The larger, a man, stands upright on his knees, the smaller leans over on all fours. Both figures are naked and, as they separate from their passion, de Morales sees the erect member of the kneeling man slide out of the cabin boy.

The man, a sailor wearing a look of shock and terror, meets Elcano's eye. De Morales notices the thin rivulet of blood spattering onto the wooden floorboards from the crouched cabin boy.

'Salamon, you squalid paederast.' Elcano cries.

The Basque rushes forward. He takes the man by the throat and crashes into him. The two men fall to the floor, crates tumbling on top of them as the smaller figure scrambles to a gloomy corner. De Morales is rooted to the spot, watching Elcano and Salamon struggle, fighting across the boards. They separate and spring to their feet.

Elcano stares at the naked Salamon, the Basque's doublet is ripped at the shoulder. 'It is over,' Elcano says breathlessly. 'Come peaceably and we'll say nothing of your violence.'

Salamon's eyes dart between Elcano, the boy and de Morales. He seems to recognise he is undone. 'Very well,' he says simply, then holds his hands up in surrender.

'You have clothing?' Elcano asks, looking the naked man over.

Salamon searches the floor in silence for his clothes. He turns around, takes a moment to look at the cabin boy whimpering in the corner, then dresses clumsily in the murky light from de Morales' candle.

Now fully dressed, Salamon turns abruptly and shoves Elcano aside. Taken by surprise, Elcano falls sideways into crates and sacks of supplies. De Morales instinctively rushes to Elcano to help him, dropping his candle and the hold is plunged into darkness. He senses Salamon dash past him, darting up the steep stairs into the upper hold. The trapdoor slams closed behind him.

Elcano fights against the crates, knocking them over and finally rises. He rushes after Salamon, taking the stairs two at a time as de Morales follows as swiftly as he can, tripping and stumbling on fallen crates. The cabin boy, curled up in the dark corner, is forgotten.

De Morales bursts into the upper cabin and a dozen eyes stare at him out of the gloom. 'Where did they go?' He asks desperately.

One of the sick men points behind de Morales towards the stairs leading to the deck of the Victoria. He hears a cry from the main deck and the thudding sound of footsteps rushing around above him.

When he emerges into the daylight, breathless and sweating, the deck is in chaos. Two sailors hold Salamon by the arms, forcing him to his knees. Men shout over one another, scuffling and jostling to see what the disturbance is. Elcano is lost in the tumult of voices and bodies.

'What is going on?' The crew recognise the voice of their captain and quickly fall quiet. Mendoza pushes into the centre of the commotion and stares at Salamon.

Elcano appears beside the prisoner and says, 'de Morales and myself caught Salamon in flagrante delicto with a cabin boy. Ginovés, I think.'

Mendoza's pale blue eyes dance between Elcano and Salamon. Finally, he says, 'we need not make any more of this than we must. Put Salamon in the stocks for three days. That ought to be punishment enough-'

'Captain Mendoza,' the voice is Magalhães'. Shouting from the Trinidad, the Capitán General interrupts Mendoza's sentencing, 'what is occurring?'

'Damn.' Mendoza says quietly. De Morales turns as one with the gathered crew of the Victoria to see the crowd Salamon's escape attempt has attracted. It seems the entire crew of the Trinidad, the Capitán General in their centre, is lined up along the gunwale of the flagship, staring at the crowd on the Victoria. 'Just a simple misunderstanding,' Mendoza calls to Magalhães. 'Nothing you need to be concerned with.'

'I will not have fights breaking out on my armada,' the Capitán General calls back. 'I want all parties involved brought to the flagship immediately.'

In the afternoon, Magalhães orders his captains to stand witness at the court-martial of Antonio Salamon onboard the Trinidad. The Capitán General is in place, seated behind a small table. Kneeling before him is Salamon, already clapped in irons as if the outcome of the trial is a foregone conclusion. After all, how can it not be?

De Morales accompanied Elcano and Salamon in the skiff back to the Trinidad. On the short, choppy journey, Elcano had said to Salamon, 'why did you run? Where were you planning on going?'

'I panicked,' was all Salamon could say in reply.

On board the Trinidad, Magalhães questioned the three men, Elcano first. When he learned from the Basque what Salamon had been discovered doing, a look of appalled shock fell over the Capitán General's face.

He turned to de Morales, 'do you corroborate what Elcano has told me?' He asked. The shortness of the Magalhães' tone took de Morales by surprise, it was as if they were starting their relationship anew despite the Capitán General confiding in the surgeon all those weeks ago off the coast of Africa. All de Morales could do was confirm what Elcano had already told Magalhães.

Now de Morales is standing beside Elcano, watching Barbosa and Espinosa manhandle Salamon to his feet before the Capitán General. They stand on either side of the accused, with a hand on each of his shoulders. Both men, he notices, are fully armed.

Serrano, always the first to arrive after the Capitán General's summons, stands to Magalhães' left. To his right, Pigafetta watches in silent assessment.

It is the first time de Morales has seen the chronicler since their argument. De Morales knows Pigafetta has seen him and catches the chronicler now watching him from the corner of a contemptuous eye. He side-steps toward Magalhães and whispers something in the Capitán General's ear. Magalhães nods and turns at the thud of skiffs hitting the hull of the flagship.

The other captains board the Trinidad one at a time. Mendoza climbs over the gunwale first. Despite the sodomy happening aboard his ship, he looks surprised at Salamon standing in irons before the Capitán General.

Quesada comes next, a blue cap covering his balding head, accompanied by de la Reina. The captain of the Concepción hugs his arms tightly around himself to ward off the wind.

Of course, Cartagena is the last to arrive. He takes in the whole scene with a sneer and says, 'could this not have waited until we made land? Christ on the cross it is freezing out here.'

The Capitán General ignores Cartagena and motions with his head for him to take his place beside the other captains.

The trial is quick. Salamon has no defence. He was witnessed by two men sodomising Ginovés. Despite already telling the Capitán General what they saw, Elcano and de Morales are told to retell the tale now before the other captains.

Elcano gives testimony first and does not mention the tussle between himself and Salamon. Not wanting to contradict Elcano's narrative, de Morales does not mention it either.

Magalhães listens to the testimonies, then turns to Salamon. With barely a pause, he says, 'for the act of sodomy upon another man, contrary to the law of nature, God and his majesty, I find you guilty and sentence you to be strangled until death.'

A murmur swells across the deck of the Trinidad.

Mendoza steps forward. 'The sentence seems excessive, Capitán General,' he says. 'These things happen.'

'Not on my armada they do not,' Magalhães replies.

'Put the wretch in the stocks,' Mendoza says. 'Let him rot for a few weeks but strangulation is too far. His crime is hardly unknown at sea.'

'I have given my verdict,' Magalhães says.

'Señor-' Mendoza starts but he is cut off by the look of rage Magalhães gives him.

'I am not a señor, Captain Mendoza. I am the Capitán General.' Though he is close to rage, Magalhães' voice has become quiet, venomous. He stands quickly. 'I will have every captain in my quarters immediately.'

Red-faced, Magalhães turns quickly on his heel, then limps across the main deck of the Trinidad towards his cabin.

The Spanish captains look to one another and slowly turn, following the Capitán General. Barbosa and Espinosa, hands gripping the hilts of their sheathed weapons, follow them. The door slams heavily behind Cartagena. Espinosa and Barbosa take up positions, guarding the door on either side.

'Is it the challenge that has so offended the Capitán General,' Elcano whispers to de Morales, 'or is calling him señor one disrespect too far?'

'I have the authority. I have the king's authority to lead.' Any attempt to hide his rage has slipped completely and Magalhães is screaming at his captains for all the crew of the Trinidad, gathered on the main deck, to hear.

De la Reina, forgotten until now, moves to stand beside Elcano. 'The Capitán General has lost his composure,' he says. The two men stare in silence ahead, their eyes boring into the wooden door of the cabin.

'This brazen lack of respect will stop at once,' Magalhães is shouting. 'You, Cartagena, may be the worst culprit, but you all show wanton contempt for my authority.'

'You have no authority I recognise, you Portuguese swine.' The shrill voice is Cartagena's. All his pent-up animosity is boiling over. 'You used fraud and trickery to deceive his majesty into allowing this expedition. You have led us through storms and landed us in the doldrums where you frittered away our stores. I would say you are incompetent but, clearly you are not. You have succeeded at every turn in undermining this fleet, which I believe to be your aim from the outset.'

'You will be silent,' Magalhães shouts back, 'or you will be made silent.'

Cartagena scoffs. 'I'm not wasting his time with this any longer, let us be done with him. Gaspar, Liuz, are you with me?'

A cry comes from the cabin. Barbosa and Espinosa, their swords already drawn, burst into the room. Through the swinging door, de Morales sees Espinosa grab Cartagena by the shirt and throw him into a chair. Mendoza and Quesada jump back in shock as Barbosa, rapier raised, places himself between them and Cartagena.

'Rebel,' Magalhães says, 'this is mutiny.'

Espinosa again grabs Cartagena who spits in his face, then screeches, 'release me, you dog.' Espinosa's grip falters and Cartagena stands quickly. But then Espinosa is on him again.

The two men wrestle and flounder, finally bursting from the cabin. They whirl and tumble across the main deck, boots pounding and slipping on the slick oak boards. Finally, Espinosa overpowers Cartagena, toppling him backwards with a skilled inside trip. Cartagena is thrown to the deck and Espinosa strides over his prostrate body and puts his boot on his neck. Barbosa emerges from the cabin and reaches for a second set of stocks laying on the deck beside Salamon.

Cartagena twists and kicks his feet, but Espinosa pushes his boot down more firmly. 'Move and I will stamp on your throat,' he says.

Beastlike in his fury, Cartagena spits and snarls as he is forced into the stocks. The other captains emerge from Magalhães' cabin, their shock written plain on their faces. The Capitán General comes last, his doublet torn and his lip bleeding. Magalhães is carrying a knife with a finely carved ivory pommel. He throws it at Cartagena's feet and the blade clatters to the deck.

'I would be within my rights to execute you here and

now,' Magalhães says.

Mendoza and Quesada look shocked at one another. 'Enough trials today, Capitán General,' Quesada says. 'Do not act in passion.'

Barbosa leans towards Magalhães' ear and says simply, 'his father, Fernão-'

'Fonseca, Fonseca, Fonseca,' says Magalhães. 'Always that vindictive snake worms his way into my affairs.'

Mendoza approaches Magalhães, 'please Capitán General, release Cartagena. Put him in my custody aboard the Victoria.' While Mendoza implores with Magalhães, de Morales notices Espinosa bend down and lift Cartagena's knife from the deck. He shoves it into his boot as he rises.

'Why on earth would I do that?' Magalhães scoffs, 'You think me that stupid? You plotted with Cartagena, we all heard his rally cry to you and Quesada.'

'But we did not rally to him, did we, Capitán General?' Mendoza's voice is soft and imploring. 'Put him in my care. He will do no more harm under my watch. I swear it.'

A long silence follows as Magalhães seems to consider his position. Finally, he says, 'very well.' He nods to Espinosa. 'Release him.'

The mutinous captain is released from the stocks. Salamon looks dumbfounded as he kneels beside him. As if he thought he, too, would be released.

Cartagena rises with as much dignity as he can muster. He is silent now, like a whipped cur. He strikes a pathetic figure as he stares with evil eyes at Espinosa. He clears his throat. 'My knife,' he says.

Espinosa, looking Cartagena in the eye and the hilt of the ivory poignard sticking out from the top of his boot, says, 'what knife?'

'Mesquita,' Magalhães says. The Capitán General's cousin steps forward from where he has been standing beside Rebêlo. 'You are now captain of the San Antonio. Take Rebêlo with you.'

Mesquita and Rebêlo share a shocked, silent glance before Magalhães turns to Mendoza. 'Remove this traitor from my sight.' He says. Mendoza takes Cartagena by the arm and begins leading him away. 'Wait,' Magalhães calls. 'Take the surgeon with you.' Without turning to de Morales he says, 'check the cabin boy.'

The short journey back to the Victoria seems to take an age. Mendoza, Cartagena, Elcano and de Morales make their slow way to the ship in awkward silence. In the corner of the skiff, Cartagena seethes. His hands shake and his face is reddened with rage. He is a primed cannon, ready to go off at any time.

Finally, the fuse lights and Cartagena spits, 'the filthy, traitorous swineherd. I will get my knife and then I will plunge it through his eye.'

'Silence.' Mendoza says. Cartagena returns to his silent seething.

Mendoza turns to de Morales, puts a hand on his knee and says, 'forgive our friend,' he offers a derisive smile. 'He is, understandably, vexed.'

Vexed indeed. Mendoza is covering for Cartagena, that much seems clear.

Onboard the Victoria, Cartagena stamps into Mendoza's cabin. The door slams behind him

Elcano, standing beside de Morales for a moment, turns to him and says, 'in all my years at sea, I have never known a sailor to be put to death over such a thing.'

Now all the excitement is over, the main deck clears as the crew slowly dissipate back into the holds. De Morales makes his way back down to the trapdoor, in search of Ginovés. He takes another candle and follows the same route Elcano and himself took not two hours earlier. Amaya has long since scarpered. In the corner, at the prow of the ship, he finds the curled-up body of Ginovés. The cabin boy, still naked, shivers in the gloom.

'Are you injured?' he asks gently.

The cabin boy's body convulses and he sniffs, crying as he hugs himself.

'Ginovés, are you hurt?' De Morales says, more firmly this time. 'Did he harm you?' Realising the question is absurd, he adds, 'anywhere else?'

The cabin boy rolls over, tears streak his cheeks and wipes his eyes. Finally, he says, 'is he to die?'

'He has been sentenced to be strangled,' de Morales says, he reaches out his hand and places it gently on the boy's shoulder. 'You need not worry. He cannot harm you again.'

Ginovés turns over, the topography of his spine showing through the taut skin of his back. He cradles himself, weeping quietly into the darkness.

Chapter 5

December 1519

The colony of Terra do Brasil fills the horizon.

As the armada nears the endless coastline, a spate of confused activity takes hold of the Trinidad. It seems they are off course. Estêvão Gomes and the armada's astrologer, Andrés de San Martin cannot fathom what has happened.

The five black ships of the armada pull in close. So small and insignificant, they hug together in the massive expanse of ocean now fringed by this unknown jungle. Confused shouts and signals pass from ship to ship. Wherever it is they have found themselves, it is almost certainly under the control of Portugal.

A cry from Quesada on the Concepción cuts through the chaos. 'My pilot knows this land. He says it is called Cabo de Santo Agostinho in Portuguese.

Gradually, the captains, pilots and San Martin, piece

together their confused route across the Great Ocean. In the course of the tempest and the overcast days and nights of the crossing, the armada has been blown off course northwards by some three hundred leagues.

If it was Magalhães' hope that, by sailing south along the well-charted coast of Africa, he could avoid the southerly journey down the troublesome coast of the New World, with its unknown shoals, acicular corals and roving Portuguese caravels, his hope was empty. That journey must be made now regardless of whatever well-laid plans the Capitán General had.

Magalhães orders the Concepción's Portuguese pilot, João Lopes Carvalho, to transfer to the Trinidad. He will substitute Gomes who has guided the flagship so assuredly through relentless storms as they crossed the Great Ocean. The swiftness of the decision is matched only by the callous nature in which Gomes is told. His job done, the pilot is cast aside by the Capitán General and left to while away his uneventful days in the hold below.

The presence of Carvalho onboard the Trinidad alters the mood of the ship almost instantly. He is a greedy, self-serving man who speaks of nothing but past glory and base desires. He says he built a great trading post in Rio de Janeiro, that he made his fortune felling Brasilwood and was greatly respected by the local tribesmen. He goes so far as to claim he married a local chief's daughter and was granted a myriad of beautiful concubines who tended to his every desire.

The men, working on the main deck of the Trinidad as the coast of the New World slides by in the distance, grow concupiscent as they listen to Carvalho's ribald tales of the licentious appetites of the native women. He claims they would do anything he desired. That there were no limits on what he could do with them. That they were his property.

Carvalho is a disgusting, amoral creature but he is cunning and crafty, taking care never to allow his unchristian boasting to be heard by Magalhães. De Morales does not doubt, however, that the Capitán General is well aware of Carvalho's tales. Magalhães, after all, seems to know everything that happens in his armada.

Barbosa has certainly heard Carvalho's depraved boasts. De Morales knows this for sure because Barbosa was opposite him on the aftcastle of the Trinidad as Carvalho boasted that if one wishes to rape the maidenhead of a native woman, one should make it a young girl with plenty of fight. 'For when they fight,' he said, 'their coño clenches, increasing the pleasure tenfold.' The whole crowd of rowdy, randy men on the main deck laughed heartily, Barbosa included, with no few clearly committing the advice to memory.

De Morales suspects that even if Barbosa has passed on Carvalho's impiety to Magalhães, the Capitán General simply does not care. Magalhães has placed great trust in Carvalho to guide the armada safely on this part of the voyage. It seems Carvalho is the only one who knows the course and, so long as he successfully guides them, he can say and do as he wishes.

Despite being at sea for almost three months, the sight of land brings no joy to de Morales' heart. This land is Portuguese and who knows what awaits the armada around every corner of the coastline. The very waters the fleet now surges through could be teeming with Manuel's caravels.

Indeed, they should be. It is only some stroke of luck they are, for now, the only ships within sight. But that could change very quickly.

Despite his anxieties, de Morales does feel it is at least good to have something against which to judge their progress. For months the armada has sailed in an endless and featureless ocean. To a sailor, de Morales is sure, it is easy to tell how fast they were travelling and how good their progress was. But to a layman such as himself, the journey may as well have been made entirely in absolute darkness.

The two-week journey down the coast of this Portuguese colony is one of fraught anxiety. Aboard the Trinidad, the shared sense of concern is amplified. The flagship by far has within its ranks the greatest number of Portuguese. Magalhães has brought with him a veritable household of friends, confidants, family members and illegitimate children. Should the armada be intercepted by the Portuguese, they will be done for. The Spanish will be thrown in jail and kept in chains until Castile barters for their freedom but the Portuguese, Magalhães foremost, will be executed as traitors.

Added to these concerns are worries about the way ahead. The waters of the Terra do Brasilian coastline are deep but largely unexplored by the Spanish and, therefore, dangerous. Though the Portuguese regularly sail these coasts, they keep their charts secret, as the Spanish do theirs of New Spain. Certainly, the French are known to have traded in these waters, either buying brasilwood from the Portuguese ashore or illegally felling it and shipping it back to France. Though Carvalho boasts he can sail these waters with his eyes closed, Magalhães, clearly concerned by what lies beneath the water's surface, orders frequent soundings.

But his concerns are largely unfounded. All along this lush

coastline, the ocean reaches to a depth of up to thirty fathoms and few shoals hamper their progress. The water is clear and warm and a strong southerly wind pushes the ships quickly towards Rio de Janeiro, a port that could well be filled with those ominous Portuguese caravels that stalked them from the Cape Verde islands.

Evening falls and a knock sounds at de Morales' cabin door.

He opens it and is surprised to find the worried face of Enrique looking at him, his brow furrowed and eyes glazed over. To see the slave without his master seems strange; as if Enrique is more an appendage to Magalhães than a man in his own right. Outside, the deck is eerily quiet, the sun sinking behind the hills of the New World, giving the slave's skin a warm glow.

'Can you see me, señor doctor?' Enrique asks quietly. When de Morales silently nods his head, Enrique slips into the cabin quickly. He moves to the far wall of the room between crates of medicines and the desk. De Morales gently closes the door.

'What can I do for you, Enrique?' He motions for the slave to sit on Pigafetta's empty bed as he reaches for a candle, placing it on a chest of medicines beside the bed. The slave remains standing.

'I need you to phlebotomise me, señor doctor.' Enrique's Spanish is excellent with only the slightest accent. De Morales is surprised to find it gives the slave away not as a Malacca, but as Portuguese.

'Why ever would you need me to do that?'

'I have an illness. The ague,' Enrique says. 'I have had it

for many years. It is not infectious, for I have passed it to no man my whole life.' De Morales takes Enrique by the shoulders and moves him toward the bed. The slave finally sits down.

'How do you know it is the ague?' De Morales asks, studying the Malacca's worried face.

'A doctor in Lisboa told me. It comes in bouts. For months I will be fine before it returns once more, seemingly for no reason at all. It has happened so for many years. So long that I can recognise the earliest symptoms long before they take hold.'

'Does the Capitán General know of this?'

'No, señor' Enrique's face hardens at the mention of his master, his body stiffening, his eyes dart to the door. 'He cannot know. I saw the physician in Lisboa secretly while I was at an apothecary collecting treatments for the master's wife. The physician bled me and did so any time I have needed since. If the master finds out, he will cast me into the sea. I may not be free, señor doctor, but I am alive.'

'And bloodletting helps?'

'Yes.'

'Very well,' de Morales says gently, trying to calm Enrique, for the slave appears on the verge of panic. 'I can do this for you. The Capitán General need know nothing of it. What did the physician in Lisboa use to bleed you?' This is important, different techniques yield different results and should only be used for certain illnesses.

'A very sharp knife,' Enrique says. 'Shaped like a key.'

De Morales leans under his bed and lifts his case of surgical tools. He carefully removes a fleam and shows it to Enrique.

The slave nods quickly. 'That is the tool. We should do it

now, and quickly, señor doctor,' he says frantically. 'Before the master wonders at my absence.'

De Morales stands up. He lifts the small brass bowl used for collecting blood from a crate against the wall. 'You should remove your shirt,' he says to Enrique.

Enrique turns and lifts his shirt over his head. The fabric is damp with sweat, either from the beginnings of the fever or from heat, and clings to him as he struggles out of it. White scars crisscross the slave's back and shoulders. He has been whipped mercilessly and many times.

The Malacca sits back on the bed and holds his arm out, ready for de Morales. Clearly, as he said, Enrique has been through this procedure many times. De Morales holds the brass bowl tightly to Enrique's arm and makes a sharp nick in the slave's forearm with the fleam. Blood, thick and dark, streams from the wound.

Enrique sits silently watching his blood fill the bowl. The slave has calmed down now, his eyes have ceased their worried glances to the door.

'Are you treated unkindly?' de Morales asks, still focusing on the bowl.

'No worse than most.' Enrique's voice is dead of all emotion.

'What of the scars on your back?'

'They are old scars and long healed, señor doctor. No few were by the master's hand if that is your question.'

De Morales sighs. It is hardly news to him that slaves are whipped. Perhaps he was foolish in hoping Magalhães would be among those who treat their slaves well. 'How long have you been with the Capitán General?' He asks.

'Many years,' Enrique says, a dismal, half-smile on his face.

'Where are you from?'

'My master bought me in a place you call Sumatra, but I was not born there. I do not wish to speak the name of my true home, to do so brings me only pain.'

The bowl is almost filled and Enrique's eyes have become heavy. He blinks slowly and he wavers from side to side. Enough blood has been let, any more will do the slave no good. De Morales takes a length of clean bandage and tightly wraps it around the slave's forearm, covering the wound. He leans down and places the bowl carefully on the floor. He will empty it into the sea later after the slave has been gone for some time, so no one will know from whom it came.

Enrique seems to come to his senses and he rises slowly from the bed, dressing himself. 'Thank you, señor doctor,' he says. The thanks are simple but heartfelt. The slave turns toward the door.

Before he opens it, he stops and turns back to de Morales. 'Señor doctor?' De Morales looks up. Enrique is looking him directly in the eye. 'Be careful. The master trusts no one and the Italian has given him cause to doubt your loyalty.'

De Morales' eyes widen but before he can ask Enrique what he means, the slave is gone.

He is standing outside his cabin, as out of the way as he can, watching the armada's slow approach to the port named Rio de Janeiro. Heat surges from the jungle inland, sweeping into the ocean and hugging him tightly. The air is heavy with humidity – oppressive and inescapable.

His mind drifts to the sentencing that will be carried out once they reach land. Somewhere on this ship, Salamon is in chains. By now he will know land has been sighted and he will be counting down the hours until his execution.

Barbosa appears beside him. 'You know,' he says conversationally, 'we have continuously been at sea longer than any other voyage in history.'

'I can well believe it,' de Morales says. He looks hard at Barbosa, searching for the distrust Enrique warned him of. But the eyes he looks into are warm and friendly. Barbosa must share none of Magalhães' distrust. Or he is hiding it well.

'Though I cannot think of a more troubled crossing of the Great Ocean,' Barbosa says. 'We are fortunate there are no Portuguese here. Welcome to the New World,' he adds brightly.

'What surprises me most about life at sea,' de Morales says, 'is the boredom. Most of the time is spent waiting for something to happen. When it finally does, a flurry of such furious activity occurs as to leave one's head spinning before another long stretch of nothing. It ebbs and flows, like the tides of the sea.'

'That is how it gets you,' Barbosa says smiling. 'You are falling into a sailor's life.'

He smiles in response, not wanting to tell Barbosa that he feels less like a sailor than he did when they left Los Cristianos three months ago. True enough, he has found his sea legs, but he never joined the armada to become something new. He joined it to escape something old.

Magalhães limps about the deck, fierce eyes darting this way and that and shouting orders in Spanish and Portuguese at his crew. Every so often he says something to Carvalho and they point to far off features of the approaching landscape. The Capitán General is frantic and his agitation is becoming infectious, its bad airs spreading across the Trinidad vitiating the crew.

'You ought to go into your cabin, de Morales,' Barbosa says. 'Fernão is anxious, it is only a matter of time before he orders you to leave the deck. Better to stay on his good side.'

He removes himself from the chaos of the deck into the darkness of his cabin. Outside, the muffled shouts and cries of the sailors continue. *Better to stay on his good side.* Was Barbosa hinting at more than the Capitán General's temperamental mood?

Enrique warned him that Pigafetta had given Magalhães cause to question his loyalties. But what could Pigafetta have told the Capitán General? Surely it cannot simply be de Morales' morose musings in the midst of that tempest in the Great Ocean, before St. Elmo's Fire burst from the mainmast of the Victoria. Nothing he said during that great storm could be construed as questioning or undermining Magalhães' leadership, at least by anyone not searching for a reason to dislike him.

De Morales searches his memory for something, anything, that Pigafetta could have used against him. He finds nothing.

Whatever Pigafetta is telling Magalhães must be untrue. The chronicler always gave the impression he would go to any lengths to earn the Capitán General's favour. Doubtless, he already has that favour, but to what lengths is the chronicler now going to keep it?

Like most learned people in Europe, de Morales has heard rumours of the marvellous Portuguese colony of Terra do Brasil. For almost twenty years, every court in Europe has been rife with gossip of the riches Manuel has accumulated from his portion of the New World. Gold, silver, turtle shells, brasilwood, feathers, dyes, all of it floods Europe and most of it passes through Lisboa.

Doubtless, the common sailor's heads in the ships now lining the empty harbour of Rio de Janeiro are filled with Carvalho's tales of voluptuous women who can be bought for a handful of glass beads.

For his part, de Morales is focused on Vespucci's accounts of a utopia. A garden of Eden of immense scale crowded with decadent fruit and teeming with life. Paradise on earth.

This is what he wished for when he joined the armada all those months ago in Sevilla. To see something so extraordinary as to pull him out of his desolation, something so miraculous as to breathe faith back into his heart.

But, in the back of his mind, he cannot shake the stories that have filtered back to Castile. They describe the natives here as a cruel people governed by barbarism and with a taste for cannibalism. The rumours say these Brasileiros eat their enemies, salting and smoking their remains and feasting on the human flesh for months. Then there are the rumours of the jungle, a vast and impenetrable labyrinth that lures men deep into its midst before wrapping them in living vines and crushing the life from their bodies.

But when he emerges from his cabin into the muggy air and vivid light, the land he lays eyes on is not the paradise Amerigo Vespucci declared it to be, nor is it a ferocious and sentient jungle.

Instead, it is a land long since raped of its bounty. A miserable place in the grip of a brutal drought that has stripped all colour and life from the immense jungle. A land of death and disease.

As he looks upon it, de Morales' hopes are stripped from his heart, leaving nothing but those sinister rumours.

Chapter 6

December 1519

De la Reina is bored.

The Capitán General has trouped out their entire contingent of two hundred and thirty-nine men for a grand show of unity and strength. They are gathered beneath a hastily built cross rising some eight yards from the cracked earth of Rio de Janeiro. The sun is high, the cross barely casting a shadow, and the men are sweating and in an ill mood in their armour and regalia.

There is a noticeable divide in the captains. Quesada and Mendoza, flanked by Cartagena, stand apart from Magalhães, Mesquita and Serrano. Despite Magalhães' best efforts, their unified body has its factions plain for anyone to see. Although the crowd of fifty-odd natives seem utterly indifferent to the politics of the pale men before them.

Everywhere evidence of the Portuguese occupation of this land is clear. The cross has been erected in an unnaturally empty clearing in the jungle of the New World, stripped of all trees and foliage. A chaotic pile of half-rotten brasilwood lies beside a dilapidated shack made of uglier and crooked planks. From the mess of timber to the shore, deep furrows scar the earth where the brasilwood has been dragged to Portuguese ships to be transported back to the markets of Lisboa.

Wherever de Morales turns his eyes, he finds the broken bodies of a broken people, eking out a life under the yoke of the Portuguese empire. They mill about in irregular groups or watch, with vacant eyes, the Christian ceremony taking place before them. All around, the swollen bellies and sunken cheeks speak to the deprived lives they live.

Several natives are missing ears and noses, their faces left haunting and empty by their absence like the skulls of the dead. One man has no hands, a pregnant woman, her toes sliced off, shuffles in the sand along the shore. Everywhere are mangled stumps and missing limbs, testimony to a depraved form of justice. Almost all bear the scars of chains around their ankles, wrists and necks and wear brands on their cheeks like cattle. For that is all they are to their masters, livestock to be used until their usefulness has passed.

He would help them. His heart longs to do so. But what relief could he bring? Against such wickedness what can a single man do? These people need more than medicine and food, neither of which he has enough of. They need freedom and justice.

The Portuguese claim when they found this land, nineteen years ago, the people were naked. Either that is untrue, or they have forced them to dress in the time since. Both the men and women wear skirts made from strips of variously coloured fronds and feathers. While the men are shirtless, the women's chests are covered with brightly painted grasses, weaved into sleeveless tunics.

Despite their terrible condition, De Morales finds himself feeling a fit of absurd jealousy at their simple clothing. Here he is, sweating and itching, dressed from head to toe in wool and linen, while they look cool and comfortable. It is hotter and more humid here than the oppression of a Sevillian July when the leaves shrink and in the afternoon heat nothing is done but siesta. But it is December, it ought to be cooler. The New World is so strange; as if everything of the old world has been turned on its head. Even the seasons here are confused.

Magalhães, flanked by Valderrama and de la Reina, asks those who wish to be converted to Christianity and accepted into the bosom of Christ to come forward. None of the natives move. Surely the Capitán General must realise these people have almost certainly already been converted by the Portuguese. They know what comes next. A christened man is a saved man, and a saved man must work further for the complete redemption of his soul. Then there are the endless rules and the endless forms of punishment that exist for breaking those rules.

Nevertheless, Magalhães is resolute and stern in his serious evangelism. De Morales is well aware of the precedent set by those who have come before to this new world. Natives, first and foremost, must be converted. The King will want to know his Capitán General has kept up the pretence of soul-saving so that his Majesty can report to the Pope of his wide-reaching Christian impact on a savage world. Another feather in the hat of their philanthropic potentate.

The ceremony is finally over and the crew share a sigh of relief. The sailors on duty return to the ships and continue repairing the damage done during the crossing of the Great Ocean. Those who remain ashore head to the tree line, searching for relief from the heat. The natives, keeping their distance, follow. De Morales stays nearer the ships beside Barbosa.

'You are to remain on the Trinidad after sunset,' Barbosa says. 'Fernão is sceptical of these people. He wishes to trade, repair the damage to the ships and leave as soon as we can. In the meantime, he worries about the safety of his surgeon.'

Though he hardly dares admit it to himself, let alone Barbosa, being confined to the Trinidad is something of a blessing. Terra do Brasil is a disheartening and depressing place and there is something ominous about its emptiness.

For now, the Trinidad seems the better option.

'And the crew?' De Morales asks. Those ashore lounge in the sandy dirt beneath the sparse fronds of palm trees at the very edge of the jungle. They seem reluctant to go any deeper.

'All will do the same,' Barbosa says. 'We cannot risk anything untoward happening here, to the ships or the men.'

Realising those who have remained on the shore have no food, the natives slowly begin to disperse. They melt into the jungle, quickly disappearing among the leaves and branches. De Morales makes for the skiffs waiting on the shore. He will find no relief from the sun in the clearing and something about the surrounding jungle seems sinister to him.

If Magalhães worries for de Morales' safety, he does not worry enough to tell de Morales himself. Whatever wedge has been driven between the Capitán General and de Morales by Pigafetta is, it seems, only growing now. That said, Magalhães' concerns are understandable. De Morales' death would leave the entire crew at the mercy of Bustamante's unskilled hands.

Under the savage sun, the men work as hard as they can

76

be driven to repair the damage to the ships. They continue long into the night, focusing their efforts on the Santiago. The smallest ship of the armada is in the worst state, knocked about as if it were a spinning top by those violent storms.

The next day, when daylight comes, De Morales decides he will go ashore once more. Perhaps he was wrong, he tells himself. Perhaps his first impressions were influenced too much by his disappointment that the reality of the New World did not match his expectations. Of course, he reminds himself, Vespucci would have exaggerated. After all, he was trying to impress royalty and secure a second expedition.

But when he does go ashore, de Morales instantly regrets it. His hopeful realism cannot divert his attention from the hostility of the New World. This place is no paradise.

Terra do Brasil is nature recalcitrant. Though the armada has arrived during a drought it is clear that, when nourished by water, the surrounding jungle grows with an aggressive and choking ferocity. The brittle foliage lies in wait for the first kiss of rain, when it will spring back to life and grow wild and rampant.

For now, though, the ground is parched and wide fissures are scarred across it like some drunken imitation of a chessboard. Tall palm trees, which must once have been great towers puncturing the heavens, are now depressed, limpen shapes arcing towards the earth and surrounded by fallen fronds. The endless jungle beyond is thin and parched, the crisp grasses crackle against each other despite the lack of wind. It seems there is absolutely no water whatsoever to be had here.

The land may be dead, but the air is alive. Melodious birdsong, chittering and squawking, is broken every so often by the ferocious bellow of some unseen beast. And beyond it all, a constant chorus of supernatural shrieks and calls from wild creatures of the deeper jungle fills the air.

In lieu of sustenance, the Capitán General has turned his attention to information. He has taken Enrique ashore with him on the off chance his slave can make himself understood to these people in their native tongue. De Morales wanders in the direction of the Capitán General and Enrique, hoping to overhear some snippets of information.

Magalhães, Espinosa and Enrique stand before a group of native men, trying to make themselves understood. They try everything, even Portuguese, but there seems to be no understanding. The Malacca is as foreign to the natives as the Spaniards are. Carvalho, leaning against the shack, appears to be useless despite claiming to have worked in these lands before. For all his being Portuguese, Magalhães genuinely seems to have no idea who the natives are.

Barbosa appears beside Enrique and quickly has more luck. Through hand gestures and sign language, he learns the last ships to leave the port departed sixty-seven days ago. Assuming the Portuguese plan to return to this place, their trade ships will likely already be on their way back. Unless they were sunk during the storms that ravaged the armada.

'For all we know,' Espinosa says, 'these savages could be in league with the Portuguese and not merely their slaves. They could have been told to keep watch for five Spanish ships coming from the east. They could right now be planning to scuttle the ships, damage the rudders or murder us in our sleep.'

Espinosa's grim thoughts attract a crowd of sailors, their eyes wide with fear. They look to their Capitán General for comfort, but de Morales knows they will find none there.

'We should take some precautions,' Barbosa says.

Magalhães glares into the parched jungle, thinking hard. 'Issue new orders to the men,' he says finally. 'No man is to go ashore under any circumstances. We will remain on the ships. This place has nothing for us anyway.'

Depressed at the news, the men nearby hang their heads. True enough there is little here, but it is, at least, terra firma. Despite the state of it, de Morales is sorry to be denied the opportunity to walk on solid ground any longer.

After several days filled with the clatter and bang of hammers, sporadic sawing and anxious glances ashore to the empty beach, the natives visit the armada as one.

Magalhães, with Espinosa, Barbosa, Enrique and Valderrama meet them on the sand. They take with them bags of glass beads and small bundles of coloured cloth. The Brasileiros take the gifts and return later with trinkets of their own. But, despite Vespucci's accounts, the natives do not come bearing armfuls of food to trade with the Armada de Molucca. Instead, they bring brightly coloured feathers, beaded necklaces and crude, though sharp, obsidian knives. The feathers are especially popular amongst the crew, they will bring a handsome price back in Sevilla.

After that, the natives begin making a daily pilgrimage to the shore. As they show themselves more, and the pathetic nature of their existence is revealed, Magalhães becomes more comfortable with them. Gradually, more and more sailors join Barbosa and Espinosa in following their Capitán General ashore and the blanket order that none are to visit the land is forgotten.

De Morales senses the land calling him, urging him back to its solid, immovable weight. Finally, he can resist the temptation no longer and ventures ashore. Natives wander towards him, clutching trinkets in calloused hands, but de Morales has nothing to trade and so they quickly abandon him for other, more promising, prospects.

He drifts between groups of natives and Europeans exchanging goods and novelties. Each side believing they are fleecing the other. There are more native women among them now and many in the crew eye them. Their greedy stares take in bare thighs and bellies, ignoring the scars and missing limbs.

'The Portuguese dogs,' Cartagena says loudly, looking in the Capitán General's direction. De Morales finds himself between the two men. 'They have raped this country for all it is worth. Why else are there no caravels at port?'

Though he surely heard him, Magalhães ignores Cartagena. But the message is clear. Every chance Fonseca's bastard gets to undermine the Capitán General he snatches at with both hands.

De Morales, however, is reminded of Bartolomé de las Casas and is astonished at Cartagena's blind hypocrisy. There are native men and women in Isla Juana, Hispaniola, Taino and Puerto Rico in the same condition. He has seen woodcuts of them and the terrible tortures inflicted upon their bodies in de las Casas' pamphlets. At this very moment, they are being worked to death in sugar fields, choking on gold dust in mines and having their ears ripped from their heads for the slightest infractions.

'They have food,' declares Carvalho who has come upon de Morales unawares. 'They hide their stores in the jungle.'

Trying his best to hide his disgust for Carvalho, de Morales replies, 'they seem to have nothing at all.'

'I have seen this in every pitiful savage native enclave I

have been to,' Carvalho says. 'The locals do not have the constitution of us Spanish. Their bodies are of low stock and cannot make the most of that which is provided. Hence, they are smaller, swarthier, uglier. Even Moors and Africans are stronger. They are not worthy of the paradise in which they live and so God sends us to enjoy the bounty He has provided.' The pilot saunters across the clearing towards a native woman.

What astounds de Morales is that Carvalho's words are no empty boast. He truly believes every word he says. De Morales has yet to hear Carvalho say one sentence that is not derogatory or self-aggrandising. Surely Magalhães will soon recognise Carvalho's evil.

After three days of near-ceaseless, hedonistic living, Carvalho's appetites are still unquenched. He goes ashore daily and rarely returns to the Trinidad. Few others keep their heads amongst the dizzying abundance of carnal delights and they become wild-eyed with desire as all pretence of discipline soon disappears. The nights are filled with moans of ecstasy as sailors, several at a time, make their way ashore to fornicate with the native women. Sailors boast of how many women they had, who had the most beautiful, who had the youngest and what the women allowed them to do. Pigafetta tells the tale of a young woman who climbed aboard the Trinidad and disturbed him in the dining room. There, he says, she slipped a clove into her vagina before allowing him to ravish her. A childish story told by a childish man, but it is just one among a hundred others.

De Morales is not alone in his abstinence. To his knowledge, Magalhães, Serrano, Mendoza, Quesada,

Valderrama, Espinosa and, of course, Enrique, who Magalhães keeps close by him at all times, have not partaken of the bounty of which Carvalho boasts.

But the rest of the men, driven on by Carvalho's boasts, are mad with lust and driven to exhaustion by their loins. Magalhães seems content to allow their rampant copulation. After all, a man who has spilt his seed is a man who is content and unlikely to cause him any problems. The Capitán General can scarcely afford for his crew to become resentful and disenchanted in the heat of Rio de Janeiro and flock to Cartagena's cause.

Though de Morales does not judge or begrudge those who have slept with women. Were he a younger man, he is sure he would have been tempted at the very least. But his mind is elsewhere, focused on the lengths he has gone to escape the ghosts of his past. Did he overreact? He has found himself on the far side of the world, as lonely as he ever was in Castile and, now, with nowhere else to run.

Late one afternoon, de Morales is making his way back to the Trinidad when he hears a cry. He turns to find Barbosa struggling against the grip of the Capitán General while Rebêlo claws at the sand, trying to stand. Barbosa, his back to de Morales, shifts his body, trying to free himself from the Magalhães' grasp.

De Morales hurries over, thinking perhaps some fight has occurred and Rebêlo may be injured. But before he reaches the group, Rebêlo rises from the sand. 'She is not yours to own, Barbosa,' he cries. I'll have who I want.'

Barbosa pulls his arm back, preparing to strike Rebêlo but Magalhães slaps him across the face with an open hand. Barbosa shakes his head, regaining his senses. 'You are not yourself,' Magalhães says.

Glancing over Barbosa's shoulder, the Capitán General sees de Morales approaching. 'Accompany my brother-in-law to Trinidad,' he says.

Barbosa looks stricken, his mouth opening and closing silently before he finally says, 'am I under arrest, then?'

'No, Duarte,' Magalhães replies, 'but will go there nonetheless.' Barbosa silently concedes to the Capitán General. He turns away, shoulders slumped and head bowed.

As they make their way to the black ships in silence together, de Morales sees three figures watching from the aftcastle of the San Antonio. He knows their silhouettes immediately: Mendoza, Quesada and Cartagena.

'For God's sake, call me Duarte. How many times must I tell you?'

Barbosa was disconsolate for an hour or so after the altercation with Magalhães. But, now onto his second cup of wine, he has begun to cheer up.

'Forgive me,' de Morales says. 'I do not wish to step on anyone's toes. Especially on this voyage, which already seems to lie on a knife-edge.' He thinks back to Mendoza, Quesada and Cartagena lining the aftcastle of the Victoria, incisive eyes searching for a chink in Magalhães' armour. A chink they may have found.

Barbosa sighs. 'A knife-edge indeed. It is Cartagena. After what happened at Salamon's trial, one would think he would have more sense and keep quiet. But, if anything, he has become more constant in his undermining since then.' Barbosa rubs his temples. 'He will slip up,' he says. 'The conspirators will give themselves up. Maybe in your presence.' He looks up, finds de Morales' eye in the gathering gloom.

'Fernão is grateful to you for your help. As am I, for that matter'

If Magalhães is so grateful for his help, why is the Capitán General so distant, so cold? Worrying he may let some irritation slip into his voice, de Morales offers a nod in reply.

Even after being scolded by Magalhães on the beach, Barbosa still speaks faithfully of him. He has shown not the slightest hint of anger at his brother-in-law. The Capitán General breeds such respect from his allies and such hatred from his enemies.

In the corner of the dining cabin, beside the trunk upon which Espinosa sat at the dinner so long ago, lies a buddled mess of clothing, parchment and bedding. Surely this is where Pigafetta has been living. De Morales wants to ask what the chronicler has been saying since he left their cabin. He wants to know, for certain, what Enrique hinted at.

Barbosa sees de Morales staring at it now and says, 'Pigafetta's.'

'I suspected as much.' De Morales does not mean to sound as curt as he does, does not mean to take out his own sense of betrayal on Barbosa who, he truly believes, is innocent.

As if he senses de Morales' hurt, Barbosa says, 'we cannot get along with everyone. What Pigafetta is is plain for anyone to see: a backslapper and a hanger-on. He is a leech, gripping tightly to men stronger than himself. In the presence of greatness, men like Pigafetta will do anything to endear themselves, go to any lengths to curry favour. But if he believes that you offer no advancement for him, he will not bother. I am sure it will come as no comfort to you, but he is the same with myself. I think he sees me as competition for Fernão's esteem. Espinosa has his measure,' he adds.

'Then, at least, I am in good company,' de Morales says. 'But I would have thought the Capitán General would see right through Pigafetta. He is no unintelligent man.'

Barbosa scoffs. 'Fernão is under much strain. You yourself have known this for almost as long as we have been at sea. Between the Portuguese, Fonseca, Cartagena and the other captains, not to mention the stress he is under to find his strait, is it any wonder? Fernão is a great man, but he is not friendly. He never has been. There has always been a distance between himself and even his closest confidants. If Pigafetta is searching for friendship, he will find none.'

'Maybe that is the point, maybe he enjoys the chase of great men.'

'Perhaps. But it matters not either way. Keep in mind that Fernão forgets not his allies. And take care not to mistake his coldness for enmity.'

Barbosa knows more than he is letting on. But de Morales gets the sense he means no harm in hiding all he knows. It is merely Barbosa's loyalty that is holding his tongue.

The two men sit in silence for some time. From outside come the staccato noises of the coopers and carpenters continuing their repairs in the relative cool of the night. From below the sound of waves slapping against the hull of the Trinidad echo through the ship. On the table, the small candle lighting the room flickers. Barbosa finishes his wine.

'I have travelled through India,' Barbosa says finally. 'I have seen the Moluccas, held cloves picked fresh from the tree in my hands. But to circumnavigate the world, as Fernão intends, is something else entirely. We are making history with every step we take, every league we sail will be studied and retraced for generations to come. I just wish the other captains could see beyond patriotism and rivalry. There is enough at stake already.'

Of course, he is right. 'Although day to day,' de Morales says, 'it does not seem such a noble enterprise. So much conniving, so many arguments.'

'It is an impossible thing, to be a leader,' Barbosa says. 'Upon every decision rests not only your fate but the fates of those you lead.'

A contemplative quiet follows, broken only by the hammering. The ships are almost ready to leave. Perhaps tomorrow, perhaps the day after, they will be gone from this place.

Barbosa shuffles in his chair, finally breaking the silence. 'You are not tempted? By the women, I mean?'

De Morales sighs, staring at the floor and remembering a youth that has long since passed him by. 'When one gets to my age, one rather loses interest.'

Barbosa smiles at that. 'All the more reason to partake now,' he says with an ironic grin.

An agonised scream fills the air. Both de Morales and Barbosa jump from their seats, the wooden legs of their chairs screeching across the floorboards. They look at one another in the dim candlelight, both knowing what the other is thinking: is this the start of the massacre they have all feared?

He is called to the Victoria. A sailor's hand has been crushed beneath the wheels of a cannon. The sailor's screams fill the air as de Morales approaches the swaying bulk of the Victoria in a skiff. The night is dark, giving only the barest hint of the massive height of the ship towering above him, silhouetted against the stars.

Elcano is waiting for de Morales on the deck. He leans

over the gunwale, first lifting the surgeon's case and then taking de Morales' hand and helping him climb over the taffrail.

The deck of the Victoria is quiet and almost empty with only two watchmen keeping a lookout, they stare in silence into the vast jungle spilling over the land before the armada. The cannons, standing in silent sentry, have been moved towards the starboard side of the ship, offering no hint of whatever accident befell the sailor. 'The men are ashore?' De Morales asks.

'Yes,' Elcano says. 'It is just myself and the watchmen for now. The injured sailor is one of them. Come señor, he is in my cabin and is in great pain.'

With an anxious look upwards to the mainmast where St. Elmo's Fire burned, de Morales turns and follows Elcano. They make their way across the main deck towards the cabins in the aftcastle.

Elcano's cabin is almost the twin of de Morales' and in the same location as his own, on the port side of the ship. The designs of the Trinidad and the Victoria are similar and, yet, different in small ways. There is no dining room onboard the Victoria but the result is that the two cabins in the aftcastle are larger, with a storeroom between them, open to the elements.

Inside Elcano's cabin, the sailor has been dumped onto a table where he is sweating and bleeding profusely onto the rich Spanish wood. For now, the sailor must have gone into shock because his screams have subsided, replaced by a whimpering murmur.

'Ma mein,' he says over and over between ragged breaths. A Frenchman, then.

Tears streak the sailor's face. The hand of the Frenchman

is a disorder of bloody, misshapen lumps that were once long, agile fingers. This man could have been a musician had he not been swept away to sea on the promise of adventure and fortune. Instead, his hand has been mangled and he lies now drooling, crying and bleeding on Elcano's charts and letters.

'Give him wine,' de Morales says to Elcano.

Elcano flings the door wide and calls for wine. While they wait, de Morales lightly slaps the Frenchman's face, waking him from his shock. Elcano sits on a chair beside the table, tugging on his pointed beard and watching the sailor. His cat, Amaya, wanders across the room, indifferent to the Frenchman's agony, before curling up on the bed.

The wine is brought and de Morales puts the cup to the sailor's mouth. The Frenchman drinks deeply as if he knows or suspects what he is about to endure. Next, de Morales turns and lifts one of the candles from a short stool against the wall and places it beside the Frenchman on the table. The light is dim and desultory, but more than enough for him to do the job.

'I am going to reset his fingers and stitch the wounds,' de Morales says to Elcano. 'He will scream, he will curse and thrash around. I need someone to hold him down firmly.'

'I will hold him.' The offer surprises de Morales. It is a job beneath a ship's pilot and, certainly, most other señores on the armada would have found some sailor to do the dirty work while they go elsewhere. But then, the Frenchman was put in Elcano's cabin, almost certainly under his orders.

De Morales takes out a piece of wood from his case, already marked and scarred by the teeth of previous patients.

and puts it into the Frenchman's mouth. Compliantly, his eyes pleading, the Frenchman takes the wood between his teeth.

De Morales nods to Elcano. The Basque takes a firm grip on the Frenchman's shoulders. 'Firmer,' de Morales says.

The fingers crunch as de Morales manipulates them. The bones grate and grind over each other as he twists the mess into something like the shape of fingers. The Frenchman's screams are terrible and he kicks wildly at the air. His bare feet slam and bounce off the table.

De Morales does not know how long it takes. He rarely does during surgery. He becomes focused, ignores all else around him. By the time he is finished, Elcano is sweating and breathing heavily, and the Frenchman has long since fainted. The fingers have swollen from the mistreatment and blood oozes freely from the torn skin.

Elcano is still pushing all his weight down on the Frenchman's shoulders, forcing them down onto the table. 'I don't think he will be moving, señor,' de Morales says.

The Basque looks at the Frenchman's face. His eyes are closed and he breathes heavily but is no longer moving. De Morales takes a fine thread and needle from his case. 'I will stitch these wounds, but time will tell if gangrene will take the hand,' he says.

Elcano wipes his brow and takes a seat beside the table, watching as de Morales works. After a while he says, 'how come you by this profession?'

'I am the youngest son of a low born lord,' de Morales says, avoiding eye contact. He must not tell the complete story: the mad father, the begging before an indifferent brother for the money to learn medicine. 'My family has lands in Llorona but I had little to hope for in the way of inheritance. First I became a barber, but it was not enough to merely mend bodies. I wanted to do good in the world, bring solace and comfort. When my father passed, I used what small inheritance he left me to pay for a place at Salamanca to learn medicine and eventually become a physician.'

'And what brought you to the Armada?'

'My wife passed six years ago while giving birth to our daughter. I could stay in Sevilla no longer after that and so became a physician to Juana of Castile.'

Elcano's eyebrows raise at the mention of Juana's name. It is always the same. Most people believe caring for royalty is a higher cause, something noble. In reality, they are no different from anyone else. In fact, in many ways, they are worse.

'It was a thankless job,' de Morales says. 'Obviously, Juana is mad but to treat a mad person day after day wears one down. Add to that the constant meddling and bickering by courtiers…' he shakes his head. 'It was not what I entered the medical profession to do. I saw the request from the Casa de Contratación for physicians for the armada and took the chance.'

'And your child? She is with your family?'

De Morales swallows hard before replying. He tries to not be so open with anyone, but something about Elcano's direct questions and friendly tone has made him reply up to now. 'No. She passed with her mother on that awful day.'

'God grant them peace,' Elcano says.

They fall silent. De Morales cannot help fantasies springing to his mind of his child and a life unlived. He feels the emptiness in his soul where she ought to be.

'Have you children?' He asks, moving the conversation away from things he would prefer not to speak of.

'I have a daughter, though I have not seen her for many years.' There is deep regret in Elcano's voice. 'But I have been at sea too much to find a wife as yet.'

'From one who never had the chance to hold his own,' de

Morales says, 'I tell you this: find your daughter.'

Elcano nods. There is a deep understanding in his eyes. De Morales recognises the regret and the sorrow he sees in them. He leans down and continues to stitch the Frenchman's wounds. Below him, his patient groans as the wound oozes globs of clotting blood.

Elcano is clearly a man who understands the need for medical knowledge. He could have asked for Bustamante. In truth, he probably should have. De Morales is supposed to be here to treat the señores and captains, not lowly sailors. But both he, and seemingly Elcano, know that had Bustamante come instead he would have burst in, hacked away the hand, thrown it in the sea and would have been rutting with the local woman by now. Few would care for the pain inflicted, but Elcano seems different.

From the deck outside, the muffled sound of heavy footsteps and voices breaks the silence. 'He was a Jew, after all,' a muffled voice is saying. 'Castile is still full of tornadizos of his ilk. We all knew it. He got what was coming to him.'

'What we all know for sure is he was a traitor.' A second voice says, 'Afterall-'

The door opens and de la Reina ducks into the cabin, Cartagena stomping after him, mid-rant. '-this is a Portuguese port,' he continues, not bothering to look up and see de Morales is in the room. 'He intends to betray us. He is loyal only to Manuel and his sordid little Portugal.'

'We have company,' Elcano says, motioning towards de Morales. De la Reina and Cartagena look from him to the body of the Frenchman and back to Elcano. De Morales hunches down lower over his patient, trying to appear as focused on the work as he can. 'Forgive me señores, my work is nearly complete,' he says.

'I care not,' scoffs Cartagena. 'Surely we all of us share the same thoughts on this Magalhães.' He spits the name, twisting it into a curse.

'Where is Mendoza?' Elcano asks.

'The captain is trading with the locals,' Cartagena says.

'Ought the armada's Inspector General be there?'

'He can handle it himself,' Cartagena says. 'I have full faith in Mendoza's abilities to swindle these ignorant locals. Unlike our engañoso Capitán General.' Cartagena cannot help himself. Every unrelated remark is twisted back to Magalhães. He is like a lover scorned.

De la Reina moves beside de Morales. He stands uncomfortably close and, it seems, deliberately so. The priest's breath stinks of wine. He leans over the Frenchman. 'This is the man whose screams we heard from the shore. Will he lose the hand?' He asks in an indifferent tone.

'Possibly. Time will tell,' de Morales says, pretending to be fixated on a job that is already complete. He dabs at the wound, smearing the blood in greasy streaks across the swollen hand and fingers. De la Reina inhales deeply as he straightens up, moving away from the carnage.

This is what Barbosa said would happen, that Cartagena would eventually let slip explicitly mutinous words. De Morales has surely heard enough already to pass on to Magalhães and be done with this spying. Perhaps then, de Morales can prove his innocence against whatever Pigafetta has been telling the Capitán General.

Cartagena slaps Elcano on the chest. 'Did you see the fight?' He asks with boyish glee.

'Fight?' Elcano asks.

'Magalhães struck his own brother-in-law,' Cartagena says. 'The man is unhinged. Unfit to lead.'

'I can bear that stench no longer,' De la Reina says. 'Is he finished with, señor doctor?' He asks, jerking his head at the sailor. De Morales nods in reply and de la Reina slaps the Frenchman in the face. 'Out,' is all he says.

The Frenchman rolls off the table and staggers out of the cabin swaying and nursing his hand. So much for Christian charity.

De Morales starts packing away his tools into his case and catches Elcano's eye. 'Thank you for your help,' the Basque says.

He offers a quick smile in reply and leaves the cabin to Cartagena's poisonous schemes.

Chapter 7

December 1519

Antonio Ginovés is missing. Magalhães orders a search to be made of the entire Victoria from the crow's nest to the ballasts. Still the boy is not found. Next, comes a full day of questioning. None of the crew have seen the boy and all maintain the same story: Ginovés disappeared soon after he was sodomised.

Salamon cannot be to blame. He has been chained up in the orlop hold of the Trinidad since the trial. If there is villainy at play, it seems the entire crew of the Victoria is in on the conspiracy. For they all maintain the same story. Some say Ginovés may have disappeared in the jungle but that seems implausible. How could a cabin boy have remained unnoticed on board the Victoria for so long before making his escape?

As if the disappearance of Ginovés has spurred him into action, the morning after the questioning the Capitán General orders Salamon to be brought ashore. The convicted man has not seen daylight since November. His eyes are dark, his skin

pale and his hair is a knotted mess. The shackles tightly
clasped around his ankles force him to hobble and stumble,
hunchbacked, across the furrowed sand of the shore to the
base of the cross.

The sky is heavy with clouds, oppressive and ominous
they weigh down on de Morales. Though the sun is hidden
behind the thick shroud, the air is still unbearably hot and
humid. The entire crew who are not on duty, perhaps some
fifty men, are called to attention before the cross.

The Capitán General, with Serrano, Mesquita and
Valderrama at his side, stands behind Salamon, facing the
gathered crew, their backs to the condemned. As is becoming
habit, Mendoza, Quesada, de la Reina and Cartagena are
notable only for their absence.

With his back to the crew, Salamon makes for a sorry
sight, but he draws a crowd of Brasileiros nevertheless. They
emerge from the jungle, curious as to what this new oddity
presages.

The sentence, carried out in the emperor's name, requires
the Capitán General to list the king's many titles. 'On behalf
of his majesty Carlos, by the grace of God, Holy Roman
Emperor, forever August, King of all Spains, of Castile,
Aragon, León, Navarra, Grenada, Toledo, Valencia, Galicia,
Majorca, Sevilla, Cordova, Murcia, Jaén, Algarves, Algeciras,
Gibraltar and the Canary Islands. King of the Two Sicilies, of
Sardinia, Corsica, King of Jerusalem, King of the Western and
Eastern Indies, Lord of the islands and Great Ocean,
Archduke of Austria, Duke of Burgundy, Brabant, Lorraine,
Styria, Carinthia. . .'

The list goes on, endless and exhaustive.

How many more domains will Magalhães add to the
King's titles? How much further will Carlos' reach stretch

around the world? Will he soon be king of the Maluku Islands? King of Ternate, of Tidore, of the Banda Islands? Only then will Spain truly compete with Portugal for dominion over the world.

Done with the list, Magalhães repeats the sentencing he first passed in the middle of the Great Ocean.

'. . .you, Antonio Salamon, are found guilty of the crime of sodomy upon the cabin boy, Antonio Ginovés, for whom we pray for salvation. For this affront to God and his Majesty, you will be strangled until your death. God have mercy on your soul.'

To maintain anonymity a hood, cut from sackcloth, has been brought from the Trinidad. Salamon is made to remain facing the cross while a cabin boy brings a sack filled with fifty glass beads. All but one of the beads is green. The crew will take turns picking a bead without looking and whoever picks the single clear bead will act as executioner while wearing the hood. The crew may guess as to who will strangle Salamon to death, but Salamon will never know. So much planning has gone into this execution.

Valderrama steps before the men as they organise themselves. 'I hereby absolve the man who is to do this deed we are gathered today to witness of all sin, culpability and guilt,' he says loudly. 'Know you do God's work and walk in His light as you do so.'

One by one, the men step forward. Each man takes a bead from the sack, gripping it tightly in a closed fist before revealing it to the Magalhães, Serrano and Mesquita. As his turn approaches, a weight grows in de Morales' stomach. If he had the choice, he would not be here, but he was told the Capitán General himself requested his presence. His professional services would have been required anyway to confirm Salamon's death, but playing the part of executioner sickens him.

It is his turn to take a bead. Green. He breathes a sigh of relief and tries to work moisture back into his dry mouth. He shows his bead to the gathered captains. Magalhães looks at the stone and returns his gaze beyond de Morales. A blank, unreadable look on his face.

The lot casting seems to take an age, fifty is a lot of men. Eventually, the sound of footsteps and the clink of beads behind him ceases and the captains come to stand below the cross before Salamon. The crowd of curious natives has grown and all stand in silence, watching the strange ceremony as it unfolds.

A moment passes and a hooded figure moves through the sailors. The figure stops beneath the cross before Salamon who is made to look up to face his executioner's shroud. De Morales can imagine the fear in Salamon's eyes now. The ragged breathing. The desperate eyes flicking this way and that in sunken sockets, searching for an escape and landing on the inevitable conclusion: there is none.

The executioner is quick in his movements. He reaches forward swiftly, taking a tight grip of Salamon's neck. The veins and sinews of his hands bulge against his skin as his grasp grows tighter still.

For a moment, it is as if they are carved in relief: the executioner's powerful hands and Salamon's clawed hands bound behind his back. But the scene is quickly broken as Salamon gives a choked, rasping cry and pulls away.

The executioner is leaning over now and Salamon's back is arched into a hideous shape, revealing his face to the crew behind him. The veins of his neck swell and pulse. His begging eyes, filled with panic, have turned red and bulge as his face darkens to a deep purple. A flash of silent lightning fills the sky with light for a split second and thunder rolls. The heavens open. Rain crashes in a fierce torrent into the parched earth, filling the cracks and fissures.

The sandy dirt below the executioner's feet has already turned into a quagmire and it looks for a second as if he will lose his footing. But the mock executioner is sure-footed and he increases the violence of the strangulation, pushing toward Salamon, squeezing the life from him.

There is a crack.

The executioner was efficient, despite his inexperience. He releases Salamon and the body crumples to the sodden dirt. Rain drums onto the corpse, filling the unnatural hollows in its broken neck.

De Morales slowly moves through the crowd of sailors. He kneels over the body, his knees sinking into the mire. He puts his fingers to Salamon's crippled neck.

Nothing.

'He is dead,' he says.

Valderrama solemnly crosses himself. De Morales rises slowly from the body. The thrumming sound of the torrent of rain is lost. All he hears is his heartbeat pounding in his ears.

He notices the natives. Their scrawny arms are upraised, hands clasped tightly above their heads. Even those with no hands have raised what the Portuguese have left them. The rain lashes down from the sky, soaking the silent Brasileiros.

The crew turn from the body, making for the ships and the native crowd press in around the sodden cadaver of Salamon. They reach out, hands hovering over the paederast, none daring to touch him. The sound of their muttering lost in the ceaseless beating of the rain.

Dawn and still the rain falls. The beach is empty of Brasileiros. The fissures stretching across the shore are torrents of muddy water rushing into the sea. The corpse of Salamon lies where it was left, soaking and sinking into the earth.

Magalhães gives the order for the captains to make ready their ships to leave. They have tarried long enough in Portuguese waters and it is inevitable that caravels will soon return to the port. Better the armada is long gone before they do.

Whistles are blown, shouts and cries fill the air. The sails, heavy and sagging with rainwater, are unfurled. The anchors are lifted and the sodden sails heave, pulling the ships away from the New World and the corpse of Salamon: a final gift to the Brasileiros.

As the armada pulls away, natives gather on the shore. Some push long canoes carved from whole trunks of brasilwood into the sea, but most stay on the land. Those in the canoes follow the armada a short distance, then stop. They stare in silence, looking out at the fleet, the rain still falling around them, still drumming against Salamon's corpse.

Behind him, de Morales hears Pigafetta say, 'they praise us as savours for we brought the rain. We delivered them from their drought with our coming.'

The natives are lost, then, in the falling rain. The last de Morales sees of them, they turn as one toward the prostrate body of Antonio Salamon.

Chapter 8

December 1519

He is standing outside the Trinidad's dining cabin. Inside, muffled by the oak door, he can hear voices talking quietly. He hears Magalhães and Valderrama, but he knows Pigafetta is also inside.

He knows he must report to the Capitán General the conversation he overheard between Cartagena and de la Reina. He has put it off too long already and to delay any longer will only arouse more suspicion in Magalhães.

Silently, he curses that Espinosa and, most importantly, Barbosa are not on board the Trinidad. Since the armada left Rio de Janeiro, they have been aboard the San Antonio, ensuring Mesquita's crew fall in line under their new captain. Magalhães, perhaps justifiably so, worried for his cousin who took over command from Cartagena. Who can tell how many men aboard the San Antonio remain loyal to their fallen captain?

De Morales takes a deep breath, knocks and the conversation falls silent.

'Enter.' The voice is Pigafetta's. His heart sinks.

He pushes the door open and is greeted by the silent, staring eyes of the Capitán General, Pigafetta and Valderrama. They are sitting around the table, chairs pushed back, shirt buttons undone, the remains of a meal before them. Scattered across the table are pages of parchment, all of them bearing scribbles intersected by geometric lines. Charts, no doubt. Enrique, standing behind Magalhães, greets de Morales with a silent nod.

'What do you want, de Morales.' Magalhães' tone is reticent, his eyes severe and his temperament distant.

De Morales swallows hard and says quietly, 'I would speak with you, Capitán General. Of things I heard on board the Victoria while at Rio de Janeiro. In private, perhaps.'

He should not have added that. Pigafetta's eyebrows raise, either in shock or anger.

'What you have to report, you can do so before my comrades,' Magalhães says. The Capitán General is already set against him, either by mood or by Pigafetta's whispering. Now he has given Magalhães one more reason to dislike him.

De Morales takes a step forward and closes the door behind him. He stands before the three men, searching for words he has practised to himself these past two days but finding none. Pigafetta smirks, enjoying De Morales' discomfort.

'Well?'

'At Rio de Janeiro, the day you asked me to accompany Barbosa back to the flagship, I was called to the Victoria,' de Morales says, settling into the narrative despite the cold atmosphere and Pigafetta's sneer. 'A sailor had injured his hand moving a cannon across the deck.'

'I know of this,' Valderrama says. 'I was in my cabin and heard the screams. After you had left, Barbosa came to me. He let me know my services might be needed.'

'I mended the hand with the help of Elcano,' de Morales continues. At the mention of Elcano's name, Pigafetta turns to Magalhães but the Capitán General does not return his conspiratorial look. 'Once the bones were set, as I stitched the wounds, de la Reina and Cartagena came aboard. They must not have been on the Victoria before for Elcano said, but for a handful of watchmen, he was alone. They came into Elcano's cabin where I was mending the sailor's hand. They did know I was there and, as they approached, I overheard their conversation. They were speaking of someone, saying he was a Jew and deserved death. As I have replayed the conversation in my mind since, I wonder if they might have been speaking of Ginovés, or maybe the sailor murdered on the San Antonio in the Great Ocean. Then I heard Cartagena's voice. He called you a traitor, Capitán General. He said you were lingering in Rio de Janeiro in hopes that the armada would be captured by the Portuguese. When they entered the cabin, Elcano pointed out my presence. Despite this, Cartagena went on, implying everyone in the armada was of the same opinion. He was hinting at a conspiracy to mutiny-'

Magalhães interrupts him, waving a hand. 'This is not news to me.'

'You asked me to,' de Morales hesitates, looking at Valderrama and Pigafetta. He lowers his voice, 'be your spy.'

'Of course, we know already,' Pigafetta says derisively.

'And this is all you have discovered,' Magalhães says. 'I say it again, señor doctor, this is not news to me. Cartagena spoke ill of me, so what? Cartagena is a gelding. He has no power now and Mesquita is bringing the San Antonio to heel. I know Mendoza and Quesada conspire every chance they get and as for de la Reina, I have had his measure since Fonseca dumped him in my armada six months ago. I know their intentions and I do not need a doctor feeding me snippets of information when he had the chance to discover the exact nature of their schemes.'

'Not to mention the Jew they spoke of,' Valderrama says. 'You could have asked who they spoke of, or at least turned the conversation in a direction that might have revealed his identity.' Pigafetta nods slowly to the rhythm of Valderrama's words. De Morales knew he faced an enemy in the chronicler, but Valderrama is an adversary he does not need.

He focuses instead on Magalhães. 'You told me not to put myself in danger,' he says desperately.

'Be that as it may,' Magalhães says. He stops and stares into de Morales' eyes. Unblinking and severe, the Capitán General waits for de Morales' nerve to break, for unchecked words to come spilling from him.

De Morales tightens his lips and stares back at Magalhães, vowing to himself to say no more.

Finally, the Capitán General leans back in his chair and shrugs as if in careless indifference. 'This is not news to me, de Morales. Do not waste my time with Cartagena. You are excused.'

Magalhães turns to the parchments before him, focusing intently on them. De Morales, face reddened with embarrassment, turns to leave the dining cabin. Before he does, he notices the Machiavellian smirk on Pigafetta's face has grown to a full smile. The chronicler delighted in every moment.

In his cabin, de Morales curses himself for even reporting what he heard to Magalhães. But what difference would it have made if he had not? Magalhães would have found out what he overheard Cartagena and de la Reina say and would have used that against him anyway. And what then? The Capitán General would only have demanded why de Morales did not report it and the result would be the same, if not worse.

He curses himself for not staying longer in Elcano's cabin. He could have found some pretence. De la Reina and Cartagena had no idea whether he was truly finished treating the Frenchman. Cartagena, especially, was obstreperous that night. He would certainly have said more, maybe even tried to include de Morales in whatever plans he has formed. Perhaps Magalhães would then have not been so dismissive.

But, as it is, Magalhães' mind has been utterly turned against him and almost certainly it has been turned by Pigafetta. The chronicler has used the Capitán General's paranoia to ingratiate himself to him, to gain power and prestige at the expense of de Morales.

He curses Pigafetta, curses the armada and the king and the whole foolish expedition. But most of all he curses himself for being caught up in the conspiracy and egotism he left Castile to be free of.

Though a favourable wind pushes them south, each day, when night falls, the armada drops anchor. These are uncharted waters and continuing after dark is far too dangerous. Magalhães stands sentry on the starboard side of the ship from the moment they set sail each morning to the moment the anchor is dropped each night. He looks west, searching, in the tangled mass of jungle, for the strait.

Though Carvalho was brought to the Trinidad to lend his supposed expertise on piloting the coastlines of the New World, he has been strangely absent since they left Rio de Janeiro, disappearing for hours at a time. Surely Capitán General has been informed but he seems unconcerned with anything that is happening aboard his ship. His focus instead is entirely aimed at the coastline and the charts he keeps with him at all times. There were certainly some in the armada who believed the Capitán General would search for a southern cape of the New World and find the Moluccas that way, but even those who held most steadfastly to that theory have surely dropped it by now.

To fill the void left by Carvalho during his absences, Barbosa orders Estêvão Gomes back to the whipstaff. Gomes, freed from the cramped life he no doubt lived in the crew's quarters below, seems content to return to piloting the Trinidad. De Morales likes Gomes' company. The pilot was kind to him when he suffered seasickness at the start of the voyage. Not to mention he is talkative and told de Morales many things about Magalhães' past he would otherwise never have known.

'I did not get a chance to thank you,' de Morales says to him now. 'Your cure for seasickness was a saving grace.'

Gomes shrugs, 'perhaps, one day, I will need your help and you can repay the favour.' The pilot slowly turns the whipstaff in response to some current unfelt by de Morales. Though he was replaced by Carvalho, Gomes' skill is clear.

De Morales catches Gomes watching the Capitán General. Magalhães is standing at the gunwale, his hands clenching the taffrail tightly, crumpling the charts in his hand. Though his back is to the two men, it is clear from his tense posture that the Capitán General is worried. Espinosa stands nearby. The master-at-arms has closely guarded Magalhães since his return to the flagship, not allowing anyone other than himself or Barbosa to even approach the Capitán General. Even Pigafetta has been spurned. For the time being the chronicler waits in the dining cabin for Magalhães to return each evening.

'Our Capitán General does not know where the strait is,' Gomes says quietly

'You think Faleiro's charts are wrong?' De Morales asks.

'I think Faleiro's charts do not exist. Or at least that the Capitán General does not have them with him.'

De Morales looks again at the crumpled charts in Magalhães' hands. He saw them before, spread across the table in the dining cabin, but their chaotic patterns were incomprehensible to him. What if they cannot be comprehended? What if they are not charts of any real landmass and are entirely fabricated? What if Faleiro really was mad?

The thought is a chilling one. If Magalhães does not have the charts, or they are incorrect, then he is blindly searching for a strait in an unexplored land. They could be thousands of leagues from their destination. They could already have passed it. Or, worse still, the strait could not even exist. The New World could stretch unbroken and endless from north to south.

Carvalho appears, rising from the hold below. He saunters across the main deck, towards the aftcastle, and pushes Gomes away from the whipstaff.

'Where have you been?' Espinosa demands. He stamps

across the deck, his eyes filled with rage and his rapier swinging at his side.

'I was resting,' Carvalho says innocently. 'Gomes handled things while I was away.'

'You are a pilot, Carvalho,' Espinosa says. 'When next you go missing, you will be flogged.' He points a finger at Carvalho, poking him in the centre of his chest. 'I will chain you to this staff if I have to.' He turns his furious eyes on Gomes and de Morales. 'Clear the deck,' he says.

The southerly winds are consistent. They drag at the armada each night and the rodes creak and complain as the ships long to be free of them. It is as if the New World is pushing them ever onwards, towards triumph or death.

The armada is now many leagues south of the equatorial line and in waters rarely, if ever, explored by either the Spanish or the Portuguese. When night falls, the vast empyrean blackness above is studded with strange, blushing constellations, rendering the astrolabes San Martin brought with him utterly useless.

On the shore, life is abundant. The massive rainforests that surrounded Rio de Janeiro have stretched onwards, broken only by rivers choked with low hanging trees and impenetrable swamps. From the jungle's midst comes the constant chatter of creatures and the call of birds. Tropical and mystic, their unfamiliar calls drift out to the fleet, never ceasing their cacophony all day and night.

Every few days, once they have anchored for the evening, the Capitán General sends a contingent of men ashore to find wood and food. The men dare not venture far into the sinister jungle. But even if they wanted to, de Morales doubts that they could. The jungle is a labyrinthine morass of creeping vines and great, creaking trees. Its floor is almost always kept in darkness by the towering canopies of the brasilwood trees, even at midday. Where the slightest ray of sunlight manages to filter through to the underbrush, a bounty of vegetation explodes.

Fortunately, it is not necessary to travel too far into the primaeval jungle. Even on its outermost fringes, where it spills into the ocean like an unattended pot boiling over, there is a wealth of wild fruits. Every time the men are sent into the jungle, they return carrying a bounty of food and loaded down heavily with dense wood collected from the jungle floor. The timber and fruit are dripping with moisture and even the men return drenched, as if the forest itself sweats with the exertion of its rampant growth.

The fruits of the New World they bring back to the Trinidad are like nothing de Morales has tasted before. Huge and swollen, every single one is of the most decadent and delicious flavour.

There is a plant, similar in shape to a pod of peas but much larger, its fruit is of a sweet, cream-like taste and is indulgent and remarkably moreish. Then there is a smaller ball-shaped fruit, similar to a Genoan lemon but of a deep purple colour. Within it are many black seeds robed in fleshy nectar much like a pomegranate, but its taste is fiercely sharp, though highly refreshing. It alone has satisfied a great thirst de Morales has had for weeks.

They celebrate Christmas with a feast in the muggy air on the main deck aboard the Trinidad. Two tables are clothed in fresh fruit from the jungle, raisins and nuts, a double ration of wine and, of course, the ever-present food at sea, hardtack. The captains, all disagreements and transgressions of the past four months forgotten, at least for a time, eat at the same table.

De Morales is sitting at another table on the deck of the flagship with Barbosa, Espinosa and an empty chair for Elcano. All in all, he would be in good company, were it not for Pigafetta and Carvalho, laughing at each other's immature jokes at the centre of the table.

Elcano finally arrives. When he sees Pigafetta boisterously laughing at some crude joke of Carvalho's, the Basque animatedly rolls his eyes at de Morales. He sees the fruit, wine and nuts spread across the table. 'Mayhap the food will compensate for the company,' he says.

The giggling stops abruptly. Carvalho straightens his back, his lip curling into a snarl. 'And who would you mean by that?' He asks.

'Well, de Morales, of course,' replies Elcano innocently. 'I truly hate the man.' He winks at the surgeon who smiles at the joke. Barbosa and Espinosa laugh. Carvalho sneers. He grabs a handful of nuts and raisins and shoves them greedily into his mouth.

'Well met Elcano,' Barbosa says. 'How do things fare aboard the Victoria?'

'They fare fairly,' Elcano says jovially, taking a sip of wine.

Barbosa passes Elcano a bowl of fresh fruit from the jungle. 'We were talking of past lives and some of us,' he looks to Carvalho, 'of past loves. What brings you to the Armada de Molucca?'

'Now there is a story,' Elcano says, selecting a particularly ripe, yellow fruit from the bowl the crew have taken to calling maracuyá. 'I fought for Castile in the Italian Wars. When I had my fill of Ferdinand's rampant bloodletting, I moved to Sevilla and became captain of a merchant fleet. I had my own ship, but the rest of the fleet was owned by a Genoese merchant. We travelled between Sevilla, Genoa and Turkey trading spices and silks.'

'A lucrative trade, no doubt,' Barbosa says, reaching for his wine.

'Lucrative indeed, for some.' Elcano says. 'I took on all the work, all the dangers, while other men took home the profits.'

'The merchant class are a scourge on Europe,' Espinosa says. 'Some are richer even than their sovereigns.'

'Is it not a good thing, Gonzalo?' Barbosa says. 'Their wealth speaks to their nation's stability. If not for a strong and stable monarch, they would not exist.'

Espinosa flings a hand in the air derisively. 'Be not naive. How can a monarch claim strength when his subjects have the wealth to raise private armies larger than his own?' The master-at-arms stabs his forefinger onto the table. 'Mark my words, their riches will be the downfall of all Europe unless they are kept in check.'

'One should see how they live,' Elcano says. 'Words cannot do justice to their lavish lifestyles.'

'How did you go from captaining a merchant fleet to piloting a ship?' Barbosa asks.

'I fell on ill-luck,' Elcano says. He slices through the maracuyá, juice and seeds spill from it, forming a sticky puddle on the table. 'One of the fleet was wrecked in a storm off Antalya. The merchant who owned the ship demanded payment, saying it was my fault.'

'You see, Duarte,' Espinosa says. 'They are lecherous vermin to a man.' Barbosa rolls his eyes.

'I could not pay for the ship,' Elcano continues, 'for all my profits were laying at the bottom of the Aegean. I was forced to sell my ship to a Genoan banker to pay the debt which, I learned later, was against Castilian law. The king offered me a subordinate position on this armada to pay for my crime.'

'So you are a criminal,' Espinosa says.

'Of a sort,' replies Elcano lightly. 'But who among us is not?'

Espinosa scoffs, 'a fair point.'

'If you believe the King of Portugal,' Barbosa says, 'the Capitán General is a criminal. Obviously, he is not,' he adds quickly, glancing at the captain's table.

'What of Amaya, your cat?' De Morales asks, 'how goes her hunt?'

'Amaya is without a peer on that ship for her diligence,' Elcano says smiling. 'Would that the sailors work as hard as her.'

'A cat? Clever,' Espinosa says. He turns to Barbosa, nudging him in the side. 'Why did we not think of that?'

'Because we are not Basque,' Barbosa says. 'Elcano has more experience at sea in his fingernail than we have in-'

'Do you know, Antonio,' Carvalho interrupts loudly, 'another name for a cat is a pussy.' Pigafetta guffaws at the joke. Espinosa lets out an exasperated sigh.

'Were you born ignorant, Carvalho?' Elcano asks with mock politeness. 'Or did you develop it along the way?'

Carvalho's chair loudly scrapes across the deck as he stands suddenly. He reaches for the knife at his belt but his hand is stayed by Espinosa before he can draw the blade. The scene seems to freeze, charged with tension, as Carvalho stares into Elcano's eyes.

Not moving from his seat, Elcano looks coldly back at the pilot, a spoonful of maracuyá flesh halfway to his mouth. 'What are you going to do, Carvalho?' He asks quietly.

From across the main deck, the captains are watching them. 'Is there a problem?' Magalhães asks firmly.

At the sound of the Capitán General's voice, the tension dissipates. Carvalho pulls his arm free from Espinosa's grip. He grabs a handful of nuts and fruit and meets Elcano's eye for a moment. 'I have a long memory for insult,' he says. A shrug from Elcano is all he receives in reply before he turns and loudly stomps across the deck towards the trapdoor to the hold.

Watching Carvalho stroppily disappear below, de Morales' heart jumps for joy. 'You had my friendship,' he says to Elcano, 'now you have my respect.'

'This factionalism is an affront to the Capitán General,' Pigafetta says. The chronicler rises from his seat. He passes a venomous glare across the table, then follows Carvalho.

With Carvalho and Pigafetta gone, de Morales can enjoy the meal. The exquisite, decadent fruits of the New World soon lighten the mood and Barbosa, Espinosa, Elcano and himself enjoy a long meal of excellent food and intelligent conversation. The hardtack, of course, remains untouched as the four men savour the recherché fruits of the New World, nectar dripping down their chins as they eat well in good company.

Chapter 9

February 1520

The feast of St Agatha has come and gone like the jungle and de Morales is warding off a chill wind. The great, sweating forest of the New World has given way to a barren stretch of land with high coasts and harsh, haggard foliage. With the passing of plant life so, too, have the sounds of animals and birds ceased. The atmosphere is now one of absence, lonely and empty and so much like the landscape. The temperature is much cooler, the wind more persistent as its thieving fingers steal what warmth his body can make.

The armada is anchored in the mouth of a wide, silty river and has been here for three days. Magalhães has convinced himself that this river is his strait. He, along with Enrique and Espinosa, accompanied Serrano onboard the Santiago into the river three days ago to scout the way ahead.

On board the Trinidad, a search is underway for Carvalho.

As soon as the fleet anchored in this river mouth and the Capitán General was gone, the pilot disappeared. In the time that has passed, no one has seen anything of him. It has become apparent he has simply abandoned his post.

Barbosa, left at the helm of the Trinidad while Magalhães is away, wants to keep the search for Carvalho as quiet as possible. As is usual in these cases, Barbosa began his search at the ship's highest point: the crow's nest of the mainmast. Doing so leaves the missing man, if he is avoiding capture and not injured, fewer places to hide and no chance of leaping overboard as the search closes in on him.

Under the pretence of thoroughly cleaning the flagship, Barbosa has ordered men to the masts, the deck, the fore and aftcastle and the upper hold. There is now only one place Carvalho can now be hiding: the orlop hold.

Barbosa comes to de Morales, asks him to accompany him below. 'With Espinosa and Enrique gone,' he says, 'you are the only man aboard the ship I feel I can trust. And if Carvalho has had some accident, you will be needed anyway.'

De Morales agrees but as they head below into the crew's quarters, he is reminded of his previous visit to a ship's orlop hold, of what he and Elcano found there, and of the enormous ramifications of what followed.

Barbosa stops before the trapdoor, where the Trinidad's supplies of food, water, wine and trade goods are kept. He kneels, stopping short as he reaches for the padlock. 'This door should be locked at all times,' he says, 'but someone has broken the lock.'

A broken lock. It is like the Victoria all over again. De Morales swallows hard, wild imaginings spring to his mind of what new horror awaits them below.

Barbosa lifts the trapdoor and turns to him before they

descend into the darkness below. 'We must proceed quietly from here,' he says softly. 'We do not know what we will find. If Carvalho is performing some evil, we must catch him in the act. I will go first,' he says, barely above a whisper. 'Stay close behind me.'

Slowly, carefully, Barbosa descends the stairs, de Morales following as quietly and closely behind as possible. The staircase into the orlop hold is so steep as to be more like a ladder, forcing de Morales to carefully search for the next step as silently as he can. The air becomes thick and dark, filled with the smells of musk, mould and rat urine. The supernumerary holds the candle loft before him. Its murky light casts a pathetic glow, barely puncturing the absolute darkness of the hold. De Morales strains his eyes and ears, searching in the silent gloom of the hold for human shapes and voices.

Barbosa begins pushing further into the shadows ahead. De Morales' eyes are becoming more accustomed now to the darkness and he can see the shapes of sacks and crates lining the walls of the hold, forming a narrow corridor down which they are making their way.

Ahead, another path splits from the main one in which they are walking, leading to the left. Barbosa reaches it now and stops suddenly, his head cocked as he stares at something de Morales cannot see.

He takes a step to the left into the path he was looking down. De Morales follows and, as he rounds the corner, the light of Barbosa's candle catches on the glint of an eye. The light spills further, filling a clearing in the stacks of supplies. In the centre of the clearing are two completely naked women, side by side. One is laying on her side, her hands and feet bound and her mouth gagged. The other is kneeling, the ropes which surely bound her lie frayed and coiled on the boards of the hold. She must have freed herself and was working at her companions' ropes when they were disturbed by Barbosa's candle.

'What-' is all Barbosa can manage to say. De Morales shares his shock as he stares in horror at what is before him.

The women are in a terrible state. Their faces are bruised from severe beatings, they have burst lips, blackened and bloodshot eyes and tear-stained cheeks. Burns and gashes ring their wrists and ankles where the ropes that bound them have cut into the skin. Their legs are stained with faeces and urine, their privates with menstrual blood. Their bare breasts bear arcing cuts and bruises where they have been bitten savagely by a human mouth.

'God's death,' Barbosa says finally, shock rendering his voice weak. 'What have these women endured?' He kneels, the shadows cast by his small candle lengthening as he does so. The bound and gagged woman on the floor attempts to move away from him, desperately struggling against the ropes. The other stares in silence, her eyes wide with terror.

'Carvalho.' Barbosa says.

De Morales looks into the darkness beyond the candlelight, searching for something, for anything, that would give some clue as to Carvalho's whereabouts. He is certainly down here. Somewhere. He is filled with a resolve to find the pilot, to see him face justice for what he has done to these women.

De Morales calls into the darkness. 'If you are down here, reveal yourself and it will go a lot better for you.' His voice, shaky, small and pathetic in the massive hold, has none of the resolution he had hoped it would.

There is no reply.

Barbosa stands. 'It will be best if we split up,' he says, turning to de Morales. 'You stay near the stairs, in case Carvalho tries to escape.

De Morales nods then moves slowly back to the staircase, searching the darkness as he does so. Behind him, he can hear Barbosa, no longer hiding his presence, stepping heavily. Like a beater, Barbosa is trying to corral Carvalho into revealing himself.

Standing at the base of the stairs, watching Barbosa's light wavering and flickering in the darkness, de Morales thinks about Carvalho. He always knew the pilot was a hedonist, a voluptuary, but even he could not have guessed the depths of his depravity. Carvalho must have bought or kidnapped these women from Rio de Janeiro. Since then, he has been using these women whenever he wished. He thinks back. All those times the pilot was absent, when Gomes was guiding the Trinidad and the time Carvalho stomped into the hold at the Christmas feast, he was coming here to repeatedly violate and abuse these women.

And Pigafetta followed him. At the very least, the chronicler must know something of this crime.

The heavy footsteps stop and everything inside the hold becomes silent. All that can be heard is the gentle slap of the ocean against the hull outside and the moaning wind. Light is snuffed out and the hold is plunged into absolute darkness.

The silence drags on.

No one moves.

Slowly, de Morales begins to see the familiar shapes of crates, barrels and sacks swelling out of the darkness as his eyes become accustomed to the small amount of light spilling into the hold from above.

There is a crash to his right followed by a loud thud and a

cry from Barbosa and the silent hold breaks into discord and dissonance. Sacks and crates spill their contents over the wooden boards and a shape tumbles into the centre of the hold. Another shape, surely Barbosa, leaps forward, despite the low ceiling. He lands bodily on what must be Carvalho who squirms, desperately trying to escape.

The two men wrestle and tussle in the darkness. 'A light,' Barbosa cries. 'Fetch a light.'

De Morales turns and leaps up the staircase into the upper hold, mad eyes searching for a candle. He finds one, turns and dashes down the staircase once more, shielding the flame before him.

He stops, breathing heavily and holds the candle aloft. Almost at his feet, Barbosa holds Carvalho down, pushing his full weight down onto the pilot's shoulders. Carvalho's mad eyes flick from side to side, searching for a way out of Barbosa's grip.

'You wicked wretch,' Barbosa cries. He turns to de Morales. 'Hold him,' he says.

The surgeon, hands shaking and breathless, puts the candle down on a crate and leans over Carvalho, pushing him down as Barbosa rises. Sensing an opportunity, the pilot snaps and twists beneath him, fighting for freedom. For a moment de Morales is sure Carvalho will break free of his hold, weak as it is.

But then Barbosa is upon Carvalho again, one hand around his neck and another twisting his ear. Carvalho cries out as he is hauled to his feet. The pilot struggles again as Barbosa releases his ear. Again, de Morales is certain Carvalho will break free, but Barbosa punches the pilot hard in the stomach and Carvalho doubles over, gasping for breath.

When he finally catches it, he says, 'I know you are

jealous, Duarte, you filthy dog. I saw you going at those native girls like a mad man in Rio de Janeiro. Take one now, I'm done with them anyway.'

Barbosa moves to land another blow, aiming for Carvalho's face this time. De Morales moves quickly, stopping Barbosa's fist. He stares into Barbosa's eyes, trying to appear as resolute as he can. 'You have him. There is no need to harm him further,' he says.

De Morales is sure Barbosa will push him away, but the anger in his eye passes. He turns back to Carvalho. 'Did you break the lock? You will be pilloried until the Capitán General returns. Mayhap that will cool your rampant libido. You could hang for this,' he adds. Barbosa pushes Carvalho towards the stairs.

'Can I look to the women?' De Morales asks.

'Leave them for now.' Barbosa says. 'I will put a guard on the trapdoor then return and give them water to wash with. Once the men are asleep for the night, I will take them ashore myself.'

'They need care. We cannot leave out there,' De Morales says. 'They are hundreds of leagues from their home. Surely they will die here.'

'Their deaths will not be my sin,' Barbosa says. He turns Carvalho's face to his own. 'You brought these women here. You stole them from their homes for your own pleasure. Their deaths will not be on my conscience.'

'It is no sin to kill that which is not human,' Carvalho says. 'Their deaths will lie on my conscience no more than a fly's.'

Disgusted, Barbosa pushes Carvalho onwards up the staircase. With a reluctant look back into the darkness and the women he knows are somewhere within it, de Morales follows.

The hold above is bright and crowded with men, drawn to the sounds that came from below. They stare in confusion at Carvalho, hands behind his back and hunched, as Barbosa pushes him from behind.

Barbosa orders two seamen to lead Carvalho onto the main deck and put him in the stocks. He looks at the gathered crew, staring slack-jawed, then bellows, 'have you no work? Out of my sight.' The crew quickly disappear, either tumbling into hammocks or else heading back up onto the main deck.

'What about the food?' De Morales asks Barbosa quietly as the Trinidad returns to its usual bustle. 'Surely they will steal whatever they can find.'

Barbosa is already heading back into the hold. He stops and looks up at de Morales, 'I will bind them once they are cleaned.' He lifts a candle and continues down into the lower hold.

The simplicity of Barbosa's reply belies his true purpose, and it is clear what he intends. Barbosa himself admitted his weaknesses at Rio de Janeiro and de Morales senses he will not be able to control himself. Barbosa will use the women before he takes them ashore.

'What about their clothing?' De Morales says. But he receives no reply.

On the main deck, de Morales finds the two seamen standing over their prisoner. Carvalho makes for a defeated sight, chained and in the stocks with his legs splayed before him, he sulkily stares into his lap.

De Morales crouches on his haunches beside the pilot.

'Do they have clothes?' he asks quietly.

'Of course, they do not have clothes,' Carvalho says derisively. 'They are savages. Anyway, what need would they have for them? Their purpose requires none.'

'You are a brute,' de Morales says. Carvalho shrugs in reply and turns his smirking face to the horizon.

De Morales turns away from the chained pilot and heads back down into the hold, hoping to convince Barbosa to allow him to check on the women. As he descends the stairs, he considers the best approach to stop Barbosa from doing what he is sure the supernumerary intends to do. Surely, he cannot strike him, as Magalhães had in Rio de Janeiro. Words must suffice. But what words will bring him around?

He is surprised, however, to find Barbosa kneeling over the trapdoor to the orlop hold, fiddling with the broken lock. De Morales' thoughts are written plain on his face. 'You think less of me than I deserve,' Barbosa says, closing the trapdoor. He points to a sailor watching them from across the hold. 'You, stand guard,' he says. 'No one is to enter the orlop hold' The sailor slides from his hammock, grumpily making his way towards the trapdoor.

'I thought-'

'I know what you thought.' Barbosa lowers his voice before continuing. 'I would not act as Carvalho has. To kidnap women, to treat them that way and take them at your leisure…' He trails off, appalled by Carvalho's actions.

'They have no clothing,' de Morales says, trying to change the subject. He is embarrassed and ashamed for judging Barbosa. 'Carvalho probably threw them overboard at some point. He had but a single purpose for them and boasts of it still.'

'That does not surprise me,' Barbosa says.

De Morales hears and sees nothing of Barbosa returning the native women to the shore. He is in no way surprised by what they found and who the culprit was. At the very least, he can now say Carvalho is not a liar in every aspect. Clearly, his lust is as infinite as he boasted. The depths of the disgraced pilot's depravity seem to know no bounds.

But Carvalho cannot have acted alone. After all, he can hardly have been slipping into the orlop hold unnoticed for the past six weeks. Who knows how many more of the crew traded their silence for pleasure?

De Morales is disappointed in himself for assuming Barbosa had evil intentions when he returned to the lower hold to bind the women. Staring into the darkness now, he admits to himself that finding Barbosa closing the trapdoor was a relief.

Surely the women will die as he had worried, but Barbosa's position is impossible. They cannot be kept aboard the Trinidad. Their presence will drive the men mad with lust, not to mention they are, technically, Portuguese property. Not only that, the Spanish captains, when they inevitably found out, would have cried deceit, and surely blamed the Magalhães.

Perhaps the women will be fine. Who is to say this whole New World is not governed by one single tribe? But de Morales quickly realises how foolish that assumption probably is. The New World is vast and, even on an island as relatively small as Hispaniola, its people are many and varied. It would be like dumping a Spaniard in England and expecting him to be welcomed with open arms.

The Santiago returns in the late afternoon of the following day. When Magalhães boards the Trinidad, his mood is sour. His eye catches Carvalho, ankles bound and his arms and neck in the stocks, at the base of the main mast. 'Why is this man in chains?' He asks.

Barbosa steps forwards. 'Carvalho is guilty of a crime of the flesh, he-'

'Release him,' Magalhães snaps. 'We leave this place immediately.'

Barbosa looks incredulous. Pigafetta, appearing in the doorway of the dining cabin, asks the Capitán General for news of the strait. But Magalhães, depressed and weary, shoves past the chronicler and enters his cabin, closing the door behind him.

De Morales cannot help but enjoy the small wave of pleasure in the look of sadness and shock that falls across Pigafetta's face. *See how you suffer at your master's whims, as I do?* He wants to say. But he thinks better of it.

The chronicler turns, making to follow Magalhães into the cabin. 'Leave him, Antonio.' The voice is Espinosa's.

'What happened?' Barbosa asks.

'The river is just that, a river,' Espinosa says, wrapping his arms around himself. 'We travelled fifteen leagues inland. The land is much the same as here. Not desolate but not welcoming either. The river's width remained the same, perhaps stretching just short of a league at its widest point. It is deep and fast-flowing, but its water is not salty. It just meanders inland. It is clear this is no strait.'

Below the mainmast, Carvalho is released from the stocks. He rubs his wrist as he waits for the ropes around his ankles to be untied. Barbosa falls in beside Espinosa. He watches

Carvalho as he is released, ignoring the satisfied sneer the pilot gives him. 'We must find the strait, Gonzalo.'

The two men turn to the other ships, silent and imperious guards in the ocean. Surely their captains now know what de Morales has suspected for months: Magalhães does not know where the strait is.

Chapter 10

March 1520

The Trinidad groans as another wave crashes into its hull, wrenching it sideways. De Morales imagines the sailors outside, desperately fighting to keep the ship upright and in one piece as the sea and the tempest rages around it.

The creaks, squeaks and thuds echoing through the Trinidad have become so regular as to be as commonplace as the wind wailing through the shrouds. But that does not mean they have no effect on de Morales. His ear has become attuned to each new noise, lest it be the flagship's last. He listens day and night for the final crack he knows can come any minute, when the ship will fall apart in the heaving water and cast him into the depths of these frigid seas.

Violent, volatile winds have battered the ships mercilessly. They increase into fierce squalls then abruptly die down or change direction before another blast slams into the ship. This whole corner of the New World is a chaotic land of savage weather. Utterly inhospitable and, it seems, hell-bent on devastating the ships and the men.

Their furious crossing of the Great Ocean is nothing compared to the storms here. Relentless and callous, they have bombarded the fleet since they left the river mouth five weeks ago. It is as if their stout ships are Granada, that last great city of Moorish Castile, under siege from the unremitting assault of the armies of Ferdinand and Isabella. Like those last Muslims, huddled together in the cellars and sewers of their once-mighty city, de Morales cowers in his cabin.

It can be doubted no longer: the armada must seek shelter. To continue on in the storms that have raged for the past five weeks is too great a risk. At any moment, any one of the ships could be torn asunder by the waves.

On the now rare, calm days he dares to venture out onto the main deck, the world he finds is fierce, austere and unearthly. Terrifying, enormous sea elephants lounge on the cold shore, their squat trunks framed by ferocious teeth rising up from their lower jaws, like inverted tusks. They are brutish and violent, fighting often. When they do fight, their clashes are savage and horrifying. They club their heads together, spearing each other with their tusks and sending blood and saliva spraying into the air as the creatures around them bellow and growl. Crowds of flightless black and white birds waddle to the shore before sliding under the waves. While inland, others huddle together, their backs to the storm, sharing one another's warmth. Their chicks, hidden in their midst, shriek as their parents return from the ocean.

Twice, de Morales has witnessed the great jet of water and foam erupt into the air from the sea beside the Trinidad that is the tell-tale sign of the beast that swallowed Jonah. Their long, arcing bodies seem endless and sailors rush to the gunwale to watch them glide beneath the waves. Some of the sailors claim to have witnessed one of those beasts leap a full fifteen feet into the air from the water before slapping its massive weight back down into the ocean. When they do this, the sailors say, the beasts are aiming for the ships in order to smash them to pieces like a walnut and devour the men as they pour from the ship's bowels.

These beasts must only be young for de Morales has heard tales that, at their greatest size, they will lay on the ocean's surface. There, they lure desperate seamen to their deaths who mistake their huge bodies for land. They even go so far as to allow the seamen to walk atop their backs, light fires and build shelters before finally throwing the hapless men into the sea and crushing them in their immense and toothy jaws.

Word filters to the Trinidad at the rear of the armada from the Santiago: Serrano has sighted a sheltered harbour.

Magalhães' reply, sent through signal lights back to Serrano, is simple. 'Lead the way.'

The land ahead rises sharply into great cliffs bracketing the harbour. Its entrance faces northeast and is guarded by crashing waves, fierce rocks and spray. The armada approaches in high, blustering winds.

The Santiago goes first. It lurches starboard, towards the massive cliffs. De Morales watches in horrified helplessness as the tiny ship, drawn by the current and the wind, tosses towards a violent end against the barbed rocks. His heart is in his mouth but, miraculously, the Santiago slides past those towering cliffs and disappears beyond the spray into the harbour.

One by one, the other ships of the armada, buffeted and battered by the wind, follow the Santiago's course. When the flagship's turn finally comes, the Capitán General orders the main decks of Trinidad to be cleared.

De Morales hides in his cabin, listening to the creak and groan of the Trinidad as it is bent and battered by the waves. The ship rocks erratically on the surging ocean below, sending his possessions and medicines falling to the floorboards. De Morales grasps his case of medical instruments, hugging them to his chest, while he sits on the floor against the wall, helplessly hoping for his end to come swiftly and his lungs to fill painlessly.

But the rocking ceases to a slow pitch and he hears the clash and clang of the rode as it passes through the hawsepipe, followed by a colossal crash as the anchor splashes into the harbour. When he finally leaves his cabin, shaken and pale-faced, the sails are being drawn and tied in place. Those crew not working, stagger about the main deck in shared disbelief that they still draw breath.

The day is auspicious. It is Holy Saturday. The final day of Christ's death, when he descended into the abyss of Hell. Like him, they have passed through the churning, lurching chaos and found salvation at its end.

This harbour is a desolate and desperate place.

De Morales is on the main deck of the Trinidad, surrounded by the other captains and señores of the armada, waiting for news from Barbosa of the Capitán General's plans.

Mesquita saunters across the deck and stands beside him. 'That compress has done nothing,' he says, holding his jaw and wincing. 'Have you nothing stronger? I cannot stand this pain much longer.'

'I will see what I can do,' de Morales says and turns back to the bleak surrounding landscape. The shale covered shore. The low, rolling hills, treeless and empty. The desolate grass, thin, patchy and blasted flat by freezing wind. On the strand lies a pile of brasilwood, so rich and out of place here, meant for the erection of another cross. Around it, shivering sailors are attaching lines from the ships to huge iron spikes driven deep into the shale. The anchors alone were not enough to keep the fleet from being swept out to sea with the turning tides.

As he watches the men struggle with the soaked lines, a realisation hits de Morales: all these preparations seem concerningly permanent.

Barbosa appears from Magalhães' cabin. 'The Capitán General,' he says to the gathering on the main deck of the flagship, 'has named this place Puerto San Julián. The fleet will overwinter here.'

'Is he mad?' Quesada's incredulity is matched only by his outrage. 'We cannot overwinter here. We know nothing of this place.'

'Madness would be to sail on in that tempest.' The voice is Mesquita's. He is defending his cousin, but there is little conviction in his voice. He, too, is clearly concerned about the decision.

'Then turn the fleet around,' Quesada says. 'Sail back to New Spain.'

'We do not have the supplies to sustain us here,' Mendoza

says.

'We can hunt and fish for food,' Mesquita says.

'Hunt?' Quesada sweeps his hand across the desolate landscape. 'I never took you for the fool you apparently are, Álvaro. A lackey, maybe,'

'Gentleman.' Serrano says. He steps between Quesada and Mesquita, holding up his hands, trying to keep the peace.

'The decision has been made,' Barbosa says.

All eyes turn to the opening door of Magalhães' cabin. Already, de Morales can sense the outraged comments about to begin. But they are stopped short when Espinosa steps over the threshold.

'Where is the Capitán General?' Mendoza asks.

'He is busy, making preparations for the fleet's overwintering.' Barbosa's excuse is pathetic but one surely coming from Magalhães, not himself.

'Cowardice,' Quesada says.

Espinosa rounds on Quesada, 'what did you say?'

'He will kill us all.' Quesada meets Espinosa eye to eye, squaring up to him. 'We will all starve here before those winds cease.'

'Return to your ships.' Espinosa says.

Quesada stares into Espinosa's eye, his face reddening. 'You do not order me, señor,' he says.

'Prepare your ship for the winter,' Espinosa says slowly.

The crew of the flagship, perhaps more loyal to Espinosa than their Capitán General, gather around the two men. Quesada's stare falters. His eyes flicking to the crew crowding in around him.

Finally, Mendoza takes hold of Quesada's arm. The two captains are outmatched and outmanned on the Trinidad, and Mendoza seems to recognise it. If Quesada were to strike

Espinosa, he would surely be overpowered.

'You forget yourself, soldier,' Quesada says with a jeering sneer. But he slowly steps away from Espinosa, nonetheless. The two captains turn to leave and are met by a wall of the Trinidad's crew, baring their way. Mendoza haughtily raises his chin. Quesada casts his disbelieving, disgusted eye between the blank faces before him. With a nod from Espinosa, the wall parts.

'It is a cowardly act,' Mendoza says quietly, as they pass by de Morales, 'to not even tell us himself.' He cannot help but agree.

The day passes. The sun, shrouded in clouds, shrinks into the horizon. The wind picks up and the current changes, sucking the ships out towards the harbour's mouth. The taught lines of the Trinidad, stretching to the shore, creak and complain as the flagship longs to be free of them.

Late in the afternoon, a skiff rowed by a sailor and bearing a cabin boy approaches the Trinidad. The boy holds his hands against his mouth, trying to send his voice against the cruel wind that would steal it straight from his lips. 'Señor doctor, you are needed on the Victoria,' he calls. 'A sailor has fallen from the crow's nest. He is in great pain.'

De Morales hurries into his cabin to fetch his surgical case. A fall from the crow's nest is a long way down and the sailor has likely broken many bones. The troubles of that accursed ship are relentless. He stops before leaving and reaches for his heavy cloak. The weather outside is cold and getting colder. He does not want to be caught without it after dark.

He turns to leave his cabin and finds Barbosa in the

doorway, blocking his way. 'Another boat, this time from the San Antonio,' he says. 'It seems you will have your hands full this day.'

De Morales pushes past Barbosa and bursts from his cabin onto the windswept main deck. Pitching on the choppy waters, two sailors from another skiff hail him with a wave. 'Doctor, it is Captain Mesquita. He complains of a great pain in his jaw. He is prostrate with it, unable to even raise his head.'

'To whom do I go first?' de Morales asks Barbosa desperately.

'The boy from the Victoria arrived first so-'

The Capitán General appears beside Barbosa, seemingly out of nowhere. 'No,' he says, with more than a hint of desperation in his voice, 'you will go to the San Antonio and treat Mesquita, the captains are your chief concern.' He turns to the cabin boy in the rocking skiff. 'Go to the Concepción,' he calls. 'Bustamante can handle your fallen sailor.'

Though it is short, the journey to the San Antonio is one of fraught uncertainty. The tiny skiff feels utterly outmatched by the errant currents, turbulent waves and tearing winds. De Morales feels like a cork in the Cascada del Cinca, whipped, battered and tossed this way and that, absolutely powerless. By the time they reach the San Antonio, the two poor sailors, each working an oar, look exhausted from fighting the tumult.

Standing gingerly in the pitching skiff, de Morales throws his satchel over his shoulder, then lunges toward the San Antonio's hull and grasping the Jacob's ladder. He then begins the daunting climb up the ladder towards the gunwale of the massive ship. Behind him, one of the sailors pushes at his legs as he climbs, while the other tightly grips the ship, desperately trying to hold the skiff steady.

The rope is slick from seawater lifted out of the harbour by the whipping wind and the climb is treacherous. Wide-eyed and panting, de Morales stumbles over the gunwale then looks back, taking in the lurching Puerto San Julián. He can only hope that, by the time he is finished with Mesquita and returns to the Trinidad, the weather and currents will have calmed.

He turns and is shocked to find de la Reina is also aboard the San Antonio. The bishop rarely leaves the Concepción, it is uncommon to even see him leave his cabin. De la Reina looks equally shocked to see him here too. Stranger still, Valderrama is already on board the San Antonio and has been for some weeks, supporting Mesquita and Rebêlo in keeping the ship in line. Why would a ship need both priests?

'The messenger said only that Mesquita has a toothache. Is he near death? Have you already given him the last rites?' De Morales asks him.

De la Reina stares back at him, a look of confusion on his face and silence upon his lips. A sense of unease settles in de Morales' stomach. Something strange is afoot here. Finally, the bishop stutters, 'I. . .came. . .for-'

'Señor doctor.' The call comes from behind de Morales. He turns away from the stuttering bishop and finds Magalhães' son, Rebêlo waving to him. There is something peculiar about de la Reina. He may be sullen, he may be bored, but he has never been simpleminded.

Rebêlo grasps his arm and pulls his satchel from his shoulder, then leads de Morales into Mesquita's cabin. The captain's room is dark, falteringly lit by a short, stuttering candle.

'I need more light,' de Morales says. Rebêlo hurries around the cabin, collecting candles and lighting them one by one before placing them at intervals around the room. Gradually, the shadows recede.

The captain is not dead, nor is he near to it. Mesquita is lying on his bed with a piece of muslin stuffed into his mouth. The smell of wine fills the cabin. De Morales suspects the captain is already drunk, which is probably a good thing.

With Rebêlo nervously watching over his shoulder, de Morales leans over the captain and removes the muslin from his mouth. The cloth is heavy and soaked in wine, seawater and the captain's phlegm.

Immediately, he can see the problem. A tooth on the right of Mesquita's mouth is badly inflamed. The surrounding gum, grotesquely swollen, has turned a deep and livid red. There is a large, milky abscess the size of a chickpea protruding from beneath the tooth, leaking pus.

'Who slit this abscess?' He asks Rebêlo.

''Twas not I señor doctor,' Rebêlo says. 'I think perhaps he did that to himself. His knife is here on the floor and I was alerted to his condition when he fell to the ground with a loud crash.'

'Fainted with the pain,' de Morales says, more to himself than to Rebêlo. He takes Mesquita by the temples and turns his head, being careful not to touch his jaw which has swollen considerably.

He looks into the captain's rolling eyes and says sternly, 'I need your permission to remove your tooth.' Mesquita does not answer. Drunkenness or pain has rendered him mute. 'A nod will suffice,' de Morales says.

The captain nods his head.

De Morales turns to Rebêlo. 'Pass me the blue vial from

my case.' Rebêlo reaches down and lifts the vial, passing it to de Morales. 'This is Aqua Vitae,' de Morales says to Mesquita. 'You must drink it, captain.'

He upends the vial, emptying the contents down Mesquita's throat. The captain coughs and sputters as the strong alcohol hits his tonsils. The elixir will act quickly, further dulling the captain's pain.

'Take his head firmly in your hands,' de Morales says to Rebêlo. 'Do not allow him to move.'

At the beginning of his career, every surgeon is attuned to the various agonies a human can suffer. Pain is an important thing. Not just for cleansing the soul, as Valderrama would have it, but also to tell the surgeon of the state of his patient. But, even if de Morales had succumbed to the indifference that afflicts so many of his profession, he would know that the pain of pulling a tooth is all pains simultaneously. There is no easy way to do it, however, and the alternative is much worse. No time to waste, then. Mesquita is already drunk, prolonging the matter will not help him.

De Morales takes a small, very sharp knife, a mouth prop and a set of long pliers with a serrated edge from his case. He gently places the prop in Mesquita's mouth, forcing the groaning Captain's mouth to open wider.

Holding a candle in one hand, de Morales carefully slits the abscess while Rebêlo firmly holds the captain's temples. Mesquita screams and a cloudy fluid oozes from the incision, gurgling and bubbling down the captain's throat. An abscess will quickly heal itself and double in size after being emptied. The trick, during a removal, is to pull the infected tooth before the abscess has a chance to heal and refill. After ten years of barber surgery before he earned his degree and became a physician, de Morales is well practised in this art.

He takes up the pelican for removing teeth. One touch from the cold brass sends Mesquita into a convulsive and shrieking spasm of pain. Rebêlo struggles to keep hold of the captain's head.

'Hold firm, Rebêlo,' he says.

The extraction lasts an hour or more. When the tooth finally gives, it does so with a sickening sucking sound. Hanging from the tooth is another abscess and a long, sinuous nerve, slickly coated in blood and spittle.

De Morales' hands are shaking from tiredness and his brow is damp with sweat. But Rebêlo is in a worse state. Being right above Mesquita's mouth, his face and clothes are covered in the captain's phlegm, blood and pus.

De Morales lifts a poultice of hemlock and mandragora from his case. It will provide some pain relief for Mesquita until the open wound has begun to heal. Very gently, he pushes the poultice into the void in Mesquita's mouth where the tooth was. Then he begins cleaning his tools.

Finally releasing his hold on the captain, Rebêlo gingerly walks backwards to the wall of the cabin and slides down onto the floor. He breathes heavily, spits on the floor and wipes his face on a rag.

Mesquita has already recovered somewhat from the pain and he rolls over on the bed, then tries to heave himself up onto one arm. 'Stay where you are, captain,' de Morales says, firmly pushing Mesquita back down onto the bed. 'The pain will subside.' He hands the captain a small cup of wine Mesquita left half-finished on the floor. 'Drink this when you feel able, it will help stop infection.'

Mesquita slumps back onto the bed. Holding the cup of wine in a limp hand he closes his eyes.

'I could do with a drink myself,' Rebêlo says.

'I will stay on the San Antonio until the captain has gathered himself,' de Morales says. He puts the last of his tools away. 'Sometimes an abscess returns and must be cut once more. If it does and I wait until the morning, he will not thank me for it.'

'Come and share a drink with me while you wait,' Rebêlo says, throwing the rag under the bed. He rises and, leaving Mesquita to grunt and groan his way back into the land of the living, leaves the captain's cabin. De Morales extinguishes the candles one by one and the shadows reclaim the room.

By now, it is full dark outside, but the wind has abated significantly. Signal lights flicker in the gloom from the other ships dotted across the harbour. A deep chill has settled in the air and de Morales feels it all the more for the sweat on his face after the exertion of the surgery. He crosses to the mainmast and stands at the brazier for a moment, warming his hands. Then he tightly wraps his arms around himself for warmth and follows Rebêlo into his cabin.

An hour passes in conversation with Rebêlo. He is a pleasant young man, with his father's charisma but without his hard-headed severity nor his manic temperament. Rebêlo speaks highly of his father. How he has expanded Castile's dominion already beyond all previous estimates. Were this a conquering voyage, Magalhães would have overtaken every other explorer for the extent of the lands he would have claimed.

Of course, Rebêlo is correct. By San Martin's estimates, they have sailed almost three thousand leagues south along the coast of the New World, never finding any evidence of previous European exploration nor even, for the most part, any sign of native activity. Perhaps this land is entirely untouched by humans. One could easily see why. For why would anyone choose to live in such desolation?

They have heard movement several times from Mesquita's cabin next door and de Morales decides now is the time to check on the captain. Rebêlo says he will accompany him and get some air.

They leave the cabin and find the main deck in complete darkness. De Morales looks at the cold coals in the brazier with disappointment. It must have been allowed to burn out. He looks up and notices a dark shape slide over the taffrail at the prow of the ship.

Rebêlo must have seen it too. In a whisper, he says, 'savages?'

The shape is followed by more. All of them have blackened faces and wear hoods or caps on their heads, pulled down low. De Morales is frozen to the spot, partly in fear and partly in interest, unable to do anything but watch as these stygian apparitions gather on the far side of the San Antonio.

They waste no time. The figures fan out, sweeping across the deck towards the mainmast and the cabins where de Morales and Rebêlo are standing. There is a lookout on the forecastle and another at the base of the mainmast. Both are looking directly at the invaders but neither has uttered a sound.

De Morales looks in disbelief between the lookouts and the swarm of intruders. As his eyes move between them, he notices de la Reina, standing at the gunwale in the middle of the main deck. The bishop is watching the intruders approach. He salutes one in silence with a raised hand and de Morales knows, then, that these are no natives. This is a mutiny.

Rebêlo has come to the same realisation at the same moment and disappears back into his cabin, closing the door silently behind him. It is a cowardly act but, being the son of Magalhães, he is sure to be a target of the mutineers.

The invaders are drawing ever closer to de Morales. They are not even trying to be quiet anymore as they clatter loudly across the deck. The leader of the troop, his face still obscured by a hood and blackened with coal or pitch, approaches de la Reina. The bishop wordlessly points towards the captain's cabin and the leader, followed by another mutineer, stomps across the deck.

The lead figure draws a rapier and others follow suit. The weapons are many, but all are vicious. De Morales sees knives, hatches, axes, hammers. It seems anything will do. Several have taken off their hoods and caps, revealing familiar faces smeared with coal. Mendoza's large head is revealed to him, as is his assistant, Molino. He is shocked to recognise the dark hair and short beard of Elcano towards the rear of the group.

De Morales senses he is not the target of their search, but it dawns on him that that does not mean he is not in danger. His heartbeat quickens, pounding in his chest as the two figures rush past him, towards the aftcastle.

The two men burst into Mesquita's cabin. Loud thuds, thumps and crashes come from the captain's room accompanied by cries of pain and surprise that de Morales knows are Mesquita's.

With all the noise, sailors begin to awaken in the hold below the main deck in their quarters. One or two pop their heads out of the opening. They seem to instantly understand what is happening and quickly drop back down into the darkness. De Morales would call them spineless but what difference does it make to them what happens between the captains? Better to keep quiet and keep your head.

The intruders have thus far ignored de Morales' presence. He is just thinking they must suspect he is party to their mutiny when one of the figures turns and approaches him. But before the figure can take two steps in his direction, Mesquita's body tumbles from his cabin, thumping heavily onto the main deck. Blood pours from his mouth and the captain lies, prostrate and unconscious but alive, in a growing pool of blood.

Two figures pass out of the doorway of the captain's cabin onto the deck. In the fight, the coal covering their faces has smeared and their hoods and caps have been pulled off and so both are fully revealed now. He sees the stocky shape of Cartagena, his venomous face reddened with exertion and split by a broad grin, and Quesada's balding head.

Despite the excitement in the air, there is an eerie quiet on the main deck of San Antonio. The mutineers have everything well planned and not a word passes between them. They seem to have had only one target. They went straight for Mesquita and the captain's cabin. But clearly, this is personal for Cartagena. The ship that was taken from the bastard child of Fonseca is his once more.

A loud noise erupts from the hold below. The commotion has agitated the common crew in their quarters. Perhaps the men who showed their faces earlier are in cahoots with the mutineers but, from the loud scuffle of shouts and thuds erupting in the hold, several are not.

Before the conspirators on the deck can react, four seamen spring up from the crew's quarters, tripping and slipping on the slick boards. They barely have a chance to take in their surroundings before the mutineers are upon

140

them. Three are quickly overcome but one man, the ship's master, Elorriaga, remains standing. He swings his arms, desperately spinning on the spot. Surrounded by armed mutineers, Elorriaga stands tall.

He sees Cartagena and his face sets in anger. 'Señor,' he says firmly, 'remove yourself from the San Antonio. Blood need not be spilt today. Return-'

Before he can finish Cartagena is upon him. The two men struggle and stumble before Cartagena thrusts a long knife into Elorriaga's side. He convulses and twists sideways into the blade. Cartagena wrenches the knife from Elorriaga's body and throws him against the wall of the aftcastle. The ship's master slumps against the wood, still standing shakily on bowed legs. Blood is already pouring from the wound, soaking his shirt.

De Morales jerks forward, instinctively thinking he must help him, but Cartagena is on Elorriaga again in an instant. He thrusts the blade again into the master's side, puncturing deeply into the slumping body.

'Cowardly knave,' Cartagena shrieks. He takes hold of Elorriaga's throat, 'how quick you were to accept your new captain. Filthy. Spineless. Churl.' With each word, Cartagena thrusts the knife into Elorriaga. But still not satisfied, he continues his vicious and rampant attack. Two more blows come as the knife flashes from side to side.

Finally, Cartagena releases his grip on Elorriaga's throat and the broken mess of the ship's master slumps to the deck. Blood spills from the body, spreading across the deck, and bubbles from his mouth. Cartagena, satisfied with his attack, turns to his fellow mutineers, breathing heavily.

'You cannot help yourself, can you?' Mendoza says.

De Morales rushes to Elorriaga's lifeless and bloody body,

lying unmoving on the deck.

'De Morales is here,' Quesada says bluntly.

The mutineers turn as one toward him as de Morales desperately pushes onto Elorriaga's body, trying to stop the bleeding. There are so many wounds, all of them pouring blood, he knows not where to start.

'There must have been a mistake,' Mendoza says. 'The doctor should be on the Victoria.'

'Well, he is here now,' Elcano says. 'As long as he is with us he will not be harmed in what follows.'

De Morales stares at Elcano and the other captains standing over him. They wanted him out of the way in case chaos took hold when they inevitably storm the Trinidad. A physician is too valuable a thing to lose in a clumsy mutiny.

'Can you save Elorriaga?' Elcano asks.

'He is already dead. No one can survive such an attack,' Quesada says coldly.

'All the same,' Elcano replies.

De Morales rips Elorriaga's shirt open. In the darkness, all he can see is the thick smear of blood oozing from the master's body. Valderrama appears beside him, muttering in Latin over the lifeless body. 'O mi Deus. Ego sum toto corde paenitet me...'

While Valderrama chants, de Morales works his bloody hands over Elorriaga's body, searching for the wounds. He counts five but knows Elorriaga was stabbed seven times.

Cartagena interrupts the priest, 'don't put yourself out too much,' he says, wiping his knife on the taffrail. 'He isn't worth the effort.'

Valderrama turns and looks Cartagena in the eye. 'The first chance I get,' he says, 'Magalhães will hear of all you have done this night.'

'Well,' Cartagena says, 'you won't get that chance.'

De Morales cannot stop the bleeding. Elorriaga is coughing now, choking on blood. 'You will need your tools,' Elcano says. 'Let me get them for you.'

Elcano starts walking towards Mesquita's cabin. De Morales calls after him. 'No, not in there, in Rebêlo's-' He stops short.

He looks with wide, desperate eyes to the closed door of Rebêlo's cabin. He has given Rebêlo away. As one, the mutineers stop what they were doing. In all the excitement, they had forgotten Magalhães' son. Mendoza and Molino immediately head for the door to the cabin, drawing their weapons as they do so.

The beating of Rebêlo is long and punishing. Though barely conscious, Mesquita is put in the stocks. Blood pours from his mouth, spattering onto the deck between his chained feet.

Meanwhile, de Morales works cauterising and stitching Elorriaga's wounds by candlelight. The ship's master lives for now, but de Morales does not think he will remain for very long. His hands, sticky with blood and tired with cold and fatigue, work clumsily as the dreadful pounding on Rebêlo's body continues.

All the while, the watchmen keep their silent vigil.

Chapter 11

March 1520

A weak dawn spills over the desolate landscape and the fractured Armada de Molucca. The erratic wind has picked up in the night, blustering this way and that, unknowable in its randomness. The San Antonio lies silent in the lapping waves of the harbour, offering no hint of the brutality of the previous night.

After hours of surgery by candlelight, de Morales managed to stop the bleeding of Elorriaga. That done, three seamen helped him lift the broken body of the ship's master below into the crew's quarters below. Though they were as gentle as possible, Elorriaga's wounds reopened. More hours of careful swabbing, cauterising and stitching followed.

De Morales does not think he has slept in thirty-eight hours. He is exhausted but climbs back onto the main deck of the San Antonio and the bitter wind strips the tiredness from his eyes instantly, its icy cold drawing tears.

During the night, the ship has been transformed into a floating fortress. Every weapon in the armoury has been pillaged and laid out on the deck in preparation for any possible counteroffensive against the mutineers. Arquebuses, cannons, falconets, axes, swords, bows, knives. Every imaginable tool of destruction and death will be brought to bear on any would-be attackers.

Around this arsenal, the ship has returned to its usual schedule. Seaman scrub, climb and patch the ship as orders are howled into the wind from below. The San Antonio, like the other four ships of the armada, was badly battered by the storms and requires a lot of mending. By maintaining a normal schedule, the mutineers probably hope to keep Magalhães ignorant of the night's events and whatever plans they have for the coming day.

What those plans are exactly, de Morales does not know. He does, however, notice that during the night the cannons have been turned towards the Trinidad. There is a mood of fraught anticipation on the ship and, standing amongst it now, he is sure its tense anxiety is plain to see for any who looked.

A skiff approaches, slapping against the sea, bearing a cabin boy de Morales recognises from the Trinidad.

If he calls out 'mutiny' now what will happen? Will the flagship rise up in arms? Will dozens of men spill over the San Antonio from the Trinidad and wipe its decks clean of this mutiny? He can see them now, led by Espinosa, crashing into the mutineers, their swords raised, teeth gritted, and the decks flowing with blood. Perhaps that is how it would go. But even if that did happen, he would be long dead before it even began.

The skiff knocks hollowly into the San Antonio and a seaman climbs down the Jacob's ladder, taking a sealed letter from the cabin boy. Its task done, the little boat turns around and heads off in the direction of the Concepción, a hundred feet away.

Cartagena skulks out of the captain's cabin, followed by Mendoza and Quesada. He takes the letter out of the seaman's hands and rips it open.

'Ha,' he says humourlessly. 'The Capitán General invites his captains to hear Easter Mass with him ashore.'

'Obviously, we will not attend,' Quesada says.

'We ought to think our response through carefully,' Mendoza says. 'If we do not attend, Magalhães will surely suspect something is amiss.'

'Then let him suspect,' Cartagena spits. 'While the Portuguese hear mass ashore, we can take the flagship and abandon them here.'

'A foolish plan,' Mendoza says. 'The mass is for the captains alone. The Trinidad will still be crawling with Magalhães' loyal men. Barbosa, Espinosa, Pigafetta, the slave. Countless more.' He shakes his head, taking the letter from Cartagena and reading it carefully with a furrowed brow.

Mendoza is certainly right. Yesterday, he and Quesada had a lesson in how many men aboard the Trinidad remain loyal, if not to Magalhães, then, certainly to Espinosa. Surely his pride alone would not let him suffer that ignominy again.

'No,' Mendoza says, still reading the letter. 'We would be outnumbered and outmatched. Better to lure Magalhães to one of our ships and take him hostage there. We must attend.'

146

'I will not,' Cartagena says.

Mendoza looks up from the letter. 'Well, you are not a captain, are you? At least, not officially. So, you need not worry,' he says, enjoying the jab. Cartagena's face reddens with anger at the insult. Mendoza sees Cartagena for what he is: a rabid dog, useful at times but best kept on a short leash.

'I will not go ashore,' Quesada says. 'I do not trust Magalhães. If he knows of our deeds already, this mass could be a trap. He may plan to lure us all into one place and do away with us.'

'True,' Mendoza says. 'Then our position is impossible. If we attend, and it is a trap, our endeavour is over. If we do not, Magalhães will suspect a mutiny and we will lose the element of surprise.' Mendoza looks to the eastern horizon, to the direction of Castile. He chews his lip as he works his mind around the problem.

'It is simple, then,' Elcano, appearing on the periphery of the captains, says. 'One captain goes ashore and makes excuses for the other. The Capitán General cannot take one man hostage on a hunch.'

Mendoza smiles at Elcano's clinical mind. 'Very good,' he says. After a moment of thought, he continues, 'I will go ashore then. Being the most senior amongst us, Magalhães will be unlikely to take me hostage and interrogate me. In the meantime, everyone else should return to their ships. We must maintain the upper hand in this endeavour. If I do not return by noon, Elcano, fire on the Trinidad.'

Elcano looks aghast at Mendoza's final order. 'We cannot fire on a ship full of men,' he says, 'most are blameless in this. Their allegiance to Magalhães is as brittle as straw. One push in the right direction and they will rally to our cause.'

'Then fire the cannons once.' Mendoza says. 'I care not

for your ethics, Elcano. Mark my words, the longer Magalhães remains as Capitán General, the more men will die. But any blood we spill will be on his hands, not ours.

While the mutineers prepare to leave the San Antonio, de Morales approaches Elcano. He thought he knew the Basque, he thought he could trust him. To begin with, de Morales hoped Elcano had been coerced into taking part in the mutiny but that last conversation has shown he is as complicit in it as any of the other captains. That said, Elcano's anxieties about harming innocent men are proof enough for de Morales that he is still, in some way, the man he took him to be. What's more, Elcano is the only mutineer de Morales has any relationship with.

'Allow me to return to the Trinidad,' he says. 'My absence will have already made Magalhães suspicious.'

'I think not, de Morales.' Elcano's reply is blunt, though not unkind. 'You heard Mendoza's orders, if he does not return I am to fire on the Trinidad. You are the only competent doctor we have, to lose you would cost many lives in the future. I may trust you, but the captains do not. They know you are close to the Capitán General and Quesada is convinced you are spying.'

De Morales hopes Elcano misses the look of shock that passes involuntarily across his face. A lucky guess, he tells himself. After all, how could Quesada know? 'Well, I cannot swim,' he says finally. 'So you need not worry about that.'

'Be that as it may,' Elcano says.

In the distance, on the barren shore, the hammering of nails and the sawing of wood can be heard as a small group of carpenters from the Santiago build a large cross. Like countless conquistadors before him, Magalhães' first thought is to claim the land for Christ and Castile wherever he lands. At some point, if it has not already been done, the Requerimiento will be read, as it has everywhere the armada has landed, and the land will be the kings. All the long leagues south down the length of the New World's coast, crosses have been erected. Some, put up in a hurry, were small and rickety and swayed in the breeze, others were carved from great bulks of brasilwood and stood imperious and daunting over wild landscapes. How many of those crosses still stand? Will this one still stand, waiting to be found by those who follow after them? Will anyone follow their journey, willingly coming into this awful place? If they do, all they will find here is a weather-beaten cross and the bones of two hundred men who died cold and desperate fighting amongst themselves.

He turns back to Elcano. 'Will you try,' he pleads. 'Surely you can see how my absence would be suspicious. I have been gone now all night without sending a message to Magalhães.'

'I may be involved in this insurrection, but I have no power in it.' Elcano's tone is matter-of-fact. He is the pawn de Morales thought him to be. Though a willing one, nonetheless. 'I cannot help you,' he adds.

Quesada appears beside them. De Morales wonders how long the captain has been there and what he has heard. Elcano may be a mutineer, but de Morales does not want to put him in danger.

'What are you two conspiring about?' Quesada asks. Neither de Morales nor Elcano say anything and Quesada lets the awkward silence draw on. When it is obvious neither man is going to answer he says, 'de Morales, I want you to write a letter to the Capitán General informing him you have moved to the Victoria to care for the sailor who fell last night.'

They have thought of everything. Magalhães is a dead man, only he does not know it yet.

There is no injured sailor on the Victoria. Of course there is not. The whole story of the previous night was a ruse to place the fleet's surgeon in the hands of the mutineers, ensuring his safety and, thereby, their own.

Onboard the Victoria, chaos has taken hold and the ship has descended into anarchy. The men have raided the stores, greedily filling their hungry bellies with hardtack, salted meats and fish, dates, nuts, beans and any surviving fruit from the jungle haul. Elcano bounds on board and immediately takes charge of the situation. He angrily rebukes the men for their gluttony and slothfulness, ordering them back to work and putting them on half rations.

Over the past twelve hours, de Morals has seen many sides of Elcano he would not have guessed the Basque possessed. But behind it all, he is a fiercely intelligent man. The Spanish captains made a mistake in not including him more closely in their conspiracy, that much is plain to see. Though de Morales would rather not admit that Elcano, who he believed to be good and kind and caring, would turn his mind to evil deeds. But at least he did not alert Quesada to de Morales' attempts to escape.

De Morales hopes, in all the excitement, the mutineers might forget the letter Quesada ordered him to write, but he has no such luck. Paper and quill are thrust toward him by a brutish sailor. He kneels over a short box, beside the sputtering brazier at the base of the mainmast and writes:

Señor Capitán General,

Having seen to the removal of a tooth for your cousin and captain of the San Antonio, Álvaro de Mesquita, I have relocated to the Victoria to assist Bustamante in the care of the sailor who fell from the nest yesterday evening. He is in a very bad way and requires a skilled hand.

I will report back to the Trinidad when I am able.

Your faithful servant,
Juan de Morales

He thinks of including some coded message to the Capitán General, but his mind draws a blank.

Ever a disappointment to himself, he hands the letter to Elcano who seals it and passes it to a sailor who climbs down the Jacob's ladder and into a skiff. The sailor heads off, rowing against rising waves and a powerful current, towards the Trinidad. As he watches the skiff struggle and splash against the waves, it dawns on de Morales that he is now complicit, in some small way, in this mutiny.

From the Victoria, he can see the mass being held on the shore. A sorry gathering of just four figures is huddled below the cross: Magalhães, Serrano, Mendoza and de la Reina who leads the ceremony. That is all the praise Christ will receive this day.

He finds himself watching the Capitán General. His small form is layered in heavy furs, expanding him outwards into the world. He is on his knees, praising the resurrection of Christ in this dreary, depressing place. He wonders what the Capitán General knows or suspects. Surely the presence of so few of his captains has aroused his suspicions. The absence of Valderrama, confined aboard the San Antonio, will certainly make him suspicious. He was already paranoid about a mutiny and even more so after Cartagena's bungled attempt at sea four months ago.

The mass lasts several hours. De la Reina dutifully playing the part of a loyal bishop praising the Lord God. After his actions last night, the bishop's hypocrisy makes de Morales' blood boil.

A sigh of relief comes from the mutineers in the late morning when Mendoza steps into his longboat and returns to the Victoria. When he climbs aboard, he has much to tell the conspirators and does so on the deck. Everyone onboard the Victoria knows and has been involved in what has occurred now. Hiding away in cabins, holds and stores is pointless.

'I think Magalhães suspects something untoward has happened but what exactly and involving whom, he has no proof of and so cannot act,' Mendoza says. 'I told him Quesada is ill and cannot attend. Mesquita's absence is already explained, given the physician's visit yesterday.'

'Did he believe the ruse?' Elcano asks.

'I believe he did, although he fell quiet for a time and said nothing further on the matter.' Despite the confidence in his voice, Mendoza is rattled. It is plain to see in his eyes. The captain is trying to convince himself as he fails to convince Elcano. 'He invited me to a meal in his cabin.'

'And…'

'I refused. What choice did I have? I think he was suspicious of foul play and if I went to the Trinidad, I would surely have been taken captive as Quesada worried.'

'We will need to act quickly, then.' Elcano's tone is resolute.

'No. We must be careful not to overplay our hand. We have control of three ships and the Santiago is irrelevant. Serrano only cares to locate the strait and get to the Spice Islands. I do not think he cares who leads the armada so long as he and his ship are safe. Magalhães is completely alone. We will wait until darkness falls and make our move on the Trinidad, sending longboats from both the Victoria and the San Antonio. We will attack from both sides quietly and simultaneously. Once we have overpowered Magalhães, as we overpowered Mesquita, the deed will be done quickly and quietly, and we can return to Sevilla.'

'What happened to luring him here?' Elcano asks.

'He will not leave the flagship,' Mendoza says. 'That much is clear. We will have to take the fight to him.' Elcano looks unconvinced but, as he said, he has no power in this endeavour.

Mendoza, heading now toward the captain's cabin, turns and says, 'I need you to send a skiff with a message for Quesada and Cartagena detailing the plan.'

The wind is picking up again as two men climb down into a waiting skiff bound for the San Antonio and the Concepción. Five sailors are to leave the San Antonio and are to be brought back to the Victoria to increase Mendoza's ranks. The San Antonio is by far the ship with the most weaponry and men guaranteed to be loyal to the mutineer's cause.

The skiff is knocked and rocked by the growing wind.

Freezing rain has started to fall, making the climb down the Jacob's ladder precarious, but the men make it and set off into the churning waters.

The mutineers have played their hand and now must wait for the sun to set and their plan to unfold. De Morales is filled with a deep, unsettling sense of foreboding for what will occur in the darkness tonight. Elcano and Mendoza have disappeared into the captain's cabin and, with nothing else to do, he finds an empty corner of the main deck to clean Elorriaga's blood from his tools and equipment. He has a terrible feeling they will be required again soon and dried blood dulls the blade. He senses that Magalhães knows a mutiny has occurred, too many strange things have happened over the course of the last day. But he worries the Capitán General has delayed too long. If Magalhães has bided his time overlong, it may prove to be his undoing.

That is, of course, if the Capitán General has realised something is amiss. After all, the mutineers have had reasonable answers to any concerns he may have had. Surely by this point, Magalhães will also have read de Morales' letter, which more than adequately explains his absence.

Magalhães' Easter feast must have finished. Standing on the aftcastle of the Victoria, de Morales watches the skiff carrying Serrano and de la Reina take them back to their ships. The boat drops Serrano off at the Santiago first, a devious plan by de la Reina. Serrano as yet knows nothing of the mutiny and if he saw the armoured fortress that is now the San Antonio, he would certainly know something is amiss. Serrano may side with the mutineers, but it is a risk they cannot take. Where his allegiances truly lie no one seems to know. These mutineers are a crafty lot. If people had not been harmed by them, de Morales could almost admire their cunning.

He looks across the bay in the twilight at the other ships dotted around, rocking on the tumultuous waters, their signal lights flaring. They lie in a rough zig-zag shape. The Santiago is closest to the land, next is the Concepción, the San Antonio, then the Victoria and finally the Trinidad, guarding the mouth of the harbour. Magalhães is always so careful to position the flagship at the rear of the armada, where he can see every other ship and guard against escape. One could call him paranoid, if not for the fact the Capitán General was correct all along.

The mutineers' skiff leaves the San Antonio, beginning its short trip back to the Victoria with six extra passengers, probably armed to the teeth with the San Antonio's weaponry. The little boat jolts and rocks on the waves.

De Morales' mind drifts to Elorriaga. The ship's master of the San Antonio will surely die. The brutality of Cartagena's attack flashes unbidden into his mind, the vicious little man stabbing Elorriaga again and again. He can still hear the air wheezing out of Elorriaga's lungs with each blow. And for what will he die? Following orders from the Capitán General. As if he had any impact on Cartagena's fall from grace.

He is snapped out of his thoughts by a cry from one of the watchmen standing guard at the prow of the Victoria. 'The skiff, the skiff' he cries.

Men sweep to the gunwale to see. Mendoza and Elcano burst from the captain's cabin to watch impotent and horrified as the skiff carrying the men drifts off course. Caught in the errant currents of Puerto San Julián, the boat is being sucked out to sea.

The men in the skiff call and wave at the crew of the Trinidad in terror. With night falling, if they are swept out into the ocean, they will be quickly and utterly lost. Surrounded by the indifferent cruelty of this capricious coastline, their scant skiff will be capsized or dashed upon jagged rocks.

Powerlessly, the mutineers of the Victoria watch events they can have no impact upon unfold before them. They watch the confused actions of the seaman on the Trinidad, desperately trying to save the lives of their would-be murderers. They throw out lines to the boat as the panicking sailors crawl over each other and their skiff slides past the flagship. A line finally reaches them and the skiff is hauled in towards the Trinidad, bumping against its hull.

The desperate seamen begin climbing aboard, slipping and catching their feet on the Jacobs ladder. How absurd, de Morales thinks. In six hours, the crew of that stricken skiff would have been slitting their saviour's throats.

'Damn,' Mendoza says simply.

The captain begins to nervously pace the deck, his agitated eyes darting this way and that. Elcano, apparently paralysed by what has just happened, simply stares at the Trinidad as the last of the men are hauled onto its deck, disappearing amongst its rigging and sails and rushing crew.

'What ill luck,' Elcano says finally.

'An understatement if ever there was one,' Mendoza says.

Twilight gives way to full night. As the deep darkness descends on the scattered ships, the wind abates once more. The churning currents of the harbour calm and the inky water sloshes gently against the Victoria's hull. De Morales is sure the irony is not lost on the mutineers. Had they waited another hour, the little skiff would probably not have drifted off course and their scheme would still play out exactly as planned.

Nobody seems to quite know what to do. Mendoza appears to be in favour of casting off under cover of darkness and returning to Castile. Elcano prefers to wait and see how events unfold. Sailing in darkness is difficult, even on the well-charted coastlines of the Mediterranean or on the open ocean. But navigating out of Puerto San Julián into uncharted waters is a death wish.

A loud thud echoes off the port side of the Victoria's hull. Mendoza and Elcano look aghast at one another. Whoever has piloted this boat has not announced themselves.

A moment of tense inaction passes. De Morales notices Elcano tightly gripping the hilt of his knife. Everyone onboard the Victoria is staring intently at the gunwale where Magalhães' men will surely climb over. The tension relaxes immediately as the wicked face of Cartagena emerges from the darkness. He climbs awkwardly over the rail, landing heavily on the deck.

'We saw the skiff veer towards the Trinidad,' he says out of breath. 'I think they meant to betray us.'

'They did not go there deliberately, you fool,' Mendoza says. 'They were caught in a current.'

Quesada climbs over the taffrail with more elegance than Cartagena and says, 'They won't talk to Magalhães unless under duress. It will take time for the Capitán General to torture the plan out of them and, by then, it will already be too late for the Portuguese dog.'

'This situation could work in our favour,' Elcano says. 'If Magalhães does suspect foul play then he may arrest the men and interrogate them. If he does not, he will likely let them stay aboard the Trinidad until dawn. Either way, when we make our move, we already have men loyal to us on the flagship.'

'True,' Mendoza says. 'Ought we move our attack earlier? If M-'

Mendoza is interrupted by a call from beyond the ship. He holds his hand up to his fellow mutineers for quiet and slowly walks to the starboard side of the Victoria.

'Ho,' comes the call again from the darkness beyond. 'Ah, well met, Captain Mendoza.' De Morales recognises Espinosa's voice immediately. 'I have a letter for you from the Capitán General.'

After a pause, Mendoza hails back to the voice in the darkness. 'Climb aboard, Espinosa,' he says.

'We can kill him now,' Cartagena whispers gleefully to Quesada beside him. 'Put Espinosa out of the picture before we even begin.'

'Silence yourself,' Quesada says quietly. 'Let us first see how this plays out.'

Espinosa climbs onto the deck of the Victoria and takes a sweeping glance at the gathered Spanish captains. They could not look more guilty if they tried. 'Ah,' he says lightly, 'you are all here. Well met, señores. I have a private letter for you, Captain Mendoza, from the Capitán General requiring your immediate reply. Shall we retire to your cabin?'

Mendoza nods and heads towards his cabin and the two pass through the awkward silence of the mutineers, closing the door after them.

'We need to kill him,' hisses Cartagena under his breath. 'It is the perfect opportunity. Magalhães was a fool to send him here alone.'

In the darkness, another thud echoes off the stern of the Victoria. Quesada and Cartagena start and look at one another. Elcano moves quickly to the gunwale and leans over into the darkness. 'It is our men from the San Antonio in the skiff,' he whispers, trying not to alert Espinosa in Mendoza's cabin.

'Magalhães is more a fool than even I suspected,' sneers Cartagena. 'The day is ours and he does not even know it yet.'

The five men from the San Antonio, along with the two rowers, climb the Jacob's ladder and then gather at the prow of the ship. They stand awkwardly, not knowing where they should go.

Quesada is watching them. A look of confusion passes across his face. The confusion turns to horror.

He opens his mouth, about to say something, but the door of the captain's cabin bursts open, slamming against the wall of the aftcastle. Mendoza stumbles onto the main deck. He is clutching his throat, blood gurgling from between his fingers. He takes a faltering step then falls face-down to the deck.

As the thud reverberates across the Victoria the realisation of what has happened comes over the other captains. From the prow of the ship, the seven men hurry towards them. One tackles Cartagena to the ground, another two slam heavily into Elcano who falls to his knees. A fourth man leaps at Quesada but he outmanoeuvres him, twisting away from his would-be captor. Quesada turns and dashes up the stairs towards the aftcastle, pursued by two men

'Mercy, mercy,' Cartagena cries. 'I concede. Mercy.'

Quesada fumbles at the gunwale, readying to cast himself into the ocean. Before he can launch himself overboard his pursuers grab him and throw him to the deck. He shrieks, kicks and lashes out, but the men are too strong and he is overcome.

It is all over so quickly. The mutinous captains have been

utterly overcome in a matter of seconds. The men stand over their prisoners, holding knives and rapiers to their necks. Shocked by the sudden turn, the rest of the crew of the Victoria stand in silence, defeated.

Espinosa walks calmly through the doorway of the captain's cabin, Cartagena's ivory poignard coated in Mendoza's blood held in his hand. He kneels beside Mendoza, avoiding the widening pool of blood. Espinosa roughly lifts the head by the hair and Mendoza's mouth lolls open, gore oozing from a wide wound in his neck. Seemingly satisfied, he releases his grip and Mendoza's great head thuds lifeless to the deck.

'I think you have been outflanked and outplayed,' Espinosa says slowly. He wipes the bloody poignard on Mendoza's coat. 'Every man on this ship is under arrest.'

Chapter 12

April 1520

The trial begins at dawn and de Morales is in chains. During the night, the temperature plummeted leaving slushy chunks of ice to bob at the shore. A small gathering of large birds, similar in appearance to gulls, preen themselves while they bounce on the choppy waves. They are the first wildlife de Morales has seen since the fleet arrived in this place and the lives they lead seem desperate and cheerless. He sees so much of himself and the other accused in their joyless existence.

The San Antonio fell soon after the Victoria. Once they learnt they were leaderless, the rebellious crew there quickly gave up on the mutiny. The Victoria is now a prison ship with some sixty men chained up on the main deck, awaiting trial. Most are poorly dressed for the weather, and they stand now shivering and sniffing in the bitter wind. De Morales is fortunate to be warmer than most, having left the Trinidad in his cloak, but even he can feel the biting cold picking its way through his layers of clothing.

The table has been dragged from Elcano's cabin and placed on the starboard side of the main deck of the Victoria. But it is not the Capitán General who will preside over this trial. Instead, Mesquita, rescued from the San Antonio, sits behind the table and will act as judge. After all, the only successful uprising was against him.

The prisoners make for a sorry sight. A long length of chain binds them together, señores, sailors and cabin boys alike. Cartagena and Quesada suffer the ignominy of being pilloried. Despite the events of last night Quesada seems accepting of his fate, whereas Cartagena spat at his gaolers and now silently seethes in the stocks.

Already the body of Mendoza swings gently from a yardarm, a noose around its neck. The livid tear in his throat where Espinosa stabbed him has turned pale, the folds of flesh peeling back as the body dries out in a harsh wind that blasts across the main deck. The feet are barefooted, the boots removed by some opportunistic sailor. It would be a shame, after all, for them to go to waste.

It seems Elorriaga, miraculously, still lives. Though in what condition de Morales has not been told. Rebêlo is also still alive, although bruised and swollen from the beating Cartagena and Molino unleashed upon him. Mesquita seems himself despite his ordeal. He does, however, have a large green-brown bruise on the right side of his face and speaks through a swollen and split jaw.

Flanking Mesquita on either side are the remaining captains of the armada: Serrano to his left, his face resolute and unreadable. While to his right Magalhães is seated, his arms folded across his body, his stern eyes flicking between faces in the crowd before him. Barbosa and Pigafetta hover nearby and Espinosa, the hero of the day, is seated beside the wall of the forecastle. Cartagena's ivory poignard, cleaned now and gleaming, hangs from his belt. A cabin boy of the Trinidad is acting as scribe, taking careful notes of every word spoken.

Several suspected men are immediately released. Valderrama pleads his innocence, of which Mesquita is well aware. The captain heard him defy Cartagena and threaten to tell Magalhães everything that transpired if he survived, and he does so now. The priest's narrative is long and thorough, and he puts the majority of the blame squarely at Quesada, Cartagena and Mendoza's feet. Elorriaga is also absolved in absentia. Valderrama witnessed Cartagena's brutal attack on the innocent man and, at the very least, Mesquita must have heard it.

Content with Valderrama's tale, Mesquita moves on. He reads from a sheet of paper before him, looks up and says, 'Luis de Mendoza. . .'

Incredible, de Morales thinks, they are trying a corpse.

'. . .you are found guilty of leading this mutiny and of treason against the captain of the San Antonio, Álvaro Mesquita, against the Capitán General of this Armada de Molucca and his illustrious majesty. You are sentenced to be brought before this congregation where your head shall be struck from your body. Thereafter your body shall be drawn and quartered, and your limbs shall be displayed in prominent places about this area.'

In disbelief at what he is witnessing, de Morales watches as several members of the Trinidad's crew, under Espinosa's watchful eye, release the body of Mendoza from the noose. The corpse thuds onto the main deck.

Next, one of the men, panting under the strain, drags Mendoza's body across the deck before placing its chest onto a crate. The head lolls lifelessly over the edge. Espinosa, whose skill with a blade has already proven itself upon Mendoza once, approaches the corpse, carrying a rapier. The slender blade looks hardly capable of separating Mendoza's great head from his neck. He plants his feet and with one resolute swing, the body is decapitated. The head thumps to the deck, rolling in an arc until it faces the cabin door through which Mendoza stumbled the night before. Blood, thickened after hours of clotting, lazily seeps from the mess of tubes, muscle and bone.

A sailor steps forward and lifts Mendoza's head by the hair. The corpse is flipped over onto its back, the crate kicked away, and the bloodstained shirt ripped open. The head is dumped into position at the top of the body.

Like a butcher setting to work on a swine, Espinosa plunges a knife into Mendoza's body, just below the ribcage. He slices downwards, drawing the blade almost to the pelvis. Though only twelve hours have passed since Mendoza died, his corpse has already begun to putrefy while it was hanging from its makeshift gibbet. Rotten air, rank with the smell of blood, death and faeces, seeps from the tear.

His work done, Espinosa hands the disembowelment over to Bustamante. For all to see, the barber displays his rude surgical skills as he rips and tears at Mendoza's body, pulling dripping chunks from the cavity and throwing them over his shoulder. De Morales can only hope Bustamante has more respect for the living than he does the dead, for he makes a great show of eviscerating Mendoza.

Arm deep in the stinking cadaver, Bustamante holds his breath as he cuts and wrenches before, finally, the organs separate. He rises, sweating despite the cold, and throws them carelessly into the brazier beneath the mainmast, they hiss and spit in its coals. Intestines hang from the rim, dripping blood and shit onto the deck.

Mendoza's lifeless eyes stare indifferently at their former body as four men tie thick ropes around the wrists and ankles. The ropes are then attached to the capstans in each corner of the Victoria's deck. On Espinosa's mark, sailors begin turning the trundle-heads, and the ropes tighten. As if in the arms of unseen angels, the body rises from the deck as the men turning the capstans struggle against its weight. It is difficult to tell where the groaning of the ropes ends and the creaking of Mendoza's joints begins.

The left arm gives way first. A slow ooze of blood leaks from the severed limb and the body thuds to the deck. The left leg follows, then almost immediately the right. Mendoza's blood, having settled at the base of his body over the past twelve hours while it hung from the yardarm, pours from the legs in a thick sludge of stinking gore. The right arm is severed with a knife after several attempts.

De Morales finds himself feeling faint, swaying on his feet. He has witnessed countless fights, battles and tortures, or at least the aftermath of them. It is the brutality of this desecration, combined with his growing hunger and the lurching ship, he thinks, that makes the scene affect him so. He notices the cabin boy acting as scribe has vomited quietly at some point during the spectacle.

Mendoza's limbs and head are gathered up clumsily and dumped into a sack. The body is simply thrown overboard into the harbour.

So ends the first day of the trial.

That night, in the frigid cold of the Victoria's hold, the prisoners are chained and kept quiet. A large seaman standing guard strikes Quesada when he tries to speak. They are fed a thin porridge of hardtack mixed with boiled seawater and a mouthful of fortified wine.

In the silence, the depravity of the day settles in de Morales' mind. He stares unseeing into the gloom of the hold, lit only by the murky torch light filtering down from the main deck.

He must find a way to prove his innocence. Maybe, when he is called before Mesquita, he will have the chance to speak. He goes over in his mind all that he can say. Of the trickery that led him to the San Antonio, of plans the mutineers made before him, of the letter he was forced to write.

But at the back of his mind, de Morales knows Pigafetta has turned Magalhães utterly against him. The realisation hits him that he may have to hope someone else will vouch for him. Someone who witnessed the mutiny and will attest that de Morales took no part in it. With cold dread, he realises there is no one.

The trial begins in earnest the following day with the señores and leaders of the mutiny. There is nothing for it but to wait his turn, and there are a lot of accused yet to stand trial. For the time being, Mesquita turns his attention to several members of the mutineers whose guilt is suspected but not yet conclusive.

Antonio de Coca, the fleet's accountant from the San Antonio, is brought before the judge and questioned for several hours. De Morales is not paying attention to Mesquita's questions. His eyes and mind are focused on the bloody stain Mendoza's corpse has left behind. He notices, almost casually, Mendoza's head and limbs hanging from various parts of the Victoria. Frost has gathered across them during the night, forming sparkling continents across the pale skin.

De Coca is released without punishment beyond losing his rank. He is now a humble seaman and nothing more. He is sentenced, nevertheless, to hard labour for not trying to stop the mutiny – an impossible task. Elorriaga stood up to the mutineers and look where that got him.

Hernando Morales, the pilot of the San Antonio known by his first name, is next. Despite questioning the terrified man for several hours, Mesquita is unconvinced of either his guilt or innocence. Hernando was witnessed throwing papers overboard once the mutiny was put down. Once fished out of the sea, the papers that could still be read were found to be charts and navigational coordinates for the journey thus far.

'Why,' Mesquita asks again and again, 'were you in possession of the charts and why did you dispose of them thus?'

The question is ridiculous. Hernando, as a pilot, had every reason to have the charts. In fact, it was his job to have them. Early in the questioning, the pilot answers that, panicked by the night's events, he threw them into the water without thinking. His excuse is met by a blank stare from his judge. By the end, Hernando is weeping pathetically and repeatedly saying, 'what more can I say?'

Mesquita grows impatient. Thus far it has taken almost four hours to question just two suspects. The judge wants a different answer to the question Hernando has already answered. Eventually, he gives up and stands suddenly. 'Come morning you will be tortured upon the strappado and asked these questions again. We will have the truth, one way or another.'

The poor pilot, confused, crying and terrified, faints and collapses into a heap. He is dragged to the gunwale beside the other accused men, chained up and dumped on the deck

Next Geronimo Guerra, a clerk of the San Antonio, is questioned. By this point the day is old and Mesquita cannot be bothered. Guerra barely gets a chance to answer the judge's first question before Mesquita irritably orders him to be tortured likewise.

A mockery. This trial is already a farce.

Another day has passed, then. It may not have been as gruesome as yesterday but tomorrow promises to be bloody indeed.

The torture of Guerra and Hernando begins on the third day of the trials. The terrified men, trembling with fear and cold, are manhandled into position under the mainmast. Their shirts are torn from them and thrown against the forecastle. Already weeping and pleading his innocence, Guerra can hardly stand for fear.

The prisoners' hands are bound behind their backs and the ropes are then thrown over the yardarms of the mainmast. When Guerra fights against the bonds, he is struck across the face with a truncheon. Blood spills from his nose, soaking his chest and stomach. The clerk begins to weep but stops fighting.

With Guerra beaten into submission, sailors take hold of the other end of the ropes and haul Guerra and Hernando into the air. Their shoulders, supporting their entire body weight, twist into inhuman shapes. Their cries are terrible, filling the empty harbour with the sound of human suffering. Mesquita asks his questions and, between agonised screams, he receives the same answers as yesterday.

With a nod from the judge, the men holding the ropes release their grip. Guerra and Hernando fall freely to the deck but are stopped at the last second by the men grabbing the ropes once more, catching them mid-fall. The two men shriek in agony, but Guerra's cries are especially piercing. His arms have already dislocated. With his torso bare, the twisted skin and bulging shoulders are plain to see.

The process is repeated.

Again and again, the prisoners are raised and dropped. Eventually, Guerra and Hernando no longer have the energy to scream and just convulse in silent agony as they are lifted and dropped repeatedly.

Having received the same answer to his questions for what must be an hour now, Mesquita releases Hernando from the torment. The pilot falls to the deck, begging forgiveness between ragged breaths.

Guerra is not so lucky.

For some reason, Mesquita seems intent on torturing the clerk beyond reason and he orders cannonballs to be tied to Guerra's feet. This new torture begins at three balls apiece suspended from each foot.

When he is raised once more, Guerra finds energy anew to cry out in pain. His already dislocated arms stretch horribly at the shoulder. De Morales cannot imagine the depths of such pain and the callousness of the men inflicting it.

'Mercy. Mercy.' Guerra cries, coughing on the blood still pouring from his broken nose. But Mesquita is indifferent to the clerk's pleading. He orders more cannonballs be added.

Two more balls are added to each foot. This time, when he is raised Guerra shrieks in agony, an awful, appalling sound the likes of which de Morales has never heard. Guerra begs God, Mesquita, Magalhães, anybody to end his torment but his cries fall on deaf eyes.

When he is dropped this time, Guerra faints and his screams fall silent. The lifeless body is raised and dropped nonetheless, swinging and spinning as it plummets to the deck.

Eventually, the unconscious clerk soils himself and, appalled by the stench, Mesquita gives up. Guerra is dumped onto the deck and dragged drooling and convulsing into the crew's quarters below.

That night, the prisoners sit in the hold in shared shock at the disgusting torture unleashed by Mesquita. No one speaks. De Morales stares into the darkness, unable to eat his cold gruel, replaying the awful screams in his mind. He sees Guerra's desperate eyes, pleading for mercy and finding none. The tortured men have been removed from the hold. The guards could not put up with Hernando's moans and Guerra's stink.

De Morales begins to worry will not have the chance to defend himself. If such wanton violence can be exacted upon so obviously innocent men, what punishment will Magalhães demand of him, who he already has cause to mistrust?

Seemingly bored with questioning men whose guilt he cannot prove quickly, Mesquita turns his attention the next day to Cartagena. Pilloried like a common criminal, Fonseca's bastard is surely now completely undone and Magalhães' retribution against this persistent foe has finally come. No amount of wheedling, whining, shrieking and spitting can save him.

'You are brought here to stand trial for the act of mutiny,' Mesquita says to Cartagena once he has been brought before him. 'Also, you are to stand trial for your attacks upon the person of Cristóvão Rebêlo and Juan de Elorriaga.'

All through the reading of the charges, Cartagena's face remained impassive but at the mention of Elorriaga's name, his face twists with hatred. How the disgraced captain can hate one man who did so little so much is beyond de Morales. The attack on Elorriaga was vicious. A violent, primal act of rage.

'You are found guilty of all the aforesaid crimes. For your treasonous and brutish acts, whence this fleet departs, you shall be marooned in this place. May God have mercy on your soul.'

'I recognise no power of yours to convict me,' Cartagena says, then spits at Mesquita's feet.

'Take him away,' Mesquita says, not even bothering to look up from the list of names before him.

So Cartagena will rot here alone in this desolate place. Marooned in an unknown corner of the world without any hope of deliverance from passing ships. He will slowly starve to death. Or perhaps he will shiver and suffer in the frigid wind before he will finally succumb to the cold. Doubtless, his death will come, but it will be slow and inevitable and alone.

De la Reina is tried next and is also sentenced to be marooned when the armada leaves. He struggles against his gaoler as he is pushed towards the trapdoor on the main deck. 'Why?' He cries. 'What part did I play?'

Mesquita's temper gets the better of him. 'You are an affront to God,' he shouts back.

Still struggling, de la Reina is finally forced down into the hold, his shouts muffled before finally silencing.

De Morales looks into Magalhães' eyes and sees only spite. Let the two rot together, they say. Cartagena, the poisonous little man, and de la Reina, the sulking, bored bishop.

Luis de Molino, Mendoza's clerk, is called next. He stands where his comrades stood before him, before the bloody stain that was his master's final farewell to this world.

Mesquita turns his attention to him. 'For your attack upon Cristóvão Rebêlo and your participation in the mutiny,' he says, 'you shall be brought to this place tomorrow and, once here, your head shall be struck from your body.' Molino does not get a chance to plead before, with a wave of his hand, Mesquita confines him to the holds of the Victoria.

The rate of the trials does not let up and Elcano's is called forward. Mesquita accuses him of conspiracy, a lesser charge than those against Mendoza, Cartagena and de la Reina, but sentences the Basque to be beheaded all the same. Elcano falls to his knees, begging for mercy.

De Morales' heart sinks. He cannot deny Elcano was complicit in the mutiny. Without his quick mind, it probably would have fallen apart long before they were finally overcome by Espinosa. De Morales has struggled since the events of that night to balance in his mind the man he believed Elcano to be and the man who took part in the uprising.

But Elcano did not plan the mutiny. Any investigation, however shallow, would prove this. Not only that, but Elcano had no part in any violence. He even tried to help in saving Elorriaga's life. Maybe he was cornered, coerced, threatened. The sentence is arbitrary.

Serrano moves forwards from where he has been standing in silent witness. 'I must intercede,' he says.

Pigafetta pipes up next, speaking to Magalhães rather than Mesquita, proving who here is the true judge. 'Capitán General,' he says, 'this man conspired your death. He must be punished accordingly. Strike his head from his body and be done with his rebellious breed.'

That sycophant Pigafetta has revelled in every moment of this trial. He stood and watched impassively as Mendoza's rotting blood leaked from the headless corpse. With cold indifference he watched Guerra's body mutilated and listened to his awful screaming. He has delighted in watching Magalhães take vengeance upon those who have wronged him.

Mesquita looks to Magalhães. The Capitán General nods. 'Very well,' he says. Mesquita turns to Elcano, still kneeling before him. 'You are sentenced to be chained until we depart this place. Until we do so you will perform hard labour for the cleansing of your conscience and your soul.'

Next comes Mesquita's trial of the forty or so other conspirators still gathered shivering on the deck who have watched every moment of his depraved form of justice. It is a day without end.

Among the forty, de Morales is one. They are a motley crew of señores, cabin boys and sailors from almost every country in Europe. Mesquita does, at least, go to the effort of naming each man.

Diego Hernández, San Martín, Miguel de Rodas, Juan de Morales, Jaime Torres, Juan Rodríguez de Mafra, Pedro de Bilbao, Pedro de Sabina, Sebastián de Olarte, Juan de Francia, Pedro Hernandez, Maestre Jaques, Alonso del Río, Sancho de Heredia.

The names fall from Mesquita's lips in a steady, unbroken stream. But for all the names he does not tire nor falter. He says each name with cold precision and they pile up like the leagues they have put between Sevilla and their fates today.

Is it vanity, de Morales thinks, that he feels aggrieved to have been dumped in the middle of this list? A part of him expected to be given the benefit of an individual trial, especially after Magalhães had made him his spy so long ago. Or perhaps that is why he does not.

Mesquita's list of the condemned has finally run dry and, without even taking a breath, he moves on to the sentencing. 'For your crimes, you are all sentenced to be executed.'

And that is it. All the pomp, ceremony and planning of Salamon's trial and execution in Rio de Janeiro is forgotten in Magalhães' feverish orgy of revenge. No man of God stands before them. No cross imposes itself above them. Even the name of the king has been omitted.

De Morales finds that, as he faces eternity, he feels nothing. The image of his headless corpse being rolled into the harbour fills him with indifference. He takes in the desolate harbour, the blood-stained deck, Pigafetta's sneer and Magalhães' stern indifference, only hinting at the joy he must be feeling now he has wreaked his revenge on his enemies. It would be an end to all this, de Morales thinks.

Barbosa leans to Magalhães' ear and whispers something. De Morales' first thought is that Barbosa is reminding the Capitán General of a name amongst the prisoners before him who deserves some special death or torture for his crimes. It occurs to de Morales that it could be him.

The Capitán General calls Serrano to him and the three men speak quietly together for some time. The mutineers around de Morales watch them speaking, deciding their fates. They shiver, either from cold or fear. Whichever it is does not matter, soon enough they will feel neither.

Magalhães flicks a dismissive hand then limps towards Mesquita. He leans down and whispers something in the judge's ear. The two men share a short conversation before Mesquita holds up a hand and proclaims, 'in his benevolence, despite your sinful, corrupt actions, the Capitán General has resolved to commute your sentences to internment. So long as the armada remains at this place, you shall be chained at night and work hard labour through the day.'

The mutineers around de Morales share a sigh of relief. He knows he, too, should feel that relief. He has been saved at the last moment. Was it all planned? Is he supposed to stand here now, teeth chattering and shivering, and feel grateful to Magalhães for his compassion?

Maybe. But, still, de Morales feels nothing.

Though the sun is sinking, Mesquita presses on, seemingly wanting the trial to be done with. With Mendoza dead, Cartagena condemned, Elcano in chains and the sorry rabble of mutineers dealt with, Quesada is finally tried.

But the cold, his hunger and his tiredness are getting the better of de Morales so that, as Quesada's trial takes place before him, he feels barely aware of it, as if it is happening beyond a veil. When Mesquita's verdict is finally delivered, he sentences Quesada to be beheaded then drawn and quartered. It is only Quesada's status that saves him from the agony of being drawn alive.

Like so many of his comrades before him, Quesada remains silent as the sentence is passed. When he does not move quickly enough for his gaoler, he is shoved toward the Victoria's hold. Then, in single file the condemned are herded like cattle, following their leader below.

With the trials finished the guard has gone, leaving the mutineers to argue through the night. Instead of the night spent in silent, penitent prayer that prisoners in Castile are afforded before their executions, Quesada and Molino are forced to listen to Cartagena rant and rave.

'How can he name you the leader?' Cartagena asks. 'You couldn't lead a duck to water.' Quesada ignores him, as every prisoner in the hold of the Victoria has done since they were shackled there earlier.

It is almost as if Cartagena is jealous of Quesada's sentence. Fonseca's bastard has spat vitriol at the Capitán General across thousands of leagues of the Great Ocean. He has undermined, countermanded, insulted and subverted Magalhães at every opportunity. To be denied his place at the forefront of the mutiny is, it seems, an insult too far. While Mendoza and Quesada will be remembered as the masterminds of the coup, Cartagena will be forgotten to history. Left to rot his way out of this life, abandoned with a sulking bishop for company.

'He put himself in this position.' Elcano's voice comes out of the darkness nearby.

'Why did you do this?' De Morales asks. The question is directed at Elcano, but he could ask it of any of the prisoners he shares the makeshift gaol with.

'I did what I thought was right,' Elcano says firmly. 'I have looked death in the eye this day and, saving Serrano's intervention, I would surely have faced it tomorrow. I do not feel like philosophising on my decisions.'

'If you will not justify yourself, then I have no more words for you,' de Morales says. 'I am here because your mutiny failed. I know where the blame lies.'

'You played your part, de Morales.' The voice is Quesada's. 'You cast your lot and chance had it that you cast well. But tell me, señor doctor, where did your loyalty lead you? Were it not for Barbosa and Serrano, you would be dying with me tomorrow. So judge not Elcano. You are two sides of the same coin.'

'What does he mean?' Elcano asks.

De Morales' heart is in his throat. He opens his mouth to speak but, from the darkness, Quesada cuts him off before he can. 'Our dear surgeon was the Capitán General's spy,' he says.

De Morales feels dozens of eyes stare at him in the gloom. Though they cannot see him, his face reddens and his pulse quickens.

'For all we know,' Quesada continues, 'it was he who gave us up.'

His anger boils over at once again being pulled into a conspiracy against his will. 'How could I have done that? I knew nothing more of your plans than any other innocent man in the armada. But it would not take a genius to divine your intentions. You hid them as a peacock hides its plumes.'

Quesada lets the silence that follows draw out. Finally, he

says quietly, 'yet you were right where you needed to be, weren't you?'

With dawn, the condemned are corralled back onto the deck. The air has grown colder every day this trial has lasted and today is no different. The wind is up and the Victoria rocks and creaks on the churning waves. Above them, hanging from the masts are Mendoza's body parts. They swing and twist in the air. His head, dipped in tar to keep it from rotting too quickly, is impaled on a spike tied to the bowsprit.

The same crate, the same sword and the same sputtering brazier used for Mendoza are standing in the centre of the main deck. All else has been cleared. Mesquita's table is gone and so is Magalhães' chair. The Capitán General is standing on the port side of the rocking ship with Serrano, Barbosa, Espinosa, Mesquita, Valderrama and Pigafetta lined up beside him.

As Molino is led to the makeshift block, Mesquita moves forward. 'The Capitán General has decreed,' he says, 'that if you perform the act of execution upon Quesada, you will be spared your sentence.'

Molino can hardly believe his luck. Saved at the last moment by Magalhães' fickle mercy. But the Capitán General's change of heart is no mercy, at least not for Quesada. Molino is a clerk. How can he perform a beheading with any skill?

Molino, however, has no care for his former master's end and quickly accepts the agreement. After all, who wouldn't? His chains released, Molino is handed the rapier that severed Mendoza's neck.

As Quesada is led to the makeshift block and manhandled into position, Molino begins to play the part of executioner with fluency. With a wavering voice, the clerk says, 'I ask forgiveness for the deed I am required to do on behalf of his majesty and the Almighty.'

'You will get none.' Quesada fires back.

On his first swing, Molino almost misses the neck entirely. The blade rips into the skin and muscle of Quesada's neck. It leaves a deep, but far from lethal, cut and a crimson arc of blood spouts from the wound. A sailor is called to forcibly hold Quesada's convulsing body in place, but he can do nothing for the screams.

The second swing buries the blade into Quesada's back. The condemned captain's screams are cut short as he faints from the pain. Molino wrenches at the blade, ripping the sinew of Quesada's back as he jerks and twists the sword free. The blood already flowing from his neck, is joined by a gory expulsion of carnage from the deep gauge across Quesada's back and shoulders

The third swing and Molino finds his target but fails to sever the head completely. Quesada's head droops grotesquely over the block, still held to his seizing body by a mess of muscle. De Morales' stomach churns, mimicking the rampant harbour below.

A fourth swing and the head is finally severed.

Quesada's blood pools on the deck, mingling with the dried stain Mendoza left behind. His hacked body convulses silently, sending spats of blood through the air. Molino, white-faced and shaking, drops the rapier into the pool of gore.

Between the relentless wind, the lurching water, the rocking boat and Molino's inexperience, Quesada's execution was horribly botched. Perhaps it is Quesada's words that unnerved him or perhaps Molino was always going to fail in his task.

Molino falls to his knees and begs forgiveness from God. But all he receives is a set of manacles. He is lifted and forced to watch as the body before him is hacked to pieces. When the grisly deed is done, with tears in his eyes, Molino stares at the severed head of Quesada impaled on a halberd. But surely, he will find no forgiveness in those blank eyes.

De Morales watches the blood run down the shaft, pooling on the deck of the Victoria. Looking up to the skewered head, he, too, stares into those dead eyes. How did he know?

They are taken below. Quesada's blood has trickled through the deck and it patters softly onto the wooden floor of the makeshift gaol. All the men, even Cartagena, are silenced by the bloody days they have witnessed, each more vicious than the last. The Capitán General has beaten the insubordination out of them with his ghastly display of violent retribution. To a man, they look defeated.

But for de Morales, their silence is a mercy. For he knows that, were they not in shock at what they have witnessed, the mutineers would be questioning him now about his relationship to the Capitán General. The lesson has been taught, then. Mendoza and Quesada were to be made examples of, to put an end once and for all to the mutinies that have plagued the armada for the past six months since it left Tenerife. Cartagena, being Fonseca's child, could not be treated in the same way and neither could de la Reina, being a bishop and a man of God, at least in title.

Magalhães has disposed of his greatest enemies over the course of the past three days and struck terror into the hearts of the other mutineers with his cruel treatment of Guerra and Hernando. De Morales does not fool himself. Though Mesquita was the judge, Magalhães was behind every moment of this trial.

But Magalhães' show of authority has not had the desired effect on de Morales. He who was guilty of nothing to begin with but being in the wrong place at the wrong time.

Since the trials began, de Morales has been asking himself why, if he had had the choice before the mutiny, he would have sided with the Capitán General. Even as he watched, from the deck of the Victoria, the mutiny fail around him he found himself willing for Magalhães to succeed.

Was it some sense of obligation? Despite Magalhães' indifference, his selfish egotism, his nepotism and his partisanship, de Morales would have remained obedient. But his lingering allegiance to the Capitán General has been shattered by Magalhães' vengeful bloodlust. Elorriaga's death, should it occur, will be a travesty, but it will be a single death on the part of the mutiny. Magalhães has tortured two innocent men, one to breaking point. He has stained the New World with Mendoza and Quesada's blood. His show trial has put guiltless men, de Morales included, in chains.

Those trials were not about justice or retribution or revenge. They were about fear. The Capitán General meant to strike terror into the hearts of everyone and ensure that mutiny would never again even be imagined on his armada.

As he sits in the dim light, surrounded by suspicious mutineers, de Morales finds there is no fear in his heart. At least not for the Capitán General.

Chapter 13

April 1520

The trials over and his rivals in chains or dead, the Capitán General turns his attention the next day to the punishment of those not executed and the repair of the armada.

All five ships bear the scars of their many thousand league battle west across the Great Ocean and south down the New World. Snapped rigging limply holds torn and stretched sails in place, yardarms are twisted and buckled and masts are cracked. The gunwales and taffrails are splintered and cracked. The pitch, once thick and glistening, is now ragged and thin, in places stripped entirely from the hull, exposing soft oak beneath. Great smears of sickly green mould have taken hold across the sails where the oil was stripped right from the canvas by the cruel wind.

The Concepción, in particular, is in a dreadful state. Quesada, focused solely on planning the mutiny, spent little time seeing to the condition of his ship and it is now falling to ruin. A large crack runs almost a quarter of the length of the mainmast and one of the yardarms of the foremast is completely broken off, lost in the sea somewhere between Rio de Janeiro and Puerto San Julián.

It is with the Concepción, then, that the punishment of hard labour will begin. Such work is completely new to de Morales. He fumbles around like an infant, not knowing where to put himself or what to do. He quickly learns, however, that the work is not complicated nor particularly intricate. But it is backbreaking and made worse by the bitter cold.

The Concepción is first careened. Carvalho sails the ship to the shore at high tide and, once the tide turns, deliberately grounds her in the shale of the harbour. The ship drunkenly leans to one side, exposing a bloated hull pockmarked with all manner of sea life. The larger creatures clinging to the hull quickly fall with a plop into the waterlogged shoal, but many remain. The first task is to laboriously remove all the molluscs still gripping the ship from the great mass of slimy oak and rotting pitch.

De Morales is given a short knife with a wide blade and a dull edge to pry the sea life away. The bigger shellfish are removed easily, popping off the wood with a gentle twist of the knife, but the smaller ones are a great trial to detach. They stick steadfastly to the wood as if they, too, grew in the northern Spanish forests from which the oak was taken. His cold fingers, numb from the frigid seawater and freezing wind, make the task even more difficult. The air rings with a clattering song as the shellfish are musically dropped into buckets to be boiled and eaten later.

The buckets fill quickly with all manner of strangely shaped mussels, limpets, clams, oysters, scallops and cockles. These would be a savoured delicacy in Castile of immense value, but here they are gobbled up greedily by hungry sailors. While Magalhães' loyal men receive their fill of shellfish, the prisoners get a small serving of hardtack mixed with boiled seawater and a cup of wine to wash the revolting taste away.

The task takes the entirety of the first day and, when the tide returns, the Concepción is turned about on its pivot so that tomorrow it will be careened on the opposite side and their task will begin anew.

Evening is falling and de Morales trudges across the shore of Puerto San Julián toward the makeshift prison in the hold of the Victoria. His clothes are soaked through, his feet are numb and cold to the bone, his fingers are deadened and his back aching. As he walks in file with the rest of the prisoners, he watches the figures of Cartagena and de la Reina being led onto the main deck of the Victoria. The two remaining leaders of the mutiny were spared a sentence of hard labour, in favour of an earlier marooning. They climb down the Jacob's ladder and enter a waiting skiff, escorted by Espinosa and four armed sailors.

De la Reina, suddenly now a picture of Christian supplication, fiddles with rosary beads and mutters some prayer. Cartagena, beside him, shivers and turns a poisonous eye on the prisoners as they make their way back to the Victoria. The skiff sets off, fighting choppy waves. It heads for a lonely island at the base of one of the great cliffs guarding the entrance to Puerto San Julián.

This is where Cartagena and de la Reina will serve their sentence, then. Dumped on that tiny island, trapped from the mainland by fierce currents, towering cliffs and crashing waves. Already standing on the island waiting for them, is a squat wine barrel and a crate of food. They will have no furs, no shelter and no hope.

He has sensed eyes on him all day, watching him, judging him. The other prisoners in the makeshift goal have doubtless been chewing on what Quesada told them the night before he was executed. Now, with no guards in the hold, their fury is finally spilling forth.

He hears malicious whispers from all sides, all filled with the same rage, the same venom.

'Turncoat.'

'Traitor.'

'Judas.'

They are looking for someone to blame, someone they can get their hands on. The antipathy quickly turns to open threats.

'You will die here,' one sailor calls from the prow of the hold, indifferent to the guards above on the main deck.

De Morales' heart is pounding in his chest and he can hear the rush of blood in his ears. If he calls out, he knows the guards will not come. Why would they bother themselves? He cannot run. The chains around his ankles bind him to the man beside him, the man whispering threats into his ear.

What if one of them, somehow, secreted a blade into the hold. He can already feel the cold steel sliding into his body, the warmth of his blood pooling around him, the kicks and punches landing. His end will not be swift, they will draw it out and the guards on the main deck will not come to his aid.

'Quiet.' The voice is Elcano's. He is some way off, but de Morales can see his silhouette rising awkwardly under the light leaking down through the trapdoor. 'If any man harms de Morales, he will answer to me.'

Several sailors scoff, one laughs mockingly at the threat.

'You will fall in line,' Elcano says, 'or I will beat you into line.' The hold slowly quietens down. Whether it is out of respect or fear, Elcano seems able to keep the sailors under control. 'I am the only man here who played any meaningful part in our mutiny,' Elcano continues, 'and I say to you now, on my honour, de Morales was not involved.'

Incredulous sneers roll through the hold, but the sailors stay quiet. 'Those of you who were there on the San Antonio know the truth,' Elcano says. 'You are looking for someone to blame but there is no one here to blame. Things did not go our way. It is as simple as that. De Morales may have been told by the Capitán General to spy on us. But I ask you, how could he have passed any information to Magalhães? I was with him the whole time.'

'He wrote a letter,' a voice says. 'On the Victoria, the morning before Mendoza was killed. I saw him write a letter and give it to you.'

'You think me fool enough not to have read the letter, del Río?' Elcano says. 'He wrote exactly what Quesada told him to write. If you want to blame anyone for where you are today, blame Mendoza and Quesada and Cartagena. They planned this mutiny and it failed because they planned it poorly.'

The silhouette of Elcano slowly lowers to the floor while sailors drop their heads. Silence takes hold once more and the men fall into deep thought. They know Elcano is right, they know where the blame truly lies.

Were it not for Elcano springing to his defence, de Morales is sure he would be dead or dying by now. Even after rebuking him for his involvement in the mutiny, Elcano still leapt to de Morales' side despite being vastly outnumbered.

The next day is much like the previous. The same back-breaking, tedious work of cleaning the careened Concepción, this time on its starboard side. As the prisoners work relentlessly at their laborious task, carpenters and the fleet's cooper begin work on the damage to the masts and yardarms of the ship. Meanwhile, sailors crawl and scurry up the leaning mainmast, strapping great iron braces around it to strengthen the wood and stop the splitting.

There have been none of the enormous trees needed to replace a mast in its entirety for many leagues now. The last time they saw a tree of any real size were the gigantic, towering trees of the Terra do Brasilian jungle. Though Magalhães had ordered that several of the trees be cut down as they made their way south, there was not enough room on board the ships to keep a trunk the full length of a mast.

This deserted, barren place, meanwhile, has no trees of any useful size beyond those that can be used for kindling. Perhaps there is life out there somewhere. But if there is, it is a harsh and bitter life indeed. De Morales thinks of Cartagena and de la Reina and tries to imagine, when they are left utterly alone, how long they will last here. Will they even outlast the fleet's overwintering?

While the carpenters repair the ships and the prisoners scrape and scratch the hull removing the abundance of sea life, the Capitán General sends several groups of men inland.

One group of a dozen or so are building a shelter from the smaller lengths of timber brought from Terra do Brasil. The makeshift shelter, made by unskilled hands, looks breezy, cold and barely worthy of the name. What on earth Magalhães plans to use it for de Morales cannot guess.

Another group of six men, led by Espinosa, have climbed to the highest peak of the low hills to the north where they will raise a cross. De Morales watches from time to time, as he stretches his aching back, the small figures' slow progress up the slope, their silhouettes hunched over and set against the brutal wind.

When they finally reach the top and begin erecting the cross, De Morales is eating his congealing porridge of hardtack and seawater. He watches as the tiny figures slowly hoist the cross into position until its stands alone in empty arrogance over the impoverished, windswept landscape below.

The figures turn and begin their descent.

What is this all for? No man would ever come here again and, if they had the misfortune of coming upon this barren land accidentally, they would surely not tarry long enough to wonder who had come before. A thousand years from now, this wretched place will be the same as it is today. The only reminder of their ever being here will be a rotten cross of vanity that once stood, overbearing and pointless, above the harbour but has since been blown over by the wind. A testament to the folly of Magalhães and his deluded followers who came to this place searching for a strait to the Spice Islands.

On the third day of their punishment, de Morales is

woken early by a strong hand shaking him firmly. He opens his tired eyes and sees Barbosa looking down at him in the gloom before dawn.

'You are needed on the San Antonio,' Barbosa says quietly.

De Morales rolls over, his aching shoulders and arms complaining at the movement. He sits up slowly. Until now he had thought he had been forgotten. Not once in the entire trial did any of Magalhães' men, men he had become close to over the previous six months, even make eye contact with him.

'What is it?' he asks.

'It is Geronimo Guerra. He is still in much pain.'

He rises fully and stretches his tired arms. Guerra, the poor clerk. He is not surprised to hear the man has not recovered after enduring such terrible treatment at the hands of Magalhães and Mesquita.

'Very well,' he says standing. He goes to take a step and nearly trips on the chains around his ankles. In his tiredness, he had forgotten they were there.

'My apologies, señor, doctor.' Barbosa kneels and unlocks the length of chain stretching between de Morales and the man beside him.

De Morales looks down at the manacles still strapped around his ankles. 'I cannot treat a man with my feet chained together,' he says.

'I have been told I cannot release you.'

He sighs at the absurdity of what Barbosa has just said. Knowing there is no point in arguing, he shuffles up the stairs into the freezing air outside. Dawn has not yet come, and it is impossible to tell what time it is. There is no moon but, compared to the absolute dark of the Victoria's hold, the starlight is more than enough to see by. Spots of flickering flame, one for each of the ship's signal lights, dance across Puerto San Julián. In the distance, the Trinidad still guards the entrance to the harbour. The rocks jutting out from the lapping water and the cruel shale of the shore sparkle in the starlight. It is low tide. In the distance, the careened Concepción is a massive, incongruous mess of shadows against the landscape.

Puerto San Julián is still now, the constant hammering and scraping of the daytime replaced by an almost serene hush. Even the wind has calmed. But with the lack of wind, a heavy frost has fallen over the land. Everything has an eerie calm.

He struggles immensely against his manacles as they climb down the Jacob's ladder into a waiting skiff. Fortunately, the skiff only bobs lightly on the gentle waves, making his climb into it slightly easier.

The two men reach the San Antonio and de Morales follows Barbosa into Rebêlo's former cabin. The room offers no hint of the events of the mutiny and has been stripped of everything save a table, chair and items of clothing strewn about the place. It now seems to serve as an infirmary.

Bustamante is already here, sitting on the chair staring at a prone body lying uncomfortably on a table. The room is lit by several candles but the shadows in the corners are deep, nonetheless. De Morales notices Hernando propped against the wall, asleep but with a look of discomfort on his face.

The body on the table is that of the unfortunate Guerra. The pilot is naked from the waist up and unmoving but, de Morales thinks, not asleep. As his eyes fully become accustomed to the candlelight, he can see the extent of the damage his torturers did to him. Spread across the clerk's arms and his entire trunk is one huge bruise. There is scarcely a part of his body that is not a ghastly smudge of blue, green, purple and brown blemishes all mixed like a painter's palette. Guerra's face is also badly bruised and his nose is swollen and clearly broken.

'He has not woken since the torture,' Bustamante says.

De Morales eyes Bustamante as he takes an awkward step toward Guerra. The manacles binding his feet clatter and Hernando shifts in his sleep at the noise. As he moves closer, he fully takes in the horror of what the torture has done to Guerra. Both arms are entirely dislocated. The left has twisted around completely, stretching the skin and leaving the point of his elbow facing forwards. Where the ropes were tied around his wrists, deep cuts have split the skin in places to the bone. On the ankles, the weight of the cannonballs has stripped the skin, folding and peeling it away from the muscle.

'Why have you not reset his arms?' he asks.

'That is why you were called,' Bustamante says.

'Has he eaten and been given water?'

'As I say,' the barber replies, 'Guerra has not woken since the torture. He has not eaten, but I have managed to make him swallow some small amount of water.'

'This man will starve to death if he is not fed,' de Morales says. He looks over the body lying before him. Though he is unconscious, Guerra's brow is creased in pain. 'But to wake him would be a cruelty. I have seen this type of stupor before. Either, by the grace of God, the patient awakens or he does not. I think, perhaps, God's grace in this instance would be for Guerra to expire.'

Barbosa is still in the room, his silent presence speaks nothing of his thoughts. De Morales wonders to himself how the supernumerary can be accepting of this? The cruelty Magalhães and Mesquita displayed in torturing Guerra was completely unreasonable and Barbosa is not an unkind man.

'Then we must wait for God to show his plan,' Bustamante says rising. He nods to Barbosa, turns and exits the cabin, leaving de Morales and the supernumerary to look over the broken body before them. The clerk's breath comes in ragged wheezes through his broken nose, his chest rising and falling fitfully. Now that he notices it, de Morales would guess Guerra has several broken ribs to add to his long list of other injuries.

'I can stand it no longer,' Barbosa says. He moves to stand beside de Morales and takes up a stained shirt from the floor. 'If you wish to stay, you can do so, but know that I am about to commit a terrible sin.'

De Morales takes a step back to allow the supernumerary through but does not leave the cabin. Barbosa pauses for a second, torn between what he wants to do and what his faith will allow him to. For a moment, de Morales thinks Barbosa will not do it but then he quickly gathers the shirt into a tight ball and places it, gently at first, over Guerra's mouth and nose. Barbosa hunches over, pushing with all his strength onto Guerra's face, blocking all breath.

Guerra does not even put up a fight. No struggle or convulsion, no desperate clinging to life. It is as if his soul has already departed.

The deed is over quickly. Hernando still sleeps in the corner. Barbosa exhales and breathes heavily, straightening up. He stares at the broken body before him. 'It was necessary,' de Morales says, his voice hollow.

Barbosa ignores him. He slowly falls to his knees and crosses himself. 'Eternal rest, grant unto your child Geronimo,' he prays. 'Welcome him into your arms. . .' He falters. His breath catches. 'Forgive me'

In the freezing morning, the body of Geronimo Guerra is disposed of. He is given a Christian burial presided over by Valderrama and a small cross is erected above the churned earth where his broken body is laid to rest. The Capitán General stands watching the ceremony impassive and unmoved; as if it was not by his hand that a man has died an unnecessary, agonising death.

Doubtless, Guerra would have died of his wounds, eventually. He would have wasted away until his emaciated, battered body would have given up the ghost and shuffled out of this mortal world. Barbosa's act was a small mercy for which, de Morales is sure, Guerra would be grateful.

The funeral over with, the condemned are returned to their labour. With the entire hull of the Concepción now stripped of its accompaniment of organic drifters, they are set the task of applying pitch to its entire surface.

The pitch is to be boiled in a huge cauldron lowered from the San Antonio into a skiff and rowed gingerly across the harbour to the careened Concepción on the shore. As the prisoners wait for the cauldron to arrive, de Morales watches the little boat toss and turn on the tide like a fretful child. The waters in this part of the world are erratic and uncompromising, the tide shifts suddenly and violently, rising almost twenty feet. Over the past days, as they worked on the beached Concepción, the condemned learnt quickly to be done with their task well before the tide changes. To tarry in the water would mean drowning as the tide quickly envelopes the ship in its icy waters and hauls her, rocking and swinging from side to side, upright.

The cauldron is placed over a large fire and a dozen

buckets are scattered around it on the floor. De Morales is given the unenviable task of constantly stirring the cauldron with a short, oar-shaped length of wood.

The pitch is as hard as granite and, to begin with, almost impossible to stir. His already aching arms are exhausted and shaking after no time at all at the awful task. But as it heats, the pitch slowly turns to a coagulated liquid, heaving with heat. It loosens further, turning to the consistency of overworked porridge bubbling and spitting and stinking until de Morales' head spins.

His only saving grace is the heat it gives off. This day is cruelly cold. In the stillness of last night, a thick frost fell over the landscape and has obstinately remained all day.

With the pitch now liquified and boiling it can be taken to the Concepción. Groups of the condemned, six at a time, take a bucket from the shore and fill it with the thick stew of stinking tar. They then carry their buckets, dripping and spitting, to the Concepción lying outrageously on its side. Once there they work quickly, smearing the smoking pitch all over the hull with heavy brushes. Slowly, the entire ship is coated in its glistening, coagulating dress of mourning black.

De Morales looks up from his stirring and finds Elcano standing before him. He has had no chance to speak with him since the Basque defended him from the other prisoners in the hold of Victoria. Several guards stand around the cauldron, attracted by the heat pouring from the fire below. He must be careful, the prisoners have been ordered to work in silence, but he must take this opportunity to speak to Elcano.

The Basque puts down the empty bucket he is holding, still sticky with clotting pitch. He leans over de Morales, lifts the huge ladle used for moving pitch from the cauldron and begins refilling his bucket.

'Thank you,' de Morales says. Elcano rises from his work and, for a moment, looks de Morales in the eye.

He winks, says, 'we must stick together, you and I.' Elcano turns and heads towards the Concepción.

For all his faults, Elcano is an honourable man and a true friend. He risked death in defending de Morales. Those brutish mutineers in the makeshift prison could easily have turned on him, too. De Morales does not doubt Elcano never wanted anyone to be harmed. He would probably have tried to take Magalhães alive, though Espinosa would certainly have put up a fight. But he will never know for sure for Elcano did not lead the mutiny.

The leaky hut that was begun on the first day is finished now. Or as finished as it will ever be. With the carpenters focusing solely on repairing the ships, the hut has been built by sailors and looks the part. Wonky planks crisscross each other giving the entire structure a strange sense of drunkenness.

Fortunately, this natural harbour is plentiful with fish and other sea creatures and the hut is to be a makeshift smokehouse for curing any fish that are caught. And they are caught almost constantly. A man could simply put his hands into Puerto San Julián's water and lift them out holding a fish like a jester's magic trick. Despite the abundance of fish, de Morales doubts the efficacy of this smokehouse with its lopsided walls that all but invite the wind to steal the smoke away.

It takes two days to completely smudge, smear, spatter and stain the Concepción in pitch. With that ship done, the prisoners move onto the next ship, the Santiago, and begin the entire exhausting process again.

Almost three weeks since the mutiny and de Morales is busy scrubbing the last of the ships, the Trinidad, cleaning off its scabby growth of sea life and slime. Puerto San Julián is quiet, almost tranquil. The prisoners work in silence, the air filled with nothing but the clink of shellfish as they are dropped into the buckets. From the hills, a cry splits through the stillness.

'Gigante.' Pigafetta, resorting to his native Italian, dashes towards the shore from the hills, half a league away. Startled by the call, the prisoners stop what they are doing and stare in Pigafetta's direction as the chronicler stumbles and trips his way back to the ships. Upon his face is a look of sheer terror. Magalhães, temporarily staying aboard the San Antonio, appears in the doorway of the captain's cabin, Barbosa and Espinosa at his side.

As Pigafetta draws closer to the shore and the careened Trinidad, de Morales sees it. Cresting the small hill, upon which Pigafetta stood when he first cried out, is the silhouette of a huge man-shaped figure. Even from this distance, the size of it is astounding. This man, if indeed it is a man, must be at least seven feet tall.

The figure walks resolutely towards the shore. The prisoners and their guards, to a man, stare at the giant in disbelief. The other prisoner's faces speak to their confusion that, after all these long weeks of isolation, there are humans in this desolate corner of the world. Despite the uneven ground that Pigafetta awkwardly stumbled across, the massive figure's determined step never once falters.

As he draws closer to the shore, de Morales can make out the native with more clarity. He is wearing a cloak made from the hide of a single, huge animal that, despite his height, reaches almost to the ground. Upon his legs, he wears a pair of loose-fitting, beige trousers and, despite the piercing cold, he wears nothing on his torso.

But it is the figure's face that holds his gaze. The giant has a long face and the skin, stretched and wrinkled by the sun, is deeply tanned. The look in his eyes is one of absolute determination, startling in its proud resolve. It is impossible to tell his age. The lined face has the wizened look of an elder, yet his step is strong and his movements as graceful as a youth.

The colossal figure stops perhaps thirty yards short of the ramshackle smokehouse steaming and smoking in the freezing air. Without taking his eyes from the men gathered around the Trinidad, he leans slowly down to the ground. He delves his hand deep into the shale, takes a great handful of dirt and stones and throws it in a wide arc above his head.

He casts off the cloak he is wearing and begins to dance, hopping from one foot to the other with startling agility. Every few steps he lets forth a high-pitched cry, sending his breath pluming and misting into the air. Then he leans down, grabs more sand and dirt and again tosses it over his head.

The men around de Morales are dumbfounded. It strikes him that this is a show of savage dominance, the giant's way of warning them to leave before he unleashes a great army of these colossal, proud men upon them.

The Capitán General seems to have taken a different opinion and sends Barbosa to approach the giant. Despite his experience in dealing with natives in the Indies, there is a reluctance in Barbosa's step as he approaches the enormous figure, still dancing and shrieking.

Barbosa stops short of the stranger and the difference in size is extraordinary. No small man himself, Barbosa is dwarfed by the enormous native. The giant ceases his dancing suddenly and stares unblinking at the insignificant Spaniard before him.

Finding some resolve, Barbosa slowly reaches down into the dirt. He takes a handful of sand and shale, tosses it over his head in a wide arc and then begins dancing, leaping from foot to foot, mimicking the giant's movements as closely as he can. But where the giant moved with speed and grace, Barbosa's movements, by comparison, are clumsy and ugly.

The giant holds his hand, palm facing outwards. Barbosa stops his dancing and copies the salute. Next, the supernumerary gently takes the giant's arm and manipulates the colossal hand into shaking his own.

Though the giant maintains his proud, strong posture there is a relaxing of tension all around Puerto San Julián. It seems the native has come to them peacefully. Barbosa signals the giant to follow him towards the fleet and the native, seeming unfazed in any way by the bizarre ships and pale men before him, follows Barbosa towards the Capitán General, who now stands on the shore.

Several men back away as the colossal figure silently approaches the Capitán General. Magalhães, with Pigafetta and Espinosa at his side, stands still, his face set in resolution. Other men, de Morales notices, have begun reaching for weapons, tightly gripping knives and swords. He imagines the cannons on the ships in the harbour being turned to face this giant of a man. A knife, surely, would not stop him but a cannon? Maybe.

Pigafetta cowers beside the Capitán General who extends

a hand in salute to the giant. The native copies the movement. Magalhães then, bizarrely, informs the native that he has claimed this land for Carlos, king of all the Spains, and gestures to the cross standing high on the hill.

The giant, making no sound, looks to the cross, then returns his gaze to Magalhães. He looks over the Capitán General. He takes in the beard, the furs, the stern eyes then lifts his hand and points to the sky. With that, the giant turns and, unhurriedly, strides away, not once looking back.

The wind blows, snow falls, and time passes. They have been at this desolate harbour now for sixty days and the men have sunk into depressed boredom. On the island on which they were marooned, Cartagena and de la Reina are tiny figures, shuffling about aimlessly. They live still, but it is difficult to imagine in what state.

Had Mendoza, Quesada and Cartagena only waited a few weeks, their mutiny would surely have succeeded. With good winds, the Armada might now be anchored on the Guadalquivir and Magalhães and his cohort of sycophants would be rotting in some jail. Guerra and Elorriaga would be at home with their wives, Cartagena spewing his venom against some other wretch. Mendoza and Quesada returned to the Casa de Contratación to lead some other fleet.

But what of de Morales? What would he return to? Back to the oppression of an empty life in Sevilla. Back to the conspiracy and stress of life at court. Back to a battlefield to piece men fighting for an indifferent emperor back together.

Somehow, winter has found a way to tighten its grip on Puerto San Julián. The ice that rimmed the harbour has crept almost entirely across its width, leaving only a narrow channel of water in the centre. Inland, meanwhile, the gnarled shrubs and blasted grass on the hills are coated in frost. From the roof of the leaky smokehouse, long, sinuous stalactites of ice stretch almost to the ground. But with the drop in temperature, the winds have calmed and the wild sea beyond the harbour has melted into lapping waves.

The Capitán General is rarely seen now. He hides in the Trinidad's office with Pigafetta, Barbosa, Valderrama and Espinosa. Mesquita and Rebêlo take their shelter on board the San Antonio, along with Estêvão Gomes and San Martin. Serrano, still captaining the Santiago, keeps his crew busy with work. The Concepción, Quesada's battered and ageing vessel still without a captain, stands in the frozen harbour, abandoned and forlorn.

Over the two months they have been in this place, each ship has been scrubbed, doused, scraped, brushed, mopped, scoured, dredged and pitched and every moment of the back-breaking work has been carried out by the prisoners. They have emptied every one of the five ships of everything in their holds. As they lifted and dragged the heavy crates of preserved food, a plague of rats squirmed and fought each other, desperately trying to escape the holds at the sudden disturbance, before disappearing into some dark corner. Next, they removed the crates and barrels of knives, beads, glass, caps and cloth.

The work was exhausting. Once emptied, the prisoners scrubbed every inch of the ship's holds with vinegar, the acid stink lingering in de Morales' clothes and hair no matter what he did to wash it out. But anything is better than the sickly, organic stench of mildew and mould that has permeated into the very bones of the ships. Then came the draining task of refilling the holds after which the rats, hiding God knows where, re-emerged and continued to gorge on what little supplies remain.

Magalhães emerges from the Trinidad after five days of calm weather and announces the Santiago will be prepared to chart the waters ahead. The Capitán General must believe the time is coming when the armada will finally be able to leave this place and the smallest ship of the Armada is best suited to weather any storm, should one come.

The following day breaks to a bright and clear dawn. Heavy snowfall in the night has left the ships cloaked in white, the weighty oppression of the snow sinking the ships lower in the water. De Morales is shovelling snow off the San Antonio's decks and gunwales as the Santiago weighs anchor and unfurls its snapping sails into the breeze. The light wind catches the canvas and it billows limply, slowly pulling the ship forwards.

The Santiago lurches its way out of the harbour, past the tiny island where Cartagena and de la Reina shiver towards their deaths. Then the little ship is gone, hidden from view by the towering cliffs that separate Puerto San Julián from the Great Ocean beyond.

Chapter 14

June 1520

It is almost July and in Sevilla the streets and markets will be packed with people, shopping before the worst of the day's heat comes. The towering Catedral de Santa María de la Sede, just two years old when the armada left Sevilla, will soon be baking beneath the sun. The sound of musicians playing vihuelas, gitterns and lutes will be mingling with birdsong and the chatter of the markets. Jesters and street performers will be dancing in the streets, their bells and cymbals jingling.

In the Mercado de Feria, the stalls will be full of wool, wine, sultanas, bread, melons, figs, and dates. Merchants will be restocking sacks of cloves, cinnamon, nutmeg, pepper, mace, cassia, cardamom, ginger and turmeric. Perhaps, at this very moment, some wealthy señor is bartering with a merchant. After the long negotiations are finished, he will leave the stall, step into the sunshine and make his way home with a handful of each spice to impress his friends at dinner tonight.

Meanwhile, the Armada de Molucca's holds are empty of spices and the ships are frozen in Puerto San Julián, slowly being crushed by the packing ice. Instead of cloves, they have rats, defecating in their food. Where the crates of cinnamon bark should be, they have the murky stain of Quesada's blood that dripped through the upper deck into the hold below. Empty barrels, meant for nutmeg, are slowly being eaten away by termites. The sacks, ready to be filled with peppercorns, lie empty and stinking of mildew. Instead of the pungent scent of mace, cassia and cardamom, the ships are reeking of vinegar, mould, stale water and death.

Every one of their stowaway pets, from the rats to the fleas, to the mice, to the weevils has an abundance of food. Meanwhile, the crew waste away, gloomily nibbling on hardtack and drinking boiled seawater. On the Victoria, Amaya cannot keep up with the ceaseless breeding of vermin. She gorges herself and when she is full, murders for fun. Once murdering has lost its charm, she simply lies on an empty sack in the hold, preening herself and sleeping while the rats scurry around her and the frigid cold nips at her ears.

But in Sevilla, the weather will be warm. Children will be playing in the streets. In the countryside surrounding the city, farmers will be tending grapevines and fig trees. Women will be working outdoors in fields and yards, taking siestas in the pleasant air. The King will have moved his court to Grenada, Cadiz, Segovia, Valladolid, Ribera, Burgos or any other place that takes his fancy. And behind the King will trail an endless train of pages, merchants, jesters, courtesans, cooks and hangers-on. The entire bloated company kept in fine food and fetal through the constant convoy of ships laden with spices and gold and slaves sailing up the Guadalquivir.

Not a year ago, de Morales was part of that vast royal train and kept warm and comfortable in Castile as he cared for Juana la Loca. Even the suspicion and intrigue he so hated are beginning to fade from his mind. Now, as his fingers numb and his nose runs, he imagines if the king looks to the horizon and wonders when his Armada de Molucca will return to Sevilla, triumphantly bloated with its precious cargo. Does Fonseca, brooding in his Casa de Contratación, surrounded by piles of spices and gold like an intumescent dragon, wonder if his bastard has succeeded in ousting Magalhães?

De Morales knows the truth. He is seeing Sevilla as he has not seen it for years: vibrant and full of life and happiness. He knows the memories are empty, that if he walked the streets he would quickly remember his sorrow and loneliness. He has travelled halfway around the world to find this dismal place and understand what he already knew: there is no place in this world for him.

Still, he cannot help remembering.

But does anybody in Sevilla remember the once glorious Armada de Molucca? Or are they forgotten by the world? Are they assumed drowned, shipwrecked, lost, imprisoned or captured? In the loneliest moments of the longest nights, do the women they left behind wonder at their fates? Can any of them, in their wildest fantasies during languid days, imagine that they have now spent almost three months in this desolate place, far from the edge of any map ever drawn?

The crew have stagnated here. The flurry of activity on their arrival, the excitement of the mutiny and the violence of the trials has passed. Even the rampant cleaning and mending of the ships has slowed to a crawl. The cold has seeped into their bones and slowed everything and everyone down.

De Morales and Elcano are working in the leaky smoke, raking smouldering coals. Over the past week, sailors fishing from skiffs in the unfrozen water in the centre of the harbour have reeled in countless sea bass. The fish must migrate to breed at this harbour for they are abundant and huge, some almost two cubits in length. Despite their size, they have little usable meat but that which can be used has been hung from poles reaching the width of the smokehouse. The work is a blessing. Despite its leaky walls, the smokehouse is doing its job and the air inside is pleasantly warm, if sooty, compared to the frigid day outside.

Tending the embers below the poles, de Morales is struggling to keep himself from taking one of the fish. 'I wouldn't,' Elcano says, guessing de Morales' thoughts as he eyes them. He glances toward the closed door, outside of which their guard will be standing. 'Surely, they have taken an inventory. Most likely they are waiting for someone to steal something to make a show of punishing them. You remember what happened to del Rio?'

How could he forget? Del Rio, a sailor from the Victoria, was caught pocketing limpets he had removed from the hull of the San Antonio many weeks ago. He was flogged savagely, then bound to one of the spikes holding the Santiago's lines to the shore. There he was left, shirtless and shivering, in the blasting wind and hail for a day and a night before he was brought back and dumped into the makeshift prison in the hold of the Victoria. The prisoners had gathered around him, drawing the numbness from him with their body heat. Del Rio's survival is nothing short of a miracle.

The door swings open and Pigafetta lunges through the threshold, his cloak and hair flapping wildly in the wind. He stops short, apparently surprised to find de Morales and Elcano inside. 'I did not think we caught any swine,' he says, looking between them. The chronicler smiles to himself, pleased with his joke.

'What do you want, Pigafetta?' Elcano asks.

'The Capitán General wants fish for his supper, is that a problem?'

'Why send you and not Enrique?'

'What business is that of yours?'

Pigafetta reaches for one of the longer lengths of smoked sea bass flesh hanging from a pole. As he pulls it down, he says, 'always you two are conspiring together. You ought to have learnt some humility when the Capitán General spared your worthless lives.'

De Morales and Elcano share the same look of exasperation. This is the first time de Morales has seen the chronicler for weeks and the first time in months they have been in close contact. Absence has not dulled the dislike Pigafetta has for him and the long months the chronicler has enjoyed in Magalhães' favour have only amplified his spiteful confidence.

'You should keep better company, señor doctor,' Pigafetta says. 'But then, your choice of friends has always been poor.'

'What do you mean by that?' De Morales asks, trying not to let Pigafetta goad him to anger.

'Do you think I could not hear you on the Trinidad,

gossiping like washerwomen with that imbecile Gomes? Those walls are thin indeed, señor doctor, and four horses could not outrun your tongue.'

De Morales thinks back, all those long leagues and months ago, to his conversations with Estêvão Gomes at the whipstaff of the flagship. The faded memories slowly reveal themselves. He remembers Gomes talking of Magalhães' former life, of the disappearance of Faleiro, of the route of the Armada and the decisions the Capitán General had made. Could this be it, the reason Magalhães seemed to turn so quickly to mistrusting him? He knew Pigafetta had been behind everything. But he had never been able to discern precisely what it was Pigafetta had told the Capitán General. But now everything is clear. Magalhães was already suspicious of him, Barbosa had told him as much long ago on the coast of Africa. All Pigafetta had to do was give the Capitán General a push in the right direction and he was done for. He would never have proven his innocence at the trials, even if he had been given the opportunity, because Magalhães always believed him guilty.

'I see you thinking,' Pigafetta says.' Searching for a loose bar in your cell. But know, señor doctor, you forged this cell yourself and you made certain it was strong.'

With a final, self-satisfied leer, Pigafetta turns and opens the door. The cruel wind blasts through the threshold, sending the smoking fish on their poles dancing and ash spinning through the air. The door slams closed and Pigafetta is gone.

All these months of exclusion, all the agonies de Morales might have eased had he not been in chains. To be Magalhães' friend is to live a blessed life. He thinks of Carvalho, of Valderrama, of Rebêlo. All the men absolved of suspicion during the mutiny because they had Magalhães' trust. He thinks of the agonies faced by Guerra and Hernando, imagines how many more have suffered since they came to this place.

The smouldering coals have lost their warmth, the smoked fish, their temptation.

The giant has returned. As the weak sun rose this morning, a watchman aboard the Trinidad spotted him on the same hill, squatting on his haunches. The giant stayed there all morning, watching the men working around the fleet.

The native seemed to be alone once again and now, once again, he approaches the armada with the same determined look on his face and the same focused eyes and confident step. The giant stops in the same place and begins the same dance, tossing handfuls of snow and shale into the air over his head.

Again, Barbosa approaches the native. The same awkward dance takes place, with both men clumsily copying the other's gestures. Again, the giant approaches the armada with Barbosa but, this time, the Capitán General is not waiting for him on the beach.

After much cajoling, Barbosa is able to coax the giant into a waiting skiff, for the first time he appears awkward as he climbs into it and desperately grips the gunwales tightly. Two shaking sailors, dwarfed by the native, begin to row towards the Trinidad. When they reach the flagship, Magalhães emerges from his cabin and awaits the native.

The giant watches from the skiff as Barbosa climbs the Jacob's ladder. He turns around halfway up, smiles down at the giant and waves his hand, coaxing the native to follow him. Reluctantly, with a look back to the land, the giant begins to climb.

Even from some thirty feet away on the Victoria, the native's wonder at being onboard the bizarre mess of wood, iron, rope, canvas and men is visible. He stands in the centre of the main deck, surrounded by curious and frightened sailors gripping the hilts of sheathed swords and knives.

The Capitán General approaches the giant and makes some of the same signals they exchanged in their last meeting. Magalhães passes him something, de Morales cannot tell what, and signals for him to come into his cabin. After more cajoling, and with a final look to Barbosa, they disappear into the darkness. The gathered sailors still crowd the main deck of the Trinidad, Espinosa moving between them.

Very quickly, a commotion comes from within Magalhães' cabin. Espinosa immediately draws his sword and several sailors follow suit. They stand, quaking and nervous in the chill wind, for only a second before the cabin door crashes open and the giant bursts out into the open air. He flings his great arms around him, stumbling into the centre of the deck, surrounded by skittish sailors. He sees the swords, the knives and the crossbows.

'They are trying to capture him,' Elcano says.

The native seems to understand what they are planning and twists about on the spot, looking for an escape. Barbosa emerges and, unarmed, cautiously approaches the giant as Magalhães appears in the doorway. The Capitán General says something to Barbosa, his words lost in the wind. Barbosa stares into the giant's eyes, slowly moving closer and closer to him.

With the giant's attention focused on Barbosa, Espinosa takes a step forward. If he thrusts now, his rapier will certainly spear the giant. The other sailors are closing in too. But the giant notices their movements. He spins around wildly and sees Espinosa. He glances between the master-at-arms and the rapier in his hand. He spins again searching for an escape, but the sailors are closing in now.

The giant lunges sideways, knocking two men aside as if they were made of straw. Panicked, the other sailors falter. Even Espinosa watches in shocked inaction as the giant leaps for the taffrail. But before he can vault off the ship, three men leap towards him, knocking him into the gunwale.

The giant takes a moment to recover but it is a moment too long and Espinosa crashes into him. He strikes the giant's head with the quillion of his rapier, sending him stumbling to the floor. More men pile on top of the native, pinning his arms and legs to the deck. The giant shouts and roars in his native tongue but he is completely overpowered.

Espinosa straps manacles around the giant's feet and he is hauled upright. Next chains are attached around his wrists. The huge native struggles against his bonds but even his immense strength cannot break them and he is led into the hold of the Trinidad. A giant made small, he disappears from view.

Elorriaga has finally died of his wounds. He lasted almost three months since Cartagena's savage attack. In what condition he has lived in the time that has passed, de Morales cannot know. He can only imagine what level of care Bustamante has provided him. The barber has no malice in him, but his is an unskilled and ruthless hand.

The entire crew are gathered on the frozen, snow-covered shale of the shore. Valderrama presides over the ceremony,

210

beseeching God to welcome Elorriaga to His kingdom.

But is God listening? Does God cast his eye to this forlorn beach with its empty hills, frozen harbour and two hundred lost souls scratching around waiting for the weather to improve? 'Eternal rest, grant unto thine child, O Lord, and let your perpetual light shine upon him. Through the mercy of God, rest in peace. Amen,' Valderrama finishes.

The words done with, two seamen, convicted during the trials, begin shovelling dirt, sand and snow onto the body of Elorriaga, resting in its shallow grave. Slowly, the pale face of the former ship's master is hidden from view.

The gathered crew linger at the graveside, sharing a reluctance to leave. They are like those flightless birds de Morales saw waddling on the rocky shores all those months ago, huddled together in the wind, eking out a pointless and pathetic existence.

The grave is almost filled and a makeshift cross is pressed into the earth and still, the crew remains. That is two crosses now on this lonely beach. Will the two become four before they depart? Will Magalhães permit the rotten remains of Mendoza and Quesada to be buried in a small act of Christian charity? Or will the Capitán General simply have their shrivelled remains tossed into the sea for the crabs to pick at?

'This is ridiculous.' Elcano breaks the silence. The men stop shovelling and look to Magalhães who stares at the half-buried corpse below him.

'Elorriaga would have lived,' Elcano says. 'His death was avoidable if de Morales had been able to care for him.'

A few of the men turn to de Morales, as if the mention of his name reminds them of his existence. The Capitán General continues to stare.

Pigafetta steps forward and jabs a finger at Elcano. 'You

ought to stay silent, you scoundrel. You ought already to be silent for eternity and hanging from the gibbet like your traitorous friends.' He signals to the various rotten parts of Mendoza and Quesada swinging in the wind from the yardarms.

Undaunted, Elcano ignores Pigafetta and continues. 'Those found guilty of the mutiny must be punished, Capitán General, but punish not the innocent. De Morales' absence from caring for the men is costing lives. I cannot keep my silence anymore. I will not.'

Elcano is becoming more animated. De Morales looks to Magalhães. The Capitán General still has not taken his eyes off the grave. Beside him, Espinosa and Barbosa are silent too, hinting at their agreement. How many more of Magalhães' comrades silently agree with Elcano?

Mesquita exhales deeply. 'Elorriaga stood by his captain in the face of certain violence. It is a travesty that his murderer lives yet he has passed.' The captain of the San Antonio turns to Magalhães and says, 'he ought to have received better care than he did.'

'This public criticism of Bustamante is unfair,' Pigafetta says, piping up again. 'His skills are more than adequate. Elorriaga bravely defended his Capitán General in the face of violence, which is something every man here ought to have done. His death was an honourable one.'

'His death was an agonising one,' scoffs Elcano.

'His death was by your hand not the Capitán General's,' Pigafetta says slowly. Elcano stares open-mouthed at the chronicler. The air is alight with anger.

Mesquita moves between the two men and, facing Magalhães, says, 'there is a reason we brought both a barber and a physician, is there not Capitán General?'

Magalhães' eyes slowly move from the corpse in the ground to his cousin's pleading face.

But, as the Capitán General turns to face Mesquita, his eyes are drawn beyond his cousin's shoulder. He stares across the frozen water to the far side of the harbour. A look of confusion settles on his face.

'O que em nome de Deus?' He says.

De Morales turns to see what the Capitán General is staring at so intently. Beyond the frigid waters of the harbour, beyond the shale and the ice and the snow and the swinging corpses and the snapping sails stand two haggard, emaciated men.

Chapter 15

July 1520

The Santiago is shipwrecked.

According to the two men, who stumbled exhausted, cold and famished from the bitter landscape, all but one of the ship's crew survived. They were washed up, freezing and disorientated, in a river mouth Serrano has named the Santa Cruz. The survivors quickly set to searching the shore, salvaging what they could from the wrecked ship.

Serrano ordered his men to construct a hut from what they were able to gather of the Santiago and therein the men took shelter, regaining their strength for several days. Finally, the captain asked for two volunteers to set out north in search of Puerto San Julián, the rest of the Armada and salvation.

The two men spent eleven ghastly days trudging and stumbling across the barren landscape and sleeping in sparse hedges that offered little shelter from the constant wind, freezing rain and driving snow. They survived by eating snow and ice and ate sodden hardtack salvaged from the wreckage.

The river, this Santa Cruz, they claim to be in an even more desolate location than Puerto San Julián. There are no fish in its waters, no animals to hunt, no shellfish nor crabs nor anything of sustenance anywhere to be found. With nothing but sodden hardtack and snow to keep them alive in such an inhospitable and frozen place, their days were numbered the very moment they stumbled from the sea. By this point, some fifteen days since the Santiago was shipwrecked, the remaining castaways are surely in a desperate state, if not dead already.

An immediate rescue is planned.

The injuries, deaths, disappearances and executions of the past months have left the Capitán General with a depleted and depressed crew, and so the condemned are released from their confinement. The armada now is desperate for crew and their skills and knowledge are far too important to be left chained up in the bowels of the Victoria. Every able-bodied man must pull his weight if they are to fight their way out of this brutal harbour, survive in the wild ocean beyond and rescue the stricken crew of the Santiago.

Despite the long months of hard labour, the remaining four ships of the Armada de Molucca are far from ready to depart. They are in a constant state of disrepair and every day since the overwintering began has added a new problem to be solved, new damage to be fixed. For the first time in months, Puerto San Julián is alive with activity as the ships are stocked, repaired and freed from the ice that has frozen their sails and rigging stiff.

The Concepción, abandoned and without a captain since Quesada's execution three months ago, has spent the last months being slowly crushed as the harbour froze over around it. Sailors go to it now. They relight the braziers and begin melting ice and snow in cauldrons above them. While they slowly come to the boil, other sailors climb down onto the ice and begin hacking away at it with pickaxes. Once the ice is broken up, the boiled water in the cauldrons is thrown overboard and the Concepción is slowly released from its icy prison. Once freed, the ship is put under the command of Carvalho. There are many other men far more capable than the pilot, Elcano and Gomes are the obvious choices. But they are no friends of Magalhães and their crimes have clearly not yet been forgotten nor forgiven. The Capitán General's long memory for offence rears its head once more.

On the shore, Magalhães asks for two dozen volunteers to travel to the castaways overland. The fifteen-league journey that took the two survivors eleven days to complete ought to take the healthier men just four days or less. They will carry with them food, blankets and dry kindling for fires. The Capitán General assembles the entire crew of the armada on the beach beside the rickety smokehouse. They stand shivering and kicking snow, inching towards the warm smoke chugging out from the leaky shack. Barbosa is the first to volunteer and another eleven men quickly follow suit.

'One of you is to be replaced by de Morales,' Magalhães says. 'I want the physician to accompany you.' Startled, de Morales looks up. It is the first time he has heard his name pass the lips of the Capitán General in months. He had accepted the life Pigafetta had forced him into – one of exclusion, where no matter what he did, good or ill, Magalhães would not lower himself to acknowledge him. 'Serrano and his men will surely be in need of his services,' Magalhães continues. 'Bustamante's skill will suffice here for the time being.'

But the Capitán General is right. The survivors of the Santiago will certainly need medical help and Bustamante lacks the knowledge to treat them properly. Could Elcano's act of defiance at Elorriaga's grave this morning actually have had an impact on Magalhães? Even if it did, the Capitán General would never admit it.

'You will leave tomorrow,' Magalhães says. He turns to Espinosa at his side. 'I want you to gather everything the men will need.' The master-at-arms nods and the Capitán General limps away across the shale towards a waiting skiff.

It dawns on de Morales that the Magalhães could be singling him out for special punishment, that this is another form of retribution for his perceived betrayal. Maybe it is a punishment. Maybe de Morales will die in the frozen wasteland between here and the wreck of the Santiago. But, if he does, at least he will die away from Magalhães and his wretched fleet of doomed ships.

The group dissipates. Elcano has stayed behind. He moves beside de Morales. 'Lucky you,' he says. 'I do not think it will be enjoyable, but it cannot be much worse than what we have endured. You will write to me, won't you?' He adds sarcastically.

'I cannot deny the prospect of getting away from this place fills my heart with joy,' de Morales says.

'Serrano and his men must have been through hell,' Elcano says seriously, his face set with concern. 'To fall into the ocean in this freezing place without shelter and warmth. .

.' Elcano trails off. He stares to the south, the direction from which the two survivors came. 'Who can say how many that place has claimed in the days it has taken those men to travel here.'

De Morales follows Elcano's gaze across the frozen harbour to the expanse of tundra stretching to the horizon and the gravity of the journey hits him. The flutter of joy in his heart at leaving the armada turns cold dread.

The following morning is damp and heavy with fog but the calmest they have yet witnessed since arriving in this place. During the night, the sails of the ships have refrozen. While sailors climb the masts and smash the ice from the canvas and shrouds, de Morales, Barbosa and the other volunteers prepare to depart. Their bags, already packed for them by Espinosa's men, are piled up on the shore. They are heavily laden with all manner of supplies, both for their journey and for the castaways.

De Morales lifts his leather shoulder bag packed with his own supply of food, dry wood, a rough blanket and a few strips of linen for dressing wounds onto his shoulders. He cannot possibly carry his heavy medical bag with him – all the tools and medicines would weigh him down too much on the unknown journey ahead. If any of the shipwrecked survivors need surgery, they will have to wait until the rest of the fleet arrives.

Before they leave, Barbosa turns to Magalhães and bids him farewell and good fortune. Then, one by one, the men climb into waiting skiffs, lined up along the frozen shore of the harbour. The rowers push off and they set out for the far side, barely visible through the mist.

As the skiff stutters across the glacial water, pushing huge chunks of ice from its path, de Morales looks to the mouth of the harbour and the ocean raging against the cliffs beyond. Shrouded in fog, vague and indefinite, stands the island where Cartagena and de la Reina are marooned. He will almost certainly never see them again.

Ice stretches further into the harbour on the far shore and so the volunteers climb out of the skiffs a hundred yards from the beach. The skiffs, emptied of their cargo, turn back quickly and the two dozen men begin their journey, melting into the mist.

In silent determination, they walk for three days. To cover the ground quicker they continue long past sunset, stumbling over the loose stones and pebbles of this ruined wasteland. When full dark finally comes, they find some haggard shrub or lonely tree, stunted and bent by the relentless wind. There they lay down for a night of restless sleep with nothing between them and the chill air and tundra but their meagre blankets. Then they rise each morning, shivering and already exhausted.

The land rose steadily once they left Puerto San Julián, but it has now plateaued. Ahead, it drops off once more, descending sharply and presumably meeting the river where the crew of Santiago suffer, frozen and starving on its banks. As they have continued inland the air has grown colder and the ground, now, is covered with a thin smear of crusty snow and ice. Before them, the bleakness is absolute. Even the stunted shrubs that provided some small shelter have disappeared. Tonight, they will be cold and exposed.

If the wind was constant in Puerto San Julián, it is

relentless here. Without the surrounding hills of the harbour, they are utterly exposed and battered by the pitiless gales, blustering and blowing from all sides at once. Every so often a stinging volley of frozen hail or icy rain will launch an assault upon them.

As he walks, de Morales turns over the events of the past months. With each trudging step his anger rises and with each blast of buffeting wind it threatens to overspill. He looks ahead at Barbosa, head bowed as he leads the group, and mutters curses under his breath. With the armada far behind them now, the supernumerary stands as the only reminder of Magalhães' despotism.

Worrying someone may overhear him, he turns away from Barbosa, looking to the west. As far as the eye can see, the same dreary terrain continues on and on, endless and empty. His eye drifts to the horizon, searching for silhouettes of more giants like that taken captive by Magalhães. But eventually, ground down by the monotony of the landscape and the relentless wind, he gives up, choosing instead to hunch over and stare at the pitted earth at his feet.

The only hint of any other life in this vast desolation is the plaintive cry of an eagle that has been following the group for the past two days. It hovers in the air erratically, buffeted by the wind and tossing from side to side, waiting for one of them to perish when it will feast upon the corpse before the body is frozen to the ground.

The eagle has disappeared and the sun set an hour ago. Since then, de Morales, in the centre of the group, has stumbled and staggered over the loose stones and ice. But now full night has almost come and they can continue no further.

'We will rest here for the night,' Barbosa says.

They are standing in a shallow basin, carpeted with rough moss, sharp stones and blasted grass. It is a sorry place to sleep, but with no shelter for miles around this small depression in the earth is the best they can hope for.

De Morales drops to the frozen ground and shrugs the shoulder bag from his aching back. He can do nothing more then than sit slumped forward, hugging his arms to his body, holding desperately to what small warmth he can. Though each man has carried dry wood with him from the armada, they light no fire. Partly, it is in anticipation of the survivors of the Santiago, whose need will certainly be far greater than their own, but also it is in fear of natives. Though they have seen none, surely there are more giants in their place and surely they wonder where their comrade has disappeared to. Though it is easy to assume so, they are not alone in this corner of the world.

Barbosa, silhouetted against the horizon, appears and kneels beside him. He offers de Morales two broken biscuits of hardtack and the flagon of fortified wine. De Morales takes a mouthful of the wine. The warming alcohol hits his throat and sends tingly roots of glowing warmth through his torso, spreading down to his weary legs. He nibbles disinterestedly at the hardtack.

'We may reach the Santiago tomorrow,' Barbosa says.

'But what will we find when we get there?' De Morales asks. 'Forty half-dead men huddled together for warmth. Or simply their frozen corpses?'

'I like not your pessimism,' Barbosa says.

'Perhaps I would not be so pessimistic had I more energy.' De Morales' anger rises, mixing with the indignation he has carried since the mutiny and Pigafetta's leering boasts of the part he played. 'Perhaps had I not been worked half to death in that frigid hell Magalhães landed us in for three months, I would have more energy.'

'Perhaps had you not taken part in a mutiny you would not have been punished,' Barbosa fires back.

The final straw. 'You do not truly believe I played any role in that uprising?' When Barbosa does not reply he continues. 'How could I? You are no unintelligent man. You heard Magalhães send me to the San Antonio. Christs' wounds, you yourself almost sent me to the Victoria. You know I had no contact with Mendoza or Cartagena or Quesada or any of those fools before that night. Did you even speak with Mesquita? I removed a tooth from his skull not an hour before that futile rebellion took place. Why would I bother if I intended to mutiny against him anyway? Why did I not give Rebêlo away as soon as the mutineers climbed aboard the San Antonio? Why-'

'I know, de Morales,' Barbosa says firmly. 'It is obvious to anyone you had no part in it. I think you know why Magalhães is punishing you, though I do not. Whatever is the cause, Magalhães has kept it to himself.'

Though it is a relief to finally hear Barbosa admit his true thoughts on the Capitán General, it is not enough to quell the resentment that is overcoming de Morales. He can sense the faces of the other men turned towards him, but he continues, nonetheless.

'The cause is simple. All across the Great Ocean, Pigafetta poured poison in Magalhães' ear against me. All because I did not weigh up to whatever standards that weasel has. As for the mutiny, I was in the wrong place at the wrong time. The Capitán General's sense of betrayal is nothing but that, a sense. His obstinacy will be his downfall.'

'Is that a threat, de Morales?' Barbosa's accusation is without any real resolution.

'Call it a premonition,' he replies. 'I wish no harm to the Capitán General. But you know as well as I do that if he continues this despotic rule of his, this whole endeavour will unwind.'

Barbosa falls silent.

Though he does not reply, de Morales hopes that, by hearing it told to him so bluntly, Barbosa might try to soften Magalhães' iron grip on the armada, to right the course the armada seems to be sailing in. There has been enough death and suffering already.

That is, of course, if they ever see the armada again. The fleet could already be dashed upon the rocks somewhere. Their bloated corpses washed up on the freezing shore in some desolate place to be feasted upon by fearsome sea monsters and the disappeared eagle.

Without a word, Barbosa rises and moves on to the next man, passing him the flagon of wine. In his anger, de Morales has voiced thoughts he knows could get him executed like Quesada. But he also knows he is not the only man in the armada to harbour these thoughts. Certainly, Elcano shares them, as does Gomes and doubtless most of the other mutineers Magalhães did not execute. But does Barbosa's silence speak volumes? Could he, one of the Capitán General's staunchest allies, share those thoughts?

De Morales slumps to the ground, feels its chill seep into his body and tries his best to get some rest.

He does not sleep, instead drifting in that listlessness

between awake and asleep. More than the howling wind snatching at his body every moment, it is his impotent anger that keeps him awake.

He breaks his fast with another mouthful of fortified wine and the group set out on their way, nibbling at hardtack as the milky sun slowly rises behind thick clouds. Hours of dull daylight and relentless wind pass as they make their way in single file, stretched out across the miserable landscape.

The ground falls away and they begin their descent down from the plateau where they camped last night. In the distance, perhaps some three leagues away, a wide river materialises in the murky landscape. The dirty water, sludgy and ugly even from this distance, meanders across an empty plain ahead, stretching far into the west until it blends into the smudge of the horizon. On either bank, a small copse of brown trees and shrubs huddles together, reaching down to the shoreline. This is surely the Santa Cruz, the river baptised by Serrano, from where the two survivors left. If it is, they are almost upon the survivors, or whatever remains of them.

As they make their slow progress, drawing closer to the river, de Morales realises that what he first took to be the grove of trees is actually a precarious hut built by the survivors surrounded by the salvaged wreckage of the Santiago. The ship's structure lies scattered across the ground like a pecked corpse, its huge ribs jut out of the shoreline, piercing the freezing air. The remnants of a sail flap limply in the wind. Scattered across the ground are chunks of wood, broken crates, smashed chests, all of it destroyed almost beyond recognition.

Others in the group have recognised what is before them. They begin picking up their pace until they are almost jogging down to the shore of the river, eager to find the survivors.

With his heavy pack and aching legs, de Morales begins to fall behind the younger and fitter men in the group. Barbosa leads the charge and dashes onwards. He calls out Serrano's name but only silence greets his calls.

The shack is a sorry sight. It is conical and clearly hastily built by amateur and frozen hands. Its warped walls are patched together with random chunks of wood, dusted in frost, from the wreckage and it slants heavily to one side. Canvas sails, frozen stiff, have been slung over the roof. The whole sorry structure reeks of desperation, of men doing what little they are capable of to stave off death.

Finally, de Morales reaches the shoreline, joining the men already there. The hut is before them and there is no one to greet them. The crew of the Santiago are dead, then. Frozen by the relentless cold or, more hauntingly still, murdered by savage natives.

The shore of the river is still and silent, with nothing but an eerie sense of lifelessness filling the void. On the far side of the river lies the majority of the wreck of the Santiago. The huge, curved hull rises from the slushy waters of the river like a tombstone as slabs of ice and slush slide past.

The group of would-be saviours stand before the shack, no one daring to step forward and see what they all know is inside: the frozen remains of the shipwrecked crew.

Barbosa cautiously approaches the rickety shelter. He reaches for the strip of canvas that serves as a door. He kicks the stones from its base that hold it in place and, in one quick movement, wrenches the canvas aside.

The sight that greets them is horrifying. Clumped together, like corpses on a battlefield, lie the crew of the Santiago. From the opening light spills into the shack, glinting off an ice-filled cauldron in its centre.

The cadavers come to life, squirming and crawling over one another. In motionless shock, de Morales watches living men untangle themselves from the pile of carcasses. Their clothes creak and snap as the ice that has frozen them stiff gives way under their movements.

'Serrano,' Barbosa calls, 'are you here?' When he receives no answer, the captain repeats the question, louder this time. 'Captain Serrano. It is Duarte. The Capitán General sent us for your salvation.'

The muddled mass of living corpses stirs and a thin, haggard figure crawls out of the confusion of limbs and frozen cloth. The figure rises slowly and the face that greets them is drawn and pale. The beard, frozen in places, is scraggly and stained with frozen drool. It is Serrano. Miraculously, he lives.

The captain tumbles closer, drawing nearer to Barbosa. He has tears in his eyes and a large cut, swollen and crusted in old blood, on his right temple. He reaches out and, almost as if trying to convince himself the figure he sees before him is real and not imagined, grabs Barbosa tightly. Serrano tries to speak but his voice fails him. He falls to the ground. Hugging Barbosa's legs, the captain weeps.

Astonishingly, not one of the survivors of the Santiago has died, despite their awful condition. Beyond the fact they are alive, however, it is difficult to learn anything else about their health from them. They are too cold, too near death and too exhausted to tell de Morales of what injuries, pains or illnesses they suffer. He will learn nothing from them until they are fed.

Barbosa orders the other men to pass around the flagons

of fortified wine they have carried with them. The shipwrecked men snatch at them, taking greedy gulps as it spills into their beards and over their chests. Some immediately vomit up what they have drunk.

'Give them water, not wine,' de Morales says desperately. 'Wine is too much for their shrunken bellies to take.' He looks around the sorry shelter, his eyes settling on the cauldron, half-filled with frozen water, in the centre. 'Someone light a fire and fill the cauldron with snow and ice. Let the water boil, these men need hot water to drink.'

They follow his orders, using the dry wood they have carried across the plains from Puerto San Julián. The fire is slow to take and weak once it has, but it is something. The survivors huddle around it like an altar. The ice melts, the water boils and the men take sips from it. Gradually the shipwrecked men become more lucid. Still shivering, Serrano begins to explain what occurred once the two men set out to find the fleet.

'I sent men across the land searching for any food, but this is an unhappy and empty place. Nothing of any nourishment could be found. For the first few days after we were wrecked, we had some luck catching shellfish nearer the coastline. But our luck did not last long and there were no fish to be found in the river. There were some root vegetables, though not many, that we shared. We brought back even the smallest branch we found in hopes that it would dry eventually and we could light a fire. We even slept on them to dry them out, but it did little to help. Nothing would take to the flame. On the fifth day after I sent the men to find the armada, a storm of ferocious brutality hit.

'If a storm raged here, we knew nothing of it in Puerto San Julián,' Barbosa says. 'There cannot be more than fifteen leagues between here and the armada and yet the weather seems to be utterly different.'

'Indeed,' Serrano says. 'It seems the storms may be localised by some phenomenon we cannot fathom.' The two captains silently consider this before Serrano continues his story.

'We took refuge in here, but our rickety shelter offered little protection. The wind blasted with such barbarity it passed right through the walls as if they weren't there. Eventually, we simply gave up. Even once the storm had passed and the wind had calmed as much as it ever does, none of us had the strength or will to move. We huddled together for warmth, eating ice and snow from the ground. I think we were close to death. You have saved our lives. God bless you all.'

Serrano falls into a fit of shivering tears. The shipwrecked captain slumps into misery as he says, 'I let down my men. Had you not come when you did, we would surely have died.'

At this, Serrano breaks down once again. He is completely crippled by the experience and blames himself for something that so clearly was not his fault. Any man in his position could not claim to be able to act differently.

The Santiago's survivors silently warm themselves by the fire, drinking steaming water and eating rations of salted fish and hardtack. Their blank eyes staring into the eternity they faced, had their saviours arrived even a day later.

Dusk is falling now. The shadows in the shack lengthen, becoming deeper, the faces of the gathered men more obscure. Outside, the wind moans while inside the small fire crackles and sputters beneath the bubbling cauldron.

'We should rest,' Barbosa says.

The next day and Barbosa sends some of the men who travelled from Puerto San Julián to salvage what they can from the shore. Others he sends into the steppes and hills nearby, hoping they will have some luck hunting or fishing with crude poles made from the wreck of the Santiago. The survivors, meanwhile, stay inside the shack, huddling around the fire.

By de Morales' estimate, they came upon the survivors on the last possible day. Another night in this frigid shack would have finished many of them off. But now they have eaten, drank and had a passable night's sleep beside a fire, they are far more lucid and able to answer his questions.

He begins with Serrano. The captain is cold to his very core but reasonably healthy despite his ordeal, besides the gash on his forehead. De Morales sets to work cleaning the cut on Serrano's temple with a small strip of linen dipped into the cauldron. As he does so, Barbosa tells Serrano the armada will be here soon.

'They will not make it,' Serrano says, his eyes wide. 'They will hit the same squalls that wrecked us. I only hope they can turn back.'

'Things may go differently for them,' Barbosa says.

'You were not there,' Serrano says. 'Almost as soon as we left Puerto San Julián, we were beaten by unrelenting winds.' Serrano winces as de Morales holds the soaked linen to the gash. 'But because the wind mainly blew against the stern of the ship, I thought it unwise to turn about and return to the harbour. After all, the wind was sending us in the direction we wished to go. At night we dropped anchor offshore, certain the wind and churning sea would tear the anchor from the ship and we would be destroyed. But we were not. When morning came, we continued onwards and the following two days of our journey were much alike, not without difficulty, but hardly worse than what we had yet faced. But on the third day, something changed in the air. The storm suddenly became more volatile, the wind more ferocious. It built and built until it was a gale battering us from all sides seemingly at once.'

The dried blood around the gash on Serrano's forehead has loosened now and de Morales begins wiping it away. The wound is quite clean and already scabbing over.

'By this point, we were just north of the estuary of this river and being relentlessly battered by the wind. I had already ordered the mainsail to be stowed but suddenly the rigging gave way. The mainsail unfurled, catching the wind. We were powerless. The ship pivoted to the port side, turning us away from the river mouth and heeling at such an angle I was sure we would capsize. But then the wind changed direction, catching the mainsail and wrenching the ship in an about-turn. The men stumbled and fell. I cannot be sure, but I think that is when Diego Barrasa was swept overboard and died.'

'Finally, the mast gave way, tearing itself from the hull. We were tossed and turned, at the mercy of the wind and the current and taking water on quickly. All was chaos, hopeless. I do not know how but, as we sank, we were swept towards the coastline and smashed to pieces against the rocks. God only knows how just one man died.'

The terror of the shipwreck is palpable in Serrano's voice as he explains the ordeal. The lasting impact it has had on him is harrowing. The visions it casts in de Morales' mind of the powerlessness of man in the face of nature's brutal indifference sends his pulse racing.

Barbosa touches Serrano's shoulder. 'Be of good heart,' he

says, 'if you came to this place in just three days, then the armada will be here soon. Then we shall be gone.'

'But will the armada survive the waters?' Serrano asks desperately, his eyes wide with fear. 'I have never known such violence in a storm before. It seemed to come from all sides at once.'

'The Capitán General will liberate you,' Barbosa says, 'he will find a way.'

'But there is more bad news,' Serrano says. Barbosa furrows his brow. 'The Capitán General feared we may hit storms, so to combat the pitching he ordered more ballast be added to the Santiago. We moved food and brasilwood to the hull to weigh the ship down.'

Barbosa's face drops. 'How did I not know of this?'

'Magalhães had the supplies moved to the Santiago when the ships were being cleaned by the prisoners.' Serrano looks at de Morales, his eyes filled with worry.

'I knew nothing of this,' de Morales says. 'Other prisoners must have done that work.'

'Maybe he forgot to tell you, maybe he felt he did not need to. Either way, all those supplies are lost.'

Barbosa slides a hand through his hair in exasperation. He sighs heavily before saying, 'he could not have known.' But the defence of his father-in-law is half-hearted and unconvincing.

With Serrano seen to, de Morales moves onto the rest of the shipwrecked crew. Almost all the survivors are suffering with a chill in their bodies that no amount of outside heat seems to warm.

De Morales has seen this affliction, having treated it

successfully several times. In Castile, it seems to chiefly afflict the elderly. But in this place, the cold has penetrated even the strongest body. A cabin boy is the worst stricken by it, perhaps because of his size. As the first full day since they arrived passes, de Morales asks the men who came with him from Puerto San Julián to cover the survivors of the wreck in their blankets. When they sleep tonight, everyone must huddle close together for warmth.

He tells the survivors of the wreck to rub their chests to warm themselves from their centres. The heat will spread to their extremities. As he passes among the huddled and shivering crew, he notices the Frenchman whose broken hand he mended on the shores of Rio de Janeiro. He is not even sure how long ago that was now. The months have drawn on, endless and empty since the mutiny.

As he approaches him, de Morales notices the stump where the Frenchman's mended hand ought to be. It has been cruelly severed just above the wrist. So cruelly, in fact, that the shattered bone is visible beneath the skin. 'What happened to your hand?' he asks. 'Did it not mend?'

The man looks forlornly at the stump and sighs deeply. 'It turned gangrenous as we sailed south beside the jungle,' his Spanish is accented heavily. 'I could bear the pain no longer. Bustamante removed it for me.' From the tears welling in the corner of the Frenchman's eye, de Morales can tell it is a painful memory.

'This happened in Puerto San Julián?' He asks. 'After the mutiny?'

'Yes, señor.'

A rising sickness wells in his stomach. While de Morales stirred pitch or scrubbed shellfish from the hull of some ship, Bustamante was hacking away at this man's hand. He can see it now. The streaming blood, steaming in the cold, the cracking bone and the hand flung into the sea when the barber was done with his bloody work. But Bustamante, for all his ignorant hacking, cannot be blamed. The blame lies at the feet of the Capitán General and his hard-headed obstinacy.

'I am sorry,' he says, 'I did my best.'

The Frenchman stares at the stump. 'You are blameless,' he says

He is kind to say that. De Morales did his best when he mended the hand in the balmy heat off the coast of Terra do Brasil. Sometimes things simply do not go your way. But if the Capitán General had made him available to care for the crew, he would have ensured the Frenchman's amputation was performed in a kinder manner.

Unsurprisingly, the hunters return that night empty-handed. A few dozen shellfish have been gathered but no fish or animals were caught and no vegetables were found despite what Serrano had said. They eat a meagre meal of smoked fish, hardtack and a mouthful each of the fortified wine as well as cups of hot water from the cauldron at the centre of the hut.

At the very least, de Morales thinks as he chews on the gristly fish, water will not be a problem. While the snow on the ground lasts, they can use that and, if it ever does thaw, river water can be boiled. For all the suffering of the journey to the castaways, he is glad they did not burn any of the wood they brought. It will not last long as it is and the inaction of waiting here for the rest of the armada will turn deadly as soon as it does run out.

They pass the night in a huddled mass in the centre of the shelter. The wind picks up, whips at the walls, whistles through the holes and sends the weak flame of the fire dancing. Fearing an attack by natives or that the armada could sail right past them if it comes after dark, Barbosa sets a guard of two men, wrapped tightly in blankets, to stare out into the empty darkness of the night.

At some point, it must have snowed heavily because when de Morales awakens the following morning, the ground is coated in a crusty layer of thick snow. A huge snowdrift has been blown up against the western edge of the shelter, engulfing it almost entirely to the roof. The night's weather does not bode well for the armada.

Sailors wander around the makeshift shelter, trying to warm their frozen limbs. Barbosa orders several to check the improvised nets that were left in the river mouth overnight. They are empty. Next, he sends several hunting parties into the surrounding country.

Barbosa has not given up hope that there must be something in this place. God, he says, would not have delivered Serrano and his men from such a violent storm only to leave them to starve to death in this wasteland. But, more than that, by sending the men out in search of food he is keeping them active. They may not like being out in the cold, but if they remain motionless, they will quickly die in the freezing wind.

De Morales is still making his rounds of the shipwrecked men. He comes to one whose fingers on his left hand are severely frostbitten. It seems he was one of the men tasked with building the shelter. While everyone else was able to dry themselves, he continued working in driving rain, wind and sleet.

The sailor's hand is reddened and swollen but the ends of his fingers are pale and corpse-like. The nails of three of the fingers are beginning to come free of their beds and the skin is wrinkled, as if it has been kept overlong in water. Despite the state of his hand, the sailor has no feeling of pain whatsoever. Just a phantom sense that the hand is still there but separate from him.

The cauldron in the centre of the shelter has almost been emptied of water. De Morales refills it with snow and ice from the drift outside then stirs the fire beneath it, trying to coax out whatever small flame he can from the charred embers.

He plans to soak a piece of cloth in the water and wrap the stricken hand, thereby gently warming it back to life. He tells the sailor to wait and do nothing until he returns, then leaves the shelter and heads towards the torn remains of one of the Santiago's sails.

He is just bending down to cut the sail when a loud crack breaks through the air followed by three more. Echoes reverberate around the landscape, rebounding off the empty hills and rippling the silty river. The men working and fishing on the shore stop what they are doing and look at one another. Their brows furrowed, they strain their ears against the howling wind.

Seconds drag by and still the men stand fixed in place. Just as several men begin to rise and look around them, the sound explodes again across the landscape but this time it is louder. The colossal boom rattles de Morales' heart against his rib cage.

'Canons.' Cries Barbosa. He bursts from the shelter,

dashing towards the river's estuary.

The men drop what they are doing and look about them quickly, searching. From the north, four men sent to hunt appear at the crest of a hill, running and waving their arms frantically. They bound down the slope toward the river. 'The Armada,' they cry. 'God be praised, we are rescued.'

Smiles break across the faces of the men gathered on the river's edge. They whoop and holler as the survivors of the Santiago stagger from the shelter. Shielding their eyes from the light, they lurch towards the sea.

De Morales sees a sight he never thought he would welcome. First, the very highest point of a mainmast appears above the land to the north. Slowly, the rest of the mast is revealed as the shape of a ship is drawn towards the river. Its billowing, triumphant sails and the faded flag of Castile snap in the wind. It is the Trinidad. From the bowsprit, Magalhães' faded ensign flickers. Another volley of cannon fire cracks through the air as, following close behind, the Concepción comes into view, then the San Antonio and, finally, the Victoria.

The main decks of all four ships teem with men. They pull at the rigging, climb the shrouds and run back and forth. Below them, the sea is a tumult. The ships rock and pitch from side to side as the Trinidad leads the armada into the river's mouth. The Capitán General is there, standing on the forecastle of the flagship. He bellows orders at his men, directing the ship as it zig-zags this way and that, avoiding the jagged rocks that claimed the Santiago.

De Morales cannot deny that the Armada de Molucca, that cursed fleet of disfigured, patched-up ships and exhausted men, brings joy to his heart as he watches their anchors crash into the river. Serrano dashes past him. The wrecked captain stops on the shoreline, his breath pluming into the air, and hails the Capitán General. His castaway crew gather around him, finally finding salvation from their torment.

Chapter 16

October 1520

The Victoria's skiff is slowly lowered into the rushing murk of the Santa Cruz River and Espinosa is rowed ashore by two sailors. Barbosa rushes to him and the two men clap hands and embrace briefly. Espinosa pulls away and begins shouting at the survivors and the men de Morales travelled with from Puerto San Julián standing on the shore. 'Return to your ships.' he calls, spinning around on the spot. 'If you were aboard the Santiago, come first to the Victoria where you will be reassigned.'

Stragglers of the shipwrecked survivors are still slowly filtering from their makeshift shelter, hugging blankets around themselves to ward off the wind. They stagger and falter but all head slowly towards Espinosa, still barking orders from the shore.

Now more skiffs, filled with sailors, have been lowered from the other ships and are making their turbulent way toward the shore. They surge into the shale and the men spill from them, quickly fanning out across the river's edge. They begin sifting through the wreckage of the Santiago and the chaos of timber and rope beside the shelter while others row to the far shore. They lift anything of any worth from the debris and begin forming piles of various materials on the shore. One for wood, another for iron, more for rope and canvas and clothing and food.

Barbosa is moving now among the chaos of sailors and survivors repeating Espinosa's commands. He notices de Morales watching him and approaches the surgeon. 'The Capitán General has ordered that you be reassigned to the Victoria,' he says. It is the first time he has directly spoken with de Morales since their argument, but his tone is light as if all offence has been forgiven. 'You must collect your belongings now and move there immediately.'

He is free, then. Free from the Trinidad and the Capitán General and his horde of sycophants. Free of Pigafetta's schemes and Valderrama's sanctimony.

But what has he been freed into?

The Victoria stands in the centre of the Santa Cruz River, sludge and silt streaming past its greasy hull. From here on the desolate shore, after five days trudging across the tundra and sleeping pressed against a stranger for warmth, it appears almost welcoming. But de Morales knows what awaits him. He knows every knot of its blackened hull is filled with curses and hexes and ill omens. Worse, still, he knows what it will become.

De Morales climbs aboard the Trinidad and gets the sense immediately that he is not welcome there. The crew are busy working, but he feels their sidelong, suspicious glances turn on him as passes across the main deck. He speeds up, wanting to collect his belongings and be gone from the flagship as quickly as possible.

He pushes open the door to his former cabin and finds the room in chaos. The beds have been flipped over and Pigafetta's desk and stool are gone. His heart sinks as he takes in the ransacked mess that was once his medical supplies. The chests and crates of balms, liniments and lotions have been smashed open. The herbs hanging from the ceiling have shrivelled and rotten and the sacks of spares are torn and empty. The tiny vials of mercury and opium have been stolen. What vinegar the Casa de Contratación provided has also been plundered, leaving only a small amount to swill around the bottom of the quart barrel now resting on its side. Even the jar of quince he had so carefully rationed has been all but emptied. He lifts it now, the once overpowering scent of oranges that transported him back to Sevilla has long since faded but a small amount of quince remains.

The only saving grace is that his tools have not been taken nor tampered with. The case has been carefully placed in the corner of the room, a last outpost of calm amid the chaos. He opens it and finds all the tools inside although some are crusted with old blood. Bustamante must have been using them. With a sigh, de Morales hopes that with better tools, the workman's skill was improved.

He rises among the wreckage and his mood shifts from

despair to anger. How could the Capitán General have allowed this to happen? Whatever grudge he has against de Morales personally, he should have ensured the medical supplies were kept safe. For a moment, he considers confronting Magalhães but what would be the point? The Capitán General's comrades would close ranks and, more than likely, accuse him of conspiracy.

He finds the lid to the jar of quince, reseals it and puts it into a canvas bag he finds on the floor. He finds the few remains of dried herbs that still have life in them and adds them to the bag. Then he lifts his case of surgical tools and turns his back on the Trinidad.

Now, on the Victoria, de Morales is given a tiny cabin in the rear of the upper hold. Elcano comes to welcome him aboard. He stands in the doorway, a look of concern on his face. 'You cannot practice here,' he says.

'It is no bad thing,' de Morales says. 'I have so few supplies now there ought to be room enough.'

'And where will you operate?' Elcano asks, 'Upon the floor?'

De Morales looks again at the tiny cabin. Between the walls and himself, there is little room for another man, let alone one struggling and writhing in pain. With no window and a door that opens into the hold, the light is inadequate too. Any surgeries he might be needed to perform will have to be done entirely by candlelight, even in the middle of the day. 'It is not ideal,' he concedes. He sniffs, taking in the miasmic reek filled with mildew, rot and mould. 'The airs are unfavourable.'

'Take mine.'

'You room? I couldn't-' de Morales begins but Elcano cuts him off with a wave of his hand.

'You will do as you are ordered to,' he says in mock vexation. 'Seriously, you need a better cabin than this. You cannot work in these conditions. Besides, Amaya will appreciate being closer to her prey.'

'As long as you are sure.'

'Then we are agreed,' Elcano lifts de Morales' case.

The two men leave the cabin, making their way up to the main deck of the Victoria. They step into the chill air, the breeze catching their heavy overcoats. 'Barbosa is to be our captain,' Elcano says. 'And I, our pilot. My post is right outside your cabin door,' he says, nodding to the whipstaff.

'Happy news,' de Morales says, smiling.

Elcano enters the cabin, puts the case down on the small wooden bed and sees Amaya lying beneath it. He leans down and pulls her out from the shadows. De Morales takes in the room, it is so much like his old one on the Trinidad. 'You do not think you ought to have been promoted, given your experience?'

'Magalhães will never promote me,' Elcano says. 'You need look no further than Carvalho and Espinosa being given captaincies on the journey from Puerto San Julián. Carvalho, for all his incompetence, at least has experience at sea, but Espinosa? The man is little more than a mercenary. You've more experience than him at sea.'

De Morales can sense Elcano's disappointment. He was only made a mere pilot in the armada under the king's orders to repay the debt Elcano owed the crown. But had he been able to apply like everyone else, Elcano would certainly have been in contention for a captaincy.

'At least you are still the pilot.' The conciliatory words are empty, but what more can he say? They both know why it is this way. Though they have served their punishment and have both proven they are loyal, at least to the expedition if not to its leader, Magalhães will never forget the mutiny nor forgive those he blames for it.

Elcano sighs heavily and shifts his feet. He scratches Amaya's ears. 'Come, we have been evicted' he says, winking at de Morales. He turns and almost walks headlong into Barbosa. 'Well met, captain,' he says, startled.

Barbosa casts his eye around the cabin, taking in the surgical case on the bed and the cat in Elcano's arms. His brow furrows. 'Change of scenery, de Morales?' He asks.

'We have swapped cabins,' Elcano says. 'A surgeon could not work below in the hold.'

'Very well,' Barbosa says. De Morales, used for months aboard the Trinidad, was prepared for bluster and complaints from the captain. Barbosa's nonchalance is welcome. 'As long as you are content with a longer walk to your post, Elcano.' Barbosa's face becomes more serious before he continues. 'I bear bad news, I am afraid. We are to continue to take shelter here. Fernão worries the storms will claim more ships.'

'Then are we to go ashore?' Elcano asks.

'No. Every man must remain on his own ship until Fernão gives the order for us to depart. Parties will be sent ashore to hunt and find firewood, but only under the direction of their captains. There are to be no unauthorised crossings between ships.'

De Morales catches Elcano's eye. It is obvious why Magalhães would give such an order. He is taking steps to ensure another uprising cannot take place which can only mean one thing: he intends to remain here for some time. De Morale's mind jumps to the frostbitten sailor he left in the shelter on the shore. In the excitement of the fleet's return, he had completely forgotten about him.

He asks now, 'what of the survivors of the Santiago? Many still need my care.'

'They have already been reassigned to the other ships. Serrano has already taken over command of the Concepción and most of the survivors of the Santiago have gone there with him.'

'Then I must go there at once,' de Morales says, already reaching for his case.

But Barbosa holds up a hand, stopping him. 'For the time being, you must remain on the Victoria. Any injured or unwell sailors will be brought here where you can treat them.'

'All the better that you have a larger cabin,' Elcano says.

'So how long are we to remain here?' De Morales asks.

'Until the weather improves,' Barbosa says.

Elcano looks over Barbosa's shoulder to the growing clouds on the southern horizon. 'Then we may be here some time, captain,' he says.

His first patient is the sailor with the frostbitten hand. The sailor comes to him now, cradling his arm already wrapped in dirty rags. The sailor seems to be carrying a fever for his eyes are unfocused and his step unsteady. It could be he is still suffering from exposure to the freezing temperatures, or it could be something much worse.

Inside his cabin, by the light of a candle, de Morales peels away the rags from the hand and gasps. 'What did you do?' He asks. The skin is livid, pocked with weeping blisters.

The sailor stares dumbly at his ruined hand. Finally, he says, 'the water was boiling, I thought it would help. I thought it would bring my hand back to life.'

De Morales is horrified at himself for not returning to the sailor. With effort, he pushes the self-recrimination from his mind. 'You felt nothing when you did this?' He asks.

The sailor shakes his head, still staring at the hand. There is no sadness in his eyes and he has none of the despondency the Frenchman had when he looked upon his stump. Instead, it is with indifference that the sailor looks now upon his blistered, burnt hand and blackened fingers.

De Morales tells the sailor to wait while he goes onto the main deck and warms water over a brazier burning near the mainmast. The same brazier in which Quesada and Mendoza's entrails were burned. The linen bandages provided by the Casa were all stolen when his belongings were ransacked, so he takes a strip of canvas sail from the wrecked Santiago piled near the forecastle and lowers it slowly into the bubbling water.

He returns to his cabin and slowly wraps the hot fabric around the sailor's hand. 'Which ship have you been assigned to?' He asks the sailor.

'The Concepción.'

Then he is under Serrano's command, this is good news. 'You must tell your boatswain this linen must be reheated regularly and wrapped around your hand. We shall try to draw the cold from it, but first the burns must heal. We must do all we can to save your hand. Tell your boatswain you must be brought back to me every two days.'

Days pass by and turn to weeks. Each morning, the sea's rampant churning crushes any hope that today might be the day the fleet can finally leave the Santa Cruz River and continue on its way.

De Morales' days pass by in shivering discomfort, broken only by visits from the sailor with the frostbitten hand. He reminds himself that at least he has a cabin to himself and can do the work he is trained to do. No more freezing in thigh-deep water, scrubbing ships or choking on fumes as he stirs pitch. Often, he eats his evening meal of hardtack and a few strips of smoked fish or, if the men sent out into the surrounding wilds are lucky, rabbit meat, with Barbosa and Elcano. Their conversations are a welcome respite from the sound of the wind's dismal howling as it rushes through the rigging.

Today, a month since the Armada was reunited, he asks them something that has been on his mind since he last looked across the harbour at Puerto San Julián. 'What became of Cartagena and de la Reina?'

Barbosa stops chewing and turns to Elcano. The mention of their names seems to have reminded him of the two marooned mutineers.

It is Elcano who answers, 'in truth, very little. You know yourself de la Reina had been subdued since the trials. But I would not say he was at peace with his fate. I think, rather, he was in a state of terror for his immortal soul. The Capitán General allowed neither man to take confession before they were marooned. It was a final act of cruelty from Magalhães to men he had already defeated.' Despite the slight at the brother-in-law, Barbosa remains silent. Perhaps he shares Elcano's thoughts.

'And what of Cartagena?' De Morales asks.

Elcano laughs humourlessly. 'If de la Reina was accepting of his fate, Cartagena was far from it,' he says. 'When the ships raised anchor, he went mad with fury. While de la Reina knelt praying into the wind, Cartagena shrieked at the passing ships. He screamed horrifying maledictions at the armada. Cursing us to lose our way, to starve and stagger emaciated about the decks. He willed the ships to be dashed on the rocks in some far-off place and the men to choke on seawater. Eventually, his curses turned to inarticulate screams. He raged as I have never seen. We could hear him long after he was lost to sight, his curses and screams carried on the air, ringing in our ears.'

Starve and stagger emaciated about the decks.

Visions of that terrible ghostly ship fill de Morales' mind. The surgeon dares not look back at the Victoria's decks, for fear of seeing those apparitions again. He shivers from the cold or, perhaps, terror.

The sailor's fingers cannot be saved. In truth, de Morales knows he has waited too long already. He has been hanging onto the hope that, by some miracle, the hand will spring back to life, that blood will return to the blackened digits and that the nails will regrow. But the fingers are utterly dead and are now slowly being overrun by gangrene.

He can delay the inevitable no longer.

The best course of action, de Morales decides, is to remove all four fingers and the thumb. Fortunately, the burns the sailor caused when he put his hand into the boiling water have healed. He knows the surgery will cripple the sailor, but at least saving the palm will leave him some usage, however small.

He unwraps the hand from its bandages as gently as he can, but the sailor feels no pain. Cold to the touch and hardened, the fingers feel unnatural, like the fingers of a marble statue rather than a man.

He lifts a knife and stops short. The blade is poised above the blackened skin. His mind is filled with doubt, questioning his skill, his knowledge, his decisions. His hand is shaking. He swallows hard, tries to remind himself he has been doing this for thirty years. Despite all the patients he could not save in that time he did, at least, bring them solace, however small.

The sailor looks up. He seems to notice de Morales' uncertainty. 'Señor doctor?' He asks.

When he slices through the skin, de Morales is surprised to find the scalpel makes a clean and easy cut through the dead flesh. There is no blood and no screams of pain, no need for wine. Instead, the sailor watches in silent interest as de Morales cuts through the skin and peels it back, revealing white bone beneath. He takes a small saw from his case and carefully begins cutting through the bones of the fingers, the blade skittering and scrapping across them. Once they have been severed, he carefully places them into a small square of canvas sail, then folds the flaps of skin over the wounds.

Still, the sailor watches quietly as de Morales finally stitches the skin over the palm to aid in healing. For all the pain the sailor showed, de Morales might as well have been cutting his toenails. He takes another small strip of canvas and soaks it in what little vinegar remains at the bottom of the quart barrel then holds the canvas to the stubs. The sailor doesn't even wince at its touch.

'This will clean the wound,' he says. 'Ideally, you would do this every day, but I cannot spare the vinegar. You must douse the hand each morning in warmed water. Not hot,' he adds sternly.

He follows his patient out into the open air and is immediately blasted with a volley of icy wind. No matter which way he turns, it seems the wind has conspired to hit him full in the face with its coldest, cruellest blast, as if it is punishing him for his impertinence.

He watches the sailor being rowed to the Concepción in a little skiff, clutching his hand to his chest. He shakes away the vision he has of the mess Bustamante would have made of the operation and turns away.

On the deck of the Trinidad, Pigafetta catches his eye, sitting with the captured giant from Puerto San Julián. The chronicler is hunched over, wrapped from head to toe in thick fabrics but the giant, still wearing his hides, sits upright and uncomfortable on the chair. The wind catches his long hair, whipping it this way and that, it snaps and billows in the wind like the Capitán General's tattered ensign hanging from the bowsprit.

The little Italian appears to be trying to make himself understood to the giant. He lifts different objects, a stone, a boot, a hat, a ladle. He holds them before the giant then leans over a piece of parchment perched on his lap, intently writing.

The weather calms. The wind loses its ferocity and the churning ocean lulls until its once-raging waves lazily slop over one another. A week of anxious weather watching passes and still the storms do not return.

Finally, Magalhães gives the order that, come tomorrow, the fleet will finally leave the Santa Cruz River and continue on its search for the strait. Even after all this time, all this brutal weather, Magalhães still searches for his corridor through the New World. He must be a madman, Elcano says, or at least fanatical. The thought is hardly a new one to de Morales.

A flurry of activity takes hold of the fleet as the men prepare the ships to leave at first light. It is strange that, no matter how long the armada spends at port, or how well maintained the ships are whilst anchored in some desolate place such as this, the fleet is always a hive of rampant activity before it weighs anchor and leaves. Sailors hastily climb the rigging, checking every knot and fibre, carpenters and coopers perform last-minute repairs. The captains, masters and boatswains shout orders at men sitting in skiffs, pounding oakum into gaps in the hulls before applying more pitch. Hunting parties head out on one last futile search of the barren land for food while nets are cast into the river in a final effort to fill the armada's stores.

Morning comes and, one by one, the remaining four ships weigh anchor. The surging river embraces their slick hulls and they rush towards the Great Ocean.

After over four months of stagnant boredom, first in Puerto San Julián and then here. After the mutiny, the trials, the tortures, the executions, the hunger, the thirst and the shivering. After brutal winds, driving rain and piling snow, the Armada de Molucca finally casts off into the Great Ocean once more, lugubriously leaving behind this accursed corner of the New World and abandoning what remains of the wrecked Santiago to rot into the river.

Just three days of calm weather pass before a ferocious storm hits them. The sun is blotted out as the storm spills over the horizon and daylight is all but lost, replaced by a murky grey. Great cracks of lightning flash through the sky, sending flares of white light that offer frozen glimpses of the tumult surrounding the ships.

Fearing he will go mad being cooped up in his cabin, De Morales summons the courage to open the door and glance out into the frightful storm. As soon as he releases the latch, the door is sucked outwards with great force, crashing violently against the wall of the aftcastle. Immediately in front of him, his feet set and knuckles white, Elcano wrestles with the whipstaff, desperately trying to keep the Victoria on course.

The shore is close by, within a league to the ship's starboard side, and is fleetingly lit up by flashes of lightning before plunging into darkness once more. On board the Victoria, the crew frantically fight with the ship. Their frozen hands, slick with seawater and rain, struggle to furl the sails, and their desperate cries are quickly lost in the tempest.

As he takes in the chaos, de Morales sees the Concepción and the San Antonio pitching violently in the churning ocean ahead. Their signal lights, sputtering and weak, are lost as a massive wave passes through the armada. Then they are revealed again, twisting this way and that, dancing with death as they are buffeted by random winds and rogue waves. His heart is in his mouth as he powerlessly watches both ships being drawn towards the shore. The sky flashes with lightning and lights up the landscape once more before the San Antonio and the Concepción are sucked towards the cruel coastline, disappearing into the darkness.

A great wave rolls out of the gloom, catching Elcano off guard. He has no time to react before it crashes into the Victoria's starboard side. De Morales is tossed sideways, slamming into the frame of the door as the crew hold desperately to whatever can be found. Seawater spills over the taffrail, flooding the deck, before it slides over the port side, taking three men with it. The men are lost in the darkness and foam as the Victoria rights itself, rocking back and forth.

De Morales, struggling against the wind, the rain and the rocking ship, finally stands straight once more. Desperately holding onto the frame with one hand, he reaches out into the abyss, stretching for the door. Lightning flashes again, directly above the Victoria this time, and his eyes, stinging with saltwater, are drawn up towards the masthead.

And he sees it.

St Elmo's fire. Burning again from the tip of the mainmast, dancing its wavering ballet in the churning chaos of the tempest. Whether it is from the seawater in his eyes or the terror in his heart, tears well and spill down his cheeks. His heart beats a terrible rhythm in his neck and his lungs refuse to draw breath.

Barbosa, tightly holding the taffrail, has seen it too. He crosses himself and cries, 'redemption,' into the wicked storm that steals the prayer from his lips. But again, there is no redemption in that light for de Morales. Only death and terror. The curse has found the armada once again.

He forces himself to take a breath. It comes sputtering and short but it comes nonetheless. Followed by another and another. Finally, he tears his eyes away from the light and searches blind and trembling for the door. With one last horrified look at the flickering blue flame, he slams the cabin door shut.

All night the Victoria is buffeted by the tempest while de Morales takes refuge in his cabin. Shaking with terror he curls up on his bed, waiting for the curse of St Elmo's fire to be realised and the Victoria to be cast against the barbed rocks of the shore.

But it does not happen.

Dawn breaks and almost at once the storm ceases.

With shaking hands, de Morales opens his cabin door. The main deck filled with emaciated crew he expects to find is not there. Nor is the algae, the rotten hull, the battered boards or the torn sails. There are only naked masts with their furled sails, a blustery breeze and a watery morning light.

Somehow, amid the savagery of that storm, Elcano was able to steer the Victoria out into the open ocean. The anchor has been dropped and, only a few dozen feet away, the Trinidad pitches gently on the waves.

He looks to the shore. It is a rugged coastline of pitiless rock, but the land is far more vegetated than Puerto San Julián or the Santa Cruz River. In amongst the craggy hills, smeared in a thick layer of greenery like moss on a stone, he fully expects to find the devastated remains of the Concepción and the San Antonio smashed against the rocks. But they are both nowhere to be found. The land rises and cuts inland to the north, perhaps hiding their sunken remains from view.

He finds an exhausted Elcano, staring off at the distant shore. 'Did you see them?' He asks desperately. 'Did you see where they were wrecked?'

'I think they are not wrecked,' Elcano replies. His eyes are dark and his hair and clothes are soaked through. He holds his arms against himself for warmth. 'Even if they had been sucked into the depths, there would still be debris on the surface. The ocean is empty. I think they survived the storm. But as to where they are, I do not know.'

Barbosa approaches them. 'Perhaps we have been cast

many leagues from them by the squall. I do not recognise the shoreline, so I think we must have been sent further south while they, perhaps, were sent north. We will not know until nightfall. God willing it is a clear night and San Martin can divine our location from the stars and the San Antonio will come to us.' The captain looks up. For now, it seems like wishful thinking. A thick blanket of grey clouds covers the sky.

They are startled by a loud crack of a cannon fire discharging to the north. The Capitán General, onboard the Trinidad, has heard it too, for he rushes up to the aftcastle of the flagship. The air is silent, every man on the Victoria and the Trinidad straining their ears for more cannon fire. Just as hope is beginning to ebb from de Morales' heart, another crack pierces the still air, swiftly followed by another.

Barbosa looks to Magalhães. The Capitán General waves his arms north. 'Set out,' he cries. 'Find them.'

Rather than use a skiff, the Victoria itself sets sail immediately. The heavy ship sluggishly plies the ocean. The going is unbearably slow, as if the Victoria itself is reluctant to reveal to its crew what lies behind the hills. As they near the high bank of land that meets the sea, a hollow bang of cannon fire erupts from the Trinidad behind them.

They pass around the land and there they find the Concepción and the San Antonio. Both ships are afloat and rocking on the gentle waters of a wide gulf that narrows sharply further inland. By some miracle, the ships, in the tumult and chaos of that storm, were drawn into the calm of the gulf.

'Have you ever known such luck?' Elcano asks Barbosa.

'It seems our armada is blessed,' Barbosa replies. 'We must thank St. Elmo in our prayers,' he adds. The captain stares in disbelief at the two ships rocking serenely in the calm waters before quickly crossing himself.

'This is it,' Magalhães cries. 'I can feel it. This is the strait.'

The armada was reunited in the peaceful waters of the gulf and immediately Magalhães began pacing the main deck of the Trinidad, searching the shore and his charts excitedly. Though several sailors were dragged overboard during the storm, there were cheers and hoots from the crews of all four ships as each saw one another again. Everyone, it seems, was certain of the other's annihilation.

'When we were swept toward the shore,' Serrano calls from the deck of the Concepción, 'I was certain it would be our end. Can we really have stumbled into that which we seek?' All four ships are anchored close together and the captains are able to shout to one another. From the short distance between the Victoria and the Concepción, de Morales can see the terror in Serrano's eyes as he rejoices. The same terror he saw when the captain told the tale of the Santiago's wreckage.

'How can we be sure this is the strait?' Barbosa calls. 'We know not what awaits us. I would be loath to sail into this gulf without the Santiago, the other ships are far too large to risk a reconnaissance.'

'Someone must go ashore,' cries Mesquita from the San Antonio. He turns and points at the snow-crested hills to the north. 'If someone were to climb those hills, he ought to see what lies ahead.'

'I will send Carvalho,' Magalhães says.

'It is believed,' Elcano says, watching Carvalho's slow progress as he trips and stumbles his way up the hill, 'the New World, despite its enormous length, is no wider than the island of England. If this is a strait, Carvalho may be able to see to the far sea on the other side.'

They watch the figure of Carvalho struggle up the incline in silence for a time. Finally, de Morales asks, 'how do we know this? I was given to think that no one had explored the New World extensively.'

'Vasco de Balboa crossed the continent some years ago and looked upon the new ocean,' Barbosa replies. 'As yet, no one has explored either the New World or the new ocean completely. But most cartographers agree the diameter of the earth is no larger than nine thousand leagues. With all we know of the size of Europe, Africa and Asia, the New World and this other ocean cannot be very wide. After all, we have travelled almost four thousand leagues on this voyage alone.'

'Not everyone agrees on the size of the earth, Duarte,' Elcano says.

'Waldseemüller's maps are all the evidence I need,' Barbosa says, as if he sees that as the end of the discussion.

'Waldseemüller has never left his bedroom. He is hardly reliable.' Elcano nods towards the shape of Carvalho climbing the hill. 'He could draw a better map in the sand with his member.'

'Christ,' de Morales says, 'never challenge him to that.'

The three men cheerfully laugh together. It is the first laughter de Morales has heard in the Armada since Pigafetta's shrill chortle at Carvalho's ribald jokes on Christmas day almost eight months ago.

De Morales had fears about life aboard the Victoria, made all the more real when St Elmo's fire burned yesterday. All night, the images that flame brought to his mind tortured him, reminding him of the ship's curse and the reasons for his fears. But day to day he is in good company and that, at least, goes some way to making life aboard the Victoria tolerable, more so than the Trinidad ever was.

Once he reaches the summit, Carvalho's miniature form, feet hidden in a deep bank of snow, is visible from the main deck of the Victoria. He stares for some time into the distance, turning north, south and west.

Finally, he starts to make his way back down. When he reaches the shore of the gulf, he climbs into a waiting skiff and, before he has even reached the armada, starts grinning broadly and shouting, 'it is a strait. We have found it. We have located the strait.'

Carvalho climbs aboard the Trinidad and explains so loudly that, even from the Victoria, de Morales can hear him. 'The land stretches for miles and the strait follows its entire length. It meanders but always continues westwards. I could not see the other ocean, but this is certainly a strait.'

Several men look between one another in astonishment, others clap Carvalho on the back. Magalhães, who has anxiously waited for Carvalho on board the Trinidad, heaves a deep sigh of relief. As if freed of an immense weight, the Capitán General's shoulders loosen, his beard breaks into a wide smile and he crosses himself. Pigafetta shakes the Capitán General's hand and Valderrama chants Latin prayers, palms upraised to the sky. Espinosa calls for the crew to cheer Magalhães' name as the cannons of all four ships are fired in celebration, their booming vibrations echoing off the preternatural landscape.

De Morales cheers with the rest of the crew. But does not say the Capitán General's name. He cannot bring himself to. For to do so would be to forget the misery and pain Magalhães has put his men through to prove himself right to a doubting world.

The luck of Magalhães is unbelievable. Were it not for that storm, that could just as easily have torn the armada apart, he would never have stumbled upon his strait. He would have sailed the fleet right past it into whatever unknown terrors would have awaited them further south. But he was right. His strait exists. He will be remembered and celebrated for all time for dragging these four ships and their wretched crew through hell to find what only he truly believed existed.

Chapter 17

November 1520

For once Carvalho was not lying or exaggerating, the route of the strait is meandering and confused. It twists and turns, sometimes back on itself entirely, snaking its way through a craggy landscape of tall hills rising quickly into mountains and split by rogue islands. The banks of the channel are coated in a thick shroud of conifers, pines and ferns, their branches knotted and their trunks stooped and bent, like old women in deepest winter. The vegetation is broken in places by colossal sheets of ice that spill through the valleys formed between hills and mountains, some stretching a hundred yards into the strait itself.

Often, the strait splits into two or three or more directions. Whenever the fleet approaches one such division, the Capitán General orders the Concepción to search the way ahead. Sometimes Serrano returns, informing the Capitán General that the way ahead is blocked by ice, leads to a pool or that it diminishes into little more than a stream. Thus far, however, there has always been a route onwards through the strait, even if sometimes the fleet must awkwardly turn back the way they came after discovering a dead end in the way ahead despite Serrano's reconnaissance.

The day is drawing on and they have passed several cautious leagues into the strait. Magalhães himself climbs down into a skiff beside the Trinidad, clutching a ladle in his hand. He dips the spoon into the water and lifts it to his mouth slowly, water sloshing over his clothes and face as the skiff rolls on the gentle waves.

'Salt,' he cries and the crew of the Trinidad cheer, holler and applaud. Any lingering doubts can now be completely dispelled. They have certainly found the strait and a new sea awaits them at its end.

Ecstatic, Magalhães asks Valderrama to lead a prayer of thanks to the Almighty for delivering them through countless trials to their goal. But the crew are too busy to spend time in reverential prayer and Valderrama's chanting is drowned out as the air is filled with calls from captains and boatswains, repeated all through the decks and shrouds of the ships.

De Morales has moved onto the aftcastle, out of the way of the bustle of bodies on the main deck of the Victoria. He watches them now as they frantically climb the rigging and work the halyards, furling and unfurling first this sail and then the next in response to whistles and shouts from their masters.

Below, at the whipstaff, Elcano is constantly and quietly cursing under his breath and frowning deeply. The currents in the strait are erratic and powerful, pulling and pushing the ship in different directions without warning.

Deep down, in the bowels of the Victoria where he slept in chains not two months ago, de Morales can hear the sonorous creak of the rudder as it is twisted this way and that, responding to Elcano's movements.

Whereas the Trinidad behind turns sharply and erratically, Elcano's skilful hand guides the Victoria smoothly despite the difficulty of the currents. Ahead, the Concepción and the San Antonio drift this way and that, guided by their equally skilled pilots. Carvalho is a fraud of the highest order. Despite his lack of knowledge, de Morales cannot help but agree with Elcano that the Trinidad seems the most likely of any of the ships to succumb to the currents and drift into a shoal or else become grounded.

Word filters forwards through the armada from the flagship. The Capitán General has named this strait the Estrecho de Todos los Santos, for the saint's day on which they have begun their journey through its waters. The news is met with little reception. Whether it is named or not the strait is still treacherous and, without a moment's notice, can claim any of the four ships.

The long day finally comes to an end as the sun slowly plunges behind the glacial mountains lining the western horizon ahead. The currents and twisting route of the strait are far too dangerous to pilot in darkness and so Magalhães orders the fleet to stop for the night.

Soundings are taken and the reading is not good, the strait here delves almost two hundred fathoms into the earth. Though they will certainly be useless, the anchors are dropped nonetheless. They splash into the frigid water, their calamitous song echoing off the glaciers, hills and mountains. But they drift uselessly in the current, their rodes swaying this way and that.

Instead, the great lines used in Puerto San Julián and the Santa Cruz River are stretched to the shore by sailors in skiffs. The men hurriedly tie lines to anything onshore heavy enough to hold the ships in place for the night. They work quickly and clumsily, looking over their shoulders at the drifting ships and the foreboding, impenetrable forests before them. When they are finished, they hastily scurry back to the skiffs.

During that first night, pink fires, radiant and ethereal, spring up along the shore. Like liquid, they ooze up from the earth, then sputter and spark while casting an otherworldly glow through the thick foliage of ferns and other strange waxy leaves. A sulphurous stench spreads from the shore into the strait, the caustic air chokes de Morales and brings tears to the eyes of the crew on the main deck of the Victoria.

'Tierra de Fuego,' Barbosa says, staring in fixed apprehension at this hellish phenomenon of the New World. The name is a good fit. But the crew jokingly lament that, for a land of fire, the strait is unbearably cold.

'Like Dante's Inferno,' Elcano says.

'What if the fires are not natural?' A voice says from the shroud above. 'What if men started them?'

Another voice behind de Morales says, 'what would cause a fire to burn with a pink flame?'

'Witchcraft,' the voice in the shroud replies.

That night, de Morales joins the watchmen on the main deck as they stare into the tangled shoreline, watching the fires spread and sputter. He focuses on the lines tied around rocks and strong trees holding the ships in place. If these lines were to be severed by whatever people inhabit these lands, if they are indeed people, the ships would be sent adrift into the tumultuous current.

But the lines hold fast and dawn comes, weak and pathetic. De Morales rises into the arms of the shared sense of anxiety on board the Victoria. The elation at finding the strait petered out as the day progressed yesterday and the difficulty of the sailing quickly became apparent. But now what little joy that survived has given way to a sense of oppressive foreboding. Few speak, beyond essential words, as every man focuses on the job at hand: getting out of this strait with the ships in one piece and finding the new ocean beyond.

From his cabin, with the door open, de Morales watches the ship come back to an apprehensive form of life. The lines are loosened, the anchor, swimming weightless and useless in the strait, is lifted.

It is easy to dwell on the otherworldly fires, on the creaking lines, heaving currents and tangled route of the strait. But there are, however, things to be thankful for. Though the waters below are a churning confusion of currents, at least the weather above is much calmer. It is even close to tranquil here, at least compared to the bitter violence in which they have lived for the past four months. Though the wind blows from both east and west, randomly changing direction and, incredibly, gusting from both directions at once, it has lost all of its ferocity.

And this place, for all its wild, disconcerting mystery, is undoubtedly beautiful. As the fleet has penetrated deeper into the New World, the glaciers coating the mountains have become more frequent, melding into one wide deep blue sheet of ice and snow. The cold that emanates from these glaciers is intense. Its chill pierces through the thick oak of the ship's hull, through the wool and cotton of de Morales' clothing, right down to his skin and into his bones, chilling his body from within.

Below, in the waters of the strait, life is abundant. So many fish teem in its depths that they can be sure of catching more than enough for this evening's meal. They ought to be able to salt fish by the dozen and store them in the holds of the ships, ready for the journey across the unknown ocean that awaits them.

From the aftcastle, as the armada continues onwards, de Morales sees the arcing backs of more of the leviathans he first saw in the Great Ocean before the mutiny. Majestic, fierce and unknowable and made weightless by the water, they effortlessly swim past the Victoria, blowing mist into the air from holes in their great backs before they dive into the depths. And then they are gone. Disappeared into the darkness below, where they lie in wait, readying to destroy the ships and devour the men.

Their appearance is a stark reminder of the dangers and mysteries of these uncharted waters. Who can say what horrors lie in wait in the depths of the strait below them? The church teaches the creatures of the sea are abominations, mongrels born of sin and made by the devil. Inferior creatures made by an inferior creator. Visions of the tentacled, hybrid monsters with dog-like faces and cruel fangs that line the borders of cartographers' maps spring to de Morales' mind.

He wonders again at what befell the Santiago.

Maybe the ship was pulled apart, not by a storm, but by one of these dreadful sea monsters, raging at their insolence in coming into its homelands. His imagination gets the better of him and he has visions of it pursuing them here. Perhaps it was this mysterious monster that pulled the San Antonio and the Concepción into the gulf. Perhaps their discovery of the strait was really a devious plot by this leviathan that plans to drag them under the waves and devour them in this cold and lonely corner of the New World.

The Armada comes to a fork in the way ahead. The strait splits into three directions; one on the left, one in the centre and another on the right.

The left route, by far the widest channel, turns almost back the way they came in a south-easterly direction. The central route heads due south before its direction is lost in a thick fog that has descended from the glaciers as the day has drawn on. Finally, the route to the right seems to head directly west. Between the central and rightmost route, a steeply rising landmass scoops up from the waters of the strait, coated in ice and widening until the channels are separated by what must be half a league. All three routes offer equally hopeful choices. With everything they have learned of this strait thus far, with its arbitrary twists and turns, it is perfectly reasonable to assume that even the leftmost channel could quickly twist back on itself and lead west out into the new ocean.

Magalhães orders lines to cast to the landmass, their sails furled and the anchors dropped. The fleet lies stationary for almost an hour while Magalhães consults charts, maps and San Martin. Meanwhile, the ships are hauled closer together by thick lines stretching between them until the hulls are almost touching and a man could walk from one ship to the other.

Finally, the Capitán General emerges from his cabin and orders the pilots and captains from each ship to come aboard the Trinidad. With the ships so close now, Barbosa and Elcano can simply step from the Victoria onto the flagship. From the San Antonio, Mesquita and Gomes do the same. While from the Concepción, Serrano and Gallego, his pilot, must first walk across the deck of San Antonio before finally stepping aboard the Trinidad.

'We must split the fleet,' Magalhães says when everyone has assembled before him. 'The San Antonio will head down that route,' he nods to the left-most channel. 'The Concepción will take the central route and the Victoria will take the last. You must all explore your channels and return here within four days.'

'What of the Trinidad?' Barbosa asks.

'I will remain here. Each evening, I will fire a cannon. You will fire your cannons in answer, starting with the Victoria, then the Concepción and, finally, the San Antonio.'

'Very good,' Mesquita says. 'Then we will know if an accident has befallen a ship.'

'Precisely,' Magalhães says. 'One of these routes will lead to the new ocean and I am certain it shall be found quickly enough.'

'This is absurd.' The voice is Gomes'. He is standing away from the group of captains and pilots who turn to him now.

A furious look passes across Mesquita's face. 'You will shut your mouth,' he says, rounding on his pilot.

'Let him speak,' Barbosa says.' What concerns you, Estêvão?'

'We have no idea what we are sailing into,' Gomes says. 'All of us could run aground or else be wrecked. Even if we

266

all make it out, no one truly knows how big the new ocean is beyond the strait. We will starve before we find the Moluccas.'

'You will do as your Capitán General has ordered,' Mesquita says, straightening up before Gomes.

Gomes equals his captain's glare. 'I will not. We should return to Sevilla, restock and attempt the voyage better prepared. We know the location of the strait. We risk too much by attempting to find the Moluccas now.'

Until now Magalhães has remained silent, but his staring eyes speak of his anger. After all his shows of strength since the mutiny, still Gomes is questioning him. 'Get your pilot in line, Álvaro,' he says to Mesquita. 'Return to your ships and prepare to leave at first light,' he says to the others.

'The Capitán General is wily,' Elcano says quietly to de Morales once he has returned to the Victoria. 'He remains at this crossroads in the flagship while he sends the other ships to scout the way ahead, knowing that if any of us were to abandon him, we would first have to pass the Trinidad to do so. He still clearly trusts no one.'

'With good cause,' de Morales says, nodding towards Gomes on the San Antonio. The pilot has an ill look about him. Clearly, he expected at least some of the other captains and pilots to agree with him. 'Do you think he could be right?'

'He could,' Elcano says. 'Truly, we do not know what we are sailing into.' Worry settles across Elcano's brow as he turns, looking into the waters, made vague and ghostly in the fog, of the route they are to take in the morning.

Before dawn the next day, the ships bustle with activity as

their crews prepare to depart. De Morales takes up his now familiar position on the aftcastle. He tells himself he is helping in some way, looking out for shoals or coral reefs. But he has no idea what he would be looking for and there are other, far more skilled, lookouts high up in the crow's nest and hanging from the shrouds of the mainmast. The simple truth is that he wants to experience first-hand the strait and the New World through which they are passing, not to mention the possibility of seeing a new ocean glittering on the horizon.

When all is prepared, men cautiously row skiffs to the shore to release the lines that have held the ships in place. While they dig out the huge spikes they often glance over their shoulders, searching for any sign of natives beyond the dense line of foliage. Anxious minutes pass. The men ashore know they must work quickly and not only for fear of an attack by natives. As soon as the lines are released, the ships will be dragged onwards by the current.

Elcano stands at the whipstaff, nervously looking to the shore. When the lines slacken, he quickly turns the rudder, righting the ship before it drifts off on a course of its own.

And so, the Armada de Moluccas is split and, for the first time, by choice rather than by fate. The San Antonio and the Concepción are quickly lost to view as they glide through the waters of their channels, hidden by the vast mountain of ice between the Victoria and the other two routes. The last ship to disappear from view is the Trinidad, standing stationary at the trifurcation of the strait. Its black bulk is an imposing sentry, guarding against any attempt to desert.

The route down which Magalhães has sent the Victoria is much the same as the rest of the strait. The same thick foliage of waxy leaves rustle in the breeze. In the distance, huge glaciers of ice tower over the waterway.

The strait is alive with fish, teeming and squirming over one another. Barbosa sets a skiff to trail by a line from the stern of the Victoria with two men aboard who cast a wide fishing net into the water. Beside de Morales on the aftcastle, two cabin boys stand with fishing poles. Because of the currents and the unknown way ahead their progress is slow and so it isn't long before the lines are being swept in. They throw the fish, wriggling and convulsing, onto the deck of the aftcastle. The men in the skiff behind have even more luck, pulling in such vast quantities of fish with their net they must be pulled back to the Victoria several times to unload.

As the day progresses, the current becomes more difficult to contend with. The water slides by quickly in the opposite direction they are sailing in making Elcano's job even more difficult and he ceaselessly arcs the whipstaff left and right as the whole ship creaks and groans.

As evening falls, de Morales hears the distant crack of cannon fire behind them from the east: the Capitán General's signal to the other ships. Barbosa orders a cannon to be loaded, set and fired. This is the closest de Morales has been to a firing cannon and the explosion makes a ferocious sound. The whole ship is pushed sideways by the force of the explosion as flame, sparks and smoke spurt from the barrel. Elcano, anticipating the recoil, quickly reacts and sets the Victoria back on its safe heading.

The crew wait, listening for the sound of cannon fire from the other two ships. In the distance, ice falls from a glacier nearby and sloshes into the strait. After several minutes of silence, the sound of a distant explosion echoes across the still landscape. The sound is to the south and some distance away but the nervousness on board the Victoria is released instantly. The Concepción is safe, then.

They wait again for the sound of cannon fire in response from the San Antonio. The tension builds once more.

No sound comes.

Silent, anxious, the crew gather at the port side of the Victoria, staring into the primaeval forests on the shore. Sailors climb the rigging or crouch in the crow's nest, looking into the deepening gloom of evening, searching, listening for any sign.

But no sound of cannon fire comes. The air is filled with nothing but the slap of water, the snap of the sails, the groan and squeak of the rigging and the eerie creaking of the huge ice mountains far off in the distance.

'Perhaps the San Antonio is too far off,' a hopeful voice says.

'Cannon fire would carry for dozens of leagues in this empty place,' Elcano says, tightly gripping the whipstaff.

'Perhaps they have already returned to the Trinidad,' a cabin boy beside de Morales on the aftcastle says. 'Maybe they have already found the end of the strait, or their way was blocked.'

Slowly, the crew melt into the holds and cabins of the ship. Lines are set to the shore, tied to the huge iron spikes driven into a glacier. Though it is still useless, the anchor is dropped into the strait, nonetheless.

Elcano sits on the deck, Amaya on his lap scratching her ears and back. Barbosa stands silent at the gunwale, de Morales on the aftcastle. They stare into the night and the night stares back. Silent and empty.

The next morning comes and they continue on their

cautious way. Heavy oppression hangs over the crew as the Victoria struggles against the current.

Only a few hours have passed and de Morales is in his cabin when a cry comes from the deck. He rushes outside into the chill air and looks around. The landscape looks the same, no one is injured, there is no native attack. Seconds pass as he struggles to divine where the cry came from and then it comes again, from high up in the rigging.

In the crow's nest, a watchman calls loudly and waves his arms. 'Ocean! I can see the ocean!'

The ship erupts with excited shouting. Sailors shake hands and clap each other on the back, others cross themselves, throw their caps into the air or dance, whirling and laughing across the main deck. Barbosa and Elcano smile at one another from across the deck. Sailors climb the rigging, lining the masts and shrouds like pigeons. Bright-eyed and smiling, they stare westwards, towards a glittering virgin ocean, towards the future.

Since they are only on the second day of a four-day reconnaissance, Barbosa gives the order that the Victoria will continue onward until the afternoon, charting the way ahead in preparation for the rest of the armada.

The melancholy of the previous night is forgotten and the Victoria is abuzz with excitement. The men work quickly, knowing their salvation from this awful search for the new ocean is almost at an end. But the boatswains remind them to remain vigilant. The strait is still dangerous.

They continue for several hours until the new ocean is visible even from the main deck. It spreads out, enveloping the way ahead, stretching across the horizon. By the late after the end of the strait is in sight, no more than two leagues away.

'We cannot leave the strait,' Elcano says to Barbosa, 'or we might never be able to enter it again and re-join the armada. Who can say what currents await us ahead?'

Barbosa agrees and gives the order to make an about-turn. The Victoria creaks and groans as Elcano turns the whipstaff and the ship slowly pivots around in a wide arc.

The way back is swift, the current pushing the Victoria along at a good pace. Nevertheless, it is still necessary for Elcano to carefully navigate the shoals and phantom fingers of kelp forests lurking beneath the water's surface.

They arrive back at the split where the fleet was divided before nightfall. The black silhouette of the Trinidad still standing sentry in the centre of the strait where they left it. As the hills between the channels melt away, the Concepción comes into view, rocking gently beside the flagship, its taut line stretching to the shore. Serrano must have met some obstacle on his way and turned back before them. Either that or there is another, quicker, route through to the new ocean down the channel he explored.

On the Victoria, a shared hope beyond hope the San Antonio will be waiting out of view beside the Concepción spreads among the crew. De Morales feels it and willingly falls into its hopeful embrace, surely Mesquita cannot be lost, surely his ship will be there.

But as they round the huge ice sheet that divides the channels in the strait, there is no sign of the San Antonio.

Barbosa's news that the new ocean has been located is met with cheers from the men. Ten long months of gruelling sailing since the armada left Los Cristianos and began its search for the strait is finally over. After all his long years of convincing the king, Fonseca and the Casa de Contratación, after abandoning his country and Faleiro and casting two hundred and forty-two souls into the sea, the Capitán General has been proven right again. Not only is there a strait, but it can be navigated.

The jubilation lasts into the evening and Magalhães, in one of his so few displays of generosity since they left Sevilla, orders a double ration of wine for the entire crew and an extra portion of fish caught by the Victoria. The news is met with more whoops and applause. Pigafetta leads the crew in cheering Magalhães' name three times, each more hearty and joyful than the last.

But when the Trinidad's cannon is fired that evening, still no response from the San Antonio comes. All three ships wait in the deepening silence as darkness falls. The joy fades, replaced with anguish at the fates of their comrades.

Dawn and the San Antonio is still missing. Its fate weighs heavily on de Morales' mind. Through the night, the Capitán General ordered a huge fire to be lit on the shore of the landmass as a signal to the absent ship. It crackled and sputtered brightly in the darkness, joining other fires that sprang up randomly across the landscape.

If the San Antonio is afloat and its men still living, would they feel relief at the sight of flames in the distance? Or would they see simply another fire burning in an already burning landscape of phantom flames? He imagines the crew now, lost, cold and hungry, arguing on the deck of the San Antonio at the appearance of another fire in the Tierra del Fuego. He lists their names: Rebêlo, Mesquita, San Martin, Estêvão Gomes – who argued against journeying any further for fear of disaster and who, it seems, has been proven right.

On the remaining ships, meanwhile, minds run riot with wild imaginations at the fate of the San Antonio and the Victoria is rife with rumour. Could it be that the sea monster that destroyed the Santiago has claimed another prize? Perhaps the Portuguese have followed them here. Perhaps all the astronomers, theologians and philosophers are wrong. Maybe the San Antonio has simply fallen from the edge of the world into the abyss beyond.

Relieved from his constant piloting of the Victoria, Elcano is spending the evening with de Morales. After two long days of exhaustive work, the pilot stretches his neck and rolls his shoulders, releasing the tension, aches and pains. 'Whatever happened to sailing east?' he asks, as he works a knot from his neck. 'Was that not the plan you were told?'

'I was told nothing of the plans of the armada.' de Morales replies. 'Only that the fleet would sail west searching for a route to the Indies through the New World. The location of a strait, the time it might take, what would happen should we fail, none of this was discussed with me. After all, I suppose, why would it be?'

'True,' Elcano says. 'Well, I can tell you now because what difference does it make? The plan was that, if the Capitán General failed to discover his strait, the fleet was to turn back on itself and seek the Spice Islands by the usual route, around the cape of Africa.'

'An interesting detail. But, as you say, it makes little difference now. Magalhães has his strait. His name will live in glory forever.' De Morales thinks for a moment, imagining the Capitán General's celebrated return to Castile. 'You have to admit, it has a certain charm to it,' he says. 'The driven visionary who gave up his homeland and risked everything to find a strait to the Indies. And succeeded.'

Elcano breaks the silence that follows. 'If the San Antonio is lost, we are in a lot of trouble.'

They have tried to keep their minds and the conversation away from the missing ship by talking of other matters. Hearing Elcano say the San Antonio's name aloud now, the sense of dread he has tried to avoid returns to de Morales' heart. To admit he feels that dread is to admit the San Antonio could be wrecked. He swallows hard. 'Why so?' He asks.

'It was the biggest ship. When the Santiago was wrecked, we already lost most of our provisions. If the San Antonio has followed her to the depths. . .' Elcano leaves the sentence unfinished.

'We have fished, though,' de Morales says. 'Magalhães and Serrano may not have thought to while we were away, but all three ships have set nets through the night. Surely that will help.'

'Even salted fish does not last long,' Elcano says.

Barbosa appears in the doorway, he looks at Elcano, takes in his tired eyes and pallid colour. 'You ought to rest,' he says.

Elcano nods and rises slowly, he wanders out onto the main deck. De Morales looks at the captain standing in the doorway. Barbosa looks worried, the fate of the San Antonio is clearly still on his mind.

'Captain,' de Morales says, 'are we truly as short on supplies as Gomes said? Will we make the crossing to the Moluccas?'

Barbosa runs his hand through his hair and rubs his eyes. 'Who knows what we are heading into,' he says finally. 'The hardtack is mouldy and filled with maggots. We have little fortified wine left, the chickpeas and raisins ran dry long ago.'

Barbosa's drawn face and his worried eyes mirror the look that has settled on de Morales' face. Finally, de Morales asks, 'how much will we need to make the crossing safely?'

'More than we have,' Barbosa says.

Sunset comes and again the Trinidad fires its cannon. The explosion cracks through the emptiness, echoing off the glaciers and distant hills, but there is still no sound in reply. After an hour, Magalhães fires the cannon once more.

Silence.

Evening passes into an apprehensive night. This is the last night when the ships were supposed to rendezvous by.

Magalhães himself comes aboard the Victoria, entering Barbosa's cabin without a word to anyone else. They remain inside for an hour or so and, while they speak, the crew of the Victoria gather outside.

'We must follow the San Antonio,' someone says.

'Into what will we be searching?' Another asks.

'The way may be dangerous,' comes the reply, 'but we must do all we can.'

The door to the cabin opens and Magalhães limps onto the main deck. The Capitán General stops mid-step, staring aghast at the gathered men before him. He looks frightened for a second; as if he thinks the assembly is mutinous. Barbosa appears beside him, he takes a step forward, placing himself between the Capitán General and the crowd. Behind his brother-in-law, Magalhães straightens and becomes more resolute. He says nothing, just stands staring at his men with a contemptuous look in his eye.

Finally, a voice from somewhere in the crowd says, 'what plan, then, Capitán General?'

Very quietly, as if he does not want to admit his decision to himself, Magalhães says, 'if the San Antonio does not appear by sunrise, we continue onward.' His voice is weak. Empty of all conviction.

The crew are aghast at the Capitán General's words, de Morales is appalled. Magalhães' own son, his flesh and blood, is on that ship.

'We ought to at least attempt a search,' Elcano says. 'Assuming some evil has befallen them, there are sure to be survivors.'

The Capitán General's face flushes a livid purple as he erupts into a rage. 'I do not need to justify myself. I will not be countermanded, least of all by you.'

The crowded men stare at their Capitán General, mouths agape in shock. Despite his attempt at showing strength, Magalhães looks feeble, surrounded by so many disbelieving men. The resolution in his eye and posture falters, he hunches over. The crowd parts and the Capitán General limps towards the taffrail.

The following evening, three ships exit the strait. The Victoria leads the way into an unknown, placid ocean. This new sea's coast is a far cry from the Great Ocean on the other side of the strait. The water's edge is calm, gently rolling onto the smooth rocks of the shore.

But the erratic currents of the strait catch Elcano off guard and the Victoria is dragged back towards its mouth. The Trinidad and the Concepción leer into view behind as the Victoria is drawn ever closer toward them. With a cry, the mainsail is loosened from the rigging, it catches the wind and billows wide and the Victoria heaves forwards. It wrenches itself from the grip of the strait and bursts into the new ocean. The Trinidad and the Concepción, learning from Elcano's lead, follow suit and soon the armada is free of the currents.

Darkness is falling but they sail on, turning immediately northwards until they dare go no further in the uncharted waters. They drop anchor, huddling together in the unknown.

Before the crew turn in for the night, Magalhães fires the cannons of the Trinidad one last time. The plaintive echo goes unanswered.

A new ocean is found, but the San Antonio is lost.

Part II

Chapter 18

December 1520

'Buenos días, Capitán General,' the giant says, his tongue struggling to form the unfamiliar shapes of this new language. The captains and señores, gathered on the main decks of their ships, applaud. Their sunburnt faces stretch into smiles as they shield their eyes from the dazzling sun, glinting off the ocean's mirror-like surface. Pigafetta stands at the giant's side, puffed up and proud of what he has achieved.

The chronicler passes Magalhães the dictionary of words in the giant's native tongue he has worked on for the past six months. Beneath his now unkempt beard, the Capitán General smiles broadly. He says something de Morales cannot hear, most likely heaping more praise on Pigafetta for his diligence.

His performance finished with, the giant wanders off, settling on his haunches beneath the mainmast with its lifeless sails hanging limp and useless. For a moment de Morales struggles as he tries to remember how many days it has now been since the wind stopped. Nineteen, he remembers. Almost three long weeks of heat, thirst, hunger and boredom.

Gomes was right, there was not enough food. Where they are now, no one knows for sure, but the best estimates put their progress since the doldrums hit at just a few short leagues. It is not enough. Soon, their rations will run out completely and then they will slowly starve to death. The fortified wine has long gone and even the water, now, has all but run dry. When that runs out, as it, too, inevitably will, they will be dead within days.

De Morales sighs, turns away from the sycophantic performance playing out on the deck of the Trinidad and ducks into his stifling cabin. He thinks back to the joy when the Victoria found the exit of the strait, then the despair when the San Antonio never appeared, then the wonder at the towering mountains reaching down to the very shore all along the western coast of the New World. So many leagues, so many strange and new things seen. All of them wonderful and overwhelming and savage.

He retraces the armada's path in his mind as best he can. They sailed north along the coast of the New World for almost five hundred leagues before turning west and plunging into this new ocean. Magalhães was confident it was no more than a hundred leagues wide, that they would cross it in a matter of days.

A matter of days passed and there was no land. The ocean

stretched on, endless and empty. The days turned to weeks and the temperature soared.

Now, the ships and the men are baking beneath the brutal sun, surrounded by water they cannot drink. Hunger and thirst have soured the moods of the men and, de Morales is sure, were it not for their lack of energy, the Capitán General would surely have faced another mutiny by now. As it is, no one has the spirit for something so draining. Surviving has become hard enough.

Outside, on the main deck of the Victoria, Barbosa has done what he can to help the men endure the heat. He is experienced in sailing through the searing, humid heat of the Indies, and instructed the men to loosen the lower rigging on the mainmast sail. The sail was then stretched across the length of the deck of the Victoria, sheltering it from the worst of the heat. But the relief is little. With forty men all huddled up underneath the sail seeking relief, it quickly becomes even hotter beneath it than beneath the blazing sun.

Whereas during the overwintering in Puerto San Julián the crew were worked almost to breaking point every day, the fleet quickly fell into lethargic inaction when the doldrums hit here. No one is immune to the torpor. The boatswains have given up their yelling and cajoling. Men sleep almost all day long, having neither the will nor the energy to maintain the ships. Even the Trinidad, usually a hive of activity ruled over by the iron will of the Capitán General, is falling into disrepair. With the lack of upkeep, the ships are slowly sliding into ruin. The rope of the stays, rigging and shrouds has turned crusty and solidified. Smears of algae have invaded the main deck, making even the shortest of walks across it treacherous.

The men are surviving now on just an eighth of their usual

rations. So little food is barely enough to keep them alive and so they have turned to other means. At first, they caught rats in the orlop hold, furiously chasing the vermin through the maze of crates and sacks. But eventually, they caught the ones too stupid or slow to outrun them. It will take a true predator, like Amaya, to catch any that remain. Some men, desperate to stave off the hunger cramps that grip them, have turned to boiling leather in seawater over the brazier under the mainmast.

Sitting in his cabin with the door cast open, de Morales looks down at his meagre provisions for the day: hardtack turned to powder, wriggling with maggots and the small cup of yellow water that turned stale long ago. He has no desire to eat but knows he must. He joylessly chews the rations, drinking the tiniest sip of stale water with it, resisting the urge to swallow it all in one long gulp.

He sets down the goblet and it occurs to de Morales that today is Christmas day. Those men dismally chewing on hardtack today were, a year ago, enjoying a feast of fruit from the New World. That feast was the last time he was truly comfortable, happy even. He longs for the food, the company, the laughter and, most of all, the land.

From beneath his bed, he pulls out a small box. He opens the lid and takes out the jar of quince. He has carefully rationed what little remained after his cabin was ransacked at Puerto San Julián but now, only hardened dregs remain clinging to the sides of the jar. He scrapes around it with his finger, finding the smallest morsels that remain. Though it is so little, his tongue, dulled from weeks of nothing but tasteless hardtack relishes it. Flavours of apple, pear and citrus fill his mouth. But now the jar is utterly spent, wiped completely clean. He is sorry to see it go.

Outside, nobody speaks. Few words have been spoken for weeks now. There is a sense of distance between the men; as if each man prefers to endure the heat and hunger alone. They wear their caps low and tie kerchiefs around their brows to both soak sweat and shield their eyes. Those who are not on duty do nothing, laying face down on the boards of the main deck beneath the canopy of the mainsail, trying to find some small relief from the blazing sun. They are irritable, quick to anger and, in the early days of the doldrums, fights broke out regularly. But now, no one has the energy for fighting. The crew say and do the absolute minimum, saving every last shred of energy for the slightest of tasks. One man rises slowly and staggers across the main deck, stepping carefully around his comrades and the streaks of slime. He stops at the gunwale and urinates over the side of the ship, the sputtering brown stream fills the stagnant air with the reek of ammonia.

The heat of the cabin becomes oppressive and de Morales walks outside in the vain hope some whisper of wind will cool him down. Even a moment's relief would be a blessing. In the ocean, several men bob and splash, trying to cool off. If only he could swim, he thinks to himself, as he watches them frolic in the seawater.

Pigafetta and the giant are on the main deck of the flagship. They are seated on stools and the chronicler gestures to parts of the ship, naming them one by one, while the disinterested giant copies the sounds. So far from his home, and in such unfamiliar heat, the giant is stripped bare to his waist. He would go further, stripping entirely, if the Capitán General had not forbidden it. Watching the two men, one dwarfed by the other, de Morales admits he is jealous of Pigafetta. It must be good to have something to focus on besides hunger, thirst and heat.

The men swimming in the ocean hoot and cheer, splashing one another with water. They play like children, joyful to have found some respite from the heat. Others, still on duty, watch with jealous eyes as they half-heartedly chip crusted sea salt from the rigging. More men slowly appear from the holds of the Concepción and the Trinidad, stripping off clothing as they come into the open air. With the promise of the cool kiss of seawater, they find energy anew and jostle and push one another as they make their way to the taffrails. The sea below ripples in wide circles around the men as they play in its waters. The scene would almost be idyllic, were it not for the niggling knowledge that these are fleeting joys.

A shadow slides through the water beneath the merrymaking men beside the Victoria. It turns, circling back towards their kicking legs and flailing arms. Slowly, the shadow rises until a short, sharp fin appears. One of the men gives a yell, spinning erratically in the water. He wildly kicks his legs, and splashes at the sea, struggling towards the hull of the Victoria. The other men, after sharing startled glances, do the same. They scramble up the Jacob's ladder, clumsy hands, shaking with fear, fumbling at the rope.

The first sailor climbs over the taffrail and thumps heavily to the deck, his eyes wild. 'Something brushed my leg,' he says desperately. He is shaking with fear, his breath stuttering from him. 'A monster touched me.'

Sailors rush to the taffrail, staring intently into the mirror surface of the ocean. De Morales looks but sees nothing. The shadow is gone now. A cry comes from behind him and he rushes to the starboard side of the ship. Plying the water, like a knife through milk, is a fierce curved fin of some huge fish. It is pale grey and has notches torn from it, giving it the look of an overused saw blade and the sense that it has seen many battles. A smaller fin of a similar shape follows behind its larger twin, some nine or ten feet behind. Whatever that monstrous fish is, it is huge and must be capable of swallowing a man whole.

'A shark,' Elcano says. He turns to the sailor, still panting as his companions join him on the deck, dripping and coughing. 'You are lucky to be alive,' he says to them.

No more swimming, then.

The giant dies on the twenty-eighth day of December 1520. He died sometime in the night, alone and sweating in this strange place on this bizarre ship, so far from his home and family. The evening before he had sat with Pigafetta, diligently repeating Spanish phrases and naming items the chronicler took from a small pile beside him.

The colossal corpse is manhandled into position in the centre of the main deck of the Trinidad. Pigafetta stands at the feet of the body. Shoulders slumped and face drawn, the chronicler looks genuinely heartbroken at the giant's death.

Magalhães presides over the funeral in full regalia, despite the heat. It seems important to the Capitán General that the giant, who had been baptised into the Christian faith weeks ago, be given the full rite of committal. Valderrama speaks of the blood of Christ, of salvation, of the eternal joys of heaven. As the day matures, the heat begins to become overbearing. The sailors, spread across the decks of all three ships, wilt under the sun's rampant rays.

Finally, Valderrama's service is finished and the body is dumped into the water. It sinks quickly, sending bubbles rushing to the surface as it disappears into the depths.

Pigafetta watches from the deck of the Trinidad, staring into the abyss.

Next, the Capitán General reads mass to the gathered men. His sermon is long and boring and, as he talks, he works himself up into a fit of Christian zeal. Magalhães speaks of pacifying the savagery of the native world with the Christian faith. He seems, however, to be preaching more to himself than to his congregation. As if he is convincing himself of the importance of converting native people to the Christian faith after his first baptism ended in death. Magalhães speaks of how the giant's soul has been saved from the damnation and hellfire that his heathen brethren will suffer. 'Even if we save but a single soul,' he says, 'our task is a success in the eyes of our God and our king.'

Behind de Morales, a sailor scoffs. 'The king would prefer cloves to savage souls,' he mumbles.

Another beside him stares at the Capitán General. 'All this for baptisms?' He says through cracked lips. 'Tell that to the men on the San Antonio.'

Magalhães has never yet mentioned the lost men of his cousin's ship, the men he abandoned. De Morales wonders, as he watches the Capitán General preach to his exhausted, disinterested crew, does he feel anything for the men he so quickly deserted? Does he see their faces as he tries to sleep, sticky with sweat in his stuffy cabin? Does the ghost of Mesquita come to him when he finally manages to fall asleep asking him, 'cousin, why did you forsake me?'

A man has fallen ill on the Trinidad with the terrible sickness that follows all ships at sea. The sailor's name is Maestre Andrew of England.

De Morales only came to know about it many days after the Englishman fell ill. Being aboard the Trinidad, the Capitán General decided to rely on Bustamante. The barber was well out of his depth with this illness and bumbled around bloodletting Maestre Andrew for two days before he finally called for de Morales. *How many more men must suffer before the Capitán General swallows his pride and accepts that sometimes he needs the only trained physician in the fleet?*

Word of Maestra Andrew's illness quickly spreads through the armada. Ignoring the protestations of his crew, Barbosa has the Englishman moved to the Victoria. Magalhães' order, from the Santa Cruz River, that no man is to move between the ships is still in place. In this case, it is no bad thing. At least now de Morales can treat Maestre Andrew without wasting time moving him between ships each day.

The Englishman is brought to the Victoria onboard a skiff that slides across the sea's silken surface. The stricken man is incapable of climbing the Jacob's ladder himself and must be hoisted up using a capstan.

Once onboard, he mumbles to himself in his monotone language, then flops to the deck against the gunwale. The other sailors avoid contact with the Englishman, staying well clear of him, fearing the infection he carries. All of de Morales' training, on the other hand, tells him that an individual is not infectious to the touch. Rather, once the sickness begins, it will spread through the air. With the lack of wind and cleansing herbs, a plague is the last thing he is equipped to handle.

Barbosa orders two men to lift Maestre Andrew and they obey reluctantly. Once he is on his feet again the two sailors quickly retreat, leaving the sick man to stumble across the deck. Maestre Andrew moves as if he is confused and listless, like a man with a deep fever. But he has no fever. The Englishman's joints seem to have no strength and his knees wobble as he wanders toward the physician's cabin. Once inside, de Morales lays the stricken man on his bed and examines him.

Before he left Sevilla, a physician of the Casa de Contratación named Pedro José Maldonado spoke with him of scurvy. Maldonado was a poor teacher, impatient and dismissive of de Morales' questions. But the students' assiduousness compensated for the teacher's shortcomings. Not satisfied with Maldonado's bored teaching, de Morales sought information from other physicians and apothecaries in Sevilla. There are none in the world more experienced than they in the treatment of scurvy. From them, he learnt much. How to recognise the symptoms early, how to clear the airs around the afflicted and how to treat the illness as effectively as modern medicine can. But this is the first time de Morales has come face to face with a patient suffering from scurvy and the first time he has had the chance to examine the illness.

The Englishman's skin has erupted in a mess of weeping ulcers about the size of a reál coin. The skin is pink and swollen around them and very tender when de Morales touches them. Working very carefully, he slices a small slit in one of them and immediately an oozy flow of clear pus leaks from the wound. Next, he takes Maestre Andrew's wrist in his hand and then his ankle, massaging and flexing them. The joints feel flaccid and soft, like an over-boiled chicken, and the appendages limply flop back onto the bunk when he releases them.

One of the physicians in Sevilla told de Morales how the

disease can sometimes affect the mouth. He gently parts the Englishman's lips with his tweezers. Immediately a putrid smell hits him and he recoils in disgust. The man's gums are rotting inside his mouth. Livid strips of decaying flesh hang sickeningly from his upper gums. His teeth, or what is left of them, are blackened. The whole sight is an appalling vision of illness. Every agonising symptom he would not wish on his worst enemy is tearing away at this man's body.

He bends down and lifts the lid on the quart barrel of vinegar supplied by the Casa de Contratación. He has refilled the barrel twice from the ship's stores in the orlop hold since he discovered it had been stolen in Puerto San Julián. After the long weeks since, however, it is almost half empty again. He administers a small brass spoonful of vinegar to Maestre Andrew. The Englishman sputters and coughs as the acid liquid hits his tongue and seeps into the open sores in his gums. It is a cruel treatment, but the only one that is thought to save those who suffer from scurvy.

Despite the barrels below, de Morales is acutely aware the supply of vinegar is not limitless. The surgeons in the Casa de Contratación advised him to treat any affected men with three spoonfuls of vinegar a day. Sores could be washed with the vinegar and, if many fall ill, the vinegar should be used daily to scrub the decks. He does not know how much vinegar remains in the barrels in the holds of the ships. That supply will surely have been used extensively already for cleaning since he was last in the hold, as was their main purpose. He makes a mental note to visit the hold of the Victoria and check exactly how much remains. In the meantime, he must remember to ask Barbosa to stop the usage of vinegar for anything but the most pressing need.

He has Maestra Andrew lifted from his cabin and

deposited into the hold of the Victoria where, already preparing for the worst, Barbosa has set up a sickbay at the prow of the ship. It is a laughably small corner of the dank hold and the air within is already putrid. De Morales knows, as the cramped space inevitably fills with sick men, the stink and heat and the discomfort will only get worse and so, too, will the miasmic spread of the disease. He can only hope the illness does not ravage the armada as it has others in the past. They are already so low on men.

Chapter 19

January 1520

More men fall ill in the coming days. So many that the makeshift infirmary in the hold of the Victoria is quickly overwhelmed. A second infirmary, overseen by Bustamante, is opened on board the Concepción. The barber visits the hold of the Victoria where de Morales is working.

'Captain Serrano sent me.' Bustamante's voice is muffled by the hand he holds over his mouth and nose warding off the pestilential odour of rotten flesh, faeces and urine. It is a smell de Morale has become used to, so much so that he barely notices it now. The barber moves to the centre of the hold where the weak flame of a candle sputters below a small bunch of rosemary and sandalwood. They are all the dried herbs de Morales has left and are now his vain attempt to clear the miasma in the hold.

'It is the airs of the Concepción that will decide if you win or lose this battle,' de Morales says, moving to the next man and holding a spoon of vinegar to his lips. 'You have vinegar?'

'The Casa gave me none, you have the only supply meant purely for medicinal usage.'

'Tell Serrano to give you access to the barrels on board the Concepción. The Casa told me to give three spoonfuls a day, but I have increased the dosage to six. We can ill afford more men to fall ill and those that already have must survive.'

'There is little we can do about that,' Bustamante says, pulling a sprig of rosemary from the bunch. He begins bruising it in his hand with his thumb.

'We must do all we can,' de Morales replies.

'You have more of this?' The barber opens his palm, then holds the broken herbs to his nose.

'No.' De Morales replies, not even attempting to hide his scorn for the barber. Those herbs are essential, the difference between life and death, and Bustamante blithely took them as if he were walking down a country lane in springtime.

He cannot help but be short with Bustamante. In this modern age, there are two sides to medicine and the barber is on the wrong one. His blind faith in God's plan, which conveniently absolves him of any blame for the death and suffering he inflicts, is dated and holds back medicine. It stops people from seeking the help of trained physicians.

De Morales stands and moves toward the quart cask of vinegar, already almost empty beside Bustamante. 'The disease is well studied yet still deadly,' he says. 'You must care for the ill. Bloodletting is useless, as is purging. All we have is vinegar and, in truth, I worry its effectiveness is lacking. Make sure the sick men eat and drink their rations.'

Bustamante turns, making for the stairs leading up onto the main deck. 'It is the airs,' de Morales repeats, trying to drive home the point. 'The heat is stifling and there is so little wind. You must keep the hatch open. The Concepción has grilled hatches so you should find the miasma will clear better than here. Keep the airs clean,' he urges once more to the barber's back.

Bustamante climbs the steep stairs, saying loudly, 'vinegar and air señor doctor. Vinegar and air.'

De Morales is quickly overwhelmed by the steady stream of men deposited by their friends and crew mates into the hold of the Victoria. Some of the sick groan and complain but most lie wordlessly, slowly succumbing to the disease. The dying line the edges of the hold until the edges are full. Then he starts filling whatever space can be found. Days and nights blur together until he has no idea how much time has passed since Maestra Andrew was first brought to the Victoria.

Their symptoms are manyfold and overwhelming in their cruelty. One man's leg breaks after he tries to stand to urinate. Another's arm tears open for no reason at all, the livid gash oozing blood and puss. Teeth, like fallen leaves in autumn, collect in the corners of the hold and between the prone men. Nails peel away from fingers, leaving the tender beds below swollen and bleeding. Joints become limp, bones become brittle, and de Morales becomes exhausted.

Since his supplies were ransacked, he has not the medicines to treat the vast array of injuries and illnesses that are tearing the men to pieces. The small bunch of rosemary he had hung from the centre of hold has withered, doing nothing now to clear the miasma. The pestilence is made worse by the heat that refuses to abate and the windless air that will not clear. The entire infirmary is weighed down with the scent of disease and the putrid, weighty reek of rotting flesh.

All de Morales has is vinegar. But, when he administers it to them and it touches their cracked lips and torn gums, the men scream in agony until they refuse it altogether. He tries to force those who refuse, but they lash out with their limp hands and arms, spilling the precious medicine. Now even that is running low. He reminds himself to visit the orlop hold below and refill the quart barrel once more.

The screams, the stink, the groans of pain – it all follows de Morales as he tends his growing flock of expiring sailors. He works each day until he can no longer stand with fatigue. Eventually, he must give in and leave the sick in the hands of fate while he takes what rest he can. In the open air, the crew are dotted around the deck. They keep a distance from their fellows, worrying about the spread of the contagion. Some chew joylessly on boiled leather, most stare into space, deadened to all around them.

When de Morales comes out of the hold, into the heavy, hot air, everyone stays well clear of him. They part like the sea around the fin of the shark still circling the ship as the surgeon passes between them, avoiding him and the stink of disease he knows follows him everywhere now.

Tonight, the air is oppressive, weighed down as warm air can be and all the heat, hardship and disease weigh down on him also, compressing all hope from his heart. It has not rained for weeks, months even. He needs rain as much as wind. The air must be cleaned, made new.

Elcano appears in the doorway of his cabin. 'Can I assist you?' He asks

'I would not ask you to do this,' de Morales says. 'Though I am grateful that you would offer.'

'But you are exhausted. You cannot continue like this for much longer.'

'We do not know how this disease spreads,' de Morales says. 'You must be vigilant and keep yourself safe. The ship needs you as much as it needs me.'

'You are doing good work, de Morales,' Elcano says, trying to reassure him. 'As yet none have died and so your treatments must be helping.'

That night de Morales tries to sleep as best he can. The heat in his cabin is unbearable but, with no wind and all the other men already sleeping there, he knows the deck will not be much better. Despite his exhaustion, he restlessly tosses and turns. Visions of the walking dead suffering from the disease parade before his eyes. If he counts them, he wonders, will he drift off to sleep?

He wakes with a start, facing the wooden wall. Skin hot and clammy with sweat. Moonlight spills through the door he left open to the night air in the vain hope it might provide some relief. He rolls over, thinking he will rise and try to cool himself off in the open air of the deck or check on the men in the infirmary. He turns rolls over and sees a silhouetted figure standing beside his bed.

He sits up. 'Who is it?' He asks, thinking someone has fallen ill during the night. Or worse that someone has finally succumbed to the sickness.

The figure stands still, staring down at him and not saying

a word. He notices a haziness to the body; as if it is diluted or half-formed. The sleep drains from his eyes, bringing the cabin into sharper focus. He recognises the figure. It is Antonio Ginovés. The cabin boy sodomised by Salamon over a year ago. Shock turns to confusion and then to dread, sending his heart pounding.

Ginovés' eyes hold his gaze. They stare wildly, unseeing, bloodshot and bulging. With a great effort, de Morales pulls his eyes away from that blank, unseeing stare. He sees the livid purple bruise, patterned like rope stretching around the boy's neck. He takes in the pale body before him, utterly naked, dripping sweat or seawater onto the floor of the cabin. The body is a patchwork of cuts, bruises and welts. Five clean wounds, pale and bloodless, pierce Ginovés' trunk, puncturing his rib cage and stomach. His legs are streaked with violent slashes as if they have been whipped without mercy. Tears come to de Morales' eyes and he begins to shake with absolute terror at the spectre before him.

The phantom of Ginovés opens its mouth, a toothless void, black as death. Water bubbles from the corners of his open lips. He opens his mouth wider and the bubbling turns to a flow. Seaweed and tiny shellfish fall from the boy's mouth, slapping and clattering to the floor.

The spectre lurches forwards. It grasps de Morales by the shoulders, pushing backwards. His head slams against the wooden wall and Ginovés opens his lips further still and the flow of seawater turns to a torrent, vomited directly into de Morales' face. The spew foams and bubbles, filling his mouth and nose with seawater. He cannot breathe. He coughs and spurts, tries turning his head away but he has been struck immobile with fear. He chokes at the saltwater and feels creatures crawling down his throat. Their tiny pincers tearing through his organs and burrowing into his lungs, into his heart, gnawing and snipping at all that holds him together.

He gasps for breath and his eyes snap open. The sun has risen. A bright light filters through the doorway of his cabin. Hot, clammy air pushes down on him. He wipes the sweat from his forehead, catches his breath. He stares at the wooden ceiling above, his heartbeat furiously thumping in his neck.

A dream.

But he can sense the phantom of Ginovés still in the room, watching him, pulling all hope away from him. Leaving only absence. He has felt this before, in the townhouse he abandoned in Sevilla.

'Why? He asks aloud. 'Why do you haunt me so?'

The ships groan back to life as a light wind blows from the east. The rigging creaks and complains as the wind rises. Slowly, the crew awakens from their daze. The captains and boatswains rouse first and their shouts, heckles and orders fill the dead air as they cajole and threaten the crew back to work.

The men slip and trip across the deck, unsteady on lifeless legs, but, slowly, the armada comes back to life. The sail stretching over the main deck of the Victoria is loosened and it thuds to the boards, then it is raised, creaking and cracking up the mainmast. The slime is scrubbed from the deck, the canons are rolled back into position and every door is flung wide, letting the fresh air pour through the ship. Using oars, sailors beat the salt from the sails and rigging, it falls to the deck like snow in the Pyrenees.

The breeze turns gusty, and the sails heave then settle in response to its rises and falls. Slowly, reluctantly, the armada stirs westwards. The wind gradually picks up, becoming persistent, as the gusts coalesce into a ceaseless surge, goading the armada onwards and they pick up speed. Now the crew scamper up and down the rigging, desperately repairing frayed lines and tears in the sails.

They are moving, finally. Though none of them truly knows how far they have yet to go before the rolling hills of the Spice Islands will rise out of the horizon. Any movement is welcome after those awful days of heat, hunger, boredom and disease. The wind strips all the accumulated sweat and stickiness, filtering through to the bowels of the ships and airing the whole stinking armada out. It steals its way into the infirmary, lifting the reek of death and disease from the sludge of bad airs that surrounds the dying sailors under de Morales' care.

In the oppressive equatorial heat, forgotten salted meats and smoked fish have putrefied in the lowest hold of the Victoria. Everyone knew it had happened, but as long as the air was unmoving, the stink of rot went undisturbed and no one had the energy to do anything about it. Now, stirred by the wind, the miasma is unbearable and sure to carry disease with it. The crew throw the rotten meat overboard and the ocean churns and bubbles as fish of all sizes, rising from the depths, seize upon it. They twist and turn, gnashing, snapping and tearing with cruel teeth at the meat and at each other. Those sinister fins of the shark that has circled the Victoria ever since the sailors near escape appear again. The shark spirals inwards, closer and closer, until it too is feasting on the mess of putrid flesh.

Land is sighted. But the elation of the crew is quickly cut short. These low islands are not the Spice Islands and, though the armada is in desperate need of food and water, it is impossible to make land here.

The sailors in the skiff that is sent to reconnoitre them report that the islands are surrounded by high towers of coral, whose knife-edge spires would tear holes in the ships like a butcher's blade. The armada passes by and the crew watch sadly as the desperately yearned-for land slowly slides away until it is lost.

The armada moves but little changes for de Morales. He returns to the infirmary, caring for men whose bodies continue to fall apart. He sleeps among them now, snatching what little rest he can. He cannot return to his cabin where, he knows, the ghost of Ginovés awaits him. He feels useless, futilely feeding the sick men spoonfuls of vinegar. But the medicine is doing nothing. They are dying, each and every one.

The vinegar in the infirmary has run dry again and so de Morales makes his way down into the orlop hold below, shielding a candle's flame before him. Rats scratch and skitter across the boards, retreating from the light. Darkness envelopes him. He stops for a moment, staring into the gloom towards the prow of the ship. A chill runs down de Morales' spine. This is the very place where Ginovés was found. Could this be where the cabin boy died? Is his soul still here, searching desperately for peace?

The smell of vinegar snaps him out of his thoughts, its pungent acidity cutting through the familiar fetor of mould and mildew. Following his nose, he finds the three huge barrels of vinegar, puts the candle down on a box nearby and clumsily lifts the lid from the first. This one is empty, as is the next. He must have used more than he thought he had, or else it has been used for some other purpose. De Morales' heart sinks as he moves toward the final vat. The vinegar is essential, if the Victoria has run dry of it, the men above in the infirmary will certainly die.

Something in the shape of the final barrel concerns him and de Morales lifts the candle to inspect it in the shallow light it offers. The lid is missing. A bad sign.

Slowly, not wanting to know what his heart already knows, de Morales leans over the opening. He sighs and his shoulders release the built-up tension. The candle's flame is reflected in the vinegar that sloshes in the bottom of the barrel, following the ship's movements as it rocks on the waves. He fills his own smaller quart barrel then takes a lid from one of the empty larger barrels and carefully places it onto the remaining one.

Slowly, the acidic tang clears from the hold. De Morales hesitates a moment. He thinks of calling Ginovés' name, begging forgiveness or wishing rest upon the soul. Maybe it would help. It can hardly make matters worse.

A new smell hits him, pushing Ginovés from his mind. Decaying flesh.

Surely some piece of rotten meat has been left behind by the crew when they threw the rest overboard. The candle sputters as de Morales covers his nose and mouth with his hand. This miasma cannot be allowed to remain. The carcass must be disposed of.

He makes a cursory search of the surrounding area. The floorboards of the hold are strewn with rat faeces, crumbs of hardtack and other pieces of food pilfered by the vermin of the Victoria over the past fifteen months. He crouches on all fours, feeling the floor with one hand while he holds a candle in the other.

He is about to give up when his hand brushes something soft. He repositions himself, holding the candle in front of him, lighting the space beside the barrel of vinegar. The candlelight flashes off matted white fur and four sets of red eyes. De Morales jumps backwards in shock and the light falters, almost extinguishing. He hears rats scurrying away between sacks and crates.

He saw a glimpse, but it was more than enough. The decaying, tangled pulp of sinew and curdled blood, the rats, their jaws bloody with rotten meat, the knotted fur.

De Morales slowly climbs up onto the main deck of the Victoria. The fresh sea air hits him like holy water, washing away the rotten smell from his nostrils. Barbosa enters his cabin, nodding to de Morales as he passes by. Elcano stands alone at the whipstaff, a hand lazily resting on his waist.

The Basque notices de Morales and smiles brightly. 'Do not look so morose,' he says cheerfully. 'We will make landfall soon. I did not like the look of those islands anyway.'

De Morales approaches Elcano slowly, trying to think of the right words. He stands before his friend. 'Amaya,' is all he can say.

Elcano's brow furrows and he straightens up. 'What is it?' He asks.

De Morales stutters, his mind failing him. 'Amaya,' he repeats, his voice breaking.

Elcano knows immediately. His eyes widen as the colour drains from his face, he starts away from the whipstaff. He stops, turns desperately to de Morales. 'Where?'

'In orlop hold.'

Elcano does not return to the helm that day. As he tends to the sick in the makeshift infirmary, de Morales hears nothing from the orlop below. His heart breaks as he imagines Elcano fighting the rats from the corpse, cradling whatever remains of the decayed body of Amaya.

He wants to help his friend. He wants to be there for him in his grief, but the sickness is running rampant and the men need his care. He will help Elcano. He will try to soothe him for his loss. But, for now, he must try to save those poor souls.

It is a strange thing that this disease seems only to affect the common sailors. None of the captains, masters, boatswains nor anyone else of any standing has fallen ill. Both de Morales and Bustamante, despite caring for the sick, so far have had no symptoms. It is a fickle and cruel disease that seems to attack the weakest of the crew.

De Morales had hoped that the fresh air would bring relief. But, with the movement of the ships, the sickness has found a new ferocity. It has torn through the armada, claiming several men each day. As the hold fills up with the sick, de Morales' exhaustion grows.

On the twelfth day since he first came to the Victoria the Englishman, Maestra Andrew, finally succumbs to the sickness. By the end, the Englishman had no teeth left in his mouth and his gums were rotten, in places, to the bone. His belly was distended, either from hunger or some other cruel symptom of scurvy. Scars had reopened and the livid splits in the skin quickly turned gangrenous. The poor wretch died in agony, without solace or comfort, slowly rotting away from the inside out.

Valderrama climbs aboard the Victoria to administer the last rights to Maestre Andrew, but he is too late. The priest stands over the wreckage of the Englishman's body on the deck. Barbosa, Elcano and de Morales stand by as Valderrama chants the Lord's Prayer into the indifferent void of the ocean.

The body is wrapped in a shroud of old sail, then lifted. Maestra Andrew's hands and feet hang limply from the shroud as his body is clumsily balanced on the taffrail. Then it is pushed over the edge, splashing into the sea. It stays afloat, bobbing beside the Victoria and is immediately set upon by that terrible, stalking shark. With one great bite, it rips through the canvas and skin, sending a cloud of the Englishman's putrefied blood into the ocean. More fish join the frenzy, slashing and tearing at the body. A miserable end for a man so far from his home.

De Morales turns away from the sight. As he does so he sees a figure beneath the mainmast. He focuses his attention on it and notices, with sickening horror, that the man is headless. A pulpy mess of blood, bone and muscle oozes slickly from a wound where the head has been severed. It is midday and the sun is shining bright and bold upon this horrifying vision, men come and go about their tasks, seemingly unaware of what de Morales is seeing.

The apparition is shirtless with a long, jagged tear down the length of its torso. The skin around the wound is pulled outwards and has cruelly torn the wound further at its edges. The cavernous opening is empty. He recognises the clothing of the spectre and the short stature. Before him is the headless corpse of Quesada.

The ghost's arms are drawn across its body. As if presenting them to the world, the headless phantom of Quesada is cradling its own guts. The intestines and liver of the mutineer, slick and blushing, drip phantasmal blood onto the greasy deck of the Victoria. In the very place where the

305

mutineer was clumsily executed by unskilled hands, where his blood splashed and spattered and stained the boards, he has appeared again.

De Morales' eyes water and his heart pounds in his chest. He can feel his pulse racing, drumming in his neck. He feels as if his chest will explode. He tries to breathe but the breath catches somewhere in his throat, as if he is choking on his terror. His vision blackens inward until only a small tunnel remains, lighting only the corpse of Quesada.

Obscured by the blood thumping in his ears, he hears the voice of Elcano. 'Are you okay, de Morales?' It asks. The voice is faint as if they are separated by the void of death.

He stumbles away from the small congregation of mourners. The corpse of Quesada follows his movement, staying on the same spot but twisting its body. With great effort, de Morales finally wrenches his eyes away from the apparition and flounders toward his cabin. He bursts through the door and collapses onto the wooden floor, still gasping for breath. His heart continues to race but he is finally able to take a ragged, convulsing breath. Sweat stings his eyes as he tugs at his shirt, fighting his body to take one more breath.

The door gently opens, boots echo across the boards and, in his unblinking eyes, he sees the worried face of Elcano above him. Elcano lays a hand on de Morales' shoulder and gently squeezes. His heart slows its galloping beat and he slowly catches his breath.

'Are you okay?' Elcano's face is wracked with worry as he leans over the surgeon.

'The dead,' de Morales stutters, eyes wide with terror at what he is admitting. 'The dead haunt me. This cursed ship is filled with the dead.'

He sees the horror on Elcano's face, but de Morales

cannot keep it to himself any longer. The ghost ship off Africa, the apparitions, the constant foreboding sense of doom that pervades this rotten ship has broken him. His eyes cast wildly about the cabin. They settle on the doorway, on the spot where the battered ghost of Antonio Ginovés stood before him, spewing seawater. De Morales' body convulses into a fit of ragged breaths as the panic floods over him again.

'You must try to catch your breath,' Elcano says. He squeezes de Morales' shoulder again, harder this time.

De Morales' eyes focus on Elcano and his worried face. He forces his lungs to take a deep breath. The air enters his body in ragged steps but, at last, he seems to have more control over his breathing.

He is covered in a cold sweat as Elcano slowly helps him up. Once on his feet, he shakily sits down on his bed and takes a deep, raw breath.

'You scared me, 'Elcano says.

'What did I say?' He asks.

'Something about ghosts and curses,' Elcano says gently. 'Are you unwell? Do you have the sickness?'

He takes a deep breath. He is exhausted. He looks around his cabin at darkening wood, splintered and waterlogged, at the white mould creeping up the walls, at the slime spilling under the door. 'This ship is cursed,' he says slowly, hardly believing he is saying it out loud. 'And the curse is coming true before my very eyes. St. Elmo's fire will burn us all like the fires of hell.'

'You are tired,' Elcano says. 'In this heat, you have not slept well. You have been overworked since Puerto San Julián. And now with this sickness wreaking havoc through the armada, you have exhausted yourself. These visions are nothing but fatigue.'

De Morale knows Elcano is trying to help, but his kind reassurances offer no comfort. These visions have been too many, too tangible and horrifying. Kind words cannot dispel them from his mind.

'Did Barbosa see me?' he asks desperately. 'He will commit me to the hold.' He can feel his breath becoming ragged again, his heartbeat quickening. He sees the mad sailor, face down in the ocean.

'Barbosa only saw you stumble into your cabin,' Elcano replies. 'I will tell him the heat made you light-headed. You do not need to worry, he will suspect nothing. For now, you should rest here. Try to sleep, you look exhausted.'

De Morales slowly lowers himself onto the bed. Elcano gently closes the door and he is left to the sticky silence of the cabin. Images of the ghost ship of Africa flash in his eyes as he falls into a fitful and broken sleep.

Chapter 20

February 1521

He wakes to the sound of waves crashing. Confused, de Morales lumbers out of bed. When he opens his cabin door, the startling sight before him makes him think he is still asleep and dreaming. The Victoria is anchored off what appears to be a large island choked with verdant vegetation, its huge waxen leaves, shaped like torn teardrops, sway in a gentle breeze. They spill from the island to the Victoria's starboard side and, hidden amongst their foliage, tropical birds screech and trill. The light is bright and bold, saturating the world in the brightest greens, golds and reds. The seafloor must drop away sharply, for the ship is rocking on gentle waves very close to a sheer cliff that gives way abruptly to the west onto a wide beach. The air is filled with the scent of warm sand and the faintly rotten, sulphuric smell of drying seaweed whose tendrils stretch across the shoreline.

Barbosa stands before de Morales in the centre of the main deck. Though his clothing is faded and torn, the captain looks dashing and cavalier in a wide-brimmed hat with one hand resting on the pommel of a rapier hanging at his side. He closes the door and Barbosa turns at the sound. A broad smile stretches across the captain's face when he sees the physician. 'Ah señor de Morales, well met.' He says. 'You have recovered?'

'Much improved, thank you,' de Morales says. He cannot be sure what Elcano told Barbosa and so he must be careful not to reveal too much. His eye lingers on the space beside the mainmast where Quesada's headless and bleeding phantom appeared.

'It was that frightful weather,' Barbosa says conversationally. 'With your workload from the sickness, I'm surprised you stayed upright as long as you did. But all is well now, señor doctor.'

'The men-,' he says, but Barbosa cuts him off.

'Nineteen so far have succumbed, God rest them.' The captain seems worryingly unconcerned with the loss of life. Barbosa starts forwards as de Morales hangs his head. They died while he slept. Who can know if he could have saved them? He is hit by an immense sense of guilt at the needless loss of life and all because he saw. . .

'How long did I sleep?' He asks, trying to turn his mind away from ghosts and curses.

'Two days.' Nineteen deaths in just two days. That is an appalling toll.

310

'You cannot blame yourself,' Barbosa says, seeing the distraught look on de Morales' face. 'You did what you could and exhausted yourself in the process. You know as well as anyone, perhaps more so, how fickle scurvy can be. It claims some and yet others who appear worse recover.' Barbosa. De Morales is sure many in the fleet will blame him for the deaths of their friends. After all, he knows he would.

'Be jolly, de Morales,' Barbosa says brightly, thumping him on the shoulder. 'We have located spices.' Now that is a surprise. De Morales raises his head and looks into Barbosa's joyful eyes. The captain cannot help but smile despite the deaths.

'How on earth did we find the spice islands in two days?'

'We are not at *the* Spice Islands,' Barbosa says. 'We have found dried cloves and other spices. But if they are here, it means the Moluccas are nearby.'

'I don't understand. Where did you find them? Floating in the sea?'

Barbosa laughs heartily. 'You slept only two days, but you missed so much. The day after you retired to your cabin, Serrano sighted land from the Concepción. It was this island,' he nods towards the beach, empty but for three skiffs and a few joking sailors staring at the swaying palm trees lining the beach. 'We sailed toward it, hoping we had finally found somewhere to restock the ships with food and water. But when the sun began to set, we knew we would not reach the island before nightfall. Fernão gave the order to drop anchor a league from land, planning to go ashore at first light. But while the crew slept, native scoundrels rowed out from the island and snuck aboard the Trinidad. The watchmen on board the flagship quickly noticed the natives climbing over the taffrail and sounded the alarm. But before anyone could react, the natives cut the Capitán General's skiff loose and rowed it to shore. Meanwhile, other natives who had climbed aboard ran amok on the deck of the flagship. They were trying to steal knives and clothing, anything they could get their hands on. One was killed and another wounded and captured, though he has since died, but the rest made it ashore.'

'These natives, it sounds as if they knew what they would find.'

'Precisely,' Barbosa says. 'Elcano said the self-same thing, you share his quick mind. The fact these natives climbed aboard, knowing where to find the skiffs and that they would find weapons on board speaks to their familiarity with Europeans. Probably the Portuguese.'

'How did Magalhães react to the thievery?' De Morales knows the Capitán General would take such an affront in the worst possible way.

'He was mad with rage.' Barbosa replies. 'When morning came, Fernão organised a foray of men. Serrano, Elcano, Carvalho and two dozen others led by Espinosa rowed ashore at first light, Enrique also accompanied them in case he could communicate with the locals. I stayed behind to watch the fleet in case of another attack. They found a native village not far inland and sacked it. The Capitán General's skiff was found in a hidden basement underneath one of the huts.'

'That business finished with, Fernão asked Enrique to try to communicate with the natives. Unfortunately, he could not. But he was able to describe cloves to the natives using sign language. They seemed to be familiar with what he described and one of the women went into her hut and returned with a handful of spices. The woman explained there are no clove trees on this island, these having come there

312

through trade with other peoples nearby.'

The story is incredible, de Morales can hardly believe he missed every moment of it. 'Why was I not woken?' he asks.

'Well this all happened only last night and the cloves were only found a few hours ago. In honesty, in all the excitement you were forgotten.'

That sounds about right, he thinks to himself. 'Was anyone injured in the attack on the Trinidad?' he asks.

'Fortunately not. Goodness knows we can ill afford to lose any more men. The locals did not seem to have any interest in killing anyone. Though if they had, they easily could have.'

'That is a relief,' he says. 'What of the skirmish in the village? Was anyone injured there?'

'Again, thankfully not. As the Capitán General attacked the village I fired the cannons which quite terrified the natives. Surely you heard that? Anyway, I aimed well above the village for fear of harming our men, but the sound alone struck the native's hearts cold with fear.'

'So where is the Capitán General now?'

'Fernão has stayed ashore,' Barbosa says, flicking his head in the direction of the island. He thinks the natives may be trying to mislead him about not having any clove trees. He has sent a search party to scour the land. So far as I know, they have found nothing.'

'Do you know if the Capitán General found food?' De Morales asks.

'They have food,' Barbosa says, and de Morales breathes a sigh of relief. At the mention of food, he realises his stomach is clenched tightly, he has not eaten in almost three days. 'When it arrives you must check what is suitable for those in the infirmary.'

The two men turn to the shore. Silent, it belies nothing of what is happening beyond the line of palms. But de Morales is no fool. Though Barbosa's account of the skirmish sounds bloodless enough, he knows precisely what will have happened beyond those silent trees.

They remain together for some time, standing side-by-side and staring into the vegetation, neither saying anything. De Morales takes a deep breath and lets it draw out of him slowly, releasing all the pent-up pressure. The sight of land feels cathartic, as if it is a turning point. Just knowing food and water are nearby is enough to quell many worries that have wracked his mind. At length, he sighs, turns away from the island, and says, 'I will check on the men.'

The infirmary is much the same, if slightly less crowded. The bodies of the dead have been disposed of, but those that still live are strewn across the floor of the hold. He checks the vinegar and finds little has been used in the time he had been gone and so quickly sets to dispensing spoonfuls into reluctant mouths.

He comes to an older man who is still in the early stages of the illness. 'You were missed, señor doctor,' the man says after he has swallowed his spoonful of vinegar.'

'I am sorry. I was unwell myself.' De Morales sees the man's look of concern and adds quickly, 'though I am recovered now.'

'I served under Cristoforo Colombo on his final voyage,' the man says, settling back onto the bare boards of the infirmary. 'I thought we suffered then but,' he shakes his head, taking in the groaning men and stained hold. 'I have never seen a sickness such as this. So many men. . .' he trails off.

Sometimes, when she was at her most unsettled, Juana la

Loca would speak of Colombo. She would say he was returning to her soon, that he had gone to the New World to find a golden and glorious city in her name and that he would return soon, bearing parrots and silver and slaves for her. The trick was to play along. Sometimes some sycophant fool would remind Juana that Colombo was dead these past ten years and that would send her into a fit of rage and threats.

'What was he like, Colombo?' De Morales asks. He has never met anyone who knew the celebrated explorer.

'Delusional,' the man says and closes his eyes.

Carvalho is missing.

The Capitán General and his entourage of makeshift conquistadors returned a few hours after de Morales' conversation with Barbosa. They emerged triumphant from the line of lilting palms that hide the village beyond from view.

It was the first time de Morales had seen Magalhães in his full armour and, even he had to admit the fine steel breastplate of the Portuguese design, decorated with golden tassels, a fluted fauld and bordered by bronze ornamentations stretching around the placart and midriff made for an imposing picture. Its polished steel caught the sunlight and flashed reflections across the beach into his eyes from the shore, dazzling him. Once on board the Trinidad, Magalhães sent sailors ashore with a guard of armed men led by Espinosa to bring the supplies that had been traded or stolen back to the armada. The Capitán General was buoyant but no longer elated for he did not find clove trees on this island.

Now Magalhães limps across the Trinidad's deck, sighs out of his armour and enters his cabin, followed by Pigafetta

315

and Enrique.

When Elcano climbs aboard the Victoria. He notices de Morales and smiles broadly. 'It is good to see you recovered,' he says simply, not hinting that he knows the nature of de Morales' affliction.

'How goes it?' Barbosa asks.

'The island is small,' Elcano says. 'It cannot be larger than twenty leagues in total and so we were unable to explore it almost completely. The men still lack energy, though we did eat at the native village.'

'Were there any other settlements?' Barbosa asks. 'Any other people?'

'Not that we saw, though as I say we did not search extensively. There are no clove trees nor pepper, cinnamon, anise, nutmeg or mace. There is, however, plentiful fresh water in a large pool near the centre of the island fed by springs. The Capitán General paid some local men in glass beads to transport barrels from the springs down to the shore, they should be here soon. He could have stolen it, but Magalhães seemed concerned that we create as little ill-will between the locals and the armada as possible.'

'A wise policy,' Barbosa says. 'We may have need of these people in the future. The bond forged by friendship is stronger than fear.'

Elcano nods before continuing. 'The people rely on the ocean for sustenance, but they do have some produce of their own. We found coconuts, cucumbers, bananas and many other new fruits. Though it is difficult to say for sure, I get the impression these are not a rich people. We found no gold, silver or turquoise.'

'Then what do they use to trade with for the cloves?' Barbosa asks.

Elcano shrugs, 'women, maybe? Turtle shells. Who knows? They may have something of value to other tribes in the area but there is nothing here for us.'

His report finished, Elcano excuses himself to his cabin below, inviting de Morales to join him. He had forgotten how small the space was. There is no window and the tiny room, reeking of mildew and rot, is lit only by a small candle on a stool beside the bed. The cramped life Elcano has been living is well below his station.

'It is good to see you recovered,' Elcano says. He motions to de Morales to take the bed as he lights a candle and sits awkwardly on the stool.

'When I awoke, I thought I had slept for weeks,' de Morales says. 'So much has changed so quickly.'

Elcano's smile is rueful. 'We are certainly close to the Spice islands, but how close exactly we do not know. The local people say only that the spices they have on the island were traded from the west, but where exactly they either do not know or will not tell us. The Capitán General thinks they are lying.'

'And what do you think?' De Morales asks.

'I think they are genuine. Most likely the cloves passed through several islands and tribes before arriving here. They could even have been left by the Portuguese or salvaged from a wrecked ship. But, in any case, the natives here have seen and heard our artillery and, despite the Capitán General's best efforts, there was some bloodshed. Would you continue to hide information having witnessed that?'

'That would depend on what I had witnessed,' he says.

'Well imagine Carvalho carving through women and children. His appetite for violence was insatiable.'

'Did the Capitán General not stop him?'

'Espinosa did, eventually. Though he let the violence play out long enough before he did.'

They sit in silence. De Morales is not surprised. In Rio de Janeiro, Carvalho only had two things on his mind: violence and women. In the time since his passions have not changed. 'And Carvalho is missing now?' De Morales asks.

'Of course he is,' Elcano says exasperated. 'The almighty only knows what evils he is up to. Once we have what food we can take, we will depart. With or without Carvalho.'

'Why does Magalhães still place so much trust in a man who has continually proven himself to be so unworthy of it?' De Morales wonders aloud.

'For all his faults,' Elcano says, 'Carvalho is faithful to Magalhães. Since we left Los Cristianos, loyalty is all that matters to the Capitán General.'

Loyalty. How many men have suffered and died in the past seventeen months despite their loyalty to Magalhães? Loyalty goes both ways, and the Capitán General is loyal only to his own glory. Outside this very cabin, dozens of men are dying because Magalhães obstinately stuck to his plan despite Gomes' concerns in the strait, concerns that have been proven correct time and time again. Had they turned around and returned to Sevilla, how many lives could have been saved, how many agonies spared? But all that matters to Magalhães is that he has been vindicated, regardless of the price others had to pay for that vindication.

'I am sorry about Amaya,' de Morales says. Even as he says them, the words seem empty.

Elcano sighs deeply and his shoulders slump. The smile he offers is sorrowful and half-hearted. 'I have never married,' he says finally. 'I have a daughter I have not seen for a dozen years. God only knows where she is now. I am not ashamed to admit that Amaya was a refuge in this cruel world.' He wipes welling tears away with the heel of his hand. His voice breaks. 'I am glad it was you who found her. Any other man would have tossed her overboard. You cannot know how grateful I am to you that I was able to say goodbye.'

Elcano is heartbroken and, seeing his anguish, de Morales remains silent. Sometimes words cannot help and silent comradeship is all people need. So many deaths. De Morales realises he has lost count. 'This expedition has cost too many lives,' he says finally.

The two men sit in quiet, melancholy contemplation. The room is dim, lit by the small flickering candle. The ceiling of the tiny cabin thuds as men, full of energy now that cloves have been found and their bellies are filled with food from the island, stomp back and forth above them, preparing the ship to depart.

Elcano returns from the dark thoughts that were on his mind. He shifts on the stool, sighs heavily then says, 'I find myself thinking of the San Antonio.'

'Of its fate, you mean?' De Morales asks, knowing Elcano enjoys reflecting and speculating. Hoping it will cheer him up, he is trying to encourage whatever Elcano has to say.

The Basque scoffs lightly. 'Fate,' he says. He shakes his head, pulls on his beard. 'Their fate was avoidable. Even if they were wrecked, and we cannot be sure they were, a wreck rarely kills every man. Magalhães must have known that. But to abandon his son and cousin regardless is abominable.'

De Morales thinks of the child in his wife's womb. The life unlived. He thinks of the lengths he would go to protect that life. 'You think it more likely the San Antonio was not wrecked?' He asks.

'I keep thinking of Gomes,' Elcano says, looking de

Morales in the eye. 'I keep hearing him talk of the foolishness of continuing and I wonder, could he have taken matters into his own hands?'

De Morales' mouth falls open. 'A mutiny?'

Elcano shrugs. 'It is possible,' he says. 'Gomes was no friend of Cartagena, but he certainly saw the Capitán General in the same light as Fonseca's bastard.'

Cartagena. The name is like a phantom now. He and de la Reina marooned together on that tiny rock in Puerto San Julián. Could they have survived this long? Sure not.

'Either way,' Elcano says, 'Magalhães ought to have gone to the San Antonio's aid. But instead, he abandoned forty men and all because he is obsessed with his strait and proving to the world he was right.'

'But he found his strait,' de Morales says, playing the devil's advocate. 'And now he is within reaching distance of the Spice Islands.'

'True,' Elcano says. 'Men like Magalhães never linger on their errors.'

The holds of the ships are stocked with food from the island and the huge barrels of water are once more filled to the brim. In his zeal for revenge and sustenance, Magalhães forgot his duty of erecting a cross and claiming the land for the king. He sets to the job now.

Perhaps it is because he is afraid of losing men to desertion, but the Capitán General allows no one but himself, Valderrama, Barbosa and Serrano to go ashore as well as two sailors to carry the cross. The ceremony is short and witnessed only by the swinging palm trees. Once done with, the small group trudges across the deep white sand towards a waiting skiff.

Carvalho appears in the tree line. Sauntering out of the jungle, his rapier resting on his shoulder. Dried blood stains the blade and he carries his shirt in his hand as he meanders across the sand towards the shore.

The pilot stops before Magalhães, addresses him and continues into the skiff seemingly without recrimination or rebuke from the Capitán General.

'A friend of Magalhães can do as he pleases.' Elcano says. 'So long as he remains loyal.'

When everyone has returned to their ships, they raise anchor, drop the sails and cast off from the island that has been their salvation and Carvalho's playground. Their heading is due west, seeking the Spice Islands.

There is no farewell gathering from the locals as in Rio de Janeiro, only the cross, minute and forlorn against the towering palm trees. But Magalhães orders a volley of cannon fire to be shot over the empty beach, nonetheless. The furious explosions shudder and shake the ships. The palm leaves on the shore of the island ripple and wave. The echoes fade, an empty display of power over a powerless people.

As the ringing in de Morales' ears fades, the sound of screaming fills the void left behind. At first, he thinks the screams are coming from the shore but, from the chaos onboard, it is clear they are from the flagship. Sailors desperately wave their hands and run the length of the deck. The armada, having travelled all of a few feet, grinds to a halt once more.

'So much for a triumphant exit,' Barbosa says, rushing to the gunwale.

'Someone is injured,' Elcano says, moving away from the whipstaff and following him.

A skiff splashes into the turquoise sea from the Trinidad and the men inside furiously row towards the Victoria, calling de Morales' name. This cannot be good. The Capitán General would be loath to call de Morales instead of Bustamante. Someone is severely injured.

When he arrives on the flagship, the scene de Morales walks into is reminiscent of the battlefields of Naples. An exploded cannon, its barrel split open like a roasted chestnut shell, lies on its side at the edge of the main deck. Smeared across the worn planks is a trail of blood leading to the port side gunwale. Leaning against it, with his chin on his chest is the body of a sailor. The sailor's face is covered with a dirty cloth, heavily blotted with blood.

De Morales approaches the sailor. The crew of the Trinidad part before him, treading carefully around the blood staining the main deck. 'What is his name?' He asks.

'Jean Bautista,' a voice says behind him. 'French.'

De Morales kneels beside the body and carefully lifts the rag. The already congealing blood jealousy holds the fabric as he peels it away. The face that is slowly revealed to him is a ruin. The nose is utterly missing, leaving an oozing, open wound in its wake. The whole left side is slanted downwards, the eye lolling in a socket blown open. Shreds of skin and muscle are all that is left of the cheek and the bone and teeth below are blackened and burned. The body gives off the sick, nauseating scent of burnt flesh and the sulphuric musk gunpowder. Through the hole in the sailor's cheeks, de Morales sees his tongue moving.

'You are alive?' He says, incredulous. He senses the crew step backwards away from the wreckage before them.

The sailor raises his hand and stretches what is left of his fingers to the sun. Blood and saliva bubble from the corner of his ruined mouth. 'J'étais,' he stutters and his hand falls to the deck.

Silence descends over the Trinidad. De Morales lets go of the breath he has been holding. Slowly, he lifts the rag back to the sailor's face.

'The canon exploded,' a voice in the crowd says. 'Jean took a face full of iron and gunpowder.'

Another voice, 'did he feel pain, señor doctor?'

'Until his last moment.'

Chapter 21

March 1521

The armada makes its slow way through a maze of islands. Some are no bigger than the ships they have called home for eighteen months now. Others are far larger, with wide beaches fringed by deep palm forests and mangroves of spear-shaped fronds, ferns and other waxy plants. But all are either inaccessible, being surrounded by jagged, towering cliffs of coral that would tear the ships apart or else simply deserted.

De Morales, meanwhile, continues to tend to the sick men in the makeshift infirmary. Since the armada left the nameless island ten days ago, no new cases of the illness have occurred and there is much hope that it has passed. It is an easy thing to believe when one is on the main deck in the clean air, with your belly full and watching beguiling paradise islands slide by in the sunshine. But in the hold below, the illness still runs rampant through the bodies of the stricken men.

In order to nourish the ill, de Morales brings fresh fruit and vegetables taken from the nameless island into the infirmary. The men are reluctant to eat the harder vegetables, fearing the pain it would cause their wobbly teeth and tender gums. Instead, they choose the softer fruit, hungrily sucking the flesh from cucumbers and wincing at the pain in their mouths as the juices seep into their wounds. The smell of death and disease that has choked the hold since Maestre Andrew was first brought there is replaced, for a time, with the sticky sweetness of tropical fruit.

But, for some, it is too late. Another three who refuse any food die, their broken bodies finally giving up the ghost. Their remains, rotten and wrecked, are wrapped in strips of old sail and hauled onto the deck. Then they were dumped into the sea like so many of their comrades before them. De Morales knows better than to watch the sorry ceremony. He cannot face seeing the spectre of Quesada again with his drawn, bloody body glistening in the sun.

Finally, they reach an island that allows the fleet to drop anchor and the men to go ashore en masse. Magalhães orders half a dozen men to remain on the ships and stand guard. Perhaps as some form of punishment for his actions on the last island, the Capitán General forces Carvalho to stay with the fleet along with other men capable of operating the cannons and crossbows in the event they will be needed. The pilot sulkily stalks into the dining cabin of the flagship, slamming the door behind him.

For the first time since the eighteenth day of October 1520, de Morales' feet touch solid ground. The land feels stable under his feet, and he is suddenly aware of the immense weight of the earth beneath him. It holds him tight to itself, as if it is welcoming home a long-absent child.

'Six unbroken months at sea,' he says to Elcano. 'I can hardly believe it.' He kneels on the beach strewn with thick tendrils of dried seaweed and lifts a handful of sand, savouring its warmth and its coarse familiarity.

Elcano thumps him on the back as he rises. 'We'll make a sailor of you yet, señor doctor,' he says smiling.

'The natives of the Indies keep their villages close to the sea, even on the largest islands,' Barbosa says. 'We would do well to prepare for an unfriendly welcome.' A nod from the Capitán General nearby and Espinosa gives the order to the crew to draw their weapons. Rapiers, knives and axes glint in the bright sun, casting dazzling reflections across the sand.

The men, some ninety in total, begin moving forward. Fallen palm fronds littering the ground crunch beneath their feet and birds in the canopies scatter at their coming. Slowly, the makeshift conquistadors pass into the deep shadows as the silent and foreboding palms press in around them. Tensions rise as daylight fades. De Morales stays at the rear of the crew, wanting to be well clear of any violence should it occur.

But as he, too, passes into the deeper shade, it becomes clear this island is most likely uninhabited. All around them there is nothing but fronds, ferns, mosquitoes and silence broken by only crashing waves and birdsong.

'There is no one here,' Pigafetta says. 'We are quite alone.'

'Suppose there is a village on the opposite side,' Espinosa says.

Barbosa shakes his head, 'even if that were the case, they would have huts and lookouts all around the island to watch for invaders. Even the most savage native wouldn't allow their home island to fall into this level of disarray. Pigafetta is right, we are alone.'

As word filters along the line, the men in front of de Morales relax and the tension dissipates. He takes the opportunity to study the jungle more thoroughly. It is almost as choking as the rainforests of the New World and so many trunks surround them as to overwhelm one's eyes. The palms are riddled with vines, twisting and creeping towards the light above. Lower to the ground, almost no light breaks through the tangled fronds high above leaving the ground a bare mess of fallen branches and curling leaves.

Calmed by Barbosa's certainty, the crew begin marching quicker through the thick jungle. They hack and slash at leaves and branches blocking their way with their weapons, no longer trying to keep quiet. Between the swaying heads and swinging weapons ahead of him, de Morales is sure the trees ahead are becoming sparser, the sunlight brightening.

'Food.' The voice, almost swallowed by the jungle surrounding them, is far ahead.

The men ahead of de Morales begin jostling for position, pushing forward towards what he can now see is a break in the jungle. He follows them, the vines and clinging leaves grappling with his clothing as he pushes onwards.

He bursts out of the tree line into a wide space cleared of all trees and shrubs. The sunlight, so bright after the darkness of the jungle, stings his eyes and he blinks several times, hardly believing what he is seeing.

Before him, planted in rows as if cultivated by farmers, are low trailing plants, bright green and verdant. Every few feet are taller, deeply green bushes. At intervals all around the clearing are stocky trees, similar to palms but much shorter with swollen, yellow fruits clumped together in the shade offered by their sparse foliage. They have been well cared for and have grown strong while the furrowed earth around them has been carefully picked clean of weeds.

'This makes no sense,' Barbosa says. He stands at the edge of the clearing staring in disbelief. But the men are not listening, they surge forwards towards the crops and begin wrenching them up out of the ground. De Morales follows, his hunger urging him onwards.

The men sit apart from one another, harvesting whatever fruit and vegetables are within reach of them. De Morales digs in the dirt beneath one of the stocky bushes with broad leaves and finds a large root vegetable, its skin blackened as if charred by fire. He wipes the dirt away with his hands, revealing a brown skin beneath, and bites into it. It is starchy and very bitter, so much so that he spits the mouthful out onto the floor.

Thinking perhaps it was not yet ripe, he digs deeper, pulling more and more of the vegetables up from the earth. His attention is quickly distracted from his crop when he sees other men tearing into swollen yellow fruits hanging from one of the trees. He joins them, pulling down a fruit the size of his fist. The flesh within is orange, its liquor sweet and moreish. He and his comrades stand at this altar like pilgrims, gluttonous and grateful.

The kings of Europe would pay thousands of maravedis for a feast like this and guard it jealously behind tall walls and fierce guards. Here they are, two hundred exhausted sailors, closer to beggars than kings, eating their fill of delicacies most would likely never taste back home.

A distant cannon fires, startling the peaceful gathering. The Capitán General stands immediately and reaches for his sword. Espinosa, Barbosa and Serrano follow suit, exchanging anxious glances. The men stop eating, looking between one another, waiting. Another explosion shudders through the air and more men jump up.

Now everyone is rushing for the shore and the waiting skiffs. All around de Morales, men stumble forwards, trying to carry armloads of fruit and vegetables while desperately reaching for their knives and tripping over roots and vines. Espinosa leads the way, furiously hacking and tearing through the thick vegetation with his rapier. In the rear, Magalhães lags behind, limping and calling orders to the men ahead of him. As de Morales emerges into the blinding light of the beach, he sees the ships are alive with activity.

The sailors left behind on the armada run about on the decks like men under siege. They reach for arquebuses, crossbows, swords and spears and man cannons, aiming everything out to the sea over the taffrails. Carvalho is among them. His back to the beach and his sword drawn, the pilot is staring out to sea.

Once they reach the beach, the troupe of men fan outwards across the sand, craning their necks to see what those on the ships are aiming at. Whatever it is, it is hidden behind the bloated bulks of the ship's hulls.

Being completely unarmed and next to useless should a skirmish break out de Morales remains at the rear of the line of sailors and captains close to the tree line. The Capitán

General bursts through the trees behind him, Enrique at his side. Unsteady on the sand, he limps forwards before stopping between Barbosa and Espinosa breathing heavily.

'Carvalho, o que você vê?' The Capitán General, in his agitation, returns to his native Portuguese as he calls out to Carvalho.

'Men,' Carvalho answers in Spanish, remembering himself better than Magalhães. 'Men in canoes carved from the hollowed trunks of trees. They came across the sea from some island. I know not where.'

'Are they armed?' Cries Magalhães, this time in Spanish.

'I think not,' comes the reply from Carvalho. 'If they are, we have the measure of them anyway.'

A charged silence follows as the men on the beach nervously anticipate what the ships hide from their view. De Morales has seen giants, sea monsters, huge storms and colossal leviathans off the coast of the New World. He struggles to imagine what new horror and hardship awaits on the other side of those ships.

Magalhães finally comes to a decision. 'Signal for them to come to the beach,' he calls to Carvalho. 'Keep your weapons at the ready,' he adds hastily.

Carvalho turns back to the open ocean, points animatedly and waves his hand in the direction of the beach. Very slowly, the men on the ships following their every movement, three long, sleek canoes come into view from behind the armada. They are similar to those the natives in Terra do Brasil used, though far more pointed at the prow and of a deeper design. Most bizarrely, the boats have wide arms reaching out into the ocean on either side of their hulls, giving them the look of water striders. The arms, de Morales supposes, are to balance the small crafts in the open ocean, stopping the boats from capsizing in errant waves. Even to a novice sailor like himself, it is clear these canoes are made for long voyages across deep water and that they must be skilfully crafted by knowledgeable people.

The men inside the canoes look as shocked to find these strange white men here as the crew are to find them. Perhaps more so, de Morales thinks, because what stands before them is something so alien and bizarre, that they likely lack the language to explain it. Their canoes, beautifully carved though they are, are dwarfed by the behemoth ships standing sentinel beside them.

The canoes surge onto the shore, the men who climb out of them are of average height but with a powerful build and deeply tanned and immaculate skin. One of them moves to the front of the group. His hair is long and smoothed from careful combing and is held back from his face with a bandanna of material coloured like gold and smooth as silk. His entire upper body is coated in tattoos of varying shapes and symbols. Like a livery collar, intricate birds are tattooed around his neck. More stretch down the lengths of his arms in geometric patterns, coating them like sleeves. He has a furrowed, worried-looking brow and high cheekbones below dark eyes. Despite his age, which must be around fifty, there is a handsome power to his features.

The Capitán General moves forward to greet the natives and the contrast is startling. Magalhães, exhausted, short and burly with his long bushy beard, stained shirt and limp, and this powerful and handsome native whose every movement is full of grace and hidden power. De Morales is suddenly very aware of the state the crew are in as he looks around and takes in the tattered clothing, the bare feet, the sores and wounds and the unkempt hair.

The two leaders approach one another. Magalhães clicks his fingers and Enrique dashes forwards, joining them at his master's side. As the leaders approach one another, de Morales finds himself moving closer as well, the better to see and hear what passes between them. The native leader holds his hand up, perhaps in greeting or perhaps as an order to Magalhães to stop moving. The Capitán General, erring on the side of caution, stops mid-step and imitates the movement.

'Greetings,' Magalhães says in a loud and clear voice, 'I am Fernão de Magalhães, Capitán General of the Armada de Molucca. I have been sent by the King of all the Spains and the Holy Roman Emperor, King Carlos.'

Enrique repeats Magalhães' words in his native tongue. The leader nods. He understood every word of it.

The leader's name is Rajah Kolambu. Through eavesdropping on Enrique's translations, de Morales learns the Rajah is the king of several islands in the area: Mazaua, South Leyte, Masao, Mindanao, Butuan, Amihanang Agusan, the list goes on. The longer Enrique lists the Rajah's domains, the more de Morales thinks they have found the emperor's counterpart in this part of the world. Even the language Kolambu speaks has the same guttural poetry to it as the Flemish that has taken over Castile since Carlos' arrival.

The Rajah gestures broadly across the island, then speaks as Enrique translates. 'This island's name is Homonhon and it, too, is part of my domain. My territories are so vast that Homonhon is but a plantation, feeding my other islands.'

They are trespassers then, not to mention thieves.

'Rajah Kolambu,' Magalhães says while, beside him,

Enrique translates, 'please accept my humblest apologies for taking from your stores. We knew not this island was governed and took it for a wild place. Please accept these fine gifts as payment for the food we took.' The Capitán General offers the Rajah a finely carved wooden box. The Rajah, fascinated by the intricate engravings upon its sides, opens the lid and is further intrigued by its contents. Glass beads, several silk hats, a small wooden crucifix and, most impressive to him of all, two well-crafted but simple knives.

Sailors snicker as the Rajah examines the gifts. Their pockets and bellies full of this king's food, the sailors mock him as he examines each one, spellbound at their craftsmanship. Few of the señores, however, find humour in the Rajah's reaction. These are merely new things to him and speak not of his simplicity, but of Castile's innovation.

The Rajah speaks and Enrique translates. 'I consider you a friend, Fernão de Magalhães. Friends cannot steal from one another. Let us feast properly together, you and I.'

And so, for the second time that day, de Morales eats his fill of the fine foods of this peaceful and quiet island. The Rajah's men bring more food from other clearings, food more familiar to him. They eat beans, cucumbers and coconuts as well as more of the yellow fruits hanging from the trees. The charred tubers de Morales dug up that tasted so bitter are collected and boiled in a large pot brought from some hidden place in the jungle. Gingerly, he puts a slice of one into his mouth expecting to spit it straight out again. But through cooking the crop is utterly transformed. It is starchy and sweet and almost melts in his mouth.

The captains, Magalhães, Serrano and Barbosa, are seated on a raised part of the land with the chief, Rajah Kolambu and Enrique who diligently translates as the two leaders speak. De Morales is seated, much to his disappointment, with Pigafetta and Carvalho who gaily talk amongst themselves, making ribald jokes and poking each other in the ribs as they tear at whatever food is within reach.

'You know,' says Carvalho, spitting as he talks through a full mouth, 'if this Rajah is so forthcoming with gifts for the Capitán General, I only hope he forgets not the common men and their needs.' Pigafetta laughs heartily, a look of rampant lust in his eyes.

Elcano is seated with the other pilots of the ships. They are engaged in a serious conversation, perhaps sharing notes of one another's experiences of the waters of this part of the world thus far. De Morales looks to them with jealous eyes as Pigafetta cackles away beside him. The Italian is the worst kind of adulator. The kind of sycophant who changes his personality to match whoever he is with. If, that is, he deems them worthy of the effort. In the Capitán General's company, Pigafetta will play the part of the noble explorer and chronicler. Put him with Carvalho, however, and he becomes a bawdy, foul-mouthed buffoon. He gets the sense that Pigafetta is deliberately overstating his merriment as a strange way of reminding de Morales of his exile.

Despite his present company, the mood of the feast is light and joyful. After all the trials and difficulties of the last eighteen months, they have found, at the very least, the general area of the Spice Islands. Surely the Capitán General is, at this very moment, discussing with Rajah Kolambu the exact location of the Tidore, Ternate, Buru and all the other Moluccan islands. De Morales has noticed a box of cloves that Magalhães always carries with him now, resting on the mat in front of the Rajah. When the Capitán General shows them to the chief, the Rajah Kolambu looks at them, but not very closely – a sure sign he is already familiar with them.

The meal is finished and the Magalhães stands awkwardly. Rajah Kolambu springs to his feet and the Capitán General shows the Rajah how they shake hands in Castile and then they part ways. Magalhães towards the ships, Rajah Kolambu towards the trees to the north of the clearing. He must have some dwelling on this island, hidden away among the thick foliage of tropical trees and ferns swaying in the gentle breeze.

The captains stand and call to the men to return to the armada. They follow, slowly at first for there is a shared reluctance to go back aboard the ships upon which they lived so long. They are sped along by the Espinosa and the boatswains cursing, cajoling and threatening them.

A sailor appears beside de Morales, holding a woven basket in his hand. 'Barbosa explained the illness to the Rajah,' he says, passing the basket to de Morales. 'He says you must fill this basket with extra food and take it to them.'

'Pass on my gratitude,' de Morales says. He takes the basket and begins filling it with as much leftover food as will fit.

'No women, then,' Carvalho says to Pigafetta as they rise slowly. 'We are forsaken by the Rajah.'

'And we asked for so little,' Pigafetta says laughing.

Wanting to get away from Carvalho and Pigafetta, de Morales waits at the edge of the clearing for Barbosa and Elcano to catch up. He falls into step beside them as they head towards the Victoria.

'What plans, then, captain?' Elcano asks jovially.

'We have learned a great many things from this Rajah Kolambu,' Barbosa says. 'He recognised the cloves and when the Capitán General described ginger, nutmeg, pepper and every other spice, the chief understood everything. It seems

335

there is a great trade in this part of the world in the same spices that we seek. Though not by the Portuguese.'

'So that would be how the other islanders had cloves.' Elcano says.

'Indeed. So far as we could tell, the main trade is from an exceedingly wealthy people to the north. The spices do not grow here, however. Nor do they grow on any island the Rajah presides over.'

'So do we have a heading?' Elcano asks.

'Not as yet,' Barbosa replies. 'The Rajah has invited the Capitán General to the seat of his kingdom, an island to the south-west named Limasawa. He would not say where exactly the island is located, but it cannot be far. It seems he and his entourage travelled from there yesterday, stopping overnight at another island on the way.'

'Do you suppose he mistrusts us?' Elcano asks.

'I think he is a careful ruler and a careful ruler trusts no one,' Barbosa says seriously.

'Hmmm,' Elcano says, jabbing de Morales in the ribs with his elbow.

They continue onwards, the silence broken by the sounds of men shouting and birds calling. De Morales deliberately walks slowly to prolong his freedom from the Victoria's oppressive presence, ghosts and rampant disease.

'I do not think this Rajah means harm to us,' Barbosa says after some time. 'He seems fond of Fernão.'

The following morning, the Capitán General meets the Rajah on the beach once again. This time, he orders the crew to stay behind on board the ships while he, Enrique and Valderrama go ashore to perform mass. The native chief watches with interest as Valderrama begins his performance before the two leaders on the shores of the island.

The routine ceremony seems out of place on the sands of the tropical island fringed by the unruly jungle. When the time comes to kneel before Valderrama, Rajah Kolambu is reluctant, standing unmoving. It is clear he feels the show of deference is beneath him. Magalhães explains, through Enrique, that the Rajah kneels not before Valderrama, but before God, for Valderrama is but a vessel through which God can be praised. It is only when Magalhães takes the knee first that the Rajah also drops to his knees.

The rest of the ceremony passes by, with the Rajah mimicking Magalhães' actions. The chief plays the part, obediently taking the Eucharist despite the fact the ceremony must be meaningless to him. An empty ceremony, on an empty beach.

The Capitán General invites Rajah Kolambu onboard the Trinidad and they come to some agreement de Morales cannot hear. The chief stands proudly in the centre of the deck of the Trinidad, but his roving eyes belie his astonishment at the colossal ship and the intricacies of its workings. Four of the Rajah's guards remain on the flagship with him while the others climb nimbly down the rigging and into their canoes

Already the day is warm despite the early hour, and the horizon is enveloped with heavy clouds as the Capitán General gives the order to raise anchor. Despite the state of the flagship, with its torn sails and splintered rails, the ship lurching to movement doubtless makes for an imposing and impressive sight to Kolambu. Magalhães and the native king stand at the prow of the Trinidad on the forecastle, the Rajah guiding to his home island as Enrique translates.

With the wind behind the fleet, the sails swell and the armada picks up pace. The canoes are quickly left behind and the Rajah's four guards, standing on the main deck of the Trinidad never far from their ruler, exchange worried looks and anxiously speak to one another. But the Rajah seems unconcerned. He waves his hand, dismissing his warriors. De Morales is struck by how complete the Rajah's faith in the Capitán General already appears to be.

What is it about this Portuguese man that inspires such devout trust? Barbosa, Espinosa, Pigafetta, Rebêlo, Mesquita, the entire crew of the flagship and now this native chief. For all of them, the Capitán General can do no wrong. Not once, through all the awful journey thus far, through the tempests and the doldrums, through the endless freezing wait at Puerto San Julián and the Santa Cruz River, through the brutality of the trials and the hardships of the punishments and the abandonment of the San Antonio, not once did any of these men question Magalhães. It cannot be simple fear. Fear breeds contempt and contempt, at sea, breeds mutiny. There is something else afoot here. Something de Morales does not feel. Something Mendoza, Cartagena and Quesada recognised and, perhaps, feared. Fonseca saw it. Elcano must recognise it, too. Clearly the king did not, for he must be equally under the Capitán General's spell to launch so much money behind the armada on nothing more than Magalhães' word.

The journey to Limasawa takes only a few short hours. De Morales makes his way into the infirmary and hands out handfuls of fruit and vegetables from the basket. The men especially enjoy the root vegetable he dug from the ground. The mild taste and soft texture make them easy for them to chew and they do not hurt their open sores and swollen gums as some of the sharper fruits do.

When he climbs back onto the main deck, the heavy clouds lining the horizon have spilt across the sky, leering over the armada, dulling the sun and promising rain. During the journey, the armada rounds a huge landmass, its towering hills coated in thick foliage stretch for miles northwards until it is lost in the haze. The Trinidad does not stop, implying this land is not under the Rajah's rule.

Once they have rounded the cape of this island, Limasawa is revealed in the distance. It is a long, low and thin island, tiny in comparison to the massive one they have just passed by. On its northern border, it rises out of the ocean but steadily falls away as the island stretches southwards towards a wide shore cleared of palms and dotted with locals scattered across the beach.

The armada drops anchor as close to this shore as possible and Magalhães and the Rajah climb down into the Capitán General's skiff, accompanied by Enrique, Valderrama and the Rajah's guards.

On the shore, Kolambu's subjects gather in a close group. Their clothing, mostly made of grasses with some small silk adornments, is dyed bold and colourful. The men and women alike are shirtless but some of the women wear small flowers in their hair and brightly coloured beads around their necks. The men wear neck pieces, fashioned from palm leaves folded into intricate shapes that fall to their hips.

The native people seem transfixed as they take in the colossal ships of the Armada de Molucca and the peculiar-looking men running to and fro about the decks. But their greatest reverence, despite all the new and strange things before them, is reserved for the proud figure of the Rajah

Kolambu, sitting noble and erect beside the small white man in the skiff.

'I do not like this,' Barbosa says watching the skiff head towards the beach. 'Fernão has a priest and a slave to protect him. He could be walking into an ambush.'

'They would not be foolish enough,' Elcano says. 'They saw our weaponry at Homonhon.'

'They had no idea that what Carvalho pointed at them were weapons,' Barbosa says, still staring at the skiff. He shakes his head. 'I like this not. I want the men armed. I want every canon turned on that island.' Barbosa turns quickly and waves desperately to Espinosa on board the Trinidad. 'Send a message to Espinosa to do the same.'

'This is unwise,' Elcano says. 'If they see the weaponry, even if they suspect what it is, you could bring about that which you are trying to avert.'

Barbosa curses. He turns back to the shore. 'You are right,' he says.

The skiff, meanwhile, has almost reached the shore and now it surges into the sand and the locals press forward to greet its occupants. Warriors push through their midst, clothed in silk skirts and carrying long spears.

Barbosa has seen the warrior's determined look and the sharpness of their blade. He anxiously moves from side to side. 'There will be violence,' he says, his voice choked.

But no violence occurs.

The warriors turn suddenly to face the locals, keeping them back from the Rajah and his companions. Kolambu and Magalhães step onto the beach. The Rajah begins speaking at length, gesturing several times towards the Capitán General and the anchored fleet standing silent and imposing offshore. Enrique diligently translates the Rajah's words into the

Capitán General's ear.

It begins to rain and Magalhães gives the order that the men should disembark from the ships and make their way ashore. Carvalho pushes his way to the gunwale of the Trinidad, joining Espinosa and Pigafetta in the lead skiff that sets out immediately for the shore. De Morales hangs back, cautious of the intentions of these people the Capitán General has so quickly trusted.

Eventually he can delay no longer, and the surgeon lowers himself into the last skiff. As the boat slaps and rocks against the waves he finds himself watching the Capitán General being led around the beach by Rajah Kolambu. Incredulously, he notices the two men walk with arms interlocked. Perhaps this is some custom of the native people, but de Morales has never seen such camaraderie from the Capitán General before. With his most trusted companions, Barbosa, Espinosa, Pigafetta, the absent Mesquita, even his own son, Rebêlo, Magalhães always seems to keep everyone at arm's length.

The first mass ever heard on this island is led by Valderrama once all the men are ashore. The seamen are distracted, looking with hungry eyes at the bare-breasted women of Limasawa, gathered in a loose semi-circle around the crew. Nobody pays attention to Valderrama's sermon besides Magalhães and the Rajah, who imitates the captain's movements and listens intently to the droning Latin.

Since they have arrived in this place, de Morales has heard more mass and more Latin than on the entire journey from Sevilla to get here. Magalhães plays the part of the pious Christian explorer well, if haltingly. Maybe the Capitán General thought it was not worth his while in the New World. After all, when he finally broke free of following in the footsteps of those who came before him, the lands he found were mostly empty. The only successful baptism he can boast of thus far is a dead giant, long ago dumped in the sea and swallowed by monsters.

As de Morales stands watching the empty show of Christianity before him, the realisation hits him that the Capitán General has no idea where he is. He blindly sought passage through a strait he never truly knew the location of until a fortuitous accident swept him right into it. He bumbled his way across an ocean hundreds of times larger than he expected. Men fell ill then died in agony around him while he pressed on, driven by his rampant obsession. But at every juncture, when Magalhães is at his most lost, his men at their last extremity, his fleet literally falling pieces, good fortune materialises in the air around him and he stumbles into salvation. Truly, the Capitán General must be the luckiest man to ever live. Now, on this unknown island in an unknown ocean, Magalhães again finds salvation in the form of this hospitable native chief who, for whatever reason, has taken an instant and seemingly unwavering liking to him.

How far will luck carry Magalhães, de Morales wonders? It has taken him so far, after all. Will it guide him through the maze of these islands to the very roots of the clove trees? Will it lead him to the merchant winds, carry him swift and true across the vast Indian Ocean, around the Cape of Good Hope, up the endless coast of Africa, past a flotilla of Portuguese caravels guarding the Cape Verde islands and onwards, past Sanlúcar de Barrameda, up the treacherous Guadalquivir to the very ports of Sevilla? Will it guide him up the steps of the Casa de Contratación, beyond the desk of the jealous Fonseca, ranting and raving at the marooning of his bastard, until, finally, after years of heat, hunger, cold and good fortune he will stand before the king?

And what of the crew? Will the Capitán General's luck carry them home too? All the trials, tribulations, pains and discomforts they have endured since leaving Los Cristianos over the past eighteen months have only taken them halfway on their journey. The Spice Islands may be nearby, but Castile is still so very far away. And what of the surgeon of the Armada de Molucca? Will Magalhães' luck carry de Morales to Sevilla? To the empty house and the ghosts. Will the headless phantom of Quesada join his wife and child in those halls? Will Ginovés haunt his dreams there?

Involuntarily he turns to the armada and sees, as though it were real, the ghostly vision of the Victoria bathed in the blue light of St Elmo's Fire, its skeletal crew and swollen hull rotting from the inside out. If that vision was a precognition of the future, is it one he wants to experience?

It is Good Friday and Rajah Kolambu has invited every man from the armada to attend a celebration in a clearing in the centre of his village. Valderrama, through Enrique, has explained the significance of Easter to Christians and the chief, wanting to maintain good relations, has organised a feast in Christ's honour.

The feast is brought to the waiting men by attendant women. They carry huge ceramic bowls like those Chinese wares sold in Venice and Genoa at exorbitant prices. Heaps of aromatic rice steam in the wide bowls. Next, despite it being a Friday, two roasted and spitted sows are brought forwards, carried by two men a piece. It seems the natives have much to learn of Christianity.

The Capitán General dutifully abstains from the pork but

the other men, de Morales included, eat it greedily. Even Valderrama cannot help himself. Pigafetta makes a great show of his reluctance, loudly bemoaning how he is breaking canon law and begging forgiveness from the Almighty. All the while, the Italian tears at the meat, grease dripping down his chin.

Elcano, sitting beside de Morales, rolls his eyes at Pigafetta's feigned hesitation. 'With all we have been through,' he says, 'I think the Lord will forgive us for eating meat on a Friday.'

Having no qualms himself, de Morales enjoys the food. It is the first fresh meat he has tasted since the meal in the Trinidad's dining cabin eighteen months ago. It is the first feast the armada has enjoyed since their meal on Christmas day long before the strait and the mutiny and the suffering really began. All the other feast days have been forgotten. Even if they were remembered, there has been so little to eat for so much of the time.

He wants to savour each bite, but he cannot help himself as he eats quickly and greedily. The crisp crackling glistens in the sun and the tender meat below is sweet and succulent, flavoured with aromatic spices and honey. For the first time in a long time, his belly feels truly full, the meat satiating his hunger in the way only it can.

Once the feast is finished, women take their pick of the men and lead them away. Pigafetta and Carvalho quickly disappear. Barbosa, too, soon takes his leave, following a woman into one of the huts dotted around the clearing.

There seems to be no sense of monogamy in this culture. Women de Morales assumed to be married, or at least their version of it, freely took their choice of the crew. Perhaps it has been ordained by Rajah Kolambu that his guests will be treated well, or perhaps it is simply how they operate here.

Either way, he has no interest in them. His belly is full and he is resting in the shade of a tree on solid ground. He breathes the clean air, savours its scent as it washes the smell of rot and mildew from his body.

Finally removed from the confines of the Armada, he sees himself anew in the bright sunshine. He looks at his hands, his broken nails, his aged skin suddenly so wrinkled, the veins and tendons popping out through tanned, paper-thin skin. He touches his body. He can feel each rib and sinew distinctly. He gasps at the plunging void where his belly once was, stares in shock at his knobbly knees and bony feet.

Beside him is Elcano. He turns to him now and sees the thinning hair, greying in places. He wonders at the gaunt shape of his friend's cheeks, the deep-set eyes and the heavy bags beneath them. It feels a lifetime ago that he first saw Elcano standing on the Victoria in Los Cristianos. The man before him is a ghost of what he once was, a man broken by the world and by the relentless hardships it has thrown at them.

They sit in silence, de Morales trying to enjoy the tranquillity of this paradise island. The warm breeze, the shade and the earth beneath him. A dozen or so native men laze about after the meal in the shade of the rippling palm trees, apparently unconcerned by the lovemaking their women are engaged in.

Valderrama, Magalhães, Enrique and Rajah Kolambu are talking seriously some distance away. Magalhães waves to Elcano 'I have need of a pilot here,' he calls.

Elcano dutifully stands, slaps the sand from his torn trousers and approaches the gathering of leaders. Unwanted and unneeded, de Morales decides he will return to the Armada, thinking he will take what food remains for the men in the infirmary. Before he can rise, however, Valderrama walks toward him. The priest awkwardly lowers himself to the ground.

'Do you wish to take confession, señor doctor?'

'Not at this time, Valderrama.' He has yet to admit it fully to himself, but whatever remained of de Morales' faith when the armada left Sevilla has withered like leaves in autumn. He has thought little of God, in truth he has hardly had the time. But if he had, he knows he would not have returned as a penitent child searching for comfort and forgiveness. Because, though he is afraid to admit it, he sees God now as the capricious, wicked tyrant he is. The trail of dead men, rotting in the ground and being eaten in the ocean from the strait to this island attests to that.

Despite the snub, Valderrama remains beside him in the sand under the palm tree. 'I thought you were with them,' he says at last, looking somewhere in the distance.

'What are you talking about?' De Morales asks.

'The mutiny. In Puerto San Julián,' Valderrama says, still focusing on the distance. 'I thought you were in league with Mendoza and all the rest. Barbosa asked me after the first day of the trial when I was cleared.'

De Morales senses a red mist descend over his eyes, feels wrath rising from his insides. He takes a deep breath and closes his eyes until it passes. He must be careful not to provoke Valderrama or speak out of turn. The priest has been Magalhães' confidant since the armada left Tenerife. In truth, he had pushed the mutiny into the back of his mind, but being reminded of it now, he feels again that same anger he felt after the trials. He knew he was not guilty. As does Elcano and Barbosa. Anyone else's opinion is irrelevant. He has served his punishment and he has been freed. At least until the armada returns to Sevilla. Then, maybe, he will be put in chains when Magalhães is done reporting what happened.

Valderrama seems to realise de Morales is not going to answer him. He pushes on. 'Barbosa wanted to know why you were there, why you remained on the San Antonio so long after you had removed Mesquita's tooth.' De Morales scoffs and rolls his eyes. 'I told him I could not answer as to that,' Valderrama continues, ignoring the affront. 'But Quesada seemed surprised you were there and not on the Victoria. And you did not speak up against the mutiny.'

'Christ's wounds,' De Morales blasphemes. 'I had a dying man in my arms, you pitiless dolt.' Valderrama, shocked by de Morales' outburst, turns to the physician.

'Men died,' de Morales says. 'Maybe I could not have saved them, but their deaths were needlessly torturous. God only knows how many men have died since because my supplies were ransacked. For a priest, you give little thought to comfort. But then, all you priests are the same, are you not?'

De Morales rises quickly. Standing over Valderrama he says sardonically, 'excuse me, father, there are still several men suffering from scurvy who must be cared for. Everyone else seems to have forgotten them, you included.'

'I did not come to argue with you de Morales,' Valderrama says piously. 'I came to absolve, to forgive.'

'I do not need your forgiveness. As for yourself, you can beg God for forgiveness of your sins, for you will get none from me.'

Before he leaves, de Morales snatches up a dish of rice and what fruit and meat he can carry for the unwell men. He leaves Valderrama under the tree alone and stamps across the

347

beach toward the armada.

Aboard the Victoria, he curses himself. He has done precisely what he knew he should not have done. Valderrama will be sure to pass on his words to Magalhães and then, once the Capitán General is done with his reports to the Casa de Contratación, the Inquisition will surely come for him. He will be racked, whipped, tortured and burned as a denier of God, an atheist.

To slow his racing heart and take his mind off a future he knows he cannot escape, de Morales turns his attention to the unwell men.

The infirmary has been slowly emptying of sick men as the scurvy has loosened its grip on the armada. The disease, it seems, has run its course and stricken those it was able to. With the fresh food the men have been able to eat from Limasawa, their constitutions have improved greatly. Their teeth will never grow back, but their gums have regained their firmness, their joints stiffened and their muscles have strengthened. The man whose leg broke is still laid up, waiting for the fracture to heal. But those who can have returned to work aboard the ships. Work waits for no man, even those who, not a week ago, were at death's door.

But there are still nine men who have refused all food and suffer greatly with the disease. Dried herbs to clear the airs might help them and food would certainly, but before they can eat they require medicine and he has none of that left. The vinegar has run completely dry and, without that to treat them, the remaining patients will surely die. He must do all he can to avert more death. Now the armada has found a land occupied year-round by what seems to be a well-organised people, de Morales hopes at least some of the medicine he so desperately needs can be found.

The disease's impact on the fleet has already been enormous. In total, thirty-two men have succumbed to it since Maestre Andrew first showed symptoms. With the loss of the San Antonio and the deaths from accidents, executions and tortures, the once two hundred and forty-two strong crew has been reduced to just one hundred and twelve. The men are spread thinly across the three remaining ships as it is and, if another outbreak were to occur, the entire armada would grind to a halt.

Easter Sunday and Magalhães decides to put on a show of strength for the Rajah and the local people. Taking the chief onto the Trinidad, the Capitán General orders the cannons to be fired. The booms echo around the island, sending birds of brilliant and bright colours screeching and fleeing into the air. The Rajah Kolambu and his guards start suddenly, jumping in terror at the violent power of the cannons. Panicked, the Rajah pushes Magalhães away and shakily makes for his waiting canoe and the safety of the shore.

It seems the decision was a poor one on the part of the Capitán General because, once ashore, the Rajah refuses his friendly advances. Magalhães, fearful that the Rajah, after all his work, will not help him locate the Spice Islands, sends Enrique ashore with a message: a fencing tournament will be held in honour of the Rajah. Of course, Kolambu accepts the invite.

To begin with, the native men are more enraptured by the craftsmanship of the Spanish rapiers than by the fencing. They admire the long, sleek steel and the inlaid filigree, the jewelled pommels and the intricate quillons. But soon enough they hoot and cheer with the crew of the Armada at each thrust and parry, each last-second dodge and desperate yield as a man is defeated.

Espinosa overcomes Barbosa in a long battle worthy of the Amadís de Gaula. Then Francisco Albo, the pilot of the Concepción, is completely outmatched by Serrano's quick, graceful movements. The Rajah enjoys the fighting greatly, cheering and clapping and presenting the winners with prizes of food and carved beads.

But the greatest clash comes when Antón Noya, a supernumerary aboard the Concepción, is overcome by an Italian sailor named Leon Pancaldo. Pancaldo wins a fine knife for his expert swordsmanship from the Capitán General and a necklace of feathers and beads from Kolambu.

Next, it being Easter Sunday, Magalhães has Enrique explain the significance of the day to the Rajah. The chief listens as Valderrama solemnly delivers the Service of Light and the Liturgy of the world, then watches with great interest and respect as Barbosa, Serrano and Magalhães renew their baptismal vows and receive the Eucharist.

As the ceremony plays out before him, de Morales searches the faces of Valderrama and Magalhães for signs of the condemnation sure to come. But their faces are blank, never even looking in his direction. If he has not already, Valderrama will report what de Morales said. Magalhães certainly has more important things on his mind than dealing with de Morales' outburst at Valderrama for now. But the time, de Morales is sure, will come.

Swept up in the incantations and prayers, the crosses and the earnest faith the captains show, the Rajah Kolambu agrees to be baptised in the faith of Christ. Magalhães baptises the native king himself. Standing with pride as he christens the first man in these islands, dubbing him Hernando in honour of the late king.

Seeing their king welcomed into God's grace, other native people step forward to be baptised. Their names, strange and beautiful, disappear and are replaced by the mundane names of Spain. This one will be Alfonso, this one Cristobal, another Diego, this child will be Isabel.

Next, the Rajah Kolambu insists that Magalhães perform a blood pact with him. The two men draw knives across their palms at the heel of the thumb then tightly clasp their hands together. Their blood mingling and falling as one in fat drops to the sand at their feet.

Enrique translates as the Rajah makes a loud proclamation to the restless Europeans and his own people. 'I will guide my brother, Magalhães, to Cebu and so to king Humabon, the greatest and most powerful king of these islands, to whom I am but a vassal. King Humabon will direct my blood brother to the Spice Islands.'

His goal finally within reach, Magalhães stands proud and noble beside Valderrama. The crew, gathered around their Capitán General, however, have eyes only for the native women. With the ceremony over, the seamen take their chance and melt away into the surrounding huts and jungle.

Evening falls and the air is filled with moans of ecstasy as a night of unrestrained orgies engulfs Limasawa. Squirming masses of bodies copulate in the open air. Walking among them, de Morales makes out the arm of Pigafetta, the discarded shirt of Barbosa, the primal rage of Carvalho as he thrusts his member into a native woman crouched on all fours.

The surgeon walks past their heaving bodies, rampant and

insatiable, and is reminded of maggots feasting on a corpse.

Chapter 22

April 1521

King Humabon will not help the armada.

Surrounded by his guards, warriors and subjects, he met Magalhães' skiff on the white sandy beach of Cebu. The Capitán General brought every power of persuasion to bear on Humabon but the king remained aloof. He waved away Enrique's greetings, listened unmoved to the Rajah's pleas and accepted the Capitán General's gifts with an unimpressed shrug. Now, the beach is deserted. The royal retinue disappeared down a pathway leading into the jungle of palms and swaying spears of a tall grass-like plant. Magalhães, Enrique, Barbosa and Espinosa followed them into the darkness. None have been seen since.

De Morales is standing with Elcano on the aftcastle of the Victoria. They are staring into the jungle, waiting. 'How long has passed?' He asks.

'An hour or so.' Elcano chews the inside of his lip, pulls on his beard. His brow furrows with worry and he lets out a heaving sigh 'There is nothing we can do for now.' He swings around, pulling his eyes from Cebu and de Morales follows his gaze.

The armada is anchored in a narrow channel of water separating Cebu from a smaller island to the southeast. Whereas the beach of Cebu is orderly and tidy, the unnamed island is wild, its deep, impenetrable jungle reaching almost to the shore and its beach strewn with decaying tendrils of seaweed and sargassum.

'What if they have already met Europeans?' Elcano asks. 'You saw how little Humabon cared for the Capitán General's gifts and he seemed so unconcerned with the armada. What if he has met with the Portuguese? What if he is a vassal of Manuel? This could all be a trick to ensnare us.'

'Surely there would be evidence,' de Morales says. 'There are no crosses, no caps, no beads. No sign of punishment like there was in Terra do Brasil.'

'True,' Elcano says. 'But something is amiss about this.'

'I worry for the men who are still ill,' de Morales says. 'Some refuse to recover and I have no medicine to give them. I must get ashore. The people here might have something that can be of use.'

'For now, all we can do is wait,' Elcano says. He sits down on a low stool beside the gunwale and turns again to the silent shore of Cebu. On the main deck of the Victoria, the crew have grown restless as the day has worn on. Now they hang over the taffrails, staring with greedy eyes at the vast island of Cebu, with its food, its shade and its women.

A figure appears in the foliage, striding down the narrow pathway leading through the jungle. Elcano jumps up. 'Barbosa,' he says. The captain is carrying his wide-brimmed hat under his arm and rests his hand on the pommel of the swinging rapier at his side. He reaches the shore and climbs into a waiting skiff.

'What is happening?' Elcano asks as Barbosa climbs over the taffrail and slams onto the main deck of the Victoria. 'We were beginning to think you were all dead.'

'The king and the Capitán General have reached an impasse,' Barbosa says, rubbing the tiredness from his eyes.

'An impasse? Then we are undone?'

'Not as yet,' Barbosa says. 'This Humabon will not allow the men to go ashore until he has assurances we mean no harm. Nor will he tell us of the location of the Spice Islands.'

'Then assure him,' Elcano says.

'You think we have not tried that?' Barbosa says. The captain is exasperated but quickly holds up his hand in apology. 'Forgive me, Elcano. It has been a long, hot day. Words are not what Humabon seeks. The king wants the Capitán General to prove his fealty by fighting a chief of the neighbouring island, Mactan.' He nods his head towards the smaller island to the southeast, with its scruffy beach and choking vegetation. 'I am to fetch some of our weaponry to show this king what we have at our disposal.'

'Mactan? This is not our fight,' Elcano says. 'We know nothing of these people.'

De Morales turns again and looks at the island. It is clear, now, why its beach is so untidy, why its jungle has been allowed to grow so thick and so impenetrable. 'It is a fortress,' he says.

'We will do what we must,' Barbosa says.

The captain turns and makes to walk away but de Morales steps in his path 'You must allow me to come ashore.'

'Why? You have no place in these matters?'

'There are still nine men who have not recovered from the sickness,' de Morales says desperately. 'I have exhausted my supplies and unless they can be treated they will die.'

'We cannot afford more deaths,' Elcano says. 'Especially if the Capitán General means to involve us in this local quarrel.'

'If I can just come ashore, I may be able to find medicine to treat the men,' de Morales says. 'I need vinegar mostly, but other plants and herbs could be useful if I can find them.'

Barbosa hesitates for a moment. Finally, he says, 'very well, you will come ashore but you must stay at my side. Once Magalhães has solved the problem with this king you can speak to him or one of his advisers about your needs.'

Barbosa collects several swords and knives as well as a crossbow and an arquebus, then de Morales follows him down into the skiff. 'This is a stern chief,' Barbosa says as they make their way to the shore. 'Do not draw unnecessary attention to yourself in his presence.'

De Morales notices how tightly Barbosa has been clutching the weaponry since they pushed off from the Victoria. 'Does he mean to do us harm?' He asks.

'I do not think so, but I think we have Kolambu to thank for that. He has been arguing for the Capitán General since we arrived. Magalhães has a staunch supporter in the Rajah, his usefulness to our success may prove to be decisive.'

'What of these people on Mactan?' he asks. 'Do we have anything to fear from them?'

'I have been amongst natives in the Indies before, Barbosa

says. 'They are fierce fighters but quickly rout when they witness what our weaponry can do. One blast of the cannons or an arquebus and they will scatter like so many leaves in the wind. Kolambu has already told Humabon of the ferocity of our cannons which is likely all that is keeping him from ordering us to leave. When he sees our weaponry in action with his own eyes, he will agree to us fighting on his behalf. I have no doubt the standoff we find ourselves in can be solved quickly.' Barbosa seems to be convincing himself as much as de Morales and quickly turns away to face the shore.

The skiff thrusts into the white sand of the beach and they climb out. Barbosa gives de Morales a sword and a crossbow, saying that if he carries them into the king's hut it will at least seem as though he has a reason for being there.

They plunge into the darkness of the jungle as the weapons, clattering and tinkling against one another, mingle with the sounds of birds and creatures calling. The jungle forms a narrow wall around the perimeter of the island and so the path is short and they soon step out into the still brilliant light of the ageing day.

Before them, huts form a circle around the outside of a wide clearing leaving a large communal area in the centre dotted with cooking fires and the bare trunks of palm trees left standing for some unknown purpose. Small black pigs and plump chickens root around in the compact ground for food. Native people dressed in simple but colourful ponchos and skirts meander around while laughing children chase chickens and pointy-eared dogs lie panting in the shade.

They head towards the largest of the huts with a heavy thatched roof made of palm fronds and other leaves. The hut, guarded by two sentries, is at least twice the size of the others and is certainly the home of King Humabon who is so demanding. But for all his troublesome parsimony, Humabon's attitude is not surprising. What king of Europe would assist another without demanding something in return?

Inside the hut is dim, the air heavy with smoke and tension. From its walls hang an array of shields, painted brightly and shaped like the shells of razor clams. A large hole in the centre of the thatched roof allows light to spill into the middle of the hut and smoke to escape. To the right, a smaller side door is guarded by two tall warriors, their long spears resting on the compacted dirt floor. The Humabon is sitting on a stool placed on a platform. Beside him is the Rajah Kolambu while his guests are gathered around him.

Though he is seated, it is clear King Humabon is tall and of a similar build to the Rajah but with a flabbier body that hides a strong figure. The king wears a red bandanna tied around his forehead and a knee-length skirt, also of red. Running down the lengths of both arms are intricate tattoos, similar to those worn by Rajah Kolambu. Upon his cheeks are two large tattoos in the shape of circles surrounded by triangles, forming the rudimentary shape of the sun. His torso bears an elaborate pattern of interlocking signs and symbols.

The Capitán General meets de Morales' eye as he walks over the threshold and a look of confused anger crosses over Magalhães' face. He is clearly thinking why de Morales, of all people, is here. Barbosa nods to the Capitán General who quickly remembers himself and turns his attention back to the King.

Humabon's focus is instantly directed at the weapons Barbosa and de Morales are carrying into the hut. They place them almost reverentially, like tools of salvation rather than death, at the feet of the king.

'These are only for his highness to inspect,' Magalhães

says quickly. 'We will need them to fight the Mactanese.'

Enrique translates for the king, but Humabon seems to take no notice of him. He leans down and lifts a rapier slowly. Magalhães takes it from him and removes it from its decorated scabbard. Like Rajah Kolambu before him, Humabon marvels at the sharp blade, focusing special attention on the filigreed patterns across the quillons and grip.

The king holds the sword straight, looking down its length. As he does so, he speaks in his own language. When he is finished, Enrique translates: 'the King is impressed by your swords, though fine carvings do not help on the battlefield. The weapons of Lapu Lapu and his Mactanese warriors, crude though they may be in comparison, will cut you down just as quickly.'

Magalhães' face drops. Now the king turns his attention to the crossbow resting on the ground before him. Three bolts lie at its side, ready for a demonstration.

'With your permission, your highness,' Magalhães says. He lifts the crossbow and sets it nose down in the dirt. Notching a bolt he cocks the tension, arching his back with the effort. The Capitán General lifts the crossbow and turns from the king, then takes aim at a pillar of wood supporting the roof at the far end of the hut. Magalhães fires and the bolt buries itself deep into the pillar.

The king sits impassively on his stool, a look of unimpressed boredom on his face. Finally, he says something in his own tongue.

Enrique translates: 'these weapons are well known to king Humabon. They are slow to load and fail too often. Lapu Lapu will not be defeated with such weapons.'

'The king knows of a crossbow?' Magalhães asks incredulously. 'Where has he seen them?'

Enrique translates the Capitán General's questions before passing on Humabon's reply. 'The King trades with a people from the north. They come in their curved ships of dark wood with eyes. They ply the water like dragons and the men aboard them fire these weapons.'

The Capitán General looks at Espinosa and Barbosa, a look of confusion on his face. 'Curved ships with eyes,' he repeats. 'Does he mean the Portuguese?'

Before either man can answer, the king continues speaking. 'Their ships are superior to your own,' Enrique translates, a hint of amusement in his voice. The slave seems to be enjoying the power he holds over his master.

'Not the Portuguese, then,' Espinosa says dryly. 'Show him an arquebus, Fernão. That will impress him.'

The Capitán General has Enrique instruct the king to come outside into the open clearing in the village. They pass out of the cool shade of the king's hut and into the orange light of the growing evening, the air still bearing down with the heat of the day.

Barbosa passes Espinosa an arquebus. The master-at-arms skilfully manages the weapon's unwieldy length as Barbosa stabs its stand deep into the impacted dirt floor of the clearing. The stand set, Espinosa lights a length of rope from a small cooking fire crackling away nearby. He blows on it, extinguishing the flame to a smoulder that slowly singes the rope. He rests the arquebus on the stand and blows into the pan before carefully filling it with charge. Next, he removes the weapon from its stand, resting the butt of the stock on the ground as he fills the barrel with powder before removing the scouring stick and ramming it three times down into the barrel to compact the powder. He lifts the heavy arquebus, once more resting it on the stand and cocks the fuse to the pan, taking aim at a palm tree some thirty yards away. A silence, loaded as the firearm, fills the clearing as Espinosa's royal audience waits with interest as the bizarre ceremony is played out before him.

Espinosa releases the trigger. Smoke billows into the air silently before a loud crack fills the clearing. The lead ball hits the palm tree on its left edge, tearing a chunk of wood from its trunk and sending shards of bark scattering through the air. The chickens squeal, dashing for cover, as natives jolt in fright and children dash into their mother's arms.

King Humabon smiles at the Capitán General and wordlessly nods. Magalhães, hiding what de Morales knows must be satisfaction, says seriously, 'if I am to fight for King Humabon, he must be baptised in our faith. It is against canon law to defend a non-Christian.'

Enrique translates Magalhães' words and King Humabon waves his hand impatiently, turning his attention back to the arquebus.

They return to the king's hut and an agreement is made. But before de Morales gets a chance to ask about medicine, Magalhães turns on his heel and, leaving Enrique to collect the weapons, limps out of the hut.

Once they have passed out of the clearing and gone some way down the path through the jungle, Magalhães turns quickly. He rounds on de Morales, stopping just short of him. 'What are you doing here?' He asks venomously, knowing they are still within earshot of the village. 'Your very presence was an insult.'

'We need medicine for the ailing men, Fernão,' Barbosa says. 'The situation is dire, we cannot afford to lose more men to scurvy, especially if we are to fight a battle and fill our holds with spices.'

'Could he not have written a list?' Magalhães asks spitefully.

'We need those men, Fernão, and the men need the medicine. I knew when the king saw our weaponry he would be impressed and accept the terms.'

'Well,' Magalhães says, 'he very nearly was not, was he?'

'I do not see the problem,' Barbosa says. 'The chief does not know or care who de Morales is. If his presence can save the lives of the men still suffering from the illness, then was it not worth the risk?'

'Nothing is worth risking our endeavour,' Magalhães says sharply. And there are the Capitán General's priorities, de Morales thinks. The suffering, the pain and the death of his crew are second to his own success. 'Well, they can wait one more day,' Magalhães continues. 'We must prepare for the attack. Tomorrow we will defeat this Lapu Lapu and take Mactan for Humabon, then be on our way.'

Magalhães turns and limps along the path leading back to the beach, Barbosa and Espinosa following him. De Morales stands back for a moment, wanting to put distance between himself and the Capitán General. He hears footsteps behind him and turns quickly to find Enrique tramping down the pathway from the village. The slave is focused on a large yellow fruit he is peeling and clumsily walking down the track, crunching dried fronds and tripping on roots as he makes his way back to the beach. He looks up, notices de Morales and offers a hesitant smile before continuing onwards.

'This battle is foolish,' Serrano says desperately. The captain of the Concepción is sitting in a skiff on the shore of the beach, apparently waiting for Magalhães' return. De

Morales arrives last to the scene but gathers the substance of the conversation quickly. This is the first time he has heard Serrano be so forthcoming in his opinions and, as far as he knows, Serrano has never questioned Magalhães' decisions.

'Why are you not on your ship?' The Capitán General asks, still incensed from his argument with Barbosa moments before. 'Humabon was clear, no one but myself and my entourage were to come ashore.'

'I am not ashore, Capitán General,' Serrano says, clutching the taffrail of the boat.

'Pedantry,' Magalhães says. 'I do not need to justify myself to you.'

'We do not need to fight a battle for these people to learn the location of the Spice Islands,' Serrano says, ignoring the Capitán General. 'All we must do is continue west. There will be other islands.'

'We will not blindly bumble our way to the Moluccas,' Magalhães says. 'I am done with aimlessness,' he adds. For a moment, his stern tone falters. Is that an admission? De Morales wonders.

Espinosa takes a step forward. 'Do you want more men to die of exposure or disease?' He asks, jumping to the Magalhães' defence. 'The ships will fall apart before we can calculate where we are.'

'We would not bumble around blind, Capitán General,' Serrano says, ignoring Espinosa. 'There will be other islanders open to assisting us who do not ask such a high price. You have three ships of seamen and pilots, not a man among them besides Espinosa is a warrior. You do not need to rely on despot rulers of savage people to find the Spice Islands.'

Magalhães takes a sharp breath, his shoulder and neck muscles constrict. The colour rises on his face. 'I never had you pegged for a coward, Serrano,' he says. 'A weasel, maybe, but not the milk-sop dog's whore you are. I say we will fight these Mactanese, and we will do so. And we will succeed because we are superior in every way. We will crush the primitives and then I will strip you of your command.'

Serrano's mouth drops at the Capitán General's tirade, the colour draining from his face. Barbosa turns in shock to his father-in-law. His face reddened and hands shaking, Magalhães limps towards his skiff. From his boat, Serrano shares a look of dismay with Barbosa.

Onboard the Victoria, Barbosa is anxious. The captain is making preparations for the attack on Mactan that is to begin at dawn. Laid across the deck is a veritable arsenal of weapons and armour: rapiers, knives, breastplates, morions, arquebuses, crossbows, spears and lances. Elcano, effectively the Victoria's second in command now, follows Barbosa as he paces the deck, examining the weaponry.

'The Capitán General wants two dozen men from each of the ships,' Barbosa is saying, 'obviously I will accompany Magalhães. You will remain aboard the Victoria.' The captain turns to de Morales. 'I need you to have your surgery tools ready in case they are needed.' He turns back to Elcano. 'Ensure space is cleared on the deck for the surgeon to do his work without hindrance. He will have need of the light and space.'

'You expect to meet fierce resistance?' Elcano asks.

'What I expect is irrelevant,' Barbosa replies. 'We must prepare for every eventuality.'

'Then you do not share the Capitán General's confidence?' Elcano says.

Barbosa moves towards Elcano. He lowers his voice. 'If you want me to admit that I do not agree with this path Fernão has set us upon I will not.' Barbosa says all the right words, but his voice lacks conviction. It is the same hesitancy de Morales saw as they marched across the barren wastes of the New World to rescue Serrano and his crew.

Barbosa turns back to the weaponry, examining the armoury laid out before him. In the still evening air, de Morales looks out across the channel towards the black shape of Mactan. The island is much smaller than Cebu, just three or four leagues across. The only viable place to attack is the wide beach directly opposite Cebu. Strewn across the narrow belt of sand is a mess of dried seaweed, branches, fronds and other debris of the sea. Behind this lies a thick and tangled jungle, dark, foreboding and impenetrable. The channel is narrow and so crossing it will take little time, but it is also utterly exposed and Mactan a formidable stronghold. Lapu Lapu and his warriors will have an unobstructed view of the attacking men taking the element of surprise away from the Capitán General.

'You are to fire the cannons,' Barbosa says. 'But only if the resistance put up by the Mactanese is fierce enough to warrant it. We must defeat Lapu Lapu, he cannot scamper into that jungle and disappear.'

Remembering Humabon's reaction to the crossbow, de Morales asks, 'what if they have already seen cannons?'

Barbosa turns to him, the look of concern is quickly replaced by resolution. 'Whether Lapu Lapu is aware of cannons or not is irrelevant. He and his army will rout as soon as they are fired. Christ's wounds, every army in Europe routs at cannon fire, why would savages be any different?' He turns back to Elcano. 'But be sure to aim above their heads,' he says. 'Even the sound will be enough to strike fear into the hearts of these people and we cannot risk injuring our own men.'

Barbosa keeps speaking of Lapu Lapu and the Mactanese warriors as if he knows anything of them. In truth, since the armada dropped anchor at this place yesterday, they have seen nothing of them and heard only rumours. Magalhães requested an emissary be sent to Mactan with an offer for Lapu Lapu that, if he would allow himself to be baptised, Magalhães would not attack. The request was refused. Whatever enmity exists between Humabon and Lapu Lapu cannot be undone so simply.

The emissary's news put a dampener on the buoyant mood Humabon's baptism had put the Capitán General in. The Cebuano king had taken Eucharist and a solemn Magalhães himself had baptised him Don Carlos, named for the emperor so far away. Then followed a mass of hundreds of local men and women who waited in the clearing for the opportunity to be christened beneath the towering, newly erected cross like their king. The whole ceremony took four hours and, by the end, the sun had sunk below the horizon and Valderrama looked ready to collapse.

King Humabon has kept his side of the pledge and now the Capitán General must keep his. With Humabon a baptised Christian it is not only in keeping with his word but also in keeping with his faith that Magalhães must defend him as a brother in Christ.

'Fernão is confident that the Mactan people will be routed easily,' Barbosa says, 'their crude armour and weaponry should be no match for us.

'You do not agree, do you?' Elcano asks, again pushing Barbosa to admit what, deep down, de Morales and Elcano know he believes.

For a second, de Morales thinks Barbosa will once again jump to the Capitán General's defence, but the captain remains quiet. Finally, Barbosa rubs his temples and sighs deeply. 'I believe we need not fight these people, Elcano. Magalhães may believe they will be easily defeated, but in my experience, native peoples are fierce and brave fighters. We must remember that they are fighting to defend their homeland. To underestimate them would be our undoing.'

'I appreciate the difficulty of your position,' Elcano says, 'but you ought not put the crew's lives in danger for the sake of loyalty.'

Barbosa does not reply for some time. Again, he shows no trace of anger at the snub of his father-in-law as he says numbly, 'loyalty is everything.' The captain walks away, ducking into his cabin and closing the door behind him.

'Men are going to die,' Elcano says quietly to de Morales. His tone is blunt, his eyes sad. He shakes his head. 'I will not let more men die needlessly.'

An anxious night sluggishly passes by. Few on the armada sleep but especially those sixty men chosen by Magalhães to fight by his side wait apprehensively. They meander about the ship, restlessly fidgeting with their weaponry and armour, hardly talking.

De Morales sits on the edge of his bed, listening to them clean their blades, and checking their crossbows over and over. When sleep refuses to come, he leaves his cabin and walks out onto the main deck. He thinks he will go below into the infirmary, but there is nothing he can do for the men who remain there. He needs vinegar but he must wait until

Magalhães is done with his show of strength before he can even hope of getting any.

The night is cool, a gentle wind blowing from the southwest. On the main deck, the men are nervous and quiet as they look to the eastern sky for the first sign of dawn. From the islands on either side of the armada, come the ceaseless exotic calls of tropical birds broken every so often by the recognisable grunt of pigs and crowing of chickens. The whole world seems restless.

De Morales begins walking laps around the deck of the Victoria in the still, charged night. The ships have already been moved in a horizontal line as close to the shore of Mactan as possible, but the shallow water of the channel means they are anchored almost half a league from the beaches of the island. It is still quite some distance for the invaders to cross in skiffs while being fired upon by their enemies. Doubtless, those enemies are already watching from the blanket of jungle lining the island of Mactan. Surely, they will already know an attack is imminent, and are already planning their response.

The air is split by a screech. De Morales jumps and spins around, searching the shore of Mactan. A drove of piglets dash across the beach. Grunting and squealing, their silhouettes disappear into the jungle. He laughs humourlessly at his nervousness.

Chapter 23

April 1521

With the first blush of dawn, a bell is rung from the Trinidad. The men, wide awake all night, make their way to the decks of their ships. There is a solemn, funereal foreboding about the whole scene. Only Espinosa and Magalhães have any real experience in war, the rest of the men who will join them in battle are completely untried.

De Morales watches the men climb down into the waiting skiffs as daylight filters through the clouds on the horizon. In total, seventy men will go ashore but there is not enough room in the skiffs for all of them to travel at once with their armour and weaponry. The plan instead is four skiffs to ferry ten men apiece, then two will return to the armada for the other thirty reinforcements. The other two skiffs will remain on the shore, ready to bring any wounded men back to the Victoria and the Concepción where de Morales and Bustamante await.

The hollow tinkle of weapons and armour clattering against one another fills the air like birdsong. The armour of the Capitán General, polished by Enrique to a gleaming mirror, catches the early morning light, flashing reflections across the hull of the Trinidad.

De Morales is surprised to see Pigafetta clamber down the Trinidad's Jacob's ladder. The Italian is probably the least prepared of anyone in the fleet to fight in a battle. Nevertheless, he joins the Capitán General in the lead skiff.

Magalhães' most loyal men make up the bulk of the force. Barbosa, Pigafetta, Espinosa and many more from the Trinidad who have remained loyal to the Capitán General over the past months. The rest of the numbers are made of an assortment of sailors and other members of the crew. De Morales recognises the cook of the Trinidad, Cristobal Rodriguez and a sailor of the Concepción, not long recovered from scurvy, named Francisco Piora. Antón Noya and Leon Pancaldo, who impressed Rajah Kolambu with their fencing in Limasawa, are also among the men selected. Many other nameless men made faceless in the harsh morning sun climb down into the boats.

The skiffs push off from the ships and begin their slow journey towards the shore of Mactan. Behind them, the Cebu beach is eerily empty, but de Morales is sure Humabon's warriors are watching from the shadows.

The boats travel just a few dozen feet before running aground in the shallow water. The Capitán General leaps over the edge of the lead skiff and the men follow suit. De Morales finds that his mouth is dry and his eyes sore as he unblinkingly watches the men, led by the limping Capitán General, wade through the thigh-deep water, holding their weapons like offerings above their heads.

Two of the skiffs immediately turnabout, heading back to the armada to collect the other men waiting on the decks of the Trinidad and the Concepción. Rowers wait in the two skiffs that remain on the shore, tightly gripping the oars, ready to flee. The whole armada is wracked by an uneasy nervousness as those left behind restlessly wait for the assault to begin. The gunners kneel beside their cannons, their barrels aimed at Mactan, hunched over and ready to light the fuse at Elcano's signal. The Basque is watching the slow progress of the two skiffs as they make their way back to the Trinidad and the Concepción.

De Morales is not even looking when the first arrows fly. The sound of them pinging off steel armour startles his attention back to the men wading through the water. He searches desperately for the wounded as Magalhães and his men panic and fan out across the shore. One man falls. Then another. They fall into the sea, writhing and convulsing.

'Poison,' a sailor behind him calls.

The arrows fall like rain now on the armoured men, clinking and clattering off breastplates and morions. The Capitán General, with Espinosa just behind him, presses on as more arrows find their mark and men fall into the surf, their screams cut short as their mouths fill with water.

All this chaos and Lapu Lapu has yet to even reveal himself. The attackers are becoming frantic, they are moving faster, breaking ranks. Several fire their crossbows aimlessly at the trees. The bolts whoosh through the air before they disappear among the foliage. De Morales sees the figure of Barbosa falling back, dragging two of the writhing men behind him as he makes for the waiting skiffs.

Magalhães, despite his limp, surges for the land while Pigafetta runs back and forth, hysterical with fear. Finally, the Italian sees Barbosa loading the injured men into a skiff and dashes towards him. As the chronicler frantically splashes through the water, an arrow narrowly misses him, instead burying itself into Leon Pancaldo's throat. The swordsman, so impressive at the tournament, dies instantly. He falls into the ocean, joining the other men who have fallen to the unremitting hail of arrows flying from the tree line.

Magalhães and Espinosa finally reach the beach. But at once a low chant swells from the jungle before them. The arrows cease and figures emerge from the darkness. They wear long skirts of red, gold and brown and carry spears and vicious swords with spiked blades and feathers hanging from the grips. The warriors begin slapping their bare chests and thighs as the air is filled with their blood-curdling war cry. They are mad with fury, their faces twisting into inhuman faces filled with rage at the hubris of the pale men attacking their land.

The Capitán General sets himself, holding his rapier en guard and, beside him, Espinosa follows suit. Cristobal Rodriguez appears beside them, holding an axe in one hand and a short club in the other. Without warning, one of the figures at the tree line throws a javelin and the cruel point impales the cook through the chest. It bursts through his back, burring itself into the sand behind him and propping him up at a horrifying angle.

As the cook's body slides down the glistening spear, Antón Noya bursts from the surf and joins the Capitán

General on the shore. Other men follow, forming up into a disorganised and frantic line.

More spears arc through the air. With shocking randomness, men drop into the channel. Antón Noya falls. His lifeless body, pierced through by two spears, falls into the channel, staining the sea red with his blood. Another is hit in the head by a rock, a third cries and runs wildly into the sea towards the waiting skiffs only to be impaled in the back by multiple arrows.

A thud from the hull of the Victoria snaps de Morales out of his trance. The terrified face of Pigafetta appears above the taffrail. The Italian falls heavily onto the deck, desperately looking around him.

'Fire the cannons.' He screeches, wiping seawater from his eyes.

The other skiffs have reached the Trinidad and the Concepción, but no sailors have climbed into them. They rock weightless beside the battered hulls.

'Fire the cannons, the cannons,' Pigafetta cries again, tears streaming from his eyes. But no one listens. The men at the fuses kneel motionless, unlit tapers in their hands. Elcano stares ahead, watching the gory battle unfold, while Magalhães' loyal mongrel yaps away his heels. A shout comes from the shore and Pigafetta whips around.

De Morales also turns, searching for the source. By the time he has looked back to the beach, the Capitán General has fallen to the sand, the long shaft of a javelin impaled through his right thigh. Espinosa is still at Magalhães' side but the two men are isolated now. The other survivors are furiously fighting their own desperate battles or else wading through the ocean for the waiting skiffs. Magalhães leans on his rapier as Espinosa desperately tries to pull him up.

Then the warriors fell upon them. Espinosa swipes wildly at them, catching one across the chest. Seeing their comrade's blood arc through the air, the warriors hesitate for a moment then surge forwards. The force of the impact pushes Espinosa backwards, leaving Magalhães utterly alone.

Espinosa stumbles into the ocean as five warriors crash into the kneeling Capitán General and he falls backwards. Blows reign down on Magalhães, splashing and spitting blood and seawater into the air. The Capitán General is lost then in the flailing arms and swinging weapons. His desperate cries cut short as the sea around him turns crimson with the billowing clouds of his blood.

Espinosa desperately crawls backwards through the surf as more warriors approach him. Clawing at the water, he finally manages to stand upright and dashes through the lapping waves towards the last remaining skiff. Javelins and arrows fall around him, splashing harmlessly into the water, as he climbs into the boat.

A small group of five men huddle exposed in the knee-deep water, desperately firing crossbows at the oncoming warriors. One man tries to fire an arquebus but the soaked weapon sputters a stream of water from its barrel. The warriors fall upon the men and unleash an onslaught of violence on them.

Now the Mactanese turn their attention to the fallen bodies. One man, still somehow alive despite the spear through his stomach, is surrounded by warriors. His pleading falls on deaf ears as his head is caved in with a rock. Then they begin stripping the armour and weapons from the dead, leaving their naked bodies to lap against the shore.

A strange calm falls. Bodies bob in the waves as blood swirls, spreading out across the channel. In the last remaining skiff, Espinosa pants and coughs, his desperate eyes searching the shore for Magalhães.

The corpse of the Capitán General lies face down in the shallow water, surrounded by the crimson stain of his blood. Elcano stares at the bloody carcass. Weeping, Pigafetta slumps to the deck.

Chapter 24

April 1521

'This is a mutiny in all but name.' Barbosa rounds on Elcano pulling his arm back, preparing to strike the Basque. De Morales leaps between the two men and pushes Barbosa away as another sailor grabs the captain's wrist.

'Release me, swine.' Barbosa turns to face the sailor and spits to the deck at his feet then forces his wrist free and takes another step towards Elcano. De Morales staggers sideways from between the two men, unnerved by Barbosa's rage and surprised by his own actions.

The captain is stopped in his tracks by the voice of Serrano calling from across the deck. 'The cause was lost whether the cannons were fired or not.' Serrano must have only just arrived from the Concepción for de Morales had not known he was aboard the Victoria. Barbosa turns now to face his fellow captain. 'Magalhães was a fool,' Serrano continues.

De Morales expects Pigafetta to pipe up in defence of his paragon, but the morose figure of the Italian is still slumped sobbing against the gunwale. In the tense silence that follows Elcano and Barbosa share a venomous look broken by thuds from the hull as Espinosa finally climbs aboard the Victoria.

The master-at-arms is panting heavily, his wide eyes filled with horror. 'Where were the cannons?' He cries desperately.

'Ask Elcano,' Barbosa says. The captain turns and, for the first time since he arrived back at the Victoria, de Morales gets a clear look at Barbosa's face. Now the initial shock has passed, the gravity of what has happened seems to have hit him. His father-in-law is dead. The Capitán General is dead. The colour has drained from his skin.

Espinosa looks at Elcano hard. The Basque stands beside the silent cannons motionless, the blank expression on his face unreadable. Espinosa holds his arms out in exhortation and shakes his head quickly. 'Well, Elcano?'

'The Capitán General was dead before we could have lit the fuse,' Elcano says. 'Whether we fired the cannons or not would have made little difference.'

'Liar,' Barbosa snarls. He turns suddenly once more, 'those savages would have scattered at the first sound of cannon fire.'

Elcano turns back to Barbosa, his sharp eyes flashing with anger. 'Did you not abandon him at the first sign of trouble?'

Barbosa is taken aback by the blatant accusation and stutters before he finds his tongue. 'How dare you,' he says finally. He takes a heavy step towards Elcano, stopping short of meeting him nose to nose. 'I helped the injured men,' he says simply.

'Whilst deserting your sister's husband,' Elcano says.

Barbosa looks set to tear Elcano limb from limb. The colour rises on his cheeks, spreading across his face like Magalhães' blood filling the channel. The gunners, standing beside Elcano, take a step forward, flanking him on either side. They spread their arms and plant their feet, readying to defend the Basque. Barbosa sees them and his glare falters. Espinosa steps forwards. He takes Barbosa by the arm and pulls him away from a confrontation the captain surely cannot win.

Serrano exhales heavily. 'The native's weapons were poisoned, Duarte,' says simply. 'You saw the men thrashing around in the water. Christ, you brought two of them back here. I told the Capitán General this battle was unnecessary. Even if we could have driven them away, Magalhães would have died from that lance wound.'

'But he would not have been hacked to pieces.' The voice is Pigafetta's, woeful and broken. The Italian, his back to the main deck, has stood up and is looking to the shore of Mactan and the desolation on the beach. It is impossible, now, to tell which of the corpses is the Capitán General's. The tide and current have washed the bodies closer together. Their blood mingled in a crimson cloud slowly settling to the bottom of the channel.

As he looks upon the hacked bodies of his comrades, Barbosa's shoulders slump. 'We must retrieve the bodies,' he says flatly.

'We cannot.' Serrano says.

'My father-' Barbosa stops, recognising his mistake. 'The Capitán General must be given a Christian burial.'

'Do you really think Lapu Lapu will allow us to retrieve the corpses?' Serrano says. 'Magalhães is lost. All is lost.'

'We must treat with them, then,' Barbosa says desperately. The captain leans over the taffrail and shouts down to the sailor still waiting in Serrano's skiff, 'go to the Trinidad, bring back Enrique.'

The survivors who made it back to the safety of the armada in the same skiff that brought Espinosa, sit now on the deck of the Victoria. Pale, panting and soaked; their desperate eyes stare into the space before them. All of them no doubt share de Morales' thoughts. The Capitán General is dead. His luck finally ran out on the shores of this insignificant island, in a battle that never had to happen. Magalhães took with him the lives of twenty-eight other men. A shocking and pointless loss of life.

De Morales looks to the surgery table standing empty on the deck. His tools and wound dressings, unused, are still neatly laid out on a smaller table beside it. There is nothing for him to do. No lives to save. No wounded came back from the battle because everyone who was wounded is gone. The men Barbosa dragged into the skiff lie dead at the bottom of the boat, their faces twisted into tortured death masks.

With no lives to save, he thinks of those that are lost. The cook, Cristobal Rodriguez, Leon Pancaldo, Antón Noya, Francisco Piora and all the other nameless men now drifting face down in the current. Their bodies empty of blood and their hearts empty of love and hopes and dreams. Twenty-nine lives snuffed out in less than thirty minutes of violence.

He looks across the deck. Sees Barbosa, Espinosa, Serrano and Elcano standing separate from one another. Serrano is looking towards the shore of Mactan and the bodies bobbing on the gentle waves. But Barbosa's eye does not leave Elcano's face.

De Morales knows what Barbosa is thinking because he is thinking the same thing: was this a mutiny? Even if firing the cannons would not have saved the Capitán General, why did Elcano not even try? He thinks back, remembers the skiffs standing empty beside the Concepción. No sailors climbed down to join Magalhães in the attack. Could Serrano have been in on a plan to abandon the Capitán General?

Enrique, accompanied by Carvalho, arrives at the Victoria and approaches the scattered group on the deck.

'You will go ashore and meet with king Humabon or Don Carlos or whatever we are supposed to call him now,' Barbosa says. 'Ask him to treat on our behalf with the Mactan people for the remains of our dead. Tell him we will offer a reward to Lapu Lapu for the return of the Capitán General.'

'With all due respect,' Enrique says, 'I am a free man now.'

'What?' Barbosa says. 'What did you just say to me? You are a slave and you will do as you are-'

'My master is dead,' Enrique interrupts, his tone is soft, simple, non-contentious. 'I am a free man to do as I please.'

'You dare interrupt me?' Barbosa's anger boils over and he stamps towards Enrique. 'You are an impertinent slave. You can either go to Humabon now or I can whip you and you will go anyway.'

Enrique straightens to his full height, meeting Barbosa's eye. 'Magalhães said that if he were to die, I would have my freedom.'

'How convenient for you that your master is dead and no one but you heard this.'

Enrique shrugs. 'Nevertheless, I am a free man,' he says

380

simply. 'It is the king's law.'

Barbosa looks around at the gathered captains, incredulous. Their blank faces offer him no support. Finally, he turns to a sailor. 'Get me a whip,' he says.

Barbosa orders two men to take hold of Enrique by his arms. The slave tries to resist but a kick to the back of his legs sends him falling to his knees. The captain takes the whip from the sailor who brings it and begins rolling up his sleeves. As he does so, Enrique's shirt is ripped open, revealing the old wounds from previous lashings de Morales saw long ago off the coast of the New World.

The whip snaps against the slave's back and shoulders. Long, white welts swell up where the lash makes contact. The welts turn to sores and the sores tear open as the flogging continues. The savagery of the beating and the anger in his voice reveal the grief Barbosa must now be feeling after the death of his brother-in-law. Barbosa's breath is ragged, his eyes wide as he takes out his pain on the only man he can. Enrique is suffering Barbosa's rage because Elcano cannot. This is a new and vicious side to Barbosa de Morales has not seen.

He loses count after thirty-six strikes. Despite what can only be unbearable pain, Enrique does not make a sound as the whip strips the flesh from his back. Finally satisfied, sweating and breathless, Barbosa throws the whip, slick with blood, to the deck. Enrique is released and soundlessly falls to the boards.

'You will go ashore,' Barbosa says, panting and wiping the sweat from his forehead. 'You will treat with the king and return here whence you will be put in chains. Fernão may be dead, but you are his family's property nonetheless.'

While they wait for Enrique to return, the crew watch horrified and powerless as the Mactanese warriors return to the shore and drag the Spanish corpses from the sea. The limp cadavers have swollen up in the water and growing heat of the day, becoming bulbous and ugly. The Mactanese take everything left behind in the heat of battle from the beach, stripping it of every memory that anything happened there. Even the billowing clouds of blood have, by now, been swept away by the tide.

Despite their history, de Morales feels a pang of sorrow for Pigafetta as the chronicler watches in stunned silence the last of the bodies being dragged away. For romance's sake, it is difficult not to imagine the last pale corpse is that of Magalhães. But how can anyone really know? In amongst the chaos of the battle and the currents of the channel, the Capitán General could well have been swept out to sea by now.

De Morales replays the short fight in his mind. There was no heroic last stand. No call to arms from the Capitán General. No rousing speeches for posterity or courageous acts fit to be celebrated in literature by generations to come. Just pain, fear and death.

He had asked himself, not long ago on Limasawa, was it luck or force of will that guided Magalhães this far on his mad journey? Either way, both have run out now and the survivors are left to rebuild their own fates. For now, it seems, Barbosa will lead that effort.

Magalhães' brother-in-law took control when control was needed and, as yet, no one has questioned him. But there is a sense on board the Victoria that a power struggle is coming. By rights, Serrano has more legitimacy to be Capitán General, given he is now the longest-serving captain in the armada and the most experienced, but he has yet to put himself forward. No one has.

The most qualified men, Serrano, Barbosa and Elcano, linger in the corners of the Victoria's main deck, weighing up their opponents before the battle of wills that is certain to come. Even Barbosa, who seems so sure of himself, can be caught looking from the corner of his eye at the other candidates. It is only a matter of time, de Morales tells himself.

When he finally returns, Enrique gloomily reports to Barbosa. His tone is flat, empty of emotion. The slave has no feeling in his eyes as he delivers his message to the captain: 'Lapu Lapu will not return the bodies. He says all the riches in the world could not compel him to hand over the foreign invaders.'

The news is met with silent resignation, hardly having an impact on Barbosa or anyone else. At the end of this dreadful day, what is one more piece of bad news?

Barbosa dismisses Enrique with a curt, 'so be it,' but the slave does not move.

'King Humabon and Rajah Kolambu invite you to attend a feast this evening in honour of the fallen Capitán General,' Enrique says, looking Barbosa in the eye. 'The king says he deeply regrets Magalhães' death. Rajah Kolambu is distraught.'

'I think not,' Barbosa says. 'We need to take stock and consider our next move.'

'With all due respect, Duarte,' Serrano says, 'you are not the Capitán General.'

So, it begins. Unless they can work this out amicably, more blood will flow. A collective tightening of nerves sweeps across the ship as fury flashes across Barbosa's face. De Morales looks to the table of surgical tools yet to be packed away. He may have a use for them yet.

Elcano takes a step forward and raises his hands, 'señores,' he says, 'I-

'Shut up Elcano,' Barbosa spits. 'We are in this mess by your hand.'

Elcano, taken aback by Barbosa's brusk tone, stops mid-step. He looks across the deck to Serrano before both men look back to Barbosa. One by one, their shoulders set, their feet planted firmly onto the wooden boards.

'Duarte,' Espinosa says, Barbosa turns and looks at the master-of-arms. 'You have lost much this day already. We all have. Do not let foolhardiness take more from you. Fernão would not have us squabble.'

At the mention of his brother-in-law's name, the tension in the air drains slightly. It is a small relief, but a relief nonetheless. Barbosa's shoulders slacken somewhat, his fists unclench. The other men slowly follow his lead.

In the silence that follows, each man appears to think over his position.

'I agree,' Serrano says. 'But we need leadership.'

The three men look between one another, no one wanting to be the first to put his name forward.

'The most experienced among us is Serrano,' Espinosa says. 'I nominate him.'

Barbosa turns to Espinosa, his comrade for the past nineteen months. Under the shadow of Magalhães, they were steadfast in their loyalty, always supporting one another, never countermanding nor questioning the other. Now that shadow has been removed, Barbosa seems appalled by what he surely sees as a betrayal.

'Perhaps you have forgotten,' Barbosa says, 'but Magalhães stripped Serrano of his command.'

'What difference does that make?' Espinosa says. 'He is still the most qualified.'

'Tradition dictates that the crew vote,' Serrano says. 'I do not think any man is composed enough to make that decision today. I nominate Barbosa as co-Capitán General in the meantime. We can vote on the morrow.'

Forgotten and snubbed again, Elcano turns and climbs the stairs to the aftcastle. 'And what of this feast?' Espinosa asks as Elcano is lost among the rigging and folded sails.

'We must attend,' Serrano says. 'Magalhães failed, but he kept his side of the bargain with King Humabon. The king is a baptised Christian now and must honour his word. I argued for leaving this place yesterday, but we cannot wander aimless through these seas any longer. We have not the men now to risk being swept into more local bickering. If we attend the feast, we can learn the location of the Spice Islands and be gone.'

'And what if Humabon does not tell us the location?' Barbosa asks, content, at least for now, to allow Serrano to lead the discussion.

'Then we will destroy his sordid little village and his inbred people,' de Morales is startled by the malice in Serrano's voice. It is a malevolence he has never yet displayed. So many unseen sides of these men have revealed themselves since Magalhães' death.

Barbosa sighs. 'Very well.' He turns to Enrique, 'go ashore and inform the king we will attend his feast. The men could do with some food and cheer this day anyway.' The slave, sullen and indignant at still being ordered around by men who are not his master, climbs over the taffrail and disappears.

In the king's hut, the feast is underway. It is so large, swelled by the crew of the armada and Humabon's many subjects, that it has spilt into the clearing at the centre of the village.

The funereal march of the men as they made their way from the shore to the clearing in the centre of the village was quickly replaced by a celebratory mood. This is the first time the men have been allowed on Cebu and many would have scattered into the surrounding huts and jungle with women were it not denied by Humabon. 'First, we must eat to the Capitán General's memory,' the king had said.

Pigafetta, utterly devastated at the death of his mentor, wandered towards the clearing like a mother in mourning for a lost child. Even now, as he sits on a mat not far from de Morales, the chronicler appears to be taking no joy from the banquet. Not the women nor the piled feast of rice, pork, tropical fruit and coconut wine can distract him from his melancholy mood.

Elcano is absent, forced by Barbosa to remain on the Trinidad and guard the ships with two dozen sailors too uninterested, unwell or shaken up to attend the feast. When the time comes, de Morales knows he will confront Elcano about the events of this morning. He must. Elcano will have his reasons, and de Morales already suspects what they will be, but he must hear Elcano explain them himself. Since the mutiny a year ago, the Basque has proven himself to be a caring and gentle man who puts others' welfare above his own. But de Morales cannot say he is shocked at Elcano's

386

actions, or lack thereof. How many times has Magalhães' headstrong and belligerent leadership led to needless death and suffering? Elcano warned de Morales long ago that he would not delay in doing whatever he felt necessary if the lives of the men were gambled. Perhaps, as Espinosa said, the canons would have done nothing. Maybe the men were already dead, poisoned by the arrows that fell from the sky. Doubtless, de Morales had nothing to treat such wounds with. Most of the dead dropped in the surf where they stood, foaming at the mouth and convulsing.

For now, the surgeon forces himself to eat despite not having much of an appetite. He must make the most of a meal of this size and quality. The long months of eating little but hardtack and drinking stale water or diluted wine have dulled his taste buds so that, now, the aromatic rice and succulent pork almost turn his stomach. Or perhaps it is the visions of the spurting blood and severed limbs of the battle not twelve hours ago.

Others eat heartily and make merry. Their greedy hands grab at handfuls of rice, pork, fruit and women. The native women squeal and giggle as sailors pinch and grope them, sampling a taste of things to come.

Barbosa, Serrano and Espinosa sit at the head of the feast with King Humabon. Enrique is loitering at the king's side, translating his words and drinking coconut wine. The king made a short speech extolling the virtues of Magalhães, a man he only met a few short hours before his death and a man he manipulated into fighting a needless battle for him.

The Rajah Kolambu, however, is notable only by his absence. During Humabon's dedication speech to Magalhães, he apologised for the Rajah's absence, explaining that the Rajah was too distraught to attend. Most likely a hunger strike is his way of honouring the dead. Not for the first time, de Morales reflects on the fierce loyalty Magalhães was able to inspire in others. During Humabon's speech, everywhere sympathetic native eyes fell on the gathered faces of the crew of the armada.

But de Morales has no sympathy for the Capitán General. There was no need for them to come to this place and there was certainly no need to fight Humabon's battles. Serrano made it abundantly clear to Magalhães on the beach that there were other ways to find the Spice Islands. But the Capitán General, in his prideful arrogance and rampant evangelising, needed to convert locals and appropriate lands for the crown in hopes of honour and reward on his return to Sevilla.

And what reward did he find? Death. Such are the fruits of egotism.

De Morales' regret is reserved solely for the men the Capitán General dragged to their graves with him. Those twenty-eight men, believing the myths Magalhães and his supporters propagated about him, rushed to that godforsaken shore and were torn and hacked and slashed to pieces by warriors doing nothing more than defending their borders from invaders.

Around him, the feast continues. Night falls and torches hanging from the walls of the hut are lit, their flickering glow throwing unstable, haunting shadows across the gathered faces. At some point, Pigafetta leaves. De Morales knows not when or where he went. Perhaps the Italian went to drown his sorrows and lie in his master's cabin, curled up and crying for the lost mentor. Or maybe he crawled into some native woman's bed to find comfort at her breast.

De Morales stands up, preparing to leave the feast and join Elcano on board the Victoria. Maybe, before they are all too drunk to be of help, he can find a native on the way and try to get his hands on some vinegar for the men in the infirmary. As he rises, he notices, out of the corner of his eye, Enrique leaving the side of Humabon. The slave melts into the darkness and, as he does so, the shadow of another figure slides by him.

More shadows follow, materialising from the side door of the hut. As they pass behind the king and the captains, de Morales sees the glint of steel. He sees axes, flints, bows, spears. He sees the forgotten rapiers and knives he and Barbosa dropped on the floor of the king's hut yesterday. The weapons Enrique was supposed to bring back. He remembers Enrique, tripping and stumbling down the path, busy hands peeling the yellow fruit.

He sees the shadows gather behind the king and his guests of honour. One steps behind Barbosa and slides a blade into the captain's neck. Barbosa does not make a noise as the blade is drawn across his throat and wrenched back out from below the opposite ear. Blood fountains into his plate of steaming rice and pork and his body slumps forward.

Espinosa leaps to his feet. Another warrior jabs at him with a hatchet but he narrowly spins away from the thrust. Serrano is stabbed in the side as he tries to stand and he groans and folds to the floor.

Sheer panic hits the men as one. A cabin boy dashes for the side door just as more warriors burst through it. The boy is struck across the face with a club, his cheek exploding in a sickly spray of blood, bone, spittle and half-chewed pork. Sailors flip the low tables and fall over each other as they desperately try to escape. Native warriors begin shooting bows from the dark corners of the hut. With a dull thud, the arrows embed themselves into the bodies of the sailors.

Men are running and de Morales is running with them. He does not even remember leaving the hut, but some primal instinct has taken hold. He runs as he has never run before. The blood pumps in his ears and his breath heaves from him. Bodies flop lifelessly to the ground around him, punctured by arrows and spears.

He can see the armada and the waiting skiffs scattered across the beach. A few steps more and he can see Elcano. The figure of the Basque, lit by the Victoria's brazier, is looking to the shore, towards the screams and cries.

Is this what Magalhães saw? Did he look at the silhouette of Elcano and believe his salvation was at hand? Did he know, as de Morales does now, that one boom from the cannons would save him? When no explosion came, what did the Capitán General think? Did he feel the empty embrace of eternity wrap itself around him? De Morales feels it now, the emptiness, the blackness closing in and the cold welcoming arms of his wife.

His attention is stolen as Pigafetta crashes through the trees to his left. The chronicler's arms wheel as he tries to keep his balance. Carvalho follows on his heels, bursting through the heavy leaves and letting out a cry of terror.

He sees a flash of light and a cloud of smoke plume from the deck of the Victoria. Then the almighty blast of a firing cannon cracks through the darkness. Three more follow. He hears the air high above the jungle tear as the cannonballs rush through the sky above him.

The warriors pursuing them fall back at the bursts of light and the roar of the cannons. The arrows stop whizzing past and the war cry of the warriors dies out, leaving only the suffering wail of sailors as they beg for death. The air is filled with the acrid smell of gunpowder and the wheezing of men all around de Morales as they desperately run towards the armada.

Elcano did not abandon them. De Morales cannot help himself as a smile stretches across his face.

Chapter 25

May 1521

The night passes in silence. Every man who escaped that massacre staring into space, and every man who had remained aboard the ship stunned into speechlessness by how few returned.

De Morales had gone ashore with almost eighty men, another thirty were left aboard the armada with Elcano. Just twenty-one returned from the feast. From the chaos of that bloodbath, he and the other survivors had burst from the jungle frantic and panting and rampantly dashed for the shore. How fickle fate had been that men to either side of de Morales, of every man who made it back to the armada, were cut down by the spears, arrows and blades of the Cebuano warriors.

Now he is here, aboard the Victoria. Alive. Those who had not made it back from the feast either died immediately or will since have been captured and butchered by the natives or else put into slavery.

The dead outnumber the living.

How many more of his comrades will die? How many more can die before there are not enough left to drag the ships back to Sevilla? Their numbers are dwindling like wheat before the scythe. Magalhães: dead. Barbosa: dead. Serrano, Mendoza, Quesada, Cartagena, de la Reina, Mesquita, Rebêlo. All gone. Almost ninety men and cabin boys must have died in the last twenty-four hours alone, including two Capitán Generals and three captains.

Their ghosts already roam the main deck of the Victoria, the spirits performing an intricate dance over the wooden boards. They move like water, drifting and spinning, but never touching the living nor their ghostly fellows.

In their centre the headless corpse of Quesada stands motionless, his guts still hanging from his hands. The sight is a horror to behold but de Morales is too exhausted, too shocked, to be moved by it. He sits entranced, watching the spectres and mundanely wondering why Magalhães is not among them. He must be aboard the Trinidad, he thinks, or else wandering the shores of Mactan.

As the sun rises the ship wakes from its mournful trance. De Morales becomes aware of an argument breaking out at the prow of the ship. Elcano, Carvalho and Espinosa animatedly gesticulate at one another.

'I know the way,' Elcano is saying. 'If we sail southwest, I will find our heading. What more cause for leadership can I claim?'

'You are a filthy dog, mutinous to your core,' Carvalho says. 'You will undo the entire enterprise. It is in your nature. Besides, if you truly knew the way, we would be at the Moluccas already, wouldn't we?'

Espinosa rubs his forehead, exasperated. How he survived is beyond de Morales. Twice in the space of one day, he has stared death in the face. Once in the surf beside the hacked corpse of Magalhães and again at the feast beside Barbosa. The man ought to be dead.

'There will be an election, then,' Espinosa says finally. 'Have the men cast lots for who they want to lead the armada.'

Elcano nods.

'Fine.' Carvalho says.

'But whatever happens, the first task of the winner is to treat with Humabon.' Espinosa says. 'There may be still living men on those shores. We owe it to them to rescue them, not to mention we need them, and we must give our dead a proper burial.'

The other would-be Capitán Generals nod in silent acknowledgement.

Those who have the stomach for it break their fast. De Morales does not. Every time he looks at the hardtack gruel before him, he sees the glistening pulp of Barbosa's neck, the blood spewing from the wound. It is not the gore that disturbs him. God knows he has seen his share of that in his time. It is the violence. The cruel cutting short of countless

394

lives and his own helplessness to do anything about it. Barbosa did not deserve such a death. He was kind, he was friendly and sociable. He looked out for the men, both before and after he became captain of the Victoria. He spoke the truth and was fiercely loyal. Perhaps, as Elcano would no doubt argue, he was too loyal, that he ought to have confronted or at least challenged Magalhães before the battle. But Magalhães was, after all, not just Barbosa's Capitán General, but also his brother-in-law. There were layers to their relationship far deeper than his critics would care to admit.

The sun rises higher in the sky. Valderrama hands out small strips of parchment and a few charred sticks from the brazier. As most of the men are illiterate, symbols will be used to cast votes. A circle for Elcano, a triangle for Espinosa and an X for Carvalho.

The men around de Morales play their part in this strange democracy. As they do so, Carvalho says loudly. ''Twas I that found the strait. Remember that, men.' He ignores Espinosa's rolling eyes before continuing. 'Magalhães may have suspected it, but it was me who climbed that mountain and found it to be the strait, me who delivered us.'

Carvalho's little speech done with, Valderrama walks past the men, putting their finished ballots into a morion. 'Your vote, señor doctor.' De Morales looks up into the eyes of the chaplain. They are filled with scorn, offering the oath that he has not forgotten de Morales' words on Limasawa.

He quickly scribbles a circle and tosses the paper into the helmet. Valderrama walks across the deck and spills the ballots onto the surgical table still standing where it was left. He quickly sorts through the ballots, organising them into three piles. One visibly bigger than the others.

'João Lopes Carvalho,' Valderrama says and Espinosa turns away.

'Damn,' Elcano says.

'You have chosen well, men,' Carvalho says proudly, 'I will-'

'We do not need to hear your victory speech,' Espinosa interrupts. 'We need to treat with Humabon, retrieve our living comrades and bury our dead.'

'You shall find me a pragmatic leader,' Carvalho says. 'Therefore, Espinosa, you are now the captain of the Concepción. Elcano, you are to captain the Victoria. I want the men to return to their ships. You will each take count of what crew remain to you and we can move men to other ships as needs be.'

Men begin climbing down into skiffs and set off for their respective ships. There are just seventy-nine men left on the armada now and so the Victoria is quickly emptied. With the crowd gone, the ship seems vacant, crewed by ghosts and the memories of dead men.

The skiffs are brought back to the Victoria to ferry the captains to their ships. A shout stops Espinosa and Carvalho before they can climb down to them. Kneeling in the white sand is Serrano, blood stains the front and side of his naked torso. The captain's head hangs, limp and seemingly lifeless. But he is alive. His shoulders rise and fall fitfully with each ragged breath. The captains and what few crew remain rush to the port side gunwale.

Serrano is surrounded by a few dozen native warriors, all of them armed with spears and bows. One tightly grips his shoulder, though he clearly is not able to attempt an escape.

The warrior holding Serrano, de Morales notices, is holding a Spanish knife. More natives appear from the thick line of jungle on the shore. They carry long rapiers, more Spanish knives as well as their own spartan weaponry.

'Serrano,' Espinosa cries, 'you live?' Serrano's head lifts slightly then lolls back down again. He is near death, that much is plain to see. But if de Morales could only get him onto the surgery table, he might be able to save his life.

The crowd of native warriors on the beach parts and Humabon steps through them. He holds an arquebus in his hand, resting the barrel on his shoulder. Enrique is at Humabon's side, but he walks with none of the swagger of the king as they stand beside Serrano. The slave seems dejected, defeated somehow and he cannot bring himself to look at Serrano, kneeling and bleeding beside him.

Humabon calls out in his own language at the armada, then leans over to Enrique. The slave listens, then calls across the sea in his accented Spanish. 'He cannot understand what I am saying,' he calls. 'Before I say what he has ordered me to say, know I did not mean for it to be this way.' He finally turns to Serrano, sadness settling on his face. 'This was not my intention.'

'Traitorous dog,' Espinosa spits back. 'I care not for your regret.'

Espinosa's words seem to hit Enrique like a blow and he murmurs something to Serrano. The captain looks up at Enrique, his expression blank and his eyes unfocused.

'The other men are all dead,' Enrique calls, slowly turning back to the Victoria. 'But the Humabon wishes to prove to you that he is an honourable man. He will ransom Serrano to you.'

'Honour?' Espinosa scoffs. He turns to Elcano standing beside him. 'All this for the whipping Barbosa gave him after the battle? Serrano is blameless, not to mention the men. Why kill so many for so small a slight?'

'Where did Humabon get an arquebus?' Elcano asks.

Carvalho and Espinosa exchange confused shrugs. 'Enrique must have raided the armoury before the feast last night,' Espinosa says.

'It was never returned,' de Morales says.

'What do you mean?' Elcano asks.

'Barbosa and I took one ashore with us yesterday when we treated with Humabon,' de Morales says. 'You were there, Espinosa,' he adds.

'Christ,' Espinosa says. 'How could Magalhães have forgotten?'

'He did not forget,' de Morales says. 'He told Enrique to collect the weaponry and return it to the armada. He was too focused on the battle to think anything of it. Everyone was.'

'Then Enrique's coup was planned long before Barbosa whipped him,' Espinosa says. 'Is this his homeland?'

'No.' De Morales watches Humabon circle Serrano. 'Magalhães bought him in Sumatra, but he was not born there. He was taken from his home, though I do not think this is it. I spoke with him on the coast of the New World when he needed my care.'

'Then what is his aim?' Espinosa asks desperately.

'Freedom,' de Morales says simply. 'Maybe he knew Magalhães would fail yesterday, maybe he didn't. Either way, he never meant to leave this place.'

'Your Capitán General is dying,' Enrique calls.

'What are your demands?' Espinosa shouts back.

'Humabon demands all the trade items you brought from Sevilla. He wants your scissors, glass beads, silk hats and knives. He wants two dozen rapiers, the same again of crossbows and he wants an iron gun. You will send it all in a skiff. No one is to come ashore.'

'A high price,' Carvalho says sardonically.

Espinosa ignores the Capitán Genera and turns instead to Elcano. 'Even if we gave him a cannon, what would they do with it? Enrique would not know how to load and fire it.'

'It is the symbol of the thing,' Elcano says. 'Even the sight of one of our cannons would strike their enemies immobile with fear. Especially after the fine display I gave them yesterday. Humabon knows Lapu Lapu will avenge yesterday's failed attack and perhaps he knows he will not be victorious. But ignoring the cannon, we cannot give them everything we brought to trade. We would be ruined.'

'We are already ruined,' Espinosa says. 'Give them the cannon and the trinkets and we will return to Sevilla.'

'And have nothing to trade with?' Elcano asks. 'We would starve before we even reached the Indian Ocean, let alone the Guadalquivir.'

Carvalho has been looking at the shore, at the kneeling figure of Serrano, bloodstained and dying on the sand. 'I will not do it,' he says. 'I will not treat with savages. It is beneath us.'

Espinosa gasps. 'We cannot leave Serrano here.'

'Serrano is dying, or very close to it,' Carvalho says.

'And you are a doctor, Capitán General?' Espinosa spits the title, twisting it into an insult. He turns to de Morales. 'What is your opinion? Can Serrano be saved?'

'I would try with all my skill,' de Morales replies. 'I saw him stabbed in the side. If that is his only wound, there is a chance. He has lived this long, after all.'

Espinosa spins back to Carvalho. 'We must try,' he says desperately. 'We cannot leave him to whatever gruesome death these savages will inflict upon him.'

Carvalho inhales deeply. He holds his breath as he takes in the scene on the beach. His eyes move from the pathetic figure of Serrano kneeling in the sand, the whole right side of his body slick with blood, to Humabon, Enrique and the crowd of warriors. Finally, Carvalho exhales. 'I will not treat with savages,' he says again. 'We cannot afford to hand them a cannon.'

'Then fire a cannon,' Espinosa says. 'Rout them and rescue Serrano.'

'Enrique is no fool,' Elcano says. 'He knows we cannot harm him or the locals without destroying Serrano in the process. I do not like it, but we cannot meet his demands and besides treating with Humabon, our only other option is to attack. I believe de Morales could save Serrano, but not at the cost of the lives of every other man on the armada.'

'Capitán-' Espinosa begins but is cut off by Carvalho flicking his hand dismissively.

'I have spoken,' Carvalho says severely. 'Return to your ship. Drop the sails and raise the anchor. We are leaving this place.'

Giving up on Carvalho, Espinosa turns to Elcano. 'We cannot leave him,' he says desperately. His pleading eyes search Elcano's face. 'Fire a cannon. Better Serrano die a quick death than be tortured for days by these savages.'

'I cannot do that. I will not do that.' Elcano says quietly. He reaches out his hand and grasps Espinosa's shoulder. 'There is nothing we can do. We have been outplayed.'

'Sixty lives, Elcano.' Espinosa's eyes harden and he despairingly turns again to the shore. 'Those deaths cannot go unanswered. You were not there. You do not know the horror of that feast.'

'I am sorry,' Elcano says. 'We must look to the lives of

those who survived. We cannot risk more trying to save a dying man.'

Espinosa falls silent. He knows the truth, knows Elcano is right. There is nothing to be done for Serrano now. The price Humabon demands is too high. With one last look at the kneeling figure of Serrano, Espinosa climbs down into his waiting longboat. Carvalho follows him, boarding his own skiff.

Elcano gives the order and the Victoria lurches to life. Creaking and groaning, the ship slowly edges away from the shore. Pigafetta stands motionless on the aftcastle of the Trinidad, a dismayed look on his face as he stares at the beach where Magalhães died.

De Morales stays beside Elcano at the stern of the Victoria on the aftcastle. The ship slowly drifts away from the shore. Serrano, hunched over and staring at the sand before him, seems oblivious or indifferent to the fate they have abandoned him to.

'I do not like supporting Carvalho,' Elcano says, still watching the shore. 'But that ransom would have ruined us.'

Humabon takes a step towards the kneeling Serrano. He takes a knife from one of his warriors and lifts it, showing the blade to the retreating armada. He brings the blade down, slowly, deliberately plunging it into Serrano's neck before pulling it out again with the same slow movement. Deep red blood gushes from the wound, flowing down Serrano's torso, and staining the sand below him. The warrior holding Serrano releases his grip and the lifeless body slumps to the sand.

Another dead man. More have died in the space of the last twenty-four hours than across the many-thousand leagues the armada has travelled since it left Sevilla.

Chapter 26

June 1521

The Capitán General has been gone for four hours. When this nameless island came into view just three days after Carvalho abandoned Serrano, the local people lining the beach dashed for cover, fearful of the massive ships materialising from the horizon.

At first, as Carvalho prepared to go ashore, they hung back, remaining in the deep shadows cast by dense palms and tall grass-like trees. But once the armada had remained offshore for several hours, their curiosity got the better of them and they slowly emerged onto the sand. Children ran around their mothers, jumping and laughing as they waved and hooted to the men aboard the ships. The native men feigned disinterest. They sat on the sand, scanning the eastern horizon, but their sidelong glances betrayed their unease.

Given the Portuguese presence in the Moluccas, it seemed unlikely the native people were completely ignorant of Europeans. Judging by the children's reactions and their mother's indifference, it seemed they felt they had nothing to be too concerned about once they had the measure of their strange visitors. They were interested, but hardly in awe of the huge ships, creaking and swaying offshore. The appearance of the armada was more of a spectacle to them, firing their imaginations and their energies, like a travelling circus arriving in a small town: something they have heard stories of, yet never witnessed themselves first-hand.

Carvalho went ashore, taking with him a small box of trinkets with which to trade for food with the local people. He forbade anyone else to join him.

It seems the new Capitán General is short of allies and confidants. Whereas Magalhães would always be escorted by some combination of Barbosa, Espinosa, Pigafetta and Valderrama, Carvalho went ashore with just five armed sailors, none of them of any standing. Even Pigafetta did not accompany him.

The Italian is morose. He stalks the decks of the Trinidad, walking in the footsteps of his lost luminary. The chronicler is a wound that refuses to heal, reminding the rest of the armada of Magalhães' death and of the loss of one who, for all his faults, at least had the resolve to govern.

Right now, Pigafetta is awkwardly scribbling on parchments as he walks, writing God only knows what about the armada and its meagre crew. 'I think I misjudged him.' Elcano says, standing at the whipstaff of the Victoria. He is watching the Italian wander the deck. 'He must have some principles. I was sure he would ingratiate himself to Carvalho as he had to Magalhães.'

'Pigafetta threw in his lot with Magalhães,' de Morales says. 'He has made few friends since we left Los Cristianos.'

'True,' Elcano says. 'Could Magalhães' death have left him concerned for his own safety?'

Before de Morales can answer, the sound of crying from the island steals his attention. They turn together as Carvalho and his guard burst through the foliage of the jungle, pushing aside the leaves and branches that bar their way. The children on the beach rush to their mothers, the men stand but do not move. As they leave the tangle of foliage, de Morales sees three women trailing after them, led by a cord held in a sailor's fist. The native women are naked, almost certainly by Carvalho's hand rather than their own choice judging by the clothing their countrymen wear, and they trip and stumble over the curled palm fronds and stones scattering the beach. Several warriors carrying spears follow Carvalho and his men. They call to their people watching Carvalho pass by and the beach quickly clears of natives.

'Where is the food?' Elcano calls to Carvalho. By this time, the men of the Concepción have heard the racket. Surrounded by his men, Espinosa stares in disbelief at Carvalho gaily tramping across the beach towards his skiff.

'There was none,' Carvalho replies.

'Then why do you have these women?' Espinosa asks.

'We will trade the women for food at the next island we find,' Carvalho says, climbing into his skiff. 'We will get more for them than we will for scissors and beads.'

'You must be joking,' Elcano says to himself, exasperated.

The women are corralled into Carvalho's waiting skiff.

Their eyes, filled with horror at what life awaits them, fitfully dart this way and that, taking in the ships and the haggard crew watching their approach.

Once at the Trinidad, they are forced to climb the Jacob's ladder and stumble into the main deck. The crew of the flagship crowd around them, hooting, joking and jabbing one another in the ribs. Hands reach out, grabbing at breasts and buttocks, running their fingers through pubic hair. The women, pushed and pawed and jostled, shrink into themselves, shaking with fear.

Carvalho launches over the taffrail. 'Get away from them,' he orders. 'They are not for you. Clear a path.' The sailors step backwards, offering the barest avenue. The women are pushed towards the dining cabin and are lost to sight, disappearing behind the frayed rigging, the crowding men and the torn sails.

'He has no intention of trading those women,' Elcano says to Espinosa on the deck of the Victoria that night. 'They are his concubines. He thinks of himself as some Chinese emperor.'

'That would make us eunuchs,' Espinosa says dryly.

'Have a care, Gonzalo,' Elcano says seriously. 'We are in a dire situation. If we do not get food, we are all going to starve to death.'

'Then what do you suggest? Should we desert the flagship?'

'We cannot abandon the Trinidad. You yourself know the state the Concepción is in.'

'True, it is falling to pieces.' Espinosa looks across to the blackened bulk of his ship. Even in the darkness, it looks shabby and on the verge of ruin. 'I have done what I can since I took charge, but the ship is being eaten away by termites. The ribs are like paper, they crumble at the slightest touch. At this point, I think it is being held together with prayer.'

'Then we must take the Trinidad,' Elcano says.

The silhouette of the Trinidad stands out against the moonlit sea. The fortress of the former Capitán General has lost all its grandeur. What little remained of Magalhães' ensign was cast into the sea when Carvalho took command. Now the bowsprit is bare and, from the tip of the mainmast, only the final rags of the flag of Castile quiver in the wind. The lowered sails, tied up tight against the gibbets, give the ship a skeletal profile; as if its life has been drawn from it.

'I like it not,' Espinosa says.

'We have no choice.'

'Suppose we fail? We have not the men to spare in a failed coup. If we attempt to overthrow Carvalho and he resists he will have us killed. Then Pigafetta can add us to the list of dead men this venture has already claimed.'

It is so strange to hear these two men conspire together. A year ago, in Puerto San Julián, Espinosa would gladly have stabbed Elcano as well as Mendoza when he foiled their mutiny.

'Then we bide our time,' Elcano says. 'There is still a chance we can find the Spice Islands. We have food for a few more weeks. If we have not found the Moluccas in that time then we will have to be done with Carvalho and, by then, the crew will support us.'

Espinosa exhales heavily. When he does not reply Elcano says, 'I need to hear you say you are with me, Gonzalo.'

Reluctantly, Espinosa nods. 'If needs must, we will

remove Carvalho. But bloodlessly,' he adds. 'If we keep him alive we can turn into the Casa de Contratación in Sevilla. We must do everything to remain on the right side of Fonseca and the king.'

Later, De Morales finds Elcano in the captain's cabin. 'Do you think Carvalho knows of the condition of Concepción?' He asks.

'I think Carvalho is an intelligent man,' Elcano admits. 'He must be to have survived this long. He played Magalhães like a fool on the coasts of the New World. He knows that, if we could, we would abandon him. But he also knows the Concepción is not capable of returning to Sevilla.'

'Could we not abandon the Concepcion? Move Espinosa's men here and sail away under cover of darkness.'

'We could,' Elcano says. 'But I would be loath to attempt the return journey with only a single ship. Suppose something happened to the Victoria? Plus, the king will be expecting five ships, each one full of spices. To return with a single ship and no spices could incur his wrath. And certainly, Fonseca would not welcome it.'

'Then Carvalho is clever indeed,' de Morales says. 'You think he deliberately let the Concepción fall into disrepair?'

Elcano scoffs. 'He may be intelligent, but he is first and foremost lazy. The Concepción's decrepitude is a happy coincidence for him. A man like that makes no plans, only manipulating events to his favour.'

'How much longer will you wait?' De Morales asks. hardly believing he is now openly conspiring in a mutiny.

'Carvalho will make a mistake,' Elcano says confidently. 'All men do and men like Carvalho tend to make theirs earlier than those who are careful. When the crew are on our side, Espinosa and I will act.'

'A year ago, I was punished by Magalhães for a mutiny I never took part in,' de Morales says. 'Now I find myself in the midst of one I have joined by circumstance. How many mutinies have we had now? I lose count.'

Elcano laughs humourlessly. 'I never wanted that mutiny in Puerto San Julián,' he says. 'I was then as you are now: strung along by circumstance.'

'And in Mactan?'

A flash of anger. Elcano looks de Morales in the eye. For a moment, he thinks he has overstepped, misjudged the new reality of their relationship. Elcano is now, after all, a captain. But the anger passes. Elcano's eyes soften as he says, 'you already know what happened in Mactan.'

'I have a notion, yes.'

'Would you have done differently, had you the opportunity?'

De Morales imagines himself where Elcano stood on that day, with Magalhães' fate in his hands. 'I do not know,' he says finally. 'I think, as you said, Magalhães would have died regardless.'

'I know you are not questioning me, de Morales,' Elcano says. 'You, perhaps more than any, know the toll Magalhães' leadership took on all of us. What happened at Mactan was not premeditated. I saw an opportunity to save the lives of the men waiting in the Concepción to join Magalhães in that foolish battle. I took that opportunity and I would do so again without hesitation. Carvalho, on the other hand, must be put aside. It can either be under my leadership or under the rule of the mob. Either way, it is inevitable.'

De Morales is not blind to what is happening here. Elcano

and Espinosa are directing events to ensure a mutiny is the only available choice. Neither captain has truly tried to reason with Carvalho. They have not pressured him as Quesada, Cartagena and Mendoza did Magalhães. But when did Cartagena's tirades actually make a difference? They seemed, instead, to set Magalhães more firmly on the path he was already upon. Maybe Elcano is right. Maybe mutiny is inevitable.

'You have my help,' de Morales says finally. 'Such as it is. If there must be a mutiny I would rather it be under your direction, to ensure as little blood is spilt as possible.'

'I am grateful to you,' Elcano says. 'For your faith as much as for your support. I mean for it to be bloodless and, if we are careful, I do not see why it should not be. Carvalho is a man with few friends. When the time comes, those few he does have will quickly see the futility of their allegiance.'

The days pass by in pointless journeys from island to island. Time becomes immaterial, the days melting one into the next until they pass by almost unnoticed. Hunger grows and more weight is shed. The height of midsummer comes and goes and the heat turns humid, oppressive and unbearable. Whatever plan Carvalho has for the fleet, if indeed he has one, is beyond de Morales to decipher. It seems the Capitán General truly has no idea where he is leading the armada, randomly making his way through labyrinthine channels between scattered islands.

Where they do drop anchor the islands are featureless, empty of hope or relief or spices. Just the same palms, the same beaches, the same glimpses of suspicious people dashing away.

Since he took his harem of native women aboard the Trinidad, the Capitán General has rarely been seen. But if he has become lazy and selfish in his habits, he has lost none of the craftiness that got him leadership of the fleet. He is shrewd, careful to follow Magalhães' example in always keeping the Trinidad to the rear of the fleet, where he can keep an eye on his armada. But Carvalho seems to have no interest whatsoever in the condition of his ship and the Trinidad is beginning to fall apart as its crew becomes lazy and lax. After all, who can blame them? Why should they work and sweat in the heat while their captain whiles the days away in his cabin?

The Spice Islands are nearby, Elcano is certain of it, though he cannot say exactly where. If Carvalho would only allow anyone but himself and his guards to go ashore on the islands, they could quickly find a heading.

Despite the directionlessness of their route, Elcano keeps the crew of the Victoria well managed and organised. The decks are cleaned as thoroughly as they can be, but mould and slime slowly claim the decks and sails.

The crew certainly look the part. After almost two years of constant wear, their clothing is a ragged patchwork, worn out and full of holes. They perpetually scratch at the lice and fleas that have overrun everything. Many are shirtless in the heat, with their trousers torn off at the knee. Most wear no shoes, having either lost or eaten the leather from them weeks ago.

The disease may have passed, but it has left an indelible mark on the crew. All around are toothless smiles and gaunt cheeks as well as the scars of ulcers and sores. And of course, there is the absence. The ghosts of those men who follow in the wake of the armada now outnumber the living.

There are still the sick men below in the makeshift

infirmary. Of the nine that remained, just one has recovered and is back to his usual duties. Another three bodies have been dumped into the ocean to sink into its depths, leaving five more groaning and mumbling through their final days. And de Morales does not fool himself, these men will not recover. He eases their discomfort and pain as much as he is able, but he has nothing that will have any real impact. All he can do is watch, a silent and useless witness to their slow, torturous deaths.

On the rare occasion he does stop at land, Carvalho fails even to trade for food. He returns to the fleet each time with excuses. 'The island was pestilential,' he says or, 'there was no food to be found.' Sometimes he returns with a new native woman, seemingly to replace those who have died or add to their number. The Capitán General keeps his harem well-stocked, while even the rats starve to death in the holds.

Elcano and Espinosa, careful to always maintain that the order has come from Carvalho, heavily ration the food. The men groan and complain at the new rationing. First two thirds, then half and finally the crew are living on just a quarter of their usual ration. They become desperate, boiling whatever leather they can get their hands on. Belts, boots, gloves and hats, all of it is boiled then chewed for hours at a time.

But the men are not fools, they can see the islands, the coconut trees and the well-fed native people watching the fleet pass by.

With the height of summer, the monsoons come. They arrive without warning, huge clouds ballooning on the horizon until the sun is blotted out. The clouds burst, unleashing a torrent of fat raindrops into the sea, soaking the sails, the decks and the men. Sometimes the downpours last just minutes, other times hours and sometimes they will drag on ceaselessly. On those long and drenching days, de Morales is sure the ceaseless drumming is driving him to madness.

Everything is soaked through. The ships' hulls, already stripped almost entirely of pitch and bloated by seawater, soak up the deluge like sponges. They expand outwards, in places turning soft and pulpy. The wood has soured from black to brown to green as algae conquers every inch of exposed boards. White mould bursts in the corners of the cabins and under the eaves of the aft and forecastles, lichen creeps up the masts and slime coats the rigging.

But the monsoons, in one regard, are a blessing. Barrels are pulled onto the decks from below in the holds and are filled within days. At least they will not die of thirst.

With so few men left, there is now little for de Morales to do. He has no medicines, no vinegar, no dried herbs. He has his tools, but thus far he has had little use for them. Those who have been injured since the armada stumbled upon Limasawa have died frighteningly quickly, cut down in the surf of foreign shores and slaughtered at the feast. It is a blessing few but the surgeon appreciate that there have been no accidents since the fleet left Mactan almost six weeks ago. The explanation, however, is simple enough. With so little energy, the men have been doing as little as possible to conserve their strength. For the vast majority of the voyage, and particularly since they left the strait, the men have got by with hungry bellies.

Sensing he ought to do something constructive, if only to keep his mind off his hunger, de Morales takes up fishing. Every day, between bouts of rainfall, he sits with his legs hanging between the rails of the gunwale of the aftcastle, his deeply tanned legs and feet prickling with heat from the sun.

He has little luck. It would be a desperate fish indeed that would have interest in the stale hardtack that is all he can spare for bait, but he perseveres, nonetheless.

Sailors from the Trinidad and the Concepción follow de Morales' lead. They sit lined up like pigeons along the battlements of the Torre del Oro. Their luck is little better than his, but they too seem grateful to have something to focus their minds on.

Very rarely, someone will pull in something. Most often mackerel, sardines and small catfish. When de Morales catches three mackerel in one day he reels them in to joyous cheers of congratulations. He presents the fish to Elcano who has them cooked that night and shared amongst the men of the Victoria. De Morales savours the small mouthful he receives as if it were the finest delicacy of kings and emperors.

The buoyant mood on the ship that evening is quickly cut short when they see a commotion on board the Trinidad. A sailor is dragging something large across the deck. It is heavy and he struggles as he heaves it onto the taffrail. Though it is wrapped in a shroud of stained canvas, it is clear what it is that the sailor is lifting. A human corpse. The sailor balances the body on top of the taffrail, catches his breath, then pushes it overboard. The body slaps into the sea. The canvas drifts open, undulating on the waves, revealing the tanned skin of a native woman.

The body slowly sinks below the waves and fish gather around it, nipping at the skin. De Morales looks between the fish, already eating their fill of the corpse, and his own useless fishing line. His fellow fisherman, lining the deck of the Victoria, follow his gaze. He knows what they are thinking, for he is thinking the same thing: such a waste.

Three-masted ships, of a similar size to their own, criss-cross the horizon, sailing north to south or vice-versa. Their low, wide sails, dyed red or tan, ripple in the heat. They are like nothing any of the crew have seen, their sleek hulls, bent like a longbow, lie low in the water.

When the presence of the ships was first noticed by sailors high up in the crow's nest of the Concepción, their call was met with fear. Though no one in the armada knows precisely where they are, they are near the Spice Islands and so the possibility of stumbling into the Portuguese is very real. It is a relief when Elcano points out the differences in their shapes. Caravels, at least, is one thing they need not worry about for now.

The low, unfamiliar ships keep their distance, always staying on the horizon. They seem to have no interest whatsoever in the armada. Which is well, for they all seem to be either going to or coming from the same place. If they did choose to attack, they would greatly outnumber the armada and the exhausted men would quickly be overcome.

'Could we trade with them?' De Morales asks Elcano.

'Carvalho has no interest in that,' Elcano says. 'It will not be long. The men are losing patience. When the time is right, we will act.'

The stores, now, are at a critical level. Without Amaya to kill them, the rats have run riot through the supplies in a final, desperate attempt to stave off starvation. The crew had hung parcels of hardtack from the ceilings of the holds, but the rats had seen through their plans and simply chewed through the rope holding them in place. What food remains now is food even the vermin refuse to eat. Hardtack soaked in rat urine, mouldy peas and faeces-riddled flour. Every day these awful rations are boiled in a great cauldron on the forecastle, forming a thick and rotten stew.

The food may be ruined, but the holds are still full of items for trade. If Carvalho would just stop at one of the many islands, or intercept one of the ships, they could fill their bellies and the holds with fresh fruit, rice, even meat. For who knows what those strange ships carry in their holds? Then they could locate the Spice Islands and be gone. Carvalho would return to Sevilla a hero, celebrated as the man who completed what Magalhães began. But Carvalho has no interest in stopping at the islands and the location of the spices now seems utterly absent from his mind. He still passes his days away in his cabin, locked in a ceaseless orgy with his native women.

The armada heads west, towards the shipping lanes used by the strange ships. There is one in particular, sailing south at such a speed and direction that the armada will soon come into direct contact with it. As they draw nearer, the details of it become clearer. The ship is a similar size to their own but much lither and more pointed at both the prow and the stern. It lacks the stocky, stubby shape of their naos of the armada and pierces through the water like a swordfish.

'This design is like nothing I have seen before,' Elcano says, marvelling at the ship. 'Look at the sails. The canvas is kept in shape by those ribbed battens of supple wood. That is the same wood we have seen growing on most of the islands here. They have no need of rope, as we do, that grows heavy, cumbersome and stiff as time goes on. If a batten breaks, they could stop at any one of the islands and easily replace it.' He shakes his head at the inventiveness. 'It is ingenious.'

The Trinidad approaches and Carvalho emerges from his cabin. De Morales has lost track of the weeks it has been since he has seen the Capitan General. Despite the heat, Carvalho is wearing a ruffled doublet, a sword at his side and a pair of faded red trousers. All of it most likely stolen from Magalhães' possessions.

'We are attacking that vessel,' Carvalho says. He gestures with his head toward the ship, now less than a league north west.

'Why?' Espinosa asks.

'Because I said so.'

A look of disbelief falls across Elcano's face. He and Espinosa stare at Carvalho from their ships, waiting for the Capitán General to explain himself.

'We will attack them and requisition their food stores,' Carvalho says.

'Piracy.' Elcano says. 'I will not do it. I will not debase myself thus, nor will I put my men in danger.'

'Nor will I,' Espinosa says. 'If you want to attack that ship, you can do it alone.'

'Very well,' Carvalho says, 'I do not need cowards anyway.'

The blood rises on Espinosa's face as the Capitán General turns and swaggers across the deck. 'You dare call me a coward, Carvalho?' Espinosa shouts. Elcano turns to him and slowly shakes his head.

Though they will not take part in the seizure of the ship, Elcano and Espinosa agree that they will accompany the Trinidad. It is too great a risk to leave the men at the mercy of Carvalho's mad plan. Worse still, there is a chance the capture

416

could fail and the flagship could be lost. With the condition the Concepción is in, losing the flagship is far too dangerous. Whoever these sailors are on this strange vessel, they will surely not attempt to board the Trinidad with two other ships close by. Just to be sure, Elcano orders the cannons on the Victoria to be prepared.

The people on the ship are visible now and they know something is amiss. They dash across their main deck, shouting undecipherable words at one another in a staccato language of rising and falling tones. With the ship so close now, de Morales can make out the eyes painted on the side of its hull. This is one of the ships King Humabon spoke of in Cebu before Magalhães' death? The king's words ring in de Morales' ears as he watches the Trinidad turnabout, preparing to fire on the ship. *Their ships are superior to your own.*

Perhaps they are. Perhaps they glide across the ocean with more grace than the Spanish naos, but this is obviously a merchant ship. It has no cannons nor any other weaponry. Its only defence, if one could call it that, is a harpoon at its prow for catching large fish.

The Trinidad is beside the merchant ship now, sailing opposite it. But Carvalho does not open fire. Instead, he surges past it, turns suddenly port side and opens fire across the ship's stern.

Clouds of smoke spill into the sky as the Trinidad's cannons rage and the air is torn by their explosions. The cannonballs smash into the hull of the merchant ship, sending splinters of wood and men arcing through the air.

'He is raking them,' Elcano shouts above the chaos.

One cannonball hits a sailor directly in the chest and he disappears in a mist of blood and bone, spattering the sails, the decks and his comrades.

Seeing the gore that was once their crewmate, the other sailors quickly wave their arms in supplication. They fall to their knees and the ship grinds to a halt. The Trinidad lurches to a sudden stop as the sails are furled and the anchor dropped.

Carvalho lets out a war cry and leads an attack on the foreign ship, thrusting his rapier into the air. He boards with a dozen men, swords drawn and teeth gritted, they collide into the merchants now crouched down on all fours with heads bowed low. The blades of Carvalho and his men catch the sunlight as they cut down the defenceless men.

'This is excessive,' Elcano shouts. Up until now, the men lining the decks of the Concepción and the Victoria have remained silent, stunned into speechlessness by the violence. But Elcano's protest falls on deaf ears as the carnage continues.

In the confusion, others pour from the ship's hold into a chaos they are completely unprepared for. Their shrill cries fill the air as they, too, fall to their knees before Carvalho's bloody and unnecessary onslaught. When they see surrender holds no hope, half a dozen of the merchants cast themselves into the sea. They splash and choke in the water before their baggy clothing pulls them beneath the waves.

The deck of the merchant ship is slick with blood, the crimson tide seeping through the scuppers and spilling into the ocean. The battle was short and inglorious. His bloodlust satiated, Carvalho lines up the sailors on the merchant ship, tying them up, side by side. He then sends his men below to ransack the holds.

Now the battle is over, de Morales has a chance to take in the men on this strange ship. Their skin is of a similar colour to their Spanish captors with that familiar Iberian tan. But their faces are of a different shape, rounder with wide cheeks and their hair is abundant, a thick mass of jet black kept long and tied into a knot at the top of their heads. They wear long blouses of many different colours with short baggy trousers much like those worn by the crew of the armada.

They make for a sorry sight, tied tightly to one of the masts of their ship, their heads hanging down. They are clearly in shock at the suddenness of the attack and the viciousness with which Carvalho set about it. A shock de Morales shares. One of the men cannot take his eyes from the floating corpse of one of his comrades, drifting lifeless on the ocean's surface.

Carvalho's men haul their stolen goods out of the hold, piling them up until the deck of the merchant ship is carpeted in supplies. There are sacks of dried rice, beans, preserved fish and other strange foods whose aromatic smell creeps through the air towards the Victoria, making de Morales' stomach knot with hunger despite his horror at what he has witnessed. In amongst the supplies, they find a sloshing barrel. They split it open and the air is filled with the sweet and faintly vinegary scent of alcohol. The faces of Carvalho's men light up with glee as they dip cupped hands into the liquor, drinking long draughts.

The crew of the merchant vessel sit in silence, watching their goods being stolen from them as the Capitán General's men throw the supplies to the deck of the flagship, using a capstan for the heavier sacks of rice.

'Cut down the mast,' Carvalho orders. 'I want this ship made useless. We must keep these filthy people from chasing us and stealing back what we have claimed.'

Carvalho's men go about disassembling the ship. First, they slash the sails to ribbons with their bloody rapiers.

Several slip on the slick deck, clattering to the boards as they swing their swords while others laugh and joke. Then the beams Elcano so admired are broken, they bend deeply before they snap with a loud crack. The mast is felled with an axe. It takes seven blows to shatter the wood, the dull thuds filling the quiet air with their dead weight. Once they are finished, Carvalho's men cast the remains into the sea, adding to the debris of bodies, food and flotsam drifting away from the ship.

'Will we share the food now?' Elcano calls to Carvalho as the Capitán General climbs back aboard the Trinidad. 'Ere we raise anchor.'

Carvalho wipes sweat and blood from his face. He smiles. 'If you wanted the food, you should have aided in the taking of it. Hunger will be ample reward for your cowardice.'

'You are condemning your own men to starve to death,' Elcano shouts.

'Call me ignorant now.' Carvalho spits back. 'I told you I have a long memory for insult.'

For a moment Elcano is stricken dumb at Carvalho's pettiness. He gathers himself. 'You are playing games with men's lives,' he shouts at Carvalho's back as the Capitán General ducks into his cabin, slamming the door behind him.

Chapter 27

September 1521

The armada lies anchored on a calm sea. They sailed away from the desolation Carvalho left of the merchant ship for almost six hours; retracing their route eastwards before dropping anchor for the night off the coast of an uninhabited islet; little more than a mound of sand swelling up out of the ocean.

The night is filled with jeers and shouts, travelling on the humid air from the Trinidad as Carvalho and his men celebrate their victory. Surely now they are sharing the stolen food and indulging in alcohol. De Morales thinks of the women. Are they Carvalho's alone or will he share them also with his men tonight?

Espinosa, his reluctance replaced with resolution, is aboard the Victoria and speaks to Elcano in the open air of the deck. 'Carvalho must be replaced before he leads us all to our deaths.'

'The time is right,' Elcano answers. 'His stunt today will have gained many loyal men on the Trinidad, but they will all be drunk tonight.'

They turn to the crew. 'Do we have your support?' Elcano asks. The famished crew of the Victoria gather around the two captains. They grunt their approval.

'Do you need me to assist you? De Morales asks Elcano.

'All I ask is your skill,' Elcano says. If all goes as I hope, there ought to be no need for force. You must remain on the main deck but keep yourself to the rear of the crowd. If Carvalho is injured, you must do everything in your power to save him. He will answer for his crimes. But he must answer to the king, not to the mob.'

They wait several hours before acting, allowing Carvalho's men to drink themselves dumb. Eventually, Espinosa sends a skiff to the Trinidad with a message that Elcano has fallen ill.

More long hours pass as Carvalho takes his time responding. The crew of the Victoria grow impatient, anxious to be done with the deed, but Elcano keeps them calm. 'What's a few more hours of hunger?' He asks them.

Dawn is near by the time the Capitán General's skiff is lowered into the water. God only knows what Carvalho has been doing in the meantime. Had Elcano actually been ill, he could very well have been dead by the time Carvalho stumbles over the taffrail and wanders across the deck of the Victoria.

Perhaps it is the alcohol he has been drinking, or perhaps

it is his arrogance, but he saunters through the gathered crew, oblivious to the crowd and the anger on their faces.

Carvalho sees Elcano standing outside his cabin door. 'You are not ill.' He says incredulously. 'Why am I here, then?'

Espinosa approaches the Capitán General as hungry sailors press in around him. De Morales, following Elcano's request, stays well out of the way, far from the balled fists of the crew. He finds he is tightly clutching his case of tools, his knuckles turning white under the pressure. The only thing standing in the way of this turning bloody is Carvalho's reaction.

'You will relinquish your command, Carvalho,' Espinosa says.

'Why would I do that?' But there is little conviction in Carvalho's voice. If he was drunk when he arrived, the seriousness of the situation has sobered him quickly. His anxious eyes cast about the deck, taking in the pressing crew, their raging eyes and their tightening fists.

'You are leading us to our deaths,' Elcano says bluntly.

'This is mutiny,' Carvalho says, his voice becoming high-pitched with incredulity. 'I will not have it. I will have your heads, you mutinous dogs.'

'No you won't,' Espinosa says simply. 'If you do not relinquish your command, you will be cut down right now.'

Carvalho laughs sardonically.

He shrugs.

'Fine,' he says. He scoffs and turns on his heel, heading for his skiff.

'You will captain the Concepción,' Elcano says. 'Espinosa will relieve you of your command of the Trinidad.'

Carvalho turns and looks aghast at the faces of Elcano and Espinosa.

'Your harem will be dropped off at the next island,' Espinosa says. 'For now, they remain on board the Trinidad.'

Carvalho's mouth drops, but his shock quickly passes. 'I care not,' he says, flicking a hand.

And so ends Carvalho's reign as Capitán General. Without violence, without months of espionage, scheming or undermining. Barely without any complaint, the hedonist has his command taken from him.

Rather than call a vote, Elcano and Espinosa agree to jointly take on the role of Capitán General. There are no complaints, for there are none left who are qualified to lead. Espinosa immediately sets out to the Trinidad with a guard of seven men most loyal to him. The flagship's rowdy crew are quickly brought into line under his stern heel. Any sailors who complain or displease him are pilloried. When the stocks are full, Espinosa has them tied to the forecastle taffrails to bake in the heat until the fight is beaten out of them.

The fleet is turned south-west. Espinosa, who has not travelled to the Spice Islands before, places all trust in the fleet's navigation in the hands of Elcano. Once he finds his heading, Elcano assures the crew of the Victoria, they will soon find those lands that have seemed a myth for so long now.

Once the fruits of Carvalho's short and inglorious piracy are spread among all three ships, there is plenty to go around and they need not ration too drastically. The alcohol, a form of strong rice wine, is locked in the dining cabin of the Trinidad and doled out daily in lieu of the fortified wine that ran dry months ago.

To pass the time as the fleet retraces part of its journey around the dozens of tiny, uninhabited islands that protrude from the sea, de Morales again takes up fishing. Pigafetta, aboard the Trinidad, does the same though no one else joins them. As undermanned as the armada now is, the rest of the crew are far too busy working to while away their days fishing.

It is the first time the chronicler has done anything productive since Magalhães' death. They are both sitting on aftcastles of their respective ships, their feet dangling over the side of the hull. At the pace the armada is moving, it is unlikely either will catch anything, but it is better to keep busy if only in mind than in action. Today is a calm and fine day, as most days have been since they arrived in this region. The monsoons have settled into a rhythm now. The clouds will swell as the day draws on until, by late afternoon, they finally spill a deluge of rain before quickly melting away once more. Birds fly overhead in the morning sun and de Morales finds he is filled with a hope he has not felt for months, years even.

Elcano is an excellent leader, someone who can be trusted to put the health and the safety of his crew foremost. Espinosa, on the other hand, has matured greatly into a level-headed and cautious leader in the months since the armada left Sevilla. All his boastful bravado and showboating has gone, replaced by sensible pragmatism.

The armada is spread across the ocean in a narrow triangle, the point of which is made by the decrepit Concepción with the Trinidad and the Victoria following behind side by side. Carvalho has quickly fallen into line. He must know the slightest misstep now will bring about his complete downfall. Life, of any kind, is preferable to the alternative.

Opposite, the Trinidad carves boldly through the water. How these ships have survived this long is beyond de Morales. All three bear the scars of the almost two-year-long journey they have endured. Everywhere broken rails, patched sails, chipped wood and rusted iron tell the tale of every gruelling league from Sevilla to this place. Although the Trinidad and the Victoria are the worse for wear, the Concepción is in a terrible state. All those long months in Puerto San Julián with neither captain nor crew, are starting to tell. From behind on board the Victoria, it is obvious how much damage the Concepción has taken on by how low it floats in the water compared to the Trinidad and how it lists to the port side. Despite Espinosa's best efforts while he captained it, it is clear the ship is on its last legs. Even a layman like de Morales can tell the damage is done and there will be no going back.

Movement from the aftcastle of the Trinidad catches his attention. De Morales turns and watches Pigafetta fall into the ocean with a hollow splash. The image seems bizarre and takes a moment to register. The chronicler simply slid off the side of the Trinidad.

Could it be that Pigafetta did not fall but jumped, that he has finally decided to join his master in death?

But then Pigafetta's arms flail and flap, splashing frantically at the water. The chronicler desperately grabs at the slick hull of the Trinidad as it slides past him. With nothing to grip, his hands slip off the belly of the ship. No, it cannot be suicide. If it were, why would he grasp so desperately to life?

De Morales looks to the right, to the main deck of the Victoria. The crew are working, climbing and scrubbing and calling to one another. He is the only one who witnessed this.

Pigafetta has been an enemy to him for months now. He even argued for his death at the trials. He poured poison in Magalhães' ear across a thousand leagues of ocean, corrupting the former Capitán General against de Morales and leaving him to freeze and slave away while men he could have saved died. And he enjoyed every moment of it. True, de Morales felt sorry for the chronicler after Magalhães' death. But would Pigafetta feel the same for him? The nasty little Venetian deserves death. Why should he live when so many others have died?

'Aiuto. Aiuto.' Pigafetta's pleas pull de Morales from his dark thoughts. 'Non posso-' his cries are cut short as the chronicler's head slips below the surface.

Sailors on board the Trinidad hear the calls but glance around them, trying to find its source. Pigafetta's head bursts up from the foam once more, his eyes wide and paling face set in terror. He claws at the ocean, grasping frantically, water and life slipping through his fingers. He is struggling to keep his mouth above the waterline. It is a fight he is losing.

'Man overboard, man overboard.' The call comes from high above de Morales. He turns to face the voice and sees a cabin boy in the crow's nest waving his arms and pointing at Pigafetta desperately trying to tread water behind the Trinidad. Other men on the Victoria, hearing the commotion and seeing the drowning chronicler, join the cabin boy. Like mimes, they gesticulate to the men on the flagship, waving their arms and shouting. Espinosa bursts from his cabin, desperately trying to understand the commotion.

Finally, the Trinidad's crew understand what those aboard the Victoria are trying to tell them. They rush to the aftcastle while others furl the sails and quickly drop the anchor. The Victoria follows the flagship's lead and the two ships grind to a halt. The sailors on the aftcastle have found Pigafetta, now splashing pathetically in the sea twenty feet behind the Trinidad.

Two men dive into the water and swim with furious speed towards the stricken chronicler while others cast ropes into the sea. The swimmers reach Pigafetta and, sputtering and terrified, the chronicler clings to them. While one holds him above the water on his back, the other ties a rope cast from the ship around their bodies. The crew on the Trinidad twist the rope through a capstan and heave on it, drawing Pigafetta and his saviours back to the ship to yells and whoops from the crew of the Victoria.

As he watches the three figures being hauled onto the deck de Morales feels sick to his stomach. He watched Pigafetta fall into the sea and was prepared to allow him to drown and disappear into its depths. He, who has trained his whole life to save lives, to lessen pain and bring comfort. He who cursed Magalhães for costing so many lives in Puerto San Julián.

He is disgusted with himself, appalled at what this voyage, this ship, has done to him. It has broken him and remade him into something wicked, something he never thought he could become.

Five bodies are lined up along the main deck of the Victoria, stretching from the mainmast to the door of his cabin. They have been covered in a single sheet of old sail, already soaked through from the beating rain. The heavy canvas has stuck to the corpses, sinking into every cleft and chasm, revealing in stark relief the disseminated bodies below. They are the last to succumb to the disease. Some have

428

suffered for almost three months.

Valderrama's prayers drone, mingling with the sound of rainwater hitting the ocean. De Morales tries to tell himself at least it is over now, at least these men are dead and no more will fall ill. But there is no comfort or consolation in those thoughts. Those corpses were men once. Men with hopes, dreams and families. He has watched their slow, torturous deaths and has been able to do nothing to help them.

He is a failure.

Five lay before him, but countless bodies stretch back through the ocean. Breadcrumbs leading to oblivion.

The canvas cannot be spared and so, before they are cast into the sea, it is pulled from the corpses. He cannot look. He cannot witness what the disease and his own inadequacy did to them.

Rather than look at the corpses he stares ahead, at the mainmast, at the flickering brazier, at the headless ghost of Quesada. Maestra Andrew stands by his side now, a crippled phantom, bent and emaciated. Beside them, Ginovés leans at the gunwale looking west, the welts and cuts on his naked body glistening in the sun.

Five splashes and they are gone.

His heart racing, de Morales bursts into his cabin. He stumbles, tripping on the threshold and falls to the ground, gasping for air. He can feel panic overwhelm him. The ragged, stuttering breaths, the wild eyes, the sheen of cold sweat covering his skin. He tries to calm his heart, breathing deliberately through his nose, forcing air into his lungs.

He falters onto all fours and crawls across the boards before slumping to the floor once more, sitting with his back to the bed. He feels the panic is passing, but the image of Pigafetta slipping into the ocean appears before him and his breath catches again.

The tears come now. Hot and free they fall into his palms as de Morales hides his face with shame. Shame at his selfish grief. Shame at his failures. Shame at the man he has become. Shame that, but for that cabin boy in the crow's nest, he would have left Pigafetta to drown. Shame that he once stood at the port in Los Cristianos and believed this would be an adventure, an escape.

Chapter 28

October 1521

'What is the name of this place?' Pigafetta asks. He speaks slowly and loudly as if volume will make up for ignorance. The native people, all of them men, before him wear long skirts of dyed grasses weaved with beads and shells. Some wear wide bandanas of various colours, while others have smaller turbans-like pieces of cloth wound tightly around their heads. One man, who seems to be a leader of sorts, stands before the chronicler, a look of confusion on his face. He is saying something in a fast and lyrical language.

'Get the spices,' Espinosa says and a sailor dashes across the sand towards a skiff.

'They are uninterested in the ships,' Elcano says to Espinosa. 'Surely that is a good sign.'

'We shall see,' Espinosa says.

The native people begin talking amongst themselves, the tones of their language flowing like the tides of the sea. De Morales watches Pigafetta putting his amateur anthropology into practice as he tries to make himself understood to the natives. The chronicler seems to have risen from the ocean reborn, as if its waters cleansed him of his melancholy and gave him a renewed purpose.

The last week has been a daze. Elcano has led the armada out of the maze of islands as de Morales has slumped into despondency, distancing himself from all others. They sailed south, plunging into a vacant sea. Then the hazy visage of land bruised the offing, spreading until it filled the horizon. Now the ships creak and sway offshore, held in place by their anchors.

The sailor returns and passes a sealed box to Espinosa who waves the man who seems to be the leader towards him. Curious, the man approaches Espinosa who opens the box. The scent of cloves, heavy, warm and citric, fills the air.

'Ha,' the man says. He clicks his fingers and speaks again in his own language. Confusion passes across his brow as he tries to remember something.

'Spices,' Pigafetta says. 'Cloves.'

'Especiarias,' the man says slowly.

Elcano's face drops. 'Portuguese,' he says, his voice quieted with shock.

A smile bursts across Espinosa's face. 'He speaks Portuguese.'

'Where?' Pigafetta asks desperately. 'Onde? Onde?'

The man turns and points south. 'Tidore. Um dia,' he says

falteringly.

'Tidore is one day's journey south?' Elcano says, incredulous.

The man holds up a gnarled finger and then points toward the battered ships. 'Um dia,' he says again, smiling now.

'What is the name of this land?' Espinosa asks. 'Qual é o nome desta terra?'

'Malaku,' comes the reply.

'We have found the Malaccas. We have found the Spice Islands.' Espinosa says.

Pigafetta falls to his knees. Tears well in Elcano's eyes as his aged face wrinkles into a smile. Beside him, Valderrama bows his head and prays quietly in Latin, his shoulders shaking as he, too, weeps. De Morales stares at the native man, the news shocking even him out of his despondency, unsure whether to believe it can be true.

The native man's smile bursts into boisterous laughter at the ragged and hopeless men, praying and weeping before him. He points south once more. 'Um dia,' he says again. 'Tidore, um dia.'

Before they weigh anchor, Espinosa goes ashore in a skiff with Carvalho's harem of native women. The women's nakedness has been covered with strips of old sail but they shiver, nonetheless. He stays only the briefest time, approaching the group of men on the shore. Then he ushers the frightened women out of the skiff. They follow him over the sand to the group of men who meet them with bemused faces. The men nod and bow, smiling and opening their palms. Espinosa quickly turns around, then heads back to the Victoria.

'How did it go with the women?' Elcano asks when Espinosa is aboard.

Perhaps it is their style of leadership, or perhaps it is simply that there are so few men on board any of the ships now, but the Capitán Generals speak on the main deck, there is little secrecy between them and their crew. Everyone who wishes to listen to their conversation can do so. After two long years of intrigue, sedition and mutinous planning, the change is welcome. After all, as de Morales stood on that pier in Los Cristianos all those long months ago, was it not rivalry and conspiracy he was glad to be rid of? How naive he was.

'I tried to explain, through sign language, that we found them on another island,' Espinosa says,

'And they understood you? Elcano asks.

'I have no idea. But I think not. I did not want to admit how we really came by them. After all, we do not know if Carvalho actually traded for them or if he kidnapped them. Perhaps they speak the same language and will explain what really happened.'

'Most likely the men believe you gifted the women to them in thanks for their hospitality,' Elcano says. 'But if they do speak the same language, we must be far from this before they can tell their tale.' The Capitán Generals turn to the shores of the island, already empty. The women are gone, disappeared into whatever life they will now live. Their treatment will be better, de Morales tells himself, half-heartedly. Surely, it cannot be worse.

'The Concepción is done with,' Espinosa says. 'I think there is nothing for it but to be rid of it.'

'From five to two,' Elcano says. He sighs. 'It is truly past repair? The listing is plain for all to see but that could be righted in Tidore, while we trade.'

'The listing is the least of the Concepción's problems. At this stage, there are more termites than wood in its hull. The whole ship is infested. It springs new leaks daily because the hull is so thin from the constant gnawing of the devils.'

'It was the oldest ship to begin with,' Elcano says. 'How many men does Carvalho command?'

'Just twenty,' Espinosa says. 'In truth, the Concepción has been undermanned for months now. It was a struggle while I captained it but we got by, just about. Goodness knows the other ships could use the manpower. If we divide its crew between the Victoria and the Trinidad, it will take a great weight from our crew's shoulders.'

'And Carvalho?' Elcano says.

They turn together to the Concepción. They must know the truth. Carvalho is a liability. Espinosa seems to have held Carvalho in as low regard as Elcano and his actions during his meandering and selfish leadership have certainly soured his opinions moreso, almost to the point of open contempt.

'You think he will dissent?' Espinosa asks.

'Based on how easily he gave up command of the armada, I would doubt it,' Elcano says. 'Carvalho cares only for his own comfort. No, it is not mutiny I fear, but slothfulness. My concern is that by having him aboard either of our ships, his laziness will spread quicker than any rebellion.'

'Then what do we do?'

Elcano looks to the south, in the direction of Tidore, thinking hard. 'We work him like a dog. Neither the Victoria nor the Trinidad require a pilot and so Carvalho will do what is needed of him. I will take him,' he adds.

The Concepción will be burned before the fleet leaves for

Tidore. The crew are distributed among the two remaining ships of the armada and Carvalho comes aboard the Victoria. The former pilot, former captain, former Capitán General seems in good spirits despite the demotion. Most likely, he thinks he can disappear among the crew and do even less work now he is no longer a captain. But, if that was his hope, it is quickly dashed. As soon as he climbs aboard, a brawny seaman grabs him by the arm. Carvalho tries to wrench away from him, but the seaman grips harder still.

He leers over Carvalho. 'Work the bilge pump,' he says, shoving him towards the hold.

Carvalho drags his feet like a petulant child as he makes his slow way across the boards to quiet jeers from the scattered seamen idling about the main deck. They call him nave, slothful and churlish and the glances they cast at him are full of malice. With how they suffered while he was Capitán General, he is fortunate they do not set upon him.

Skiffs ferry back and forth all afternoon from the Concepción to the Victoria and the Trinidad, moving what little supplies remain onboard the doomed ship. The stagnant water is simply left in the holds, as are the rotten, rat-infested crates of hardtack and other mouldy foodstuffs long-forgotten about in the dark corners. Crates of scissors, bells, hats, silk, cotton, wool and knives are moved to the two remaining ships of the armada, ready to be traded with locals in the Spice Islands for cloves. As are the swords, arquebuses, cannons, crossbows, breastplates and helmets. All are dumped into skiffs and brought to the other ships. Elcano and Espinosa are sure to spread the supplies and weaponry across both ships, avoiding a repeat of Magalhães' poor logistical choices in the strait.

Come evening, the Concepción is finally emptied and the

now hollow boat bobs lightly in the sea. Purged of its immense load of cargo, weaponry and men it seems weightless despite its massive size.

Oil is spilt across the battered main deck. The last man to leave the ship climbs down the frayed Jacob's ladder into a waiting skiff. Once in the boat, he lights a torch, the red glow pulsating in the evening gloom. He turns and throws the torch onto the deck of the Concepción and quickly rows toward the Trinidad.

Slow seconds turn to minutes as everyone waits for the light to take. It takes so long, that de Morales starts to think it won't. That the Concepción is clinging desperately to its miserable existence, so much like the crew of the armada.

But finally, the flame takes and flares suddenly. Fire launches up the barren mainmast, stripped of its sails. With a ferocious roar, the fire spreads quickly, devouring the main deck of the haggard vessel. The glowing ship pulsates orange, red and yellow as the air above it ripples in the fizzing heat. What little pitch remains on the hull, bubbles and sputters before finally melting and sliding into the sea to form thick puddles on the ocean's surface. Even in the growing dark of evening, de Morales can see the multitude of rats desperately dive into the ocean from the deck, squealing and snarling. They frantically swim towards land, the water rippling in their wake, scattering the reflection of the blaze.

The Concepción, now completely engulfed in flame, cracks in two and the mainmast topples over, crashing into the forecastle, sending sparks and ash billowing into the night sky. Then the ship sinks into itself and slips below the surface with a hiss as the raging flames are finally quenched.

It is all over so quickly. The Concepción, which has carried its crew so far from Sevilla is gone, leaving only charred flotsam and a few floating crates as its final farewell. An ignominious end.

Exactly as the native man had said, the journey south from Malaku to Tidore takes only a single day. When the rolling visage of land comes into view the mood among the crew is subdued, de Morales included. After all this time, all these countless leagues, it is difficult to know what to feel now their destination is finally before them. There is a disbelieving pride at the achievement but weighing heavily upon him is the knowledge of what awaits him in Castile, as well as all those who have been lost along the way.

Emptiness fills his heart. They have come all this way across thousands and thousands of leagues, travelled for over two years through hunger and hardship and death. Now, when they will finally arrive at Tidore, there will be no fanfare. No celebration awaits them. Just those rolling, quiet hills of cloves now clearly discernible from the prow of the Victoria as tufts of deep green.

He finds Elcano on the forecastle looking to the land of spices. 'Am I to feel triumphant?' he asks.

'We have not triumphed yet,' Elcano says. 'Even when our holds are full, we must still get home. Though those waters are, at least, well-charted.'

Home. Where exactly is that? At Juana la Loca's bedside? At his own table, surrounded by ghosts? At the Castillo San Jorge?

He senses Elcano eyeing him, trying to read his thoughts. He looks back to the coast of Tidore with its deep green hills. Everything here is hyperreal, like an imitation of all he has known before. The sun, so high in the sky, burns with a vivid light, bathing the island in a brilliant glow. The vegetation is of the boldest green, its flowers, now discernible, are of the brightest whites, reds and golds. Birds spill from cliffs, whirl in the sky, then plunge into the ocean before bursting into the air once more, snapping a sparkling trail of water from their beating wings.

'You have been here before,' he says. 'Tell me, was the route we found truly worth it?'

'No,' Elcano says quickly as if he has already asked himself the same question countless times before. 'Even if I had to fight through a Portuguese armada guarding the Cape of Good Hope, I would not go through that hell again.'

'Then you will return to Sevilla via the usual route?' De Morales asks. 'You will not go back the way we came.'

'Espinosa is more open to the idea,' Elcano says. 'He has spoken in favour of heading east to New Spain and abandoning the ships there, then continuing over land and returning via the Great Ocean.'

'And you?'

'We know nothing of the New World,' Elcano says. 'Our voyage has proven only its immensity. Everything we have learnt of it since we began charting new waters and lands has only added to its unfathomable vastness. Maybe we could find New Spain. But even if we did, what would we find there? There was no settlement on its western shore when we left, yet Espinosa hopes that in the time since the Spanish presence in the New World will have spread. Maybe he is right. Maybe Cortés will have succeeded. But to act on such a gamble is at best a risk. We would likely find nothing but empty beaches and jungle. It took us six months to cross the New Ocean and you yourself know we barely made it. Can you imagine repeating that voyage, knowing that at the end of it we faced a march through jungle and hostile territory"

'But we would be on land in weeks rather than months.'

'Better months on a well-charted ocean with known ports and friendly settlements than weeks of blindness.'

Elcano is probably right. Yet de Morales cannot shake the sense that prolonging their journey, even though charted waters, is more than he can handle. More men will fall ill with scurvy as they always do and he knows he cannot save them. He is out of his depth. The Portuguese know their planned route would circumnavigate the globe. Even if the rest of Europe believe the armada to have disappeared, King Manuel would have every one of his caravels in the Indian and African oceans keeping a sure eye for rogue Spanish ships. And all the while, the Victoria will be inching towards a fate de Morales saw off the coast of Africa.

He can smell the spices before they have even dropped anchor. The whole island of Tidore is coated in a thick blanket of clove trees, their tiny white flowers ebullient in the sunshine set like stars against the lavish green backdrop of their leaves. The scent is rampant, its congesting cloud hanging heavily in the air, spilling into the sea.

The remaining two ships of the once glorious Armada de Molucca drop anchor off Tidore as dusk falls. Elcano and Espinosa order the men to prepare to go ashore the next day. This slow process, lengthening again their already long journey, even by a single night, is an extra torture for the men.

When it does finally come, the following morning, the process of bartering for the spices is mundane. It is nothing like de Morales had imagined, there is no mad exodus of raucous, celebratory men to the shores of Tidore to trade trinkets for sacks of spices worth more than gold. He realises, now, he was foolish to ever imagine it that way. After countless years of careful planning by Magalhães and the hundreds of millions of maravedis poured into the Armada by the Casa de Contratación and the court of Castile, the purchasing of cloves will be a meticulous and carefully supervised process. This will be no free-for-all.

To begin with, only a handful of men are permitted on Tidore. Despite the fact he has no real reason to be there, Elcano kindly allows de Morales to go ashore. He understands the toll the last months have taken on the doctor. If the harshness of the overwintering in Puerto San Julián weakened him, the voyage across the New Ocean broke his nerve completely. All those men, piled up in the bowels of the Victoria, moaning and weeping themselves into an empty, pointless death he could do nothing to soothe. And then the beaches of Mactan and the slaughter of so many at the feast.

As he wanders the shore of this paradise island, clothed like royalty in its rich regalia of spices, de Morales feels empty, defeated. But it is not merely exhaustion and neurasthenia that weigh upon him, nor is it merely the weight of the journey thus far. It is the knowledge, unshakable and certain in his mind, of what, if he boards the Victoria again, he will be willingly walking into.

The bartering goes on around him, but it is not the one-sided swindling he had imagined it would be. The native people know the value of what they have, and they have been doing this for hundreds of years.

The entire island is built up around the trade of spices. It is cultivated, the trees and shrubs carefully cared for. They are planted in meticulous rows, separated by wide pathways kept clear of all other foliage. The south-facing sides of several hills are left bare. Here, cloves are spread across packed dirt to dry in the sun. There are huts filled with other spices from other lands, each one pouring forth a smog of rich, earthly and tangy scents.

But this is not Thomas Moore's Utopia. It is clear from the stooped backs and plunging stomachs of those working amongst the trees, that at best they are vassals and at worst slaves. There are no horses or oxen to carry the weaved sacks of cloves to the drying hills. Instead, every moment of back-breaking work is carried out by teams of men and women, even children. They sweat under the sun, heaving masses of cloves to and fro about the island, watching from the corners of their eyes the despondent physician walking among them.

Once he would have wished to help them, as he did in Rio de Janeiro. Once he would have been appalled at their treatment. But now he sees their torment and feels nothing. Nothing but an affirmation of what he has long known but never truly admitted to himself. He allows himself to admit it now and damn the consequences. Mankind is unfathomable in its cruelty. And God made man in his image.

The other men are buoyant. They chase women across the beach, fill their pockets and trunks with spices until their very being absorbs the powerful scent. Carvalho is nowhere to be seen. This time, no one bothers searching for him.

But where the other men are relieved of the terrible burdens of the journey of discovery, de Morales is weighed down by it. As if the cares they have cast off have fallen onto his shoulders.

What now? They are where they hoped to be. But there are so few of them. He cannot help his mind drifting across the names of the dead as if their graves are before him on this perfumed beach. Magalhães, Serrano, Barbosa, Mendoza, Quesada, Elorriaga, Guerra, Cartagena, de la Reina, Rebêlo, Mesquita, Maestra Andrew. All empty names. Not all of them were friends. Most were everything but. But they were all people who lived and loved. Sons, daughters, wives, mothers and fathers are waiting in Sevilla, Castile, Grenada and every other part of Europe for their loved ones who will never return to them.

Was it worth it? Was it worth all the hardship, disease and murder? Was it worth travelling thousands of leagues through every danger and difficulty imaginable? Through hunger and illness, pain and panic, death and destruction. And for what? A handful of cloves. A few thousand maravedis of stinking spices to build an empire upon.

When his wife died giving birth to his child, de Morales ran to Castile. When that was not far enough, he ran to the ends of the earth with the Armada de Molucca. But rather than leave the ghosts behind he has gathered more about him.

Quesada's headless spectre, Ginovés, Maestre Andrew, Serrano, Barbosa, Elorriaga. The dead stand before him on the warm, white sands of Tidore, their blank eyes staring disinterestedly past the piles of spices being loaded onto the bloated and battered remains of their Armada de Molucca. His eye follows theirs, finally settling on the Victoria. He sees the ship's phantom crew staggering across the deck. Maybe Elcano is there. Perhaps that short man is Pigafetta. Could that hunched form, fiddling with rosary beads be Valderrama? The vision that has haunted him since the coast of Africa so long ago barely registers now. It is as real to him as the sand beneath his feet.

He cannot board that ship again. He cannot walk into the

heart of so many ghosts. Spirits draw others to them and he knows, if he climbs aboard the Victoria again, he will find the phantoms of his wife and child waiting for him.

He joined the armada as a physician, a surgeon, a saver of lives. But how many has he saved? Elorriaga died after three months of agony. Guerra died a wreckage, whimpering and crying. Magalhães was hacked to pieces. Barbosa and Serrano were slaughtered in a foreign land. All those nameless, faceless men lying face down in the ocean, their corpses torn apart by sharks.

He tried his best and he failed. Too many of those men died because he could not save them. He had not the skill, the supplies or the energy. He could not even offer them the mercy of comfort. They died in agony, pleading for death as they choked on their teeth, as their skin tore and split, and their bones broke with every movement.

Even now, in death, they find no relief. Their spirits and spectres relive the horror of their deaths. And those who yet live will find these brief moments of joy on Tidore quickly snatched from them. The men today who dance and cheer as they grasp handfuls of cloves and women will tomorrow be starving and dying on the deck of the Victoria as it slips into its fate.

The crew are preparing to depart and he is still in a daze. He has been in a daze since they arrived. He has eaten, he has moved, but he has never lived. He is vaguely aware of a conversation happening before him.

'-if you are to stay behind,' Elcano is saying.

'Only for a few weeks,' Espinosa says. 'Once the Trinidad is repaired, we will depart. Head east for New Spain.'

'Then the Trinidad goes east and the Victoria goes west,' Elcano says.

The Victoria. The name snaps him out of his trance.

He looks at that cursed ship. In the bright light of midday, he sees those ghostly men and the memory of St. Elmo's Fire flaring. He sees the emaciated ribs, the gaunt faces, the stumbling feet. He sees the bulging hull, rotting and stinking of mould and the sails slick with green algae. He sees Elcano, a broken man with grey hair and no teeth slowly starving to death. And then he sees himself. He sees the tears, the yellow eyes, the consumption. He sees a broken man. He sees a ghost.

Elcano is beside him. The Victoria is ready to depart. He wants to know if de Morales is okay.

He cannot answer.

Elcano speaks of the journey. He says the Trinidad must be repaired. He says the Victoria will go ahead. He says they will be home soon.

De Morales, former physician to Juana la Loca, failed physician to the Armada de Molucca, looks at his friend. A man he has clung to since Rio de Janeiro. A man guilty of mutiny but a man who saved countless lives in Cebu. A man who, for all his faults, has saved more lives than the armada's surgeon.

'I cannot come.' His voice cracks. 'I cannot board that ship.'

Elcano can see his frightened eyes, the tears forming. He can see the horror of the visions that have haunted de Morales for two years now written clearly on his face.

He understands.

445

He touches de Morales' shoulder. 'We will meet again, my friend,' he says.

De Morales stands on the beach alone and watches the Victoria melt into the horizon.

Epilogue

The ship presses low into the water, weighed down by its tremendous cargo of cloves and spices. The people of Tidore watch the crew board their ship. They watch the solitary man the sailors called señor doctor stand on the aftcastle, his haunted gaze never leaving the shore.

The anchor is raised and the sails are unfurled.

Once it leaves the harbour, the ship heads east, towards that distant place called New Spain that has been on the lips of the foreigners for months now. Black clouds build on the horizon, bruising the sky. The ship shrinks, dwarfed by the immense ocean below and the boiling storm above.

From the mainmast, a blue light shimmers in the gloom. In mesmerised silence, the native people watch the light waver and flicker, casting a ghastly, hopeless glow over the sails.

Lighting flashes. In the distance, thunder growls.

And the light glows on.

Afterword

On 6 September 1522, the Victoria finally made port on the Guadalquivir. Its cargo of precious spices was worth 7,888,864 maravedis, or over £26 million ($31 million) today.

Of a total crew of 242 men and cabin boys spread across five ships, the Armada de Molucca was reduced to a single ship and just eighteen emaciated survivors. Included among those who completed the first circumnavigation of the globe were Juan Sebastián Elcano, Antonio Pigafetta, Pedro de Valderrama and Hernando Bustamante.

Sixteen months previously, on 6 May 1521, the mutineers of the San Antonio, captained by Estêvão Gomes, returned to Sevilla with Álvaro de Mesquita and Cristóvão Rebêlo in chains. Betrayed by the mutineers of the San Antonio, the survivors on board the Victoria were greeted with suspicion and imprisonment.

Gonzalo Gómez de Espinosa failed to reach Mexico and the Trinidad returned to Tidore where it was captured by the Portuguese and later torn apart in a storm.

Juan de Morales died somewhere in the Pacific Ocean of scurvy on 25 September 1522.

Coda

The Armada de Molucca's voyage may not have been one of conquest, but the consequences of its success were long and devastating for the indigenous people of what is now known as South America, Indonesia, Malaysia and the Philippines. For over four hundred years, empire after empire followed in the footsteps of Fernão de Magalhães and unleashed wave after wave of displacement, exploitation, enslavement, ecological destruction and cultural genocide.

In the appalling history of Western colonisation, the first circumnavigation of the world is little more than a curiosity to most. But to the indigenous people it encountered and their descendants, the coming of five black ships from a faraway land signalled the beginning of hundreds of years of hardship and cruelty.

Their names may be lost, their languages silenced, and their achievements overlooked, but their place in history should never be forgotten.

Acknowledgements

I am forever indebted to my wonderful partner, Law Lok Yeng, who, for two years, has put up with my constant ramblings about the Armada de Molucca. Without your patience, encouragement and kindness, I could never have completed this book.

I have endeavoured to always remain faithful to history. As with most historical fiction, however, this is not always possible. For those readers interested in learning more about the history of the Armada de Molucca, I would point them first and foremost to *Over the Edge of the World: Magellan's Terrifying Circumnavigation of the Globe* by Laurence Burgreen – a captivating book that captures in non-fiction the drama that unfolded five hundred years ago.

Another excellent and invaluable resource can be found at www.rutaelcano.com. There, readers can learn of almost all facets of the armada's planning and journey: from the food that was taken on board to the names and fates of most of its crew members. Perhaps most interestingly of all, one can find exact GPS locations (mapped onto Google Earth) of almost every event endured by the crew of Armada de Molucca.

I hope you have enjoyed my book and would be tremendously grateful if you would leave a review of it.

Printed in Great Britain
by Amazon